Malcolm couldn't bring himself to explain. He looked away from Cassie's striking eyes and said, "I'm not certain she's the right woman for me."

Cassie's heart grew full and plump within her breast. "Why not?"

Malcolm no longer hesitated. He had spoken this much, and knew he might as well finish. "I know she's not. But something about her . . ."

Cassie did not at all like the expression that came over him then. He looked starry-eyed, as though he were remembering Priscilla's silky black hair and shimmering violet eyes. Cassie self-consciously touched her own reddish locks, as a few strands fell sloppily from her bun. She glanced down at her small, practical body, mentally comparing it to Priscilla's long and lithe one.

"Why do I pursue her?" Malcolm asked. "I can't think of anything I like about her, anything we have in common at all, and yet . . . I'm just drawn to her."

"No," agreed Cassie, folding and unfolding her hands, "but you think she is alien. She does not remind you of yourself, and therefore, you are drawn." She turned from him and faced the wall. "Someone who is nearer," she continued, her voice beginning to tremble, "someone who is less frightening, less haunting, not so . . . so inhumanly beautiful"—she took a deep breath to keep from sobbing—"may be overlooked, you see. No matter how much she may suit you, or . . . or how much she may . . . may care for you." She was trying so hard not to collapse into tears, that she did not feel him rise from his chair. She did not notice him at all until his breath tickled her hair.

He turned her around with gentle but firm hands. "Cassie," he whispered. He bent down so he could try to look her in the eye. "Cassie," he said gently, "what is it?"

Still, she could not answer.

So he studied her face carefully, and ventured, "My God. Have you fallen in love with me?"

BOOK YOUR PLACE ON OUR WEBSITE AND MAKE THE READING CONNECTION!

We've created a customized website just for our very special readers, where you can get the inside scoop on everything that's going on with Zebra, Pinnacle and Kensington books.

When you come online, you'll have the exciting opportunity to:

- View covers of upcoming books

- Read sample chapters

- Learn about our future publishing schedule (listed by publication month *and author*)

- Find out when your favorite authors will be visiting a city near you

- Search for and order backlist books from our online catalog

- Check out author bios and background information

- Send e-mail to your favorite authors

- Meet the Kensington staff online

- Join us in weekly chats with authors, readers and other guests

- Get writing guidelines

- AND MUCH MORE!

**Visit our website at
http://www.kensingtonbooks.com**

CASSIE'S ROSE

Elizabeth Doyle

ZEBRA BOOKS
Kensington Publishing Corp.
http://www.kensingtonbooks.com

One

July 1823

She didn't do it. But that hardly mattered anymore. It had stopped mattering the moment she'd set foot on this stinking vessel. She would not even be sure the ship was moving if it weren't for the nausea. There was no wind in her hair, no salt on her face, none of the sensations she had imagined experiencing in sea travel. Her eyes saw no glittering sun on bright waters, but only darkness. She could scarcely hear the thundering waves—only the wailing prayers of the women around her. She smelled neither fish nor seaweed, but only the remarkable scent of humans beings, becoming pickled in filth and captivity. It was only her dizziness and seasickness that reminded her she was at sea.

She couldn't quite see the other faces. There was so little light below deck, she had begun to imagine that her fellow passengers were not human at all, but contorted phantoms, warning of a fate surpassing the horror of any gallows. Cassie was trembling from the ceaseless rocking motion that threatened to turn her stomach. She was also scared but she did not like to seem afraid. If she were scared senseless, then *they* had won. Those who had sought to put her here, those who had laughed at her fate. If they saw her now, they would know that she was defeated, trembling like the mouse they would have her be. Cassie lifted her chin and took a deep breath, trying to draw courage from nowhere.

"Pssst." She heard a whisper in the dark. She ignored it, but then it happened again. "Pssst."

"Are you talking to me?" whispered Cassie, her voice nearly cracking, it had been so long since she'd spoken.

"Yes," whispered a young, female voice. "Can you see me? I'm to your left."

Cassie squinted into the darkness and saw an outline of long, bushy, dark hair surrounding a narrow face. "What is it?" she asked.

"Scoot closer so we can talk," instructed the voice.

Cassie inched over, as much as her chains would allow, sliding her bottom along the splintered planks. "What is it?" she repeated. She could now see that the woman beside her was about her own age, rather pretty, with dark hair and white skin, and very unkempt. Her dress did not fit, and, in fact, did not even reach her ankles. She must have had it since she was a child. Her curly hair looked as though it had never been combed.

"Is this your first time?" asked the young woman.

"Of course!" snapped Cassie in a whisper. "How many times could there be?"

The girl was undaunted by Cassie's unfriendliness. She shrugged and replied, "This is my second time."

Cassie was startled. "Really?"

"Yes. My first time, I was ten years old. My own family turned me in to the police when they caught me shoplifting."

"How long did you get?"

"Seven years."

"What about this time?"

"The rest of my natural life."

"But why?"

"Went home and tried to kill my family, of course! I failed, but received life anyway."

Cassie wanted to laugh, so dark had her humor grown over the past several weeks.

"What about you?" asked the girl.

"Murder," said Cassie with a little laugh. It was all just so stupid. She had never killed anyone in her life.

"Murder? Then you're here for your natural life as well?"

"No," said Cassie, "I was given twenty years. The barrister called it a 'victory.' He said he was very proud of himself for getting the judge to show such mercy."

Her companion looked at her quizzically. "What did you say?"

"I told him I was happy for him. I told him to think of me when he's having his celebration banquet."

That caused both women to laugh, and finally, they looked upon one another without suspicion. "My name is Sheena," said the dark-haired stranger. "I'd offer you a handshake, but . . ." She rattled her chains a bit.

"My name is Cassie."

"Are you Irish?" asked Sheena. "Your hair is red, but you sound like a Tory."

"Half Irish," said Cassie, "half Irish, and half English. I've lived both places."

"Ah, I see," said Sheena. "Then I don't think we'll see each other again after this voyage. They always split the Irish, you know. They're afraid we'll band together and rebel."

"Believe me," moaned Cassie, "I'm too worn out to rebel against anything."

Sheena studied her companion carefully. Cassie had shiny red hair, straight as a sheet of satin, and tied primly into a knot. A few strands had come loose from travel, and now wisped at her temple. Her complexion was lightly freckled, but not to a fault. Her lips were full, and her green eyes, stunningly exotic. It was hard to see her dress when she was sitting with her ankles tucked under her, but it looked reasonably new and well-made. It was not the gown of a noblewoman, but it was certainly no peasant's wear. It was unusual, indeed, to see a middle-class woman on her way to Australia. "Have you any idea what's in store?" asked Sheena, suspecting that the answer was "no."

"You must be joking," said Cassie. "I have no idea at all. Why, when the judge sentenced me to 'transportation,' I thought he was giving me a horse to compensate for all my trouble."

They both laughed again, creating a lighter mood where there had been only wailing. "There are some things you ought to know," said Sheena. "First of all, the trip is the worst part. Once we arrive in Australia, things'll get a little easier. But you've got to survive this journey."

"How long will it be?"

"About three months."

Cassie dropped her head and groaned. Unthinkable. She felt just as she had when the judge had told her "twenty years." It was unthinkable. She'd kept imagining that there would be more steps, more processes before her sentence was final. It couldn't be over. Not when the verdict had been "twenty years." There had to be a loophole, another way out. That her fate was sealed, that she would be an old woman by the time she returned home, was impossible to believe. Just as the notion that she would be chained below deck in this darkness and stench for three entire months was too awful to grasp. "I can't make it," she announced.

"Yes, you can," said Sheena, "and you must. Listen to me. It's all about sorting. When we arrive on shore, they sort us. They decide which of us will go to the Female Factory, and which of us will be given assignments. Trust me, you want an assignment."

"Why?" Cassie barely had the strength to ask.

"Because the Female Factories are horrible! Listen to

me. You get assigned to be someone's maid or servant, and the twenty years will fly by. You might have to let the head of the house bed you, but . . ."

"What?"

Sheena shrugged. "That's just the way it is. They get convict help, and they know they don't have to treat us right. But listen. They're not allowed to flog us. They can send us back to the Female Factory, or they can lodge a complaint and have us reassigned. But they cannot flog us. So it's a lot better than being at the mercy of the gaolers. And if you think this ship is dark," her memory made her shiver, "you should see that Female Factory. You'll be blind in a week, and the work is nonstop. Believe me. Get an assignment, and get a good one."

"But how?"

"That's what I'm trying to tell you. The gaolers are on board." She jerked her head upward toward the deck. "Be nice to them, and they'll see you get a good assignment. Be rude to them," she added eerily, "and they'll shave your head. Nobody wants a servant with a shaved head. They don't like to look at it."

Cassie gulped, absently touching her hair. "They'll really do that?"

"Last time I took this trip, three women were held down and their hair was shaved off. Let me tell you, none of them got a good assignment when we reached shore, even though they had a week's growth. The gaolers laughed, said they looked silly, and sent them to the factory."

Cassie was decidedly panicked, though she tried not to let it show. "Well, how do I please the gaolers on board? We never see them."

"Oh, believe me," warned Sheena, "you'll see them, all right. You'll see them at nightfall when they get restless. And it'll be you they're wanting. They never trouble the older women."

Cassie was still twisting a piece of her hair. She knew that Sheena would think she was daft for asking this question; in fact, she thought herself daft for asking it. But she wanted to make sure she understood. "What exactly will they be wanting?"

Sheena smiled. "You really haven't been out and about much, have you? It's funny. You look too bitter to be an innocent." She squinted thoughtfully at Cassie's hardened face.

Cassie replied only with a flare of her narrow, emerald eyes. "What do I have to do?" she asked. "How do I get the gaolers to like me?"

"Just lie still and don't fight them," said Sheena. "They won't ask for more than that."

Cassie's breath caught in her throat. She had never been much of a lady, it was true. She had been told a thousand times she was ill-tempered, unsociable, and, at times, downright unpleasant. She did not dress up to the best of her ability, nor did she take enough care in her appearance. She dressed sensibly, walked determinedly, and wore her hair in the most practical fashion. She didn't care to be a lady. But neither was she a whore. And even in her most desperate hour, even when she had lost all interest in propriety and all respect for righteousness, she didn't think she could bed a stranger. It wasn't a moral decision. It was a decision based on the rare appearance of her secretly tender heart. "I can't do that," she said quietly.

"But you must. If they come down here, which they will, you must do whatever they ask. Listen to me, Cassie. Three months of misery is nothing compared to twenty years of hell! What you do now will affect everything that happens when we land."

Cassie was staring at the floor, a dazed look in her eye. "I can't."

"It won't be so bad after the first time, I promise."

Cassie's head began to shake back and forth. "I can't. I really, really can't."

"Listen to me!"

It was too late. Overhead, a trapdoor opened, blinding the prisoners with painful sunlight. A rope ladder was tossed through the hole. Three sturdy gaolers climbed their way down into the filth. All of them were young and handsome, all of them strong and powerful, and all of them perfectly evil in the eye. One distributed water while another winked at Sheena. The third had eyes only for Cassie. "What a pretty girl," he said icily, his heavy boots stomping across the room. Cassie feared he might actually step on her, but he stopped just before his boot crushed her hand. "James!" he called to his friend. "I'm taking this one. Help me strip these dirty clothes off of her, will you?"

Two

It was Sheena, rather than Cassie, who panicked first. Sheena had not made many friends in her life, and rarely met anyone she liked. Somehow, almost a murderess and thief though she was, she could not bear to see a new companion, someone who would actually talk to her and laugh with her, torn apart by the likes of these gaolers. And besides, it was an opportunity she could use to her advantage. It was her only hope of escaping the factory. "Take *me!*" she blurted out impulsively.

The gaoler glanced at her with narrow eyes. "I prefer redheads," he told her, as though having a woman offer herself to him was the most normal thing in the world. He rattled some keys on a large, round ring and knelt before Cassie, fumbling to unlock her irons.

"I'll change your mind," promised Sheena, first frantically, then seductively. "That is," she added with a practiced calm in her gaze, "give me an hour, and I'll convert you to brunettes."

He sneered. "Isn't it pathetic," he asked his friend, "the way they throw themselves at us just to get a good assignment? It'd serve you right if I shaved your head," he warned Sheena.

"Then I wouldn't be nearly so enticing in your bed," she countered.

Cassie could not believe her friend's bravery. And yes, at this moment, she considered this stranger a friend, though she'd known her only a few hours. Sometimes, friendship happens that fast.

The gaoler had a bitter look in his handsome brown eyes and a cocky set to his well-defined jaw. He knew he was the boss here. He knew that these women had to do whatever he said. And this being his seventh journey, he'd gotten rather accustomed to the power. The way he saw it, prisoners were filth, prostitutes and pickpockets at best. And he was an honest man, the sort who deserved his freedom. He saw no shame in treating these miserable prisoners however he pleased. They were the root of all the troubles back in England, and he was doing his country a favor by making certain their sentence was not an easy one.

He kept looking back and forth between the two young women. He was certain he preferred the redhead, not only for the elegant color of her hair, but also for the fullness of her lips and the exotic slant of her eyes. But he could see she was frightened, and the brunette was not. Undoubtedly, the dark-haired girl would do whatever it took to please him, while the redhead would be too scared to move. He didn't like settling for his second choice, but the voyage would be three months long, after all. He didn't have to choose between them; he could have both. "All right," he relented, "I'll take you for now." He reached over and unlocked Sheena's irons.

She shook her wrists in relief, then stood up and kicked out her bare feet, trying to get her blood circulating again. "I'm Sheena," she said hurriedly.

"Oh, isn't that lovely," he sneered. "And I'm Robin. Do you think we're courting now? Just be quiet and come with me, slut." He pulled her roughly by the elbow and shoved her to the rope ladder. When she had difficulty climbing it, he rolled his eyes and muttered to his friend, "Bloody incompetent, too, aren't they?" He gave her a hoist, then watched idly as she struggled with the remaining footholds.

At last, all the gaolers were gone, the hatch closed, and Cassie was left to the darkness and the weeping. She felt guilty, utterly indebted. How could she let someone take such a battering for her? And yet, how could she not? How could she have gone with that cruel, snide man and let him touch her? That she was a maiden, and Sheena undoubtedly was not, did not ease her conscience. It did not make her feel justified in allowing such a horror to befall her new friend. She had not even tried to stop it. She had not objected to the gaoler taking Sheena in her stead. Imprisonment was making her cowardly, and this, in her mind, was unacceptable. She would have to rebuild herself; she would have to find her lost strength. But where could such a virtue as courage be found in all of this darkness?

The wailing was just awful. Sounds of women crying out to God for mercy, and reciting Bible verses from memory, was positively eerie. The oldest women wailed the loudest, for some reason. As a rule, the young women could be presumed prostitutes and the older women, crooked housekeepers. Some of them had probably, indeed, stolen from their employers, Cassie reasoned. Some of them probably had been falsely accused. But they all cried out their innocence, and it was impossible to know what really happened. The courts did their best to sort out tales, theories and evidence, but in truth, nobody could ever really know. Cassie had come to understand that.

In the beginning, she had explained her innocence to anyone who would listen, or even pretend to listen. Every time a human being neared her London cell, she would yell out, hoping to reach sympathetic ears. But it gradually dawned on her that nobody listened to anyone who lived behind bars. They knew that such a person would say anything to regain her freedom, so her words had no credibility. Even at her trial, the speeches of free witnesses were held sacred, while her own testimony was considered tainted by her desire to be found innocent. Her dearest friends had become enemies. Even Annabelle, whose heart had always been so true and who had testified in hopes of helping her childhood friend, had done nothing but worsen her predicament.

"Do you know Cassandra Madison?" the barrister had asked.

"Why, yes," said the plump young woman, her face adorned with oversized features that made her look as kind and truthful as she was. "I have known her since we were girls."

"And knowing her as you do, would you consider her a . . . good person?"

"Absolutely!" the girl beamed. "She is my dearest friend!" She shot the slouching Cassie a triumphant look as though to say, *Did you hear that? Did you hear what I said about you? Aren't I doing well?* Cassie forced herself to smile back.

"What makes you say that she's a good person?" asked the barrister.

"Well," Annabelle shifted in her seat, "she's very responsible, for one thing. Everyone knows that her parents are positively frivolous with their estate. Mr. Madison is always gallivanting about, so much so that I honestly don't recall having met him in all of these years! And Mrs. Madison is more concerned with her soirées and her social climbing than she is with her debts, or even her own children! Why, if it hadn't been for Cassie, I don't know what would have become of that family. She manages the servants, sees to the bills, pacifies the debt collectors, and has even done a great deal in the way of raising her three younger brothers! I, myself, admire her greatly."

"Indeed," he drawled. "However, would you say that

her decidedly burdened lifestyle has in any way inter-
fered with her . . . *socialization?*"

"Hmm? Why, no! Why, I don't think so anyway. It is
true that she never accepts courtship, nor will she attend
even a single dance. She says she cannot afford to ne-
glect her responsibilities at home long enough to
indulge in those sorts of activities."

"I see. And would you say that she is gifted in the art
of managing an estate, even at her tender age?"

"Absolutely!"

"How so?"

"Well, she . . . she's very forthright, you know. One
could hardly ask for a stronger head to a household,
young though she be. I've never seen a debt collector
who was able to stand up against her when she was determined that the family needed more time."

"Please elaborate."

"Well, she just stares piercingly at them, in that
staunch way of hers, and tells them, 'You shall have your
money, sir. But if you persist in this rudeness, you shall
get not a shilling.' It's very convincing, the way she says
it. I believe she scares the daylights from them."

"I see then. So she is rather threatening when need
be? Rather . . . short-tempered?"

"Oh my, yes! Why, I remember when we were girls,
some of the children teased her for being half Irish.
There was one boy who just wouldn't stop calling her
'freckle face,' and she warned him several times. But he
persisted! Oh my," she laughed. "Cassie threw that boy
across the room and sent him crashing into the teacher's
desk. We thought he was unconscious at first, but he was
only pretending so she wouldn't hit him again."

"She sounds violent. Tell me, has she ever threatened
to kill anyone during one of these fits of hers?"

"Well, I wouldn't call them fits," said Annabelle. "She
is generally very calm when she's angry."

"Then these violent outbursts are not so much outbursts at all, but in fact extensions of her already bitter
personality."

"Well, I . . . I wouldn't call her bitter. A bit jaded perhaps. A bit overworked."

"Has she ever threatened to kill anyone?"

"Well, just in passing, is all."

Cassie closed her eyes and rubbed her forehead.

"She's threatened to kill people *in passing?*" asked the
barrister.

"Well, I'm sure she didn't mean it! It's just one of her
expressions, is all. When one of her brothers, for exam-
ple, threatens to disobey her, she just says, 'Do it or I'll
kill you,' with a very calm look on her face."

"And do her brothers find this endearing?"

"Oh, goodness no! They usually run immediately to
do her bidding."

"Then they believe she might kill them."

"Why, no! At least, I don't think so. I certainly pre-
sume not." She draped a thoughtful index finger across
her chin.

"Miss Edwards. Do you believe that Cassandra Madison is capable of killing someone?"

"Well, I wouldn't have thought so," she pondered,
"but the more I think about it . . ."

Cassie was already shaking her head. So long as she
lived, she vowed, she would never, ever befriend a stupid
person again, no matter how kind her heart. None of
the friendly witnesses understood what their sloppy tes-
timonies had cost her. But did the hostile witnesses
understand the results of their lies? Why did they do it?
Who would want to get rid of her so badly? And why?

She banged her head against the moldy wall of the
ship several times until it hurt. Why?

Three

Within the hour, Sheena was tossed under deck, her irons brutally refastened by a gaoler whom Cassie did not recognize. "Sheena!" she cried as soon as the gaoler had disappeared. "Are you all right?"

"I'm fine," she panted.

"But it took so long! Where were you?"

Sheena snickered. "Believe me, it didn't take *that* long." Cassie could see this was meant as an insult to her assailant, but she had only the vaguest notion of what it meant. "He finished with me half an hour ago, but then fell asleep. I thought about jumping overboard while I was still unbound, but I couldn't work it out."

Cassie was nearly weeping in her gratitude. "Sheena, I'm so sorry. Why did you do that? Why did you volunteer?"

"It was nothing," she grinned, giving Cassie a glimpse at how hard and cool she could look when she really tried. "In fact, it's all in my favor. I'm bound to get a good assignment now."

"Oh, Sheena," said Cassie, "I know you didn't do that for yourself. I know you did it to save me, and I don't know how to thank you."

"You can thank me by toughening up!" snapped Sheena. "Listen to me. Robin will probably be coming for me from now on. But you've got to get one of the others. This is your only chance. Make nice with these brutes, or you're factory bound! It wouldn't be that way if you were a thief or such. But as a murderer? They'll never send you to be a housekeeper unless they've got a good word on you."

Cassie was adamant. "I won't do it, Sheena. I hate these men! All of them." Her eyes were narrow and hot. "I don't need their bloody favors. I just need to serve my time and get out."

"It's a new world out here," warned Sheena. "You can't afford your pride. Pride is only for the rich and the free. Now you've got to get charity anywhere you find it."

"It isn't charity," she snapped, "when they're using me in my desperation."

Sheena smiled bitterly, the corners of her broad mouth lifting without joy. "I can tell you're not a peasant. Down here in the dregs of society, Cassie, we don't turn down help just because it comes with strings attached. That's the only kind of help we get."

Cassie studied the planks beneath her feet. They were rotten, wet, and stinking. "I won't do it," she muttered. "I'll serve my time, but that's all. I won't bow down."

Sheena was able to move her manacled wrist just enough to pat her friend's hand. She understood Cassie. She understood her steel and her fire. But she also knew that this wouldn't last. The stubbornness would be beaten out of her, and she would learn to give in. When it came to the little things, at least, she would learn to bend. A person without a thimbleful of power would have to choose her battles carefully.

Days passed, and Cassie grew hungry. Sheena told her she was lucky. In the old days, the sailors would eat the prisoners' rations. But the English wouldn't pay them anymore for transporting dead convicts. The prisoners had to arrive, if not in good health, then at least alive. So while the rations were still smaller than they were supposed to be, they did come. Cassie surely would have passed out from hunger if she'd had even a minute of exercise each day, but since she could only lie still, chained to the wall in the darkness, she existed in a drowsy state somewhere between awake and asleep. Even the loudest women stopped their wailing in time, for they no longer had the energy. Not being able to see clearly across the room, Cassie wondered whether a few of the older ones had died over there. She played a game with herself, watching their dark forms for hours on end to see whether they moved.

Sheena got to leave once every day. Robin would come for her, blinding all the women with painful sunlight from above. He would free Sheena, take her to his cabin, and then return her. Cassie nearly envied her, getting to get up, getting to walk somewhere. She didn't know how it would feel to stand again. Her backside ached, and her leg muscles felt withered. Her head had a sore spot where it rubbed against the wall. She wondered whether Sheena got to lie on a real cot when she was on deck. That would be nice. Maybe, she thought on occasion, it wouldn't be so bad to be bedded by a pack of hostile strangers, if it meant ten minutes on a real cot.

Time was becoming distorted. Days and nights were the same, because there was no light. Sometimes she slept, but she had no idea what time it was when she awoke. Perhaps she only slept five minutes at a time. She wasn't sure. One of the women broke down one day, and started screaming. Cassie could barely make out the desperate woman's words, though they were deafeningly loud. She was yelling something about being innocent. Cassie chuckled. It had been a long time since she'd cared whether anyone believed her innocent. A gaoler came below and beat the poor woman until she stopped wailing. Cassie had to close her eyes against that. She remembered that this particular woman had a family. They had seen her off when the ship departed, shouting out that they would follow her, that they would come to Australia and settle so she would not be alone. They had seemed so nice. Cassie hated to see their daughter beaten ruthlessly, six of her teeth falling to the ground in a pool of blood.

No one had seen Cassie off. Her family's love for her had died the moment the judge pronounced her guilty. They were incapable of disapproving and loving at the same time. Her father had not even made it to the trial. He was undoubtedly with one of his mistresses and did not receive word in time. Her mother came, but slipped out quickly when it was done, hoping no one had seen her there. Cassie's three younger brothers, whom she'd worked so hard to raise, were not permitted to attend. Her arrest was the last time they would ever see her. Cassie had been manacled and led on board this ship all alone, friendless and forgotten. Forgotten even by the family which would undoubtedly fall apart in her absence.

All she had now was Sheena. "Does it hurt?" she asked groggily, one day or evening, she wasn't sure which.

"Does what hurt?" sniffed Sheena.

Cassie dropped her weak head on Sheena's shoulder. "When they come for you? When Robin comes?"

"Oh, that?" Sheena was surprised. "You mean you've never . . ."

Cassie shook her head against Sheena's arm.

"Oh, no, it doesn't hurt," she said. "Not at all. In fact, it's rather fun, just so long as you don't think about it."

"How do you do it without thinking?"

"Practice."

"Have you ever been in love?" Cassie was moving closer to unconsciousness, and was burdening Sheena with her weight.

Sheena's dark eyes were distant. She absently combed through Cassie's tangled auburn locks, finding that they were slippery and soft.

"Well, *have* you?"

"I'm thinking," Sheena replied stiffly.

Cassie waited.

"You know," Sheena said at last, "I don't think I've ever met a man I liked, much less loved."

"Really?" yawned Cassie.

"Yes," said Sheena. "Really."

The gaolers never managed to ravage Cassie. They came for many of the other women, but every time they threatened to pull Cassie from the group, Sheena protected her. Of course, she hated to do this, for she felt it would be in Cassie's best interest to go, but her friend didn't want it, and so she did what she could to fend them off. Sometimes she offered herself instead, sometimes she created a sudden emergency by screaming senselessly or knocking something over, and sometimes she just said, "I think she's nearly dead," and told Cassie to lie still. On one occasion, however, a gaoler managed to get Cassie out of her irons and on her feet despite Sheena's best efforts. Cassie found that she could not walk, her ankles were so weak. The gaoler was nearly dragging her to the ladder. When she felt she'd gotten some balance, she used her newly freed legs to kick him. She wasn't thinking about it, she just had the instinct to fend him off, to keep from being dragged on deck. This angered him so much that he let her go, but not without first whipping her against the wall, causing her head to bleed.

As he refastened her chains, she was crying. She thought her skull was broken, though it was not. She reached up to touch the bloodied hair behind her head, only to have her moist hand yanked away and remanacled. She was wailing out loud as he strolled away, and the strangest thing was, she felt no shame. All of the prisoners had already lost their dignity, and there was no pretending anymore. She was hurt and afraid, and she let herself weep. "Sheena," she sobbed, her face hot and red, "they won't tend this wound, will they? They'll just let it keep bleeding? I'm going to die, aren't I?"

Sheena hurriedly looked at the bloodied mass of hair. "No," she said strongly, making a part so she could examine the damage. "No, it'll stop bleeding in a minute. I promise."

"I don't want to die," Cassie wept, collapsing into her friend's breast. "I want to go home, Sheena. I want to go home."

"Someday we'll all go home," she said soothingly. "It's just that home isn't where you thought it was."

Cassie sniffed, and tried to imagine puffy, white clouds in the sky. She was still trembling, but she started to let her eyes close. "If I died, what would they do with my body?"

"It doesn't matter," Sheena whispered. "It's only a body. You'll not need it anymore."

Sheena used her water ration to clean Cassie's head. She insisted that Cassie should drink her water, for she had lost some blood. Cassie fell asleep, using Sheena's shoulder as her pillow. It was a nice, soft shoulder of porcelain white. Cassie had always wanted porcelain white skin, but hers was freckled. She was also sleeker and less soft than Sheena. These were the things she thought about in her delirium. Her freckles and her small bust. They were strange concerns, but her mind was wandering from thought to thought without reason. At one point, she giggled at a joke she'd heard when she was twelve. Her mind seemed to be breaking, or perhaps it was regrouping. For one thing that did happen that night: Cassie made her peace with death. She fell asleep, still worried over her head wound and imagining that she might not ever awaken. It was a strangely comforting notion, and she found that in her dreams, she was brought to a mythical land of clouds and bluebirds. She would never again be afraid of death, not really because she believed that clouds and bluebirds were in store, but because she had spent an entire night believing that death was an inch away, and she had found comfort in that. She knew that someday, when her time had come, she would find comfort in it again.

"Will you promise not to wake me?" she asked Sheena several hours or several days later. "Will you promise to let me sleep forever?"

"There is no such thing as time," said Sheena. "Close your eyes, and you are home again."

And within days, it was true. No one had noticed the motion of the ship until it slowed down. But now, all prisoners' eyes were wide with wonder. Something was actually happening, and none were afraid. For whatever lay ahead, at least it was not this. "My God," cried a woman whom Cassie had never noticed before, "we are in Australia!"

"Australia!"

Four

The waters were a beautiful, transparent blue. The sun overhead was scorching and healing. The town of Sydney was nothing but a quaint community of whitewashed buildings. Beyond that, yet near enough to see from the dock, was dense, lush jungle. The prisoners could barely walk, but somehow they did anyway. The sun, which burned their eyes shut, also lent energy to their weary legs and enabled them to march in line from the transport to the prison. The prison was the entire world so far as they could see. And the wild waters were its walls. Several women's ankles wobbled and gave way, but the chain which connected them to the others would not allow them to fall. Somehow, they all made it to shore, a sallow-faced horde, haggard and defeated. Gradually, eyes opened and looks of surprise came over them. This land did not look like a prison, but like a tropical haven. Gazes traveled from the sea, to one another, to the jungle, to one another again. They were all wondering the same thing: Are we still alive? And do I look as bad as you do?

A heavyset, gruff gaoler greeted his men, but did not greet the prisoners. They were dragged to vacant barracks, and all of them mourned the return of darkness. The sunlight had been stolen just as quickly as it had been given. And now, they were forced to bathe without privacy before the watchful eyes of several imposing guards. Cassie watched miserably as the women around her began to strip. She couldn't believe how quickly they had lost their modesty. She was looking at their nudity just as surely as the guards were. They splashed their bare skin with water, as though in relief, as though they did not know they were being watched. "I'll stand in front of you," Sheena offered. "I don't mind if they see me. I've done this before."

Cassie weakly nodded her thanks, then let down her hair. She was dismayed to see how much of it fell from her scalp when she loosened its ribbon. Poor nutrition, she reasoned. Poor nutrition and no brushing. She dunked her head in the communal bath water and rubbed hard, trying to scrub the dried blood from her hair. The water did feel good. And these barracks were not as dark as the ship had been. It was clear no one was intended to live here permanently, as the hammocks were few and the splinters were many. It was just a place to wash and change before the sorting. And its flimsy walls were not tight enough to properly fend off the Australian sun. Many thin rays of light shone upon tunnels of dust in the air.

Cassie lowered her ruined gown from her shoulders, then looked around. The guards were watching her. Her head bent down. Sheena saw her predicament and made good on her promise to stand in the way. Already naked and pleasantly wet, she interrupted the gaolers' view of Cassie, who knelt on the dirt floor and seemed to pray to the water. Her arms stretched out before her, she splashed its lukewarm lushness upon her neck, and then her bosom. She tore off what was left of the gray gown that had once been her favorite and let it fall to the ground, soiled, stinking, and torn. And once her sleek, freckled body tasted the bath water, it wanted more. Dirt and stench were melting from her, and rejuvenation seemed near. But she had to make it quick. Sheena could not stand there forever, and she didn't want the gaolers to observe her in such a tender state. As soon as

Sheena handed her the uniform dress and apron, she used it to regain her modesty.

Soon, all of the women were dressed alike and standing in a line like soldiers. What a joke, thought Cassie, cracking her first smirk in a long time. A bunch of poor, sickly women expected to behave like soldiers. Who were these gaolers trying to fool? Who were they trying to impress? The biggest, most bloated of them all marched before the line of women with his hands clasped behind his back. There was joy in his bulbous cheeks. This was clearly his favorite part of the job. "Hello, ladies," he said sarcastically. "Are you all very happy to be here?" He laughed at his own joke, but no one else did. Most had forgotten how to smile. "I hope you don't think you'll be getting any special treatment," he warned, "just because you're women." Cassie closed her eyes. They had received plenty of special treatment already, in the form of rape. "Because here," he continued, "you're all just prisoners. And in the Female Factory you'll be expected to work just as hard as the men. Any laziness will be punished by the whip, and don't think you'll escape that just by looking pretty." Cassie nearly moaned, but restrained herself. What world did he live in where women expected not to be whipped?

"Now, some of you will be given assignments," he went on, examining a list. Sheena nudged Cassie as though to say, *Here it comes*. "You will be expected to serve your assigned families just as though you were paid employees. Any laziness will result in immediate deportation to the Female Factory, where we will keep an eye on you and be sure that you work. Assignment is a privilege, and if you abuse it by being slothful or belligerent, you will be punished. And no, you won't be wearing chains while you clean house, but let me assure you, there is no escape from this island. Any attempt to flee will most likely result in a good hanging." A good hanging? He said it as though he looked forward to such events with relish.

"Now, when I call out your name, I want you to step forward, tell me the nature of your crime, the length of your sentence, and any special skills you possess. Christina Jean Holliday!"

A frail blonde, who might once have been Christina Jean Holliday, stepped forward in her bare feet and her kerchief-bound hair. "I am . . ." She cleared her tender throat. "I am Christina."

"Did you not hear my instructions?!" he bellowed.

"No, I did," she said quickly. "I . . . I am here for . . . for theft, though I really didn't do it!"

He grabbed her by the elbow and dragged her to his side. "Prisoners, listen!" he commanded. "When I give an order, I want it followed precisely, promptly, and without hedging! The next woman to say she is innocent will be stripped bare and flogged! Is that understood?"

"Yes, sir," came a general mumble.

He tossed Christina back in line and allowed her to finish. Sniffing, she said meekly, "I am sentenced to seven years, and I have no special skills."

"Fine," he replied sternly, making a mark on his scroll, "then you are hereby assigned to . . . let's see . . . ah yes. You'll be the housekeeper at the old Ransom household. They're a nice lot. You'll do fine there. Next! Jane Rowena Jennings!"

Christina held her cheeks in relief. Her sallow face gained some color, and she said a quick prayer to the sky. In the meantime, Jane Rowena Jennings stepped forward. She was an elderly lady who looked as though she would rather be dead than here. "I am Jane," she announced lifelessly. "I am also sentenced to seven years for theft of clothing, and I have many special skills. I can sew, knit, and make pottery. I have fifty years experience in running a house, and cleaning."

"You're too old," he snapped brutally. "You're going to the factory. No one wants an ugly, old woman."

Jane's face scrunched up and her head bowed, but she did not cry. She took her place quietly back in line.

"Cassandra Eileen Madison!" he called, then added, "Eileen? Isn't that an Irish name?"

Cassie stepped forward, her heart pounding and her knees shaking. "Yes, sir," she replied, "my mother is Irish."

"You don't sound Irish."

"My father is English."

"Hmmm, very well," he replied disapprovingly. "State your circumstances."

"I am sentenced to twenty years for murder."

His eyes bulged out comically. "Murder? You?" He studied her young, pretty face, her sleek but muscular body, and wondered whether it could be so. "Not often we get a female murderer," he muttered. "Very well. Any special skills?"

"None."

"Hmmm." He studied his scrolls with care. "How was she on the transport, Robin? Any problems?"

The despicable, evil-eyed Robin shook his head disinterestedly. "No problems. No serious ones, anyway." Cassie hated to think she was indebted to him for that reply.

"Hmmm. Biggins! I need some help with this one."

"What is it, sir?" asked a young man. Too young, Cassie thought, to be in the business of death and imprisonment.

"We only have twenty-two convicts on this ship, but we have sixteen requests for assignment. More than six of these women are too old to be handed out, so I want to use this pretty young woman, but she's a murderess. Have you got any easy assignments on there? Something with no women and children to offend?"

"I have two bachelors on hand," he answered. "One is wanting a wife. The other is wanting a housekeep."

"Well, we can't make her a bride, being a murderess and half Irish. Give her to the other gentleman."

"Yes, sir."

"Very well," he announced to Cassie, "'tis your lucky day! You will be assigned to Dr. Rutherford's home. A bachelor ought to keep you busy," he mocked, suggesting what Sheena had already warned. She would be his concubine.

"Next! Sheena O'Malley. What's this," he asked his subordinate, "Irish day? And no middle name? That's when you know your parents didn't love you," he chuckled. "Didn't even bother to think of a second name."

Sheena stepped forward without apology. "I am Sheena," she said. "I am sentenced to life for attempted murder. And I am a very good housekeep," she lied.

"Murder again?" he asked. "What is happening? With the men, I get murders all the time, but with the women? Hmmm. Robin? Any trouble with this one?"

Sheena looked at him with phony lovingness in her eyes.

"Why, yes," he said, "she was terribly violent and ill-behaved. We had to keep an eye on her at all times." There was a twinkle in his eye. This was a joke. He was playing a joke for the benefit of his onlooking gaoler friends. But he did not take back the remark.

"Very well. To the Female Factory she goes."

"You bastard!" Sheena cried out, making a dart for Robin's throat. It took several guards to restrain her. "You bastard!" she kept calling, kicking her bare feet into the air as she was held sideways.

"Do you see what I mean?" laughed Robin. "Completely out of control."

The gaolers made to carry her off, to put Sheena on the wagon to the Female Factory. Something in Cassie snapped, and she cried out, "No!!!" though she knew it might mean the loss of her own assignment. "Sheena!" she cried, and for that moment, hoped that she would get sent to the factory after her. But she had no such luck. Within moments, Sheena and her screams were gone, and order was restored to the barracks. The rest of the women were given their assignments or their dooms, and Sheena was forever absent.

When Cassie was loaded into the back of a wagon, her wrists and ankles manacled, she felt a hollowness inside. This was the first time since her sentence began that she was without Sheena. There would be no one to comfort her now, no one to give her advice. When the horses lurched forward, and dust flew into her face, she thought she would be ill, though she had no nourishment to lose. She squinted out at the dusty, winding roads, at the small stores, at the magnificent, sparkling ocean, at the perfectly clear, painfully bright sky overhead, and felt nothing but loss. Somehow, foolish as it was, she'd imagined she would spend her twenty years with Sheena. And now it seemed she would not spend one more day with her. From here on, she was alone. In a foreign land. With no friends. And she was a slave.

The wagon pulled up to a lovely white house, not far from town, that would be her private jail. It was surrounded by lush jungle on three sides, and the fourth faced the dusty road. There was a flower garden behind the iron gates, filled with bright colors that Cassie could not feel. There was a wraparound porch circling the entire house. There was even a swing near the entrance. If Cassie had been a guest here, she would have been thrilled. If she'd been an employee here, she would have been content. But as it was, she didn't care what the house looked like. She just wanted her twenty years to pass by, and so far, they were really inching. She was relieved of her irons and allowed to walk freely to the front entrance. A gaoler rapped the brass knocker while Cassie stared at her bare feet. She wondered what monster would come to the door. As though from a distance, she heard it swing open. And from over her head, she heard talking.

"Ah, Dr. Rutherford. Good day. I have brought with

me a . . . er . . . woman from the most recent . . . uh . . . shipment. Will she do?"

"Yes, yes," said a smooth, silky voice. "She'll do just fine, thank you."

"Would you like to inspect her?"

"No, no. I'm sure she's just fine."

"If she gives you any trouble . . ."

"I'm sure I can handle it. Thank you."

"Now, you understand about the payment. We can't keep jailing them without funds, you know. So . . . we'll be needing your payments without delay."

"I understand. Thank you."

The voice was so appealing that Cassie could not resist lifting her gaze, though this took a great deal of courage. She did not want to be caught staring, but . . . She nearly lost her breath. Before her, she believed, was the most handsome man she had ever seen in her life. His short hair and long sideburns were a silky light brown. His eyes were strikingly blue, and so very kind. His mouth was set in a look that said clearly, *I'm trying not to laugh.* And he was dressed stylishly in black, with a blue cravat. His tall, casual stature and handsome face were a perfect combination of character and quirk. Cassie had never known she had a particular taste in men before. But now she knew. Dr. Rutherford was everything she had ever held to be handsome.

He caught her staring, and gave her a quick smile. Then he returned his attention to the prattling gaoler. But Cassie would not forget that brief smile. It meant he believed her to be human. It meant he knew that she was thinking exactly what he was—that the gaoler was a moron. And it meant that when the gaoler stumbled away, at last leaving her alone with this stranger, she was left with the most unexpected of feelings. Excitement flickering in her belly.

Five

She couldn't help peering around at her surroundings, even though she knew that no matter how lovely the house was, she would hate it here. Her life would be filled with nothing but work and captivity, and she would be miserable. But she did like the decor. She was standing in the entrance, a cheerful red rug under her feet, and a modest but bright chandelier overhead. There was not a great deal of furniture, but what she saw was of a beautiful hardwood that she did not recognize. It was all quite shiny. The walls were painted white, and the curtains were all red. Rising from the entrance was a winding staircase with wide, carpeted stairs and a shiny banister. "Hello," said her host, or rather, her captor. He closed the heavy white door with a gentle bang. "I . . . uh . . . it's one of those oddities," he explained, noticing that Cassie was studying the house. "It looks bigger from the outside." He laughed nervously, jamming his hands in his pockets.

Cassie looked at him expectantly. He saw how pretty she was. He saw how her green eyes sparkled, and how her full lips flushed naturally. And he had always thought redheads were attractive. But these were not appropriate thoughts, so he banished them. The poor thing, after all, probably expected him to use her like an enslaved harlot. He didn't want to give her any indication that his intentions were unseemly. "I'm afraid I don't have many house servants," he apologized. "In fact, you . . . well, you're the only one," he smiled boyishly. "I uh . . . I'm not a real gentleman, you see. I'm only a doctor. I'm just what they call 'Australian nobility,' which means . . . well, it means that there's nothing very noble about me at all. I'm . . . I'm just a self-made man." He bit his lip, and stretched out his arm. "Well, enough small talk. Shall I show you your room?"

Cassie nodded and followed humbly as he lead her up the sweeping staircase. She was self-conscious about her bare feet treading on his nice rugs. She imagined she must look like a filthy stray puppy. And it did bother her. She had just met the most handsome man in the world, by her reckoning, and here she was, not at home where she might have impressed him with her sensible gowns and her chin held high, but in a wild land, with bare feet and social leprosy. Even if he fancied her, which was un-likely, he would undoubtedly use her brutally, then toss her away. She would never have romance or courtship, probably so long as she lived. Having to work for such an eligible bachelor would be torture. It would be a con-stant reminder of what could never be hers.

"I don't have any servants' quarters," he apologized, "because when the house was built, I . . ." He laughed in that charmingly awkward way of his. "I forgot them." He shrugged, flinging open a door at the end of the white-carpeted hall. "But I did remember to build a guest room or two, so . . . I hope this will do."

Cassie could not believe her eyes. The room was spa-cious, yet cozy. Light blue curtains framed the small, picturesque windows, through which she could see a beautiful rose garden. A giant canopy bed was draped in pale blue satin, and chests of drawers shone a magnifi-cent bright brown. "Who else will sleep here?" she asked, thinking that surely she could not have such a spacious room to herself.

"No one," he shrugged. "As I said you . . . uh . . . you're

it. I have a landscaper who comes and does the gardening. I have a cook, too, but she doesn't live here. I'm afraid you're my one and only housekeep. I promise I'm not very messy, though," he added quickly. "I work at the hospital most of the time. I don't . . . I hope it won't be too much work for you. I . . . I think you'll be able to manage."

Cassie nodded enthusiastically.

"Well . . . uh . . ." He looked down at her bare feet for the first time. "Is that all the . . . uh . . . all the clothes they gave you?"

She nodded.

"Hmm." He scratched a sideburn. "They used to at least give shoes. Wonder if they're out." He thought about it another moment, and Cassie thought he looked as though he were trying to remember something. "Oh, well. I'll go see whether the store has anything stocked. It isn't London here, I'm afraid. Having money is only half the battle when making a purchase. But I'll do my best."

They both stood awkwardly in the doorway for a moment. Cassie looked at the ground, and Dr. Rutherford looked at the room. It seemed an excellent time for him to say, *Make yourself at home* or *Go unpack*. But, of course, there was nothing for her to unpack, and no way for her to make herself at home. Still, he thought of something. "Are you tired? Would you like to rest?"

Strangely, Cassie wanted to impress him. So she replied, "No, sir. I'm ready to get to work."

He didn't seem to like that answer. He looked warily around and explained apologetically, "Well, I . . . you see, there's not really anything for you to do yet. I've been hiring people to clean on a one-day-at-a-time basis, and . . . well, I know I should have something for you, but . . ."

"Then I'll rest," she broke in.

"You're sure?"

"Yes, sir. Just let me know as soon as you need me."

"You're not just sleeping out of boredom, are you?

Because I'm sure I have some books . . . well, no, they're all medical books. Interested in biology?"

"No," she smiled. "No, I'm not."

"No, of course not," he replied humbly. "Well then, sleep well. I . . . I shall get you when Faith arrives. She's the cook."

"Thank you, sir."

He nodded and began his departure. The door closed behind him, but within a moment, he was back. "You . . . uh . . . you don't have anything to wear to bed," he stated with a comical expression of stupidity.

Cassie lifted her eyebrows and shook her head. She couldn't help returning his smile.

"Ahhh," he drawled, still laughing at himself. "I . . . uh . . . I'll get you something."

Cassie had thought she might never smile again when she boarded that ship so many months ago. But now, she was grinning ear to ear. She liked him. She really liked him. And she loved the room. She hurried to the small window by the dresser and looked out. Was it really possible that she could keep this assignment for all twenty years? What would she do if she were reassigned or sent to the factory? After this, it would be unbearable. She thought about Sheena. Betrayed, crying out, sent to that awful place—for life. Sheena had been so kind to her. And that had been her reward.

There was a knock at the door. Cassie opened it to find Dr. Rutherford standing there with a white gown slung over his elbow. "Found you something," he said.

It was most peculiar. She lifted the white cotton from his arm and found that it was, indeed, a woman's sleeping gown. Puffed in the sleeve and flared at the skirt, it was rather a nice one, too. What was a bachelor doing with such a garment?

"Thank you," she replied quietly. He began to leave, but she stopped him. "Dr. Rutherford?"

"Hmm? Yes?"

She looked right into his perfectly blue eyes. His face was so kind, so youthful, so full of humor that she found the courage to ask him, "How long will you be needing me?"

He gave the matter some thought. He wasn't sure what she wanted him to say. He knew that some women preferred the factory to assignments, but that was only because they didn't want to be concubines. Most women preferred an honest assignment to the regular gaol. "Are you anxious to go somewhere?" he asked with a spark in his eye.

"No," she laughed.

"Then I guess I'll be needing you indefinitely." He shrugged. "Is that all right?"

She nodded emphatically.

His eyes were filled with understanding. An understanding that Cassie would not have guessed him to have. "I won't toss you out," he assured her in a warm, fluid voice. "And . . . uh . . . Miss Madison?"

"Yes?"

He jerked his head at the door. "I won't come in here without knocking, either, all right?"

She shrugged, and did not take his true meaning.

"Do you understand?" he asked more slowly. "This room is yours. Not mine."

Now, she got it. At least, she thought she did. But she dared not reply, dared not ask him to speak more plainly. For this was much too tender a subject to be brought into the open.

He nodded his satisfaction, for he believed she had taken his meaning well enough. "I'll introduce you to Faith when she arrives," he said, eager to change the subject. He couldn't stand to see such a pretty girl feeling so terribly at his mercy. He meant her no harm, but he could think of no way to convince her of that, except to keep chattering. "I'm afraid I often have . . . uh . . . company for dinner," he grinned wryly. "Tonight it'll just be a few unruly bachelors, old friends of mine. I hope they won't frighten you. If they do, I'll tell them to settle down."

Cassie nodded her thanks, eyes cast down.

"Say, are you . . . are you Irish?" he asked.

Cassie shook her head. "Just half."

"Oh, really? Hmm. Me, too. That is, I'm half Scottish. So I know how it is," he grinned. "Neither here nor there." Offering her a friendly wink, he made his final exit for the afternoon. "I'll knock before dinner." Then, on the other side of the door, he admonished himself. He should not have winked. She was not a lady friend, she was not even a beloved servant. She was virtually a slave, and he would have to be more careful. Careful to let her know that she was safe here. Careful to help her understand that she would not be mistreated.

And careful never to let on how pretty he thought she was.

Six

Cassie's slumber was interrupted by a loud knock on the door. Heavy-eyed, she opened it to find an attractively plump woman on the other side. She was an older lady, with black-and-silver hair like partially burnt charcoal, wrapped in thick braids round her head. Her eyes were big and black, gentle and wise. "Miss Madison," Dr. Rutherford announced from behind the plump chef, "this is Faith Johnson, my cook."

"I'm so glad that the doctor has finally hired some more help!" exclaimed the woman, casting welcoming eyes upon Cassie. "I've told him a thousand times I can't do everything around here. How do you do?"

Cassie returned the handshake. "Quite well, thank you."

"Will you mind carrying in platters for me?" she asked. "I've told the doctor it is impossible to keep soup warm and stirred while running back and forth from the kitchen to the dining room."

"Certainly," replied Cassie. "Just show me what is to be done, and I shall do my best." She had spent much of her young life directing servants, and knew that the best ones were not those who promised to be superb, but those who vowed to ask many questions and do their best to hear the answers. Being on the other end of it gave her the distinct feeling of having stepped down in life, yet she found that her experience running a household made her quite confident that she could serve one.

"Such a pretty Irish girl," Faith beamed.

"Half Irish," Cassie was quick to remark.

"Such a pretty half-Irish girl," the cook corrected herself with a sly grin.

Dr. Rutherford seemed satisfied that the introductions were complete. "Now, don't be hard on her, Faith. She's had a long voyage," he said, leaning casually with one arm at the top of the door frame.

"In my kitchen everything must be just so," she said with false sternness. "I'm stern with anyone who enters." But her kind, square face told Cassie that she was not concerned with the voyage Dr. Rutherford had just mentioned. She knew Cassie was a convict, and did not seem inclined to dwell on it.

Soon, the doctor departed and Cassie found herself being led by Faith into a silvery kitchen, filled with light. In this room, there was a set of French doors leading into the rear garden. It seemed a lovely place to cook and to think. "Now don't touch any of my dishes," said Faith with kind stubbornness. "I don't like anyone interfering while I cook. What I'll need you to do for now is set the table. The silver is right here." She opened a cabinet filled with blue-and-white china. In a lower drawer, she revealed an enormous set of silver. "Do you know the proper settings for a table?" She held up two different spoons as a test.

Cassie was not offended by the question, though she knew perfectly well how to set a table. Naturally, Faith would have no idea where she had come from, or whether she had ever eaten at a dining room table. "I'm fairly confident," she reported.

"All right, then, go to it," she said sternly. "Don't mind if I check your work the first time. We'll need six settings, though likely only five gentlemen will dine. That Robert Jennings hardly ever shows up when he promises to." She shook her head with a great deal of disapproval.

"Does the doctor always have so many dinner guests?" asked Cassie.

"Oh, no!" cried Faith, clearly delighted that a conversation had been sparked. "But he has to have them in from time to time. The man has more acquaintances than I have cousins!" she chuckled. "And let me assure you, I have a lot of cousins."

"Are they nice?" asked Cassie, sensing that Faith wanted the conversation to keep rolling.

"Bah! Not likely." She narrowed her eyes at Cassie, a thought suddenly occurring to her. "I suggest you keep away from these rapscallions. I'm sure they'll be wanting to know you better, some of them. But the ones that are any good already have wives. And the rest of them, well . . . let's just say the women who've set them free knew what they were doing."

"I'm sure they wouldn't have any interest in a convict anyway," Cassie blurted out.

Faith turned away, and tended to a pot of stew. An awkward moment ensued upon her abrupt retreat. "Go set the table," she said gently. "We've got a lot to do. And Cassie?" she added as the girl made her exit. "We don't use that word here, all right? There are no convicts in Australia." She winked. "Only people, doing their best with what they've got."

"Yes, madam." Cassie went to the task of fixing the dining room table, feeling that she had never known anything so strange as this enormous island.

The dining room was small but pretty, like the rest of the house. It was the table that made it so impressive. Its top was the thickest slab of wood Cassie had ever seen on a table, and it was polished to an elegant shine. Its strong legs were accented with lovely, decorative stripes, and its feet curled like Dutch clogs. The chairs were equally impressive. All of them were wide, sturdy, and comfortable, complete with red velvet seats. Their legs precisely matched those of the table, and their backs were made of elegant columns framed at the top by a curved bow. Aside from the furniture, the room was left to speak for itself. There was not much in the way of frivolous decor. Other than the red carpet underfoot and the white paint on the walls there was no decoration. The open windows showed the beauty of nature to be more captivating than anything money could buy. Cassie took a deep breath as a hot breeze wafted through the window and through her hair. This room was exactly to her taste. As was everything about Dr. Rutherford. Pure torment, that's all it was. She busily set about the task of spreading out silverware.

Within the hour, the dining room was transformed from tranquil to boisterous. Men of all ages, with long sideburns and tailcoats, burst in one at a time to cheers from those who had already gathered. They were all very loud. Cassie had never seen English gentlemen behave so boisterously, and she wasn't sure how she felt about it. Her instinct was to feel they were being crass with their exaggerated laughs and their constant hugging and patting, but she knew that her instinct was driven by the voice of a society that had abandoned her. So she tried to accept what she saw, tried to imagine that a man didn't have to be proper to be respectable. She tried to digest that in this land, wealth was not always accompanied by a superb upbringing. It was hard.

"Malcolm, you should join us for tea tomorrow," said a stocky blond man. "We promise there will be absolutely no tea served, just rum."

Malcolm. It was the first time she'd heard his first name, and she liked it. It sounded like Mountain. Cassie stood in the corner, waiting to refill empty bowls and glasses, but all the while, she watched him. He was fascinating. He had not greeted his guests as they came in, but treated them cheerfully as expected burdens. "I'd wondered when you might arrive. I knew it was peaceful around here." This was the warmest greeting a guest could get in this house, yet no one seemed to mind. Malcolm was so kind in the face, casual in posture, and playful in the eye that even his insults felt like embraces.

Now that they were all seated and eating, he allowed conversation to flutter around him, without once joining in. He didn't speak about politics, he didn't participate in gossip about friends and family. But every time someone made a good joke, he immediately offered his full attention, a smile squinting his navy eyes as he laughed good-heartedly. He liked to tip his chair back while he ate. It was most improper, but Cassie found it charming. It was as though he were determined to be the most relaxed man in the room. His confidence and disinterest made him the natural leader of the otherwise boisterous group, for every time he graced the room with any remark at all, everyone fell silent to hear it.

"Miss Madison!" someone called to Cassie.

The voice startled her into attention, and she dazedly approached the stocky blond man who had summoned her. "Yes, sir?"

"Did you know," he began somewhat drunkenly, "that Dr. Rutherford here, Malcolm to you and me, is one of the only convicts to have survived the jungle during an escape?"

Cassie's green eyes flung wide.

"Isn't that something?" he asked boastfully. "A full month he survived out there! Before they caught him and whipped him half to death," he added with a chuckle.

Cassie looked at Malcolm, who was avoiding her gaze. He was tapping his fork absently against the table, his expression somewhere between somber and uncomfortable. She couldn't believe it. Was this a drunken tale? If so, then why wouldn't Malcolm look at her? "Oh, don't be so modest," said his friend, flinging an arm about his shoulders. "Tell the girl. You were a real hero in the barracks."

Malcolm looked to another friend for help, and his silent request was received. "This might sound strange to you, Kevin," said a curly-haired gent, "but some men don't actually like to tell their servants about their personal lives."

"Oh, Miss Madison here isn't a servant," said the drunken gent. "She's a member of the family. Isn't that right?" he asked, giving her a friendly squeeze round the waist.

Malcolm's face said plainly that he disagreed. "Miss Madison is, in fact, a servant," he countered mildly, "and I'll ask you not to touch her." He glanced pointedly at the hand which clasped Cassie's waist.

"Ah, come now," the blond man laughed, throwing up his hands, "can't a man have a little fun with a pretty lady?"

"Not when she works for me," said Malcolm, but his light smile showed that he was making allowance for his guest's drunkenness.

Cassie wanted desperately to break the tension which she felt responsible for causing. "May I get you something from the kitchen?" she asked the gentleman who'd been asked to unhand her.

"No, no, nothing," he muttered. "On second thought, more rum!"

The evening wound down, and Cassie had much work ahead of her. The men had not been delicate eaters, and they had made several scratches on the beautiful table that she would have to polish out. "I'm sorry for the clutter," Malcolm said, once the last guest had gone. "My friends are . . . well, you know," he smiled in that adorable way of his, "Well, they're . . . pigs." He broke into a full grin.

Cassie could not help sharing his smile. "It isn't any trouble," she assured him. But all she could think of was the tale she'd been told. Had he really been a convict like herself? And had he really tried to escape? How could a convict become a doctor?

"Do you need anything?" he asked. "Because I'm about to retire."

"No," she assured him, looking nervously about. "No, I'm sure I'll be fine."

"Then . . . uh . . . I'll see you in the morning."

Cassie heard footsteps outside the window. She gasped.

Malcolm turned around, then assured her, "Oh, that's nothing. That's just . . . a friend of mine. I'm expecting . . . my friend."

Cassie sighed her relief.

"Well, good night," he said, slouching from the room.

Cassie watched him move, not to the staircase but to the front door. He did not turn up the lantern. He quietly opened the door and let in a tall, slim creature who moved right into his arms. Cassie's heart sank a little as she watched. The dark-haired woman snuggled into his chest, and received loving, masculine squeezes in return. The expression on his face was that of a man in love. He lifted her into his arms as though she weighed no more than a cloud, and then he kissed her without mercy. "I have waited all day to see you," said a small voice. Malcolm did not reply, but put her down and led her to his study. There, he pinned her to the wall and devoured her lips greedily as his free arm gradually pushed the door closed behind them.

Cassie looked around at the dirty dishes, then carried them into the kitchen, and began scrubbing.

Seven

In the morning, Cassie found Faith in the kitchen, preparing breakfast. "Good morning!" said the kindly woman. "Now, don't worry, you aren't late. I just had to get a head start with this porridge."

"Good morning," smiled Cassie. The kitchen was alive with sunlight and the scents of garden flowers.

"Since you're up, you may as well set the table," said Faith, "but I've nothing else for you to do until the doctor comes downstairs."

Cassie went immediately to the task assigned her. It didn't take but a few moments, and then she rested in a wobbly kitchen chair and watched the cook at work.

"Rowdy bunch, aren't they?" asked Faith, referring to the guests last night.

"They're not bad," said Cassie politely. "They just like to have fun, I suppose."

"Ill-mannered is what I call them. In England, I wouldn't have served their like! But for the doctor, I imagine there isn't much I wouldn't do. He's a kind gentleman."

"Yes," Cassie agreed, trying to sound nonchalant. A little pause ensued, and Cassie found the courage to end it with a daring question. "Faith?"

"Yes?"

"I don't mean to sound intrusive, but I can't help wondering about the doctor's lady friend. Have you met her?"

Faith stopped what she was doing and faced Cassie with a worried sneer. "She didn't come here last night, did she?"

"Well, someone did. I didn't get a good look at her, but she was very slim and had dark hair."

"Ugh!" said the cook, licking porridge from her fingers. "That's Priscilla. I'd hoped the doctor had stopped welcoming her after the last time she broke his heart."

"She broke his heart?" asked Cassie anxiously, knowing well that she was not as sorry about that as she should be.

"Yes," said Faith bitterly. "Between you and me, the woman is no good. He loves her. He's always loved her, ever since they first met. But she doesn't love him back. She just uses him because he buys her nice things, and he knows it! He bloody well knows it! But he doesn't care. Mmm," she grunted, shaking her head in frustration, "I really had hoped that was finally over. I'll tell you this much, though. I won't serve her, and the doctor knows better than to ask. When they first began courting, I was perfectly civil to the girl. I'd wait on them hand and foot at every meal. But when she left him for a wealthier man, you should have seen how it tore him apart! I told him, 'Don't you ever bring that woman back here.' Of course, he didn't listen to me. He's stubborn as a mule. As soon as she came back to him, he took her in. It's as though the man likes to suffer." She said this with as much love as indignation.

Cassie said nothing.

At noon, Malcolm returned from the hospital, carrying some packages for Cassie. He had bought her some shoes and simple dresses, and something else, which he hid from view. She did not know whether the remaining item was for her or not, but she thanked him for the clothes, and immediately changed into them. She knew that her bare feet looked ridiculous in a house this lovely, and that her convict's gown must be an embarrassment. So she changed quickly into her new beige gown and comfortable slippers. On her way downstairs to fetch the doctor's tea, she overheard him speaking to an older colleague who'd accompanied him. "Malcolm, you're the best surgeon at the hospital," the man said.

She heard Malcolm give a low laugh. "That isn't saying much, is it?"

"No, it's not," agreed the gentleman. "Our Sydney hospital is an abomination. But you are one of the finest surgeons I have ever seen, and that's why I urge you to take heed. When someone comes to our waiting room, they are either put in your hands, in which case they live, or they are given to one of the unqualified doctors, in which case they die. That's why it's so important that you operate on the right people."

"I've no way of knowing who the right people are."

"Stop being obstinate," insisted the colleague. "You know perfectly well of what I speak. Rumor has it that respectable citizens are dying in the waiting room while you treat convicts!"

"That is terrible," Malcolm agreed. "It's horrendous. That's why we need more staff and better nurses."

"We need you!"

"But there is only one of me," Malcolm reasoned. "I can't treat all of the patients simultaneously. We simply need more help, and better doctors."

"But you are being wasted when you assist convicts first!"

"I don't assist convicts first," Malcolm insisted. "I assist those in the most dire need first, regardless of who they are. Often, as it turns out, convicts are in the worst condition when they reach the hospital. They are beaten and decrepit and bleeding all over my floor. I won't make them wait while I treat a bellyache."

"But they are convicts!"

"They are patients."

"They are *supposed* to be suffering for their crimes!"

"Not in my hospital."

"It isn't *your* hospital."

"Well, maybe if it were, you'd fire some of those doctors who are killing patients left and right with their incompetence. And where are my nurses? I thought we were going to get some more on the last ship?"

"Not enough arrests were made," the colleague said regretfully. "They're not arresting as many women as we need them to. And of the ones who came, many were too old or violent for nursing."

"I don't care!" Malcolm cried out with a half-laugh, "Give me old and violent nurses. That's fine. It's a hell of a lot better than nothing."

Cassie broke in. "Excuse me, sir. May I bring your tea?"

This broke the men's angry mood. They both slumped in their chairs and looked at each other, silently calling a truce. "Yes, Miss Madison," Malcolm said quietly. "Thank you."

When tea was over, Cassie retired to her room. But within moments, she was disturbed by a knock. "Yes?" she asked, delighted to see Malcolm on the other side, holding something in his hand. Something which had undoubtedly been the hidden gift from town.

"I . . . uh . . . I hope I didn't disturb you," he said nervously.

"Not at all."

He held out a cloth-bound book, adorned with deep red roses. "I . . . I don't know whether . . . well," he scratched his head, "I guess you overheard last night that

. . . that I've more or less been where you are. That is, imprisoned."

Cassie lowered her eyes.

"Well, . . . now that the cat's out of the bag, so to speak, I . . . well, I wanted you to have this."

She took the beautiful book in her trembling hands. The cloth felt like velvet beneath her fingers.

Malcolm shrugged. "I found that sometimes writing out my thoughts made me feel better." He smiled awkwardly. "I just thought you might want to try it. Or not," he added and shrugged again. "Anyway, just keep it." He pointed to a lovely rolltop desk in the corner of the room. "There's a pen and blotter over there." Not wanting to prolong the awkwardness, he departed. And Cassie watched him go, clutching the diary to her breast.

She wasted no time in getting started. She closed her bedroom door for privacy and took a seat at the rolltop desk. She dabbed her pen into ink a couple of times, then began to write the date. But she did not know it. She had lost track of time, and was certain of only one thing—the year. Carefully, in the most elegant hand she could manage, she wrote boldly across the top of her diary's first page: *Cassandra Eileen Madison, 1823.* Then she looked out her window and began to shake. For the first time in so terribly long, she would use her own voice, and tell this diary her own truth. She began this way:

I am in Australia for a crime I did not commit.

Immediately, she crossed out the line. This was not a biography. She did not have to explain herself to these pages. She must write what she felt like writing, not what she felt obligated to discuss. She began again:

I am so angry with my family for their abandonment.

But again, she crossed out the line. For this was not what she was feeling at this moment. If she were to write from the heart, she would have to write what seemed the most real and the most vivid at this very moment. She wrote his name.

Malcolm.

And then she wrote his name ten more times. Next, she sloppily jotted down every observation she had ever made about him, each one stupid, but each one somehow bringing warmth to her heart. She wrote:

Malcolm gives dignity to strangers. Like me. Malcolm forgot to build a servants' wing. Malcolm is a gentleman. But he survived the jungle. He stutters when we're alone. Because he's scared of scaring me. Malcolm thinks the whole world is a gruesome joke. That's why he always smiles.

Cassie bent her head back and took a deep breath.

Malcolm likes women who aren't good for him.

She closed her eyes and pictured him in the hallway last night, embracing that slender woman. And she wrote:

Malcolm kisses like a man well acquainted with death.

Eight

Far away, on an island quite different from Cassie's new home, Mrs. Caroline Madison was sprawled across a loveseat of pine-forest green. Her full, satin skirts tumbled over the edge of her seat along with a limp arm. "Oh, Christine," she whimpered dramatically, "you've no idea how these past months have aged me. Do I look older to you?"

"No, madam," said the somber young servant, dabbing a moist cloth on her mistress's brow. "You look lovely as always."

"Really?" Caroline's wide mouth grinned. "Do you mean that?"

"Absolutely, madam," replied the girl without enthusiasm.

"Well, it's a wonder." She sighed, dropping a weary palm over her heart. "For my trials have been grave. Can you imagine how I feel?"

"No, madam."

"No, no. Of course you can't. No one can, really. Even my husband, wounded as he is, cannot know the shame and the ostracism I have been forced to bear. Of course, he would if he were home a bit more often."

"Yes, madam."

A lanky young man strode past the parlour, munching on an apple picked fresh from the orchard. "Oh, Samuel!"

cried his mother. "Oh, Samuel, do come here and help your mother to her feet. I have been so weak of late."

Samuel winced as though he had been caught sneaking. "Yes, Mother," he replied.

She pressed hard into Samuel's shoulder, nearly toppling him in her efforts to rise. "That's a good boy, son. You've always been such a good boy."

"Whatever you say, Mother."

"Tell me, darling," she said, straightening her skirts, "is your father home?"

He looked at her as though she'd gone mad. "My father is never home."

"Yes, yes. That's quite right. However, I believe he was scheduled to arrive today. Have you seen any carriages?"

"None yet, Mother."

"Well, when he arrives, please send him directly to my bedroom. I simply must talk to him."

"Does he know where your bedroom is, Mother?" the boy asked snidely.

"Hmm? Oh, yes, yes. I think so. Of course he knows where it is, you sarcastic little tripe." Her eyes mellowed as she remembered she was supposed to be ill. "Now I must get my rest. Please have him sent as soon as he arrives."

"Yes, Mother."

Once the plump lady had ascended the staircase, Samuel turned his chocolate eyes on Christine. He was the only one of the children who resembled his father, sharing his pallid skin and brown hair and eyes. His sister and younger brothers all had their mother's red hair and Irish complexion. "How much does the family owe you?" he asked frankly.

Christine bowed her head. "Samuel," she implored, "my family has always served the Madisons, and you know that we wish to stay."

Samuel was bright for his age, and did not hesitate to

take her meaning. "I understand. How much must we pay to keep you?"

Christine looked ashamed. She could not even meet his eyes, she felt so miserable at having to pose an ultimatum. "It isn't that we don't understand all the troubles you've had," she assured him. "We really do, and we would like to stand by you, but . . ."

"But you need to eat," Samuel finished for her. "That makes sense. How far behind are we?"

Christine pursed her lips. "Samuel," she said gravely, "we've not seen a shilling since your sister left."

That's the answer he'd been afraid of. He turned away so Christine could not see his troubled face. First the bill collectors, threatening to take the entire estate, and now this. He wished he could get his parents to listen. But every time he brought it up with his mother, she said she felt faint, and retreated. And his father was terminally absent. It was as though the man wished he had no family at all. If he weren't careful, thought Samuel, he'd get his wish. For soon, there would be no home left for that overblown man to return to after his escapades. There would be no estate, no servants, nothing. They could all land in debtors' prison if it got bad enough. How he wished he had Cassie's business sense. How had she done it? How had she managed all those years to keep the collectors at bay, to make certain the servants somehow got their pay? She'd been no more than fourteen when she'd taken responsibility for this place. Now here he was, nearly seventeen, and he still didn't have the maturity to do it. "I'll get you that money somehow," he promised. But it was a weak promise, a promise without a plan. Christine knew it, and could think of nothing to do but nod and walk away.

When the master of the house arrived home, he was, as promised, sent to his wife's bedroom. Wilbert Madison was a small, stout man with very little chestnut hair remaining on his head. He always whistled when he arrived home, trying desperately to gain the attention of a family who routinely ignored his sporadic entrances. "Your mother wishes to see me?" he asked. "Is that all you have to say to your old man?"

"Pretty much, yes."

"How about 'welcome home'? How about 'I've missed you'?"

"Uh," Samuel scratched his head. "All right. Uh, welcome home. I've missed you."

"A little more enthusiasm wouldn't kill you," his father grumbled, beginning his waddle up the stairs. "Where are your brothers? I haven't even seen them yet."

"I don't know," Samuel shrugged. "I saw them a few hours ago, and they were trying to light a fire. Don't think it was going well, though I did see a little smoke coming from the stable a minute ago."

His father scowled. "Well, tell your sister to look after them! Oh, that's right. She's gone, isn't she? Well, go look after them yourself then!"

"Oh, speaking of that sort of thing, Father. Could you tell me where I might find some extra funds for the servants? You see, we've emptied our main account, and . . ."

Mr. Madison waved his hand in dismissal. "Ask your mother. I'm not good with money."

"But mother has taken to her bed, and . . ."

"Not now," grumbled the balding man. "This is a fine welcome home, I say. Two of my sons don't even bother to greet me, and the other starts off by asking me for money. I don't know why I ever come home." He huffed and puffed up the stairs, still muttering, until he reached the climax of his miserable welcome. His frigid wife's bedroom. It gave him shivers to have to open the door.

"Ah, Wilbert!" she cried, pretending to have difficulty opening her eyes. One hand was busily fanning herself, while the other kept reaching for bonbons. "How lovely it is to see you, my darling!"

Mr. Madison couldn't help smiling, though the sight of his much-too-familiar, titian-haired wife, collapsed dramatically on her canopy bed, caused him absolutely no romantic feelings. "I'm glad someone is happy to see me," he announced. "Two of my sons didn't even bother to welcome me, and the other, well . . . the other is Samuel." He shivered, as though the mere mention of his least favorite son gave him chills.

"Oh, my poor dear," moaned Caroline, shaking her head sympathetically, "you mustn't let those boys trouble you. They are, after all, the only children we have left."

Wilbert's cheeks grew rosy with the prospect of demonstrating his natural generosity. "My dear, I have an announcement."

"What is it?" she asked excitedly.

"I have decided that for the holidays, we shall send Cassie a shipment of sugar biscuits."

Caroline fanned herself rapidly, as though she might faint. "Wilbert! I told you not to mention her name in this house!"

"Now, my dear, that is most uncharitable of you," he lectured her nobly. "I have given the matter a great deal of thought. And it would be unchristian of us to forget our only daughter during the holiday season."

"But she is a . . ." Caroline glanced around as though to make sure she were not overheard, "a criminal!" she whispered loudly. "We mustn't send sugar biscuits to a criminal."

"Now, my dear, I think you should consider that she may not have committed that atrocious crime. Just because she was found guilty, does not mean . . ."

"Oh, of course she did," snapped his wife. "Don't be ludicrous, Wilbert. The courts are never wrong about these things. They have the evidence and the witnesses, and all the information they need. Believe me, if she were innocent, they'd have known about it."

"But doesn't it seem just a bit out of character? Of course, I didn't know her well, but she did seem awfully responsible to be running amuck in a murderous rage."

"That's how it always is with those people," she assured him. "That's what everyone says. 'But he seemed so normal!' And then boom! He goes on a murderous rampage. 'Tis always the way with that . . . element."

"But why would she murder a man she's never even met before?"

"Wilbert, Wilbert, darling. Do not try to understand the criminal mind. It is far too complex for ordinary people like you and me to understand. Let us just be thankful she did not slaughter us instead."

"Hmm." Mr. Madison had to scratch his bare head over that one. "Well, still, I think it would be good of us to send sugar biscuits. After all, it will soon be the time of year for thoughtfulness."

"Thoughtfulness?" she sneered. "When did she ever show *us* thoughtfulness? Did she think of us even once before hacking that poor man to bits? Did she think of our shame? Did she think of my social life? Oh, no, Wilbert. It's simply out of the question. It does no good to show those sorts of people kindness. They cannot be redeemed, and they are incapable of consideration for others. Do you know what I've heard?" she asked with a savvy lift of the eyebrow. "I've heard that most of those people don't even know about right and wrong. I'm not joking! They are so self-centered that they think anything they do is all good and well. Oooh, it gives me shivers to think that one of those . . . those . . . *things* lived here." She crossed her arms and trembled.

Wilbert opened his arms, imploring. "Oh, my dear, all these months must have been just awful for you."

She leaped into his waiting arms and wept into his

shoulder. "Oh, yes, Wilbert, oh my, yes. It has been perfectly awful for me."

"But if I know you, my darling, then I know that you are capable of reaching out to those in need, even when they don't deserve it."

Caroline lifted her chin proudly, and met her husband's round eyes. "You know me too well, my husband."

"I know I do," he smiled comfortingly. "Sugar biscuits then?"

"Yes, darling," she said with a bold tear in her eye. "Sugar biscuits."

Nine

It was a terrible risk, but she knew she had to take it. She could not live with herself otherwise. This, she had concluded after tirelessly pacing back and forth in her bedroom. Selfishly, humanly, she had not wanted to put herself on the line. But when she tried to settle into her decision, and live with her cowardice, she could not stand her own company. So she braved her way into Malcolm's study, her hands moist and trembling.

"Come in," called Malcolm. It was a Sunday, and he was spending his day reading books on biology. It seemed that his career was more than a job; he was genuinely fascinated by medicine. "Hello," he said, clearly startled to find that it was Cassie who had knocked. He was slumping in a heavily cushioned brown chair with his feet on a table. He closed his book and struck a more dignified posture. "What's on your mind?"

Cassie was positively pale, she was so worried. She could not believe she was doing this, could not believe that after only a few days of working here, she was asking for a favor. This could ruin her new assignment, could forever estrange her from the kind man who had taken her in. But she took a deep breath and began. "Dr. Rutherford, I . . ." She pressed her eyes closed and then let them fling open again. "I overheard you saying that the hospital had a shortage of nurses."

His expression was a startled one. Cassie knew that as

a servant, she was not supposed to be listening, even to conversations that took place right in front of her, which this one had not. Malcolm cast his gaze warily in her direction. "I see," was all he said. He was not pleased, and Cassie could feel that in her bones.

She swallowed. "I . . . I have a friend. She would make an excellent nurse! She is strong and capable, and very pretty. She's intelligent, and would learn anything she had to, I'm sure. And she has no assignment. She's completely available. I just know that she could help you!"

"Well, where is she?" he asked stiffly. Cassie had never seen him so stiff or formal with her before. She had clearly already damaged their friendly rapport, and that pained her. But she'd just had to do it.

"She's in the factory," Cassie explained pathetically, passionate pleading in her almond-shaped eyes. "But that was a terrible mistake. You must believe me. She would make an excellent nurse. They'd no right to put her in the factory. It was wasteful and irresponsible. She would make such a fine nurse. I know she would." She finished her sentence with the beginnings of a sob. Images of Sheena being dragged to the labor wagon overtook her, and fed into the anxiety of having to beg her master for a favor.

Malcolm's thoughts were unreadable. Clearly, all of this had taken him entirely by surprise, but how he felt about it was not obvious, save the fact that he was uncomfortable. "Miss Madison," he said, his blue eyes wide with unease, "the hospital put in a request for nurses. The report was that there weren't even enough house servants to go around, though the gaolers had utilized every able woman. If your friend was not considered able, then . . ."

"But she *is* able!" Cassie interrupted. "It's just that horrible Robin, he . . ."

"What was her crime?" he asked, keeping his own demeanor steady despite Cassie's obvious desperation.

"Murder," she admitted, "but . . ."

"Well, that's why," he concluded firmly. "They can't give assignments to murderers."

"They gave one to me!" she cried, and then clamped her hand over her mouth. A horrible silence ensued. Malcolm's mouth was frozen half-open. His eyes were startled, but otherwise, gave away nothing. Cassie thought she might die on her feet. Or at least, she thought she would like to.

At last, Malcolm broke the silence with a very calm, silky voice. "Miss Madison," he began, "I'm sorry, but I cannot free your friend from the Female Factory. It isn't in my power."

"But if you told them her name, told them you were willing . . ."

"They wouldn't listen," he finished for her.

Cassie thought she might weep. Her fists were clenched; her chest was hollow. She could not leave this room with nothing. She had damaged her relationship with the man whose assignment had saved her. She had confessed she was a convicted murderess. For all she knew, the moment she left the study, he would race to town and request that she be removed from his house. After all the damage she had just done to herself, she could not leave without carrying some hope for Sheena. "Dr. Rutherford," she said quietly, "please just hear me out."

There was no reply, so she was quick to continue.

"I've learned not to expect anyone to believe I'm innocent. I know that all convicts say they've been wronged, so we are all presumed liars. But just so it has been said, I will tell you. I am innocent of the crimes written beside my name."

Malcolm scratched his sideburns irritably and looked toward the window, perhaps wishing he were somewhere else.

"When I was put on that transport, it was the worst day

of my life," she explained. "I would rather have been headed for the gallows. I had never dreamed that the trip here would be so awful. The gaolers, they . . . they tried to . . . to use us. They treated us no better than animals. They would have hurt me, but . . . but Sheena came to my aid. She wouldn't let them touch me. She wouldn't let them near me. Dr. Rutherford, she kept me sane. She talked to me on all of those nights when I thought I might die. She held my hand, she . . . she was my friend." Cassie glanced upward for the first time to make sure that he was listening. He was. "When we arrived on shore, the gaolers played a trick on her, reporting bad behavior that had never occurred, even though she had . . . had bedded them to the promise of recommending her highly. They did it as a joke. They had a good laugh over it, and I had to watch the only friend I have left in this world dragged off to the place she had dreaded most. Please, Dr. Rutherford." She thought about taking his hand, but was too shy. "Please, whatever you decide to do with me, please help Sheena. I know you don't have much power, but at least you are free. And people will listen to you. Please."

"Look up," he said, kindly lifting her chin with a finger. He was smiling comfortingly. "Now, first things first," he assured her. "I'm not having you sent away. All right? Faith says you're a great help, and I've no fear that you're going to murder me." He restrained himself from laughing.

Cassie bent her head, something between a nod and a bow.

"Next thing," he said, chilling her spine by reaching out and touching a wisp of her auburn hair, "I want to have a look at that scrape on your head." His expression was casually comical. "And I think it might need some tending. Come."

Cassie touched the back of her head. She had nearly forgotten about the wound she had received on the transport, when she was so cruelly shoved against the wall. At night, she had to sleep on her side to steer away from the soreness, but during the day, she barely noticed it anymore. The doctor brought her to the window's light and asked her to sit on the sill. "Hmm." He chewed on his lip as he examined the wound, careful not to touch it. Then gently, he parted her hair, again not letting his fingers disturb the tender spot. Something about his touch was so caring and light that Cassie felt sinful in its wake. "Did you black out when it happened?" he asked, careful not to hold any worry in his voice.

"No," she replied, her voice rather soft and shy. "Does it look bad?"

"Mmm," he chewed pensively on his cheek. "No, not really. At least, it's not infected."

"I lost a little hair," she blurted out, guessing that he had already noticed.

"Yes," he replied nonchalantly, "but it'll grow back. And it's barely noticeable."

Cassie flushed at hearing him console her vanity.

Malcolm stretched out a careful finger. "I'm just going to touch some of the surrounding area," he warned her. "Stop me if it hurts."

"All right," her voice trembled.

He made a circle of firm presses around the wound.

"Ouch!" she cried, pulling away from him.

He squeezed her shoulder with affection, causing her eyes to close ecstatically. "I'm sorry," he said. "Looks like there's some bruising on the skull. I'll get you some ice."

"Bruising on the skull?!" she cried as he moved to the door. "Is that serious?"

"No," he assured her with a warm smile, "it's really not. Not if you didn't black out."

Cassie relaxed. "Well, shouldn't *I* get the ice?" she asked. "I am your housekeep, after all."

His smile broadened and reached his friendly eyes.

"No, you're my patient for the next five minutes. I'll get the ice."

Cassie felt numb in his absence. She felt like a little girl, sitting there on the windowsill, waiting for him to come back and take care of her again. When he returned, he set a cloth full of ice in her hand. "Press this against your head," he instructed gently, "Hold it there for about twenty minutes a day. And don't worry," he assured her with a comforting expression, "the wound's not as bad as I first thought."

"Thank you," she said, holding the cool bag to her sore head.

Malcolm dragged a chair to the windowsill. Arms on knees, he clasped his hands and smiled at her, waiting shyly for her attention. When she gave it, he asked, "Do you know why I was sent here, Cassie? May I call you Cassie?"

"Yes," she said. "That is, you may call me Cassie. But I don't know why you were sent here."

"I'll only call you Cassie for a minute or two," he promised. "Then we'll return to formal address." He swallowed hard and rubbed his hands together, nervously recalling the story of his own capture. "I . . . I became a doctor like my father, but I . . . I didn't think I wanted to be one. Not at first." He checked for her attention, and found he had it. So he continued. "I thought I'd raise sheep for a while, so I purchased some land on the Scotland border and made a go of it. I wasn't very good," he smiled charmingly. "I could hardly make ends meet. But to be fair, I had an enormous obstacle— my neighbor. He was a gruff man with a chip on his shoulder that far predated his acquaintance with me. He kept chopping down my trees, insisting that they disturbed his view. Kept moving his fence line deeper and deeper into my property, then pretending he hadn't done it. Worthless sod," he chuckled, with a disbelieving shake of the head. "I kept trying to talk to him, but he wouldn't listen, wouldn't even let me in his house. So, being young and reasonably stupid," he grinned boy-ishly, "I decided to get him back by putting a herd of his sheep into my own stables, so that he couldn't get them back without talking to me. I'd hold him in captive con-versation, you see. Then I could tell him to move his damned fence, and stop cutting down my trees." He sighed wearily. "Well, things didn't work out the way I'd hoped. He never did talk to me. Instead, he summoned the law, and I was promptly arrested for stealing sheep. Imagine my surprise to learn that this is a transportable offense." He laughed quietly at the stupidity of the world around him, something Cassie suspected he did a lot. "And that's how I came to be here."

Cassie looked rather speechless.

That made him meet her eyes with a smile. "A re-markably disappointing story, isn't it?"

Her lips curled in comical agreement.

"I always wished I had a better one," he confessed. "It would've earned me more respect in the barracks if I had say, killed my wife's lover or something," he laughed, "if I'd ever had a wife. But this is the story I'm stuck with. And the reason I tell it to you isn't actually because I hoped to impress you with my virile sheep-stealing story," he winked smartly, "but because I want you to understand my posi-tion here on this island. Since I had medical skills, they let me out of the barracks a tad early. At least, early for some-one who'd tried to escape a couple times," he shrugged. "And I like my work at the hospital, and I like this little house I've built. But I don't consider myself to be a free citizen." He looked at her pointedly. "I'm still a convict here. I have relatively little in the way of social status. Everyone who knows me, or even of me, knows what I am. The only friends I have are those who were in the barracks with me. What I'm trying to say, Cassie, is that you have come to me as though I were a gaoler. As though you and I were on opposite sides, and if I wished, I could help your friend. But it isn't so. I will always be a convict, as will you. We are inherently fighting the same battle, on the same side. Never expect that I can speak to the law on your behalf. I cannot."

Cassie understood. "I'm sorry," she said.

"Don't be. I'm just sorry I'm unable to help."

Cassie's eyes fluttered a bit. "That's the price you pay for being so kind," she confessed, "that I should feel obliged to trouble you for a favor."

Malcolm's face was sober. "I'm glad you find me kind," he said with absolutely no humor in his gaze.

"I do."

He reached out and brushed a red wisp of hair from her cheek, over her ear. The touch gave Cassie shivers. She could not read his thoughts, but she knew somehow that they were brilliant. She could see such intelligence in his face, and such secrecy in his slightly averted eyes. She waited breathlessly for him to speak, but just as he opened his mouth, there was a knock at the front door and Cassie was forced to rise from the windowsill and hurry to answer it. She felt murderously impatient as she swung open the heavy white door. But when she saw who was waiting there, her impatience transformed into misery and painful disappointment.

It was Priscilla.

Ten

Priscilla was more beautiful than Cassie had ever imagined from afar. Her hair was a deep charcoal, her eyes positively violet. Her face was a delicate array of fine bones, each of them placed with absolute elegance. She was tall and slender, and moved with natural grace. Cassie had never thought herself ugly, but she felt very self-conscious right now, in her plain beige gown and untidy hair. Priscilla looked surprised to see her. "I'm looking for Dr. Rutherford," she announced, as though Cassie could not have guessed.

"Yes," said Cassie with less subordination in her gaze than she usually had while working, "right this way."

As Cassie led her to the study, Priscilla drawled, "I already know the way. But if it makes you happy, then you can lead me there."

Cassie smiled broadly when she reached the study door. "I assure you it does not make me happy. But as I've been convicted of murder, I try to do what I'm told."

This comment produced the desired affect, as Priscilla looked quite shocked. The know-it-all expression fled from her face, and she may actually have been frightened, though Cassie wasn't sure. She knocked upon the study door, though it was already open, and said, "Dr. Rutherford. You have a guest."

Malcolm was not immune to the awkwardness of the situation. He had come very close to kissing Cassie a few moments ago, whether she knew it or not. He had reached out and tucked her hair behind her ear. It was not a provocative gesture, but it was one unfitting for an employer or a doctor or even a gaoler. Surely, Cassie knew, as he did, that something inappropriate had nearly passed between them. He hadn't had time to study Cassie's feelings. He didn't know whether she had been glad of his touch, or worried that he would make demands on her. He didn't know what she was feeling, but he was pretty sure he knew what she was thinking. She was thinking, as he was, that this was all a little awkward. The woman he had nearly kissed was, moments later, presenting his lover. "Thank you, Miss Madison," he said, appearing as comfortable and comforting as he could. "If you'll . . . uh . . . leave us. Thank you. And . . ." He brought her the ice pack she'd left behind. "Don't forget this."

Cassie returned his smile and made her exit. But she did not scurry off to get the feather duster, as she should have. She crossed her arms on the wrong side of that closed door, and listened, and the more she heard, the more drawn she was. "I couldn't wait to see you," came Priscilla's smoky voice.

Cassie heard shuffling, and then, "Don't talk. Just kiss me," from Malcolm.

"Your maid says she's a murderer."

"Did she? How odd." His voice was low and disinterested. Cassie thought she heard kissing.

Then Priscilla broke in. "Did you tell her you killed a man in the barracks?"

"No, why should I?" he asked casually.

"She might like to know you've something in common."

"I thought I told you to stop talking."

"Why do you speak so horribly, Malcolm?"

"Because I hate you," he said breathily, "and you know that. I've never lied about that."

"You don't hate me. You hate yourself for taking me back."

"No, I hate you."

"Then why do you welcome me into your home, night after night?"

"Because I like to punish you for breaking my heart."

"Is this your idea of punishment? Something I enjoy so much?"

"Yes. It's a punishment we can both enjoy."

"You are the strangest man I have ever known. I'm probably not safe with you."

"I've never lied about that, either."

"What happened to you, Malcolm? When you're not working with the dead and dying, you're reading about them. And then you come home to my torment. Why?"

"I told you that's enough talking. Do I have to say it again?"

"No," came the lusty reply.

There was a lot of heavy breathing and rustling of clothes. "On my lap," came Malcolm's voice. "Come here, I said. On my lap."

There was more movement, and then, "What do you want me to do, Malcolm? I'll do anything."

"I want you to stop talking. Don't talk and don't stop my hands."

Cassie thought it might be just about time to stop listening. Red-faced and wide-eyed, she raced from the hallway to the farthest broom closet, picking up whatever cleaning vessels that absently fell into her hands. She mopped and dusted and polished, not daring to think anything about what she had heard. She was completely dazed . . . and wonderfully intrigued. At last, after more than an hour had passed, she finally settled into one thought on the matter. It did not summarize all of her feelings, and it did not mean she was finished with her thinking. But it was a thought that seemed worthy to be whispered out loud: She wanted to learn about the dark side of pleasure. And somewhere in the back of her mind, she knew that Malcolm was the only man who could ever teach her.

Eleven

Samuel Madison was feeling more like a grown man every day. Today, he was dressed in a velvet coat, satin neckcloth, and top hat. He felt utterly ridiculous, and everything itched. He hated this growing-up business, but an early adulthood was the price he paid for having irresponsible parents. He had come to accept that.

"Why, Samuel! Come in, come in," said his uncle. "It is terribly wet out there."

This was true. In fact, it had been wet ever since his arrival in London. His horses didn't like to move in the rain. He'd had to lead them by the reins through much of the dark night, forcing them every inch of the way. His shoes were sloshy, and his hat soaking wet. He was all too eager to leave the dark, quiet cobblestone sidewalk in favor of a warm hearth. "Look who it is!" his Uncle Egbert called to his wife. "Why, it's our dear nephew!"

"Oh, my!" she cried, "Do come in, child. Come in and get dry! What a horrible night!"

Samuel, never having been raised with any real manners, flopped into the nearest armchair, staining it with his suit's moisture. "Ah, that is nice," he said.

Mrs. Sarah Madison turned to her husband in dismay, but he would not scold his guest for soiling their furniture. Even if it were some of the finest in all of London. "May I bring you some brandy?" offered Sarah.

"No, no, I'm fine," said Samuel, peeling off his gloves. "I never drink unless it's to get drunk."

Egbert laughed as though it must have been a joke, but he found he was chuckling alone. Samuel was quite in earnest. "Well, then. Sarah, I think I shall have a brandy for myself, thank you. What . . . uh . . . what brings you all the way to London on a night like this, young Samuel?" He settled into a nearby couch, fixing his bushy gray eyebrows into a listening expression.

"Well, it's this way," began Samuel, slouching boyishly in his seat, "you remember my sister, Cassie? Of course you do. Well, as it turns out, by all I've been able to surmise, she's the only one in our entire family with any brains. And I'm afraid we're in a bit of a fix without her."

Egbert grunted sympathetically. "Yes, she was a very sharp young woman."

"Not that it takes a great deal of sharpness to be the cleverest one in our family," Samuel was quick to point out, "but yes, she did have a way of keeping things under control. She really knew how to talk to people, how to organize things. And I'm afraid that I don't."

Egbert felt that he should argue, but didn't quite know how.

"So you see why I'm here," explained Samuel. "My family's in a great deal of trouble, and we're in sudden need of a rich relative to bail us out."

Egbert was taken aback. "I beg your pardon."

"What's the matter?"

"Well, I . . . I had rather thought you had come for a social call. I didn't expect to be asked for money, if that is what you are doing."

"Well, of course," Samuel chuckled. "Why would I pay you a social call? I don't even like you that much."

Egbert furrowed his brow. "I see why you say Cassandra was the negotiator of the family."

Samuel shrugged. "So what do you say? May we have some money?"

"I should say not!" he bellowed, just as his wife brought the brandy. "Thank you, my dear. Please leave us." He turned his angry brown eyes on his nephew. "I believe I could count on one hand all of the times you have visited me in your lifetime. That goes for your father as well, and he is my very own brother!"

"But I've already explained that," said Samuel with puzzlement. "We don't like you very much. Why would we visit someone whose company we scarcely enjoy?"

Egbert's face grew positively red, his bulbous cheeks inflating. "Then why should I give you money?!" he cried.

"Oh, all right," said Samuel diplomatically, "I see where this is going. All right. How many social visits will it take before you'll give us cash? One a year? Two?"

"I don't ever want a visit from any of you!"

"Well, of course not," laughed Samuel. "You don't enjoy us any more than we enjoy you. See, that's why I was trying to save us all the trouble. I could have stayed here all week long before asking you for the money, but that would have been torment for us both, wouldn't it?"

Egbert was stumped by that argument. "Well," he said calmly, "nonetheless, I see no reason that I should give money to such ungrateful relatives."

"Ungrateful? We don't have anything to be grateful *for* yet. But if you give us the money, then you can forever call us ungrateful, and be quite on the mark."

Egbert wiped his forehead with a handkerchief. He was feeling relieved that his own sons had turned out better than his brother's.

"You ought to be glad," Samuel explained, "that you're the one to whom grandmother left all her money. If she'd favored my father, then you'd be the one asking help."

"Your father married Irish," he grumbled. "What did he expect?"

"I think he expected that marrying in a drunken rampage would be grounds for annulment the next morning, but that's really beside the point. The point is that you have the entire family fortune. And what little my family had, to the best I'm able to tell, has been spent. So I thought it would be awfully brotherly of you to help out."

Egbert sighed heavily, then took a hardy swig of his brandy. "Are you sure the money is gone? Are you sure there aren't some hidden funds somewhere?"

Samuel shrugged. "As far as I can tell, we're on our way to the poorhouse."

There was a strangely pleasant twinkle in Egbert's eye all of a sudden. "Dear nephew," he said, as though overcome with sentiment, "I should not blame you for your abrupt demeanor. Naturally, you've not had much upbringing. What, with your family scarcely able to afford servants, much less nannies."

"Precisely," beamed Samuel. "I'm glad you're catching on."

"Well, I know I shouldn't do this," began his uncle with another heavy sigh, "but as you say, it would be unbrotherly of me to refuse. I can hardly have my own relatives sent to the poorhouse, now, can I?"

"Certainly not! Think of the shame to you."

"And the heartache," added Egbert gruffly. "It's the heartache that would be worst of all. So rest assured, young man, I shall do what I can to assist."

"Really? Why, thank you! Thank you very much!" Samuel stood up, and began shaking his host's hand most eagerly. "This is wonderful! I . . ." He looked around the room, a sudden wariness in his expression. "I uh, I don't have to stay the night now, do I? I mean, we're done here, aren't we? There's no reason to . . . to chat longer, is there?"

Egbert scowled. "No."

"Ah, good," he sighed with relief, returning to the task

of pumping his uncle's hand. "Thank you again! Thank you so much!"

Egbert watched the boy's departure, a certain mysterious look in his eyes. When all was quiet, he felt his wife's arms wrap round his waist. He patted her clasped hands with affection. "Were you listening?" he asked without turning.

"Yes," she replied, burying her face in his back. "What a horrible boy."

"But to us, he's wonderful," said Egbert darkly. "You do see that, don't you? He's everything we hoped he would be."

Sarah only sighed.

"My angel," he said, whipping around to face her, "everything will be all right."

She snuggled into his embrace, trembling in her worry. "Oh, Egbert. I'm so scared. Everything has gone so horribly wrong! It's all just . . . just awful! Sometimes I can't even sleep at night. I wake up, fearing that something terrible has happened. My stomach sinks, and I lose my breath. Oh, Egbert! Let us just flee. Let us just run from here. I don't care where we go. Anywhere! Just somewhere where no one can find us."

He grabbed her wrists and fiercely met her eyes. "This is nonsense! Do you hear me? It is utter nonsense. Nothing has gone wrong. Everything is fine. We are fine. And we will always be fine."

Her head was shaking wildly. "But . . . but it's not the way you said it would be. The girl . . ." She bowed her head. "I can't even speak her name."

"Cassandra," he said sharply. "Her name is Cassandra."

"But you said," she sniffed, "you said that . . . that she would be sent to the gallows! You said . . ."

"I don't control the courts!" he bellowed, causing his wife to cower. He immediately repented by drawing her into his arms. "It's all right, Sarah. Everything is fine."

"But she'll be back in twenty years! What will we do then?"

"Twenty years is a long time."

"But our children will have families of their own then! Think of them."

"Don't worry," he said, stroking her narrow back, "nothing is going to happen in twenty years."

"But the girl . . ."

"She won't be coming back."

"What do you mean, she won't? The judge said . . ."

"Shush, my dear. I've taken care of everything," he promised her. "Ask no more questions. Just rest assured, Cassandra Madison will perish in Australia."

Twelve

Cassie saw Malcolm more clearly every day. Each time he moved, or spoke, or refrained from speaking, she learned something about him. The more she learned about him, the more she wanted to know. And the more she yearned to understand him, the fuller her heart grew. She brought him breakfast each morning, lingering by his side, not wishing to return to the kitchen until he'd dismissed her with a smile. She had learned to read his smiles. Some of them were meant only to be comforting, others were used to share a private joke. Sometimes he smiled only to be polite. Hardly ever did his smiles express genuine joy. For Cassie was coming to understand that Malcolm, though gentle as a lamb and sociable as a tiger, was, in fact, living in a world of darkness. And any hand which reached into it might well be bitten off. Some of his smiles were a warning to back away.

"More tea?" asked Cassie, keeping her eyes averted.

Malcolm had grown increasingly uneasy around her. He liked her very much, and was pleased he had hired her. But he'd never been able to stop thinking about the kiss that didn't happen. He worried that she was afraid of him now, feared that he had stepped out of his boundaries as employer. Worst of all, he was tormented by the question of whether he should try again some day. He wanted to. Every day, she had grown prettier in his eyes. The face that he had once thought perfectly lovely, he now found positively stunning. The green eyes, which had been so striking at first glance, were now absolutely gorgeous. Her red hair no longer cute, but breathtaking. This had always been Malcolm's way of falling in love. It never happened suddenly for him, for he was not sufficiently moved by sheer appearance to experience love at first sight. His heart had a way of surrendering gradually, as a woman's warmth seeped through his outer skin. It took time, but when it happened, it was powerful. He knew all the signs, and he knew that it was happening again. If he weren't careful, he would fall in love with Cassie. "Yes, more tea. Thank you." His smile was weak and brief.

Cassie poured, her emerald eyes fixed on the teacup.

"Thank you." He dismissed her with a courteous nod.

Cassie departed, though she would rather have remained idly beside him, just so she could gaze on him while he ate and read his book. She was delighted when Faith immediately thrust a platter of toast into her hands and said, "Here. Take this to him."

Cassie returned to Malcolm, beaming with the excuse of having a platter of toast to offer. He looked up from his book and caught her eyes. "Oh, uh . . . thank you." He reached for a slice and folded it into his fist. He was not a gentlemanly eater, but Cassie didn't mind it the way she minded it from his guests. Malcolm didn't chomp casually at his food because he enjoyed being a brute. He did it because he was disinterested, always thinking about something more important than his manners.

"Will you be home late again?" she asked, imagining that she had an acceptable reason for asking this. A servant needed to know when to expect her master, didn't she?

"Hmm?" His navy eyes were always so startled by her feminine voice. "Uh, yes. Yes, I'll be late again." He reached for the jam.

"Perhaps when you get more nurses, you won't have to work so late," she suggested, though she could not come up with a rationale for a servant making this frivolous remark.

"Won't make a difference," he replied. "I'm working late because too many people are getting hurt. More nurses will only mean that more of them survive long enough to make it to the operating table." He smiled and met her eyes to see whether she appreciated his dark humor, or was repulsed. She smiled back.

"If you need help," she offered uncertainly, "I could . . . I could go with you some morning."

He bent his head in thought, as though she had either asked him a tremendous favor, or offered an enormous sacrifice. "No," he said at last, "believe me, this is a better assignment than the hospital is. We'll wait for the next shipment and see if we can rescue some women from the Female Factory. They'll be happy to do the work, and you'll be glad not to." He smiled shakily as he rose from the table. "Enjoy your day."

Cassie couldn't help wondering how it would feel if he sealed that morning farewell with a kiss. Every day he departed, bidding her a good day as though she were his wife, and all day, she waited for his return. In some ways, it seemed to Cassie, all that was missing was the kiss. She cleared the table, lonely in his wake. Then she cleaned the dishes and retreated to her bedroom for a quick diary entry before the silver polishing phase of the day. She still loved her bedroom. It really did feel as though it were her very own. In fact, there were days when she nearly forgot that she was serving penal time. She believed she was a traditional servant with unusually luxurious accommodations. There were days when twenty years didn't seem such a long time. And days when she was all too aware that if anything ever went wrong, she could be flung from this cushy assignment and sent to some unthinkable fate. For the next twenty years, she would never be allowed to relax and feel secure in her station.

She held her diary to her nose and took a deep, leathery sniff. Then she settled into her desk, let the hot breeze blow from the jungle, through the rear garden, into her bedroom window and right onto her face. She opened her diary and wrote:

I wonder that I may be in hell, for it is only ten weeks to Christmas, yet the world is deathly hot. Sometimes I look around and I see beauty in the tropical winds fluttering the trees and rippling the sapphire waves. Sometimes I see convicts (though I'm told not to use that word) limping by the roadside, beaten, hungry, and forlorn. I never watch them, but turn away, for they are reminders of what will become of me should this assignment ever expire. I live in deep terror, but I hold it at the back of my throat, where it remains no matter how often I swallow. All that keeps me sane is Malcolm. There is nothing that would rattle his deep, cynical sense of calm. Whenever the world feels too random, my own circumstances so frighteningly out of my control, I look to him as one who has made his peace with uncertainty. I know that I shall never have him. I am lower than filth in this godforsaken land, unfit to be any man's bride. But sometimes I dream of lying in his arms, of feeling his adoration. Even seeing the wish on paper makes me feel a fool. But what do I have now if not my dreams? And what a dream that would be.

Malcolm had to work so late at the hospital that he missed his supper entirely. His rambunctious friends made do by convening at someone else's house for the meal. But Faith was personally offended. She had spent her entire day preparing supper, and couldn't bear to see it cold and untouched. She went home with a grumble on her lips and a wrinkle in her brow. She muttered to Cassie something about seeing that the food didn't spoil, something about making sure he ate something before bed, and something about young men who work themselves into an early grave. Cassie was left alone in the silence of night. She never knew what to do in times like these. She couldn't bear to think. To reflect on her past was too painful, for her past had led her to this place. To think about the present was positively dreary, for she was, after all, a slave. And to think about the future was the worst of all. So she settled into a comfortable chair by a starry window, and thought of nothing. The silence of the house was beautiful.

Then, for just a moment, she thought she saw a shadow move in the garden. She leaned into the window, squinting at the rosebushes. There was definitely a shadow that did not belong. She suddenly realized how very alone she was, and how very helpless. Without Malcolm here, there was nothing to protect her from an intruder. But the shadow was so still. Perhaps it was not a person at all. Perhaps it was merely an animal scurrying about, or . . .

When she heard a knock on the door, she nearly cried out, she was so startled. But she stopped herself in time, and held her heart steady. She rushed to the front door and opened it for a very haughty-looking Priscilla. Cassie had never been so relieved to see the raven-haired vixen. "Priscilla," she said, "did you see anything outside? When you came up . . ."

"That's Miss Crane to you," said Priscilla sharply.

Cassie bowed her head, knowing she had been in the wrong. "Yes, I'm sorry," she said humbly. "Miss Crane, did you see anything?"

"Try staying out of your master's brandy," she suggested coldly. "Perhaps the phantoms will disappear."

Cassie could not help scowling. Not only was she wounded by the intended insult, but Malcolm had never since the day she arrived requested to be called "master." It didn't seem Priscilla's place to suggest the term. "May I help you with your shawl?" she asked stiffly, her green eyes biting.

"No," said Priscilla, strolling toward Malcolm's study. "I'm just going to wait for the doctor."

"By all means," Cassie whispered to the beauty's turned back. Then she tossed her hands up in the air and walked away. She returned to the window, and saw that the shadow was gone. This was more frightening than finding it still there, for now she knew it had been alive and moving, whatever it was. She sighed, and returned to her chair. She was glad she was no longer alone in the house. Priscilla was not great company, but at least she was . . . well, an alternative target for the attacker. Cassie giggled at her own shameful thoughts. She imagined herself faced with a burglar, pointing urgently at the study. "There's a prettier one in there! Go get her!" Cassie giggled for a few moments more before retreating into a thoughtless daze.

It was well past her usual bedtime when Malcolm finally came home. She felt a little excitement at hearing his distinctly masculine footsteps in the hall. He was rubbing his eyes and yawning when he caught sight of her running to greet him. "What are you doing up?" he asked, a gentle smile forcing its way through his exhaustion.

Cassie looked down at her wringing hands. She could not tell him that she'd waited just to see him before bed. "I . . . well, you have a guest. I wanted to warn you before you go in your study."

"A guest?" he moaned, his eyes narrowed in half-sleep.

"Priscilla . . . Miss Crane."

His expression changed somewhat. It seemed the mere mention of Priscilla's name had the power to awaken him. His back straightened and he now looked like a man preparing himself for an enticing battle. His eyes held a little more spark as he nodded kindly at Cassie. "You really didn't have to stay up to tell me that, but thank you. I hope you sleep well." He listened to her return the sentiment from somewhere very far back in his mind. Then he watched her beautiful face disappear into the kitchen, and thought how nice it would be if they could talk again someday, not as servant and master, but as two convicts. He really got tired of receiving curtsies from someone he wanted so desperately to know . . . as a person . . . as a woman.

Cassie was really not sleepy yet, but knew that she would be tomorrow if she did not get some rest. She stayed up, dusting clean tables and polishing silver that was already sparkling, until she felt that she could force herself into sleep if she tried. Unfortunately, to get to bed, she had to climb the staircase. And to climb the staircase, she had to pass Malcolm's study. And it was from outside his door that she overheard a most devastating conversation.

"Malcolm, why don't you marry me?" asked Priscilla's husky voice.

Cassie froze, one foot on the first stair.

"I didn't know you wanted me to," came his disinterested reply.

"Of course I do. Why wouldn't I?"

Silence. Cassie could feel Malcolm thinking hard.

"Wouldn't it be fun to have a wedding?" Priscilla asked. "A party with cake and a honeymoon?"

"You want to get married so you can have a party?"

"A party and a husband."

He gave a little laugh. "You would hate having a husband, Priscilla. Believe me."

"Malcolm, I want to marry you."

His reply was demanding. "Why?"

"Why not?"

"I can think of lots of reasons why not. Give me a reason *why.*"

"Because we're mad for each other."

"We torment each other."

"But you love it, Malcolm," she drawled seductively. "You love the excitement, the bitter pain."

"I love bringing you to my bed," he retorted. "Nothing more."

"Then why not bring me to your bed every night?"

"Don't I already?"

"Malcolm, this isn't fair to me." Her voice became more natural, less seductive. "I need a name, I need respectability."

"Oh, is that all?" He gave a little laugh. "Fine. Why didn't you just say so?"

"You mean you'll . . ."

"Certainly. Why should I care? Here I thought you were talking about marriage, and all you wanted was legality. Fine. I've no objection to lending you my name."

"Oh, Malcolm," she whispered gratefully, "you really do love me."

"No, I really don't. I don't even like you. I can't trust you."

"Then why would you marry me?"

"Because I'm bedding you, and I feel obliged to lend you respectability."

"I know you love me, Malcolm."

"Just kiss me."

"I love it when you talk to me like that."

"I know you do. Now kiss me."

There was a long pause.

"Oh, Malcolm," Priscilla sighed, "what sort of wedding shall we have?"

"You can have any kind you want. Just make the arrangements and have them bill me."

"I don't care what you say, Malcolm. I know that you love me."

Malcolm did not reply, but Cassie was sure she heard more kissing. She ran up the steps and fled into her room. Her heart sank pitifully into her gut, and she had to hold herself round the waist. It was over, her favorite dream shattered. Her bedroom door shut tightly, she paced in circles until she collapsed on the bed in a fit of silent sobs. It had been more than a dream, she realized at that moment. It had been a hope. A real, tangible hope. And now it was gone, along with every speck of goodness in her life. She would have to help with the wedding, no doubt. She would have to watch the two of them marry. And she would be left behind, to twenty more years of servitude. She was so pitifully forlorn that she could not write in her diary that night. She was so achy and quivering that she did not even notice the shadow which had reappeared outside of her bedroom window.

Thirteen

Priscilla stretched out across a rough, wooden floor, candles flickering all around her. She let down her shiny black tresses and breathed heavily, her violet eyes glowing in the dim light. Gradually, she let down one shoulder of her dress, and then the other. She loved to feel air against her bare skin. She hiked up her skirt, revealing her long, slim legs to the disinterested, shabby room. Then she rolled her weary neck. "Was she there?" boomed an unfriendly voice.

Priscilla was not surprised that she had a visitor. She barely glanced his way as she replied. "Yes, of course she was there."

A middle-aged man stepped into the candlelight, his boots thumping on the rough floor, his blue eyes glistening angrily beneath graying hair. "What did you say to her?"

"Nothing," replied Priscilla. "I didn't know I had to make small talk."

"Don't be smart with me," he snapped. "What was she doing? Was she alone?"

Priscilla sighed heavily. She wished desperately to be alone, and glared at the gentleman for invading her privacy. "She was alone until I got there, yes. And then she was no more. What she was doing, I cannot say. Possibly sweeping or scrubbing. It's hard to say what those cleaning women may be up to."

He yanked her roughly by the arm. Though she struggled, she was pulled to her feet, a sore elbow caught in his grip. "Don't you sass me," he scolded.

"Let me go," she griped, trying to pry his fingers apart. "Let me go, Miles!"

Rather than let her go, he slammed her brutally against the wall.

"Ouch!" She gritted her teeth and rubbed her throbbing head.

"Now, you listen to me," he sneered. "I sit here all day while you throw yourself at that . . . what's-his-name. I sit here, and I think about it, and it kills me. It really does. But I put up with it because I know you're getting the job done. But when you come home, I don't expect to get his bitter, tired leftovers. I expect you to be bright-eyed and happy to see me. I expect you to answer my questions and do it with a smile. Do you understand me?"

Priscilla nodded, her breath rapid and heavy.

"Good." He flung her free of the wall, and watched her stumble. "So you kept an eye on that Cassandra?" he asked firmly.

Priscilla nodded and rubbed her arm.

"Good. And things are going well with you and what's-his-name? You're not going to be expelled from his house and lose sight of the girl, are you?"

She shook her head.

"Excellent. And you thought he wouldn't take you back," he reminded her in jest. "You thought he'd have nothing more to do with you."

"That's not what I said."

He looked surprised to hear her speak. "What?" he asked with a raised, silver eyebrow.

"I didn't say he wouldn't take me back," she explained quietly. "I said that he shouldn't. I did leave him for another, after all."

"Well, obviously Dr. Rutherford was smitten enough not to mind."

"He does mind. He hates me," she confessed bitterly. "And I would hate me, too."

Miles studied his lover's beautiful, raven-crowned head bowed so humbly in the dim light. "Do you feel guilty?"

"Of course I feel guilty," she spat. "Leaving him was the biggest mistake of my life. I thought I loved another, but I was so wrong," she said passionately. "There is no one like Malcolm. I don't see how any woman who knew him could bring herself to love another. I wanted desperately to get him back, almost from the moment I left him. And then you came along and forced me to make a game of it, to trick him, to use him for your own purposes."

"I didn't force you," he said defensively. "Nobody forced you to do anything."

"My whole life has been forced on me!" she cried angrily. "It's as though you're telling a starving peasant that he's not forced to beg! Everything I do is driven by necessity. Don't tell me I'm not forced."

Miles approached her gingerly. "Oh, my poor dear," he said kindly, and with condescension. "Really, it can't be that bad."

She slapped away the hand that threatened to brush her cheek.

"So stubborn," he smiled, "so much anger trapped within so much beauty." He leaned forward to kiss her face.

Priscilla did not resist, but she winced until the kiss was over.

"You just keep an eye on that girl," he warned her, "and everything will be all right." He caressed her bare shoulder with a rough hand. Finding her skin soft and golden, he ventured to the valley between her breasts.

"Don't touch me," she said exasperatedly, but without fear.

"Now, now," he patronized her, "don't be so unpleasant. Haven't I told you how deeply I adore you?"

"That means nothing to me," she informed him.

"Well, I have something that means a great deal to you." He jingled some coins in his hand, and displayed them for her enticingly. "How about that?" he asked.

Priscilla couldn't help smiling a little, perhaps at the sight of money, or perhaps at herself for being so easily bought.

"I thought that would put a smile on your lips," he grinned, leaning in for another kiss.

This time, Priscilla allowed the assault without flinching a bit.

"Come," he said, wrapping his arms about her waist, "there's a very lonely bed in the other room."

Priscilla sighed heavily, as though preparing herself for something unbearable. Then sweetly, she nodded and allowed herself to be led to the bedroom. She looked longingly at the warm mattress. How she would have enjoyed a night of real slumber, with no one at her side! She wondered what it would feel like to awaken to her own company, just herself and the early morning sun. Privacy was one of the first things in life she'd learned to do without. As a girl, she was crammed beside seven other children in one cot. She had lived in the city, where people were forced to see, feel, and smell each other all day long. Once she reached womanhood, she learned that even her own body was not a sanctuary. If she wanted to survive, she would have to let men touch it.

As she lay beneath Miles, looking out the window, trying to ignore him completely, she dreamed about a night of complete solitude, in which she did not have to pleasure anyone but herself. The stars were twinkling so brightly out there. As a woman, she knew she could not even take a walk under cover of night. It wasn't safe. She could not be alone inside, and she could not be alone outside. She was forever trapped beneath the muscles of men. But even as this angered her, she knew that there was one man whose prisoner she would gladly be. Malcolm. He was the finest man she had ever known. The most decent, and the most utterly savage. Could it be that he would really marry her? That he would really take her away from this life? Miles would be furious if he knew her plan. She'd been told to renew their affair so she could watch Cassandra's every move. But wouldn't it be just if she could come away from this with more than money? The thought of marrying Malcolm sent shivers up her spine. And yet . . . there was guilt. That poor Cassie! If she only knew the danger she was in.

Fourteen

It seemed to Cassie that Malcolm was sulking. She wasn't sure of it. It was a scorching hot Sunday afternoon, and as usual, Malcolm spent the day in his study. Cassie disturbed him only once, to bring his afternoon tea, and it was then that she noticed his somber mood. She'd caught him staring out of the window rather than reading. There was a dullness in his navy eyes, as though he had spent too much of the day thinking, and hadn't set one foot outdoors. Cassie could remember days like that, from her own bygone life in England. She remembered those Sunday mornings when staying home seemed so luxurious for the first few hours, and then how sluggish and regretful she would feel by afternoon. Malcolm had that cloudy, unhappy look that she always had by the end of such days.

He took his tea without smiling. He thanked her without meaning it. Then, before she had even left, he returned to stroking his chestnut sideburns and staring out at the sun that did not touch his face. On the other side of the door, Cassie wondered at his behavior. She scolded herself for hoping that he regretted his rash decision to marry Priscilla. But it did seem possible. Though Cassie had overheard the proposal days ago, Malcolm had yet to mention it to anyone. Faith had remained blissfully ignorant thus far, and Cassie thanked the heavens for that. She did not want to witness the cook's reaction when she heard of the disastrous arrangement. And now, it seemed that after days of Malcolm's careful silence on the topic, he was quite vividly sulking. Cassie could not help viewing this as a sign of hope.

It was not until late that evening, however, that her optimism would be validated. She was sitting at her desk, her diary open, but her pen not moving. She was trying to decide whether she was over her heart-sickness well enough to write again. Suddenly, there was a knock on her bedroom door. She stood up immediately and scurried to open it, knowing that it could only be one person. "Dr. Rutherford," she smiled, her insides bubbling with delight.

"Hello, there. I . . ." He swallowed uncomfortably. "Don't . . . don't worry. I . . . I just came to make certain all is well. It's been a while since I checked on you." He cast his eyes pointedly toward the bed, and then quickly away again. He smiled reassuringly. He didn't want to scare her by visiting so late at night.

"Oh, I . . . I'm fine. Please come in." She widened the door so that he might venture through. She felt a thrill at watching him cross the room and settle into her very own desk chair. His long legs stretched out before him as he tried to seem at ease. She realized she had never seen him lounge in this room before. It was exciting to find him so near her bed. "Is there . . . is there anything else?" she asked.

He shook his head slowly and steadily, his elbows resting on his knees, his hands clasped together. He was such a fine and handsome man, and yet so void of vanity. His suit was so casual, his boots so worn, his neckcloth so simple. But no matter how badly he slouched, he could not help being elegant. And no matter how modestly he dressed, he could not hide his handsome face. "Just wanted to make certain you were comfortable here," he muttered. But he did not get up to move. It was clear he wasn't going anywhere, and Cassie was glad.

"And yourself?" she asked boldly. "Are you also feeling well?"

Malcolm bit his lip as he looked up. Slowly, he shook his head.

Cassie bowed hers, as though in regret. "Will you tell me about it?"

It seemed that Malcolm had come upstairs to do just this. He was not surprised by her question, and he patted his hands together while he gave it some thought. "I . . . I wondered if it wouldn't be too much to ask for a woman's perspective."

"Of course not," she said quickly. Then she slumped a bit to seem less eager.

Malcolm was watching her closely, but it was impossible to tell what he was thinking or what he was trying to decide. At last, he spoke. "It seems I have become engaged," he said to a lantern on the far side of the room. "I know I haven't spoken of this before, but in truth, I've been rather reluctant to have Faith learn of it." He caught her eye again, and cracked a smile. Cassie returned it.

"I see," she replied with restraint. "Well then, I suppose congratulations are in order."

He sighed and grinned wider at the same time, causing the sigh to sound like a laugh. "I don't know about that," he hedged.

Cassie worked hard to remain motionless, expressionless. She had a very clear opinion about this matter, an opinion that was unbefitting of a servant girl. "Why do you say that?" She tried not to sound as though she were encouraging his doubts.

Malcolm made a fist and absently punched his hand a couple of times. "I . . ." It seemed that he couldn't finish, that he couldn't bring himself to explain. But after a moment's pause, he looked away from Cassie's striking eyes and said, "I'm not certain she's the right woman for me."

Cassie's heart grew full and plump within her breast. Her eyes began to flutter in relief. "Why not?"

Malcolm no longer hesitated. He had spoken this much, and knew he might as well finish. "You've met Priscilla, haven't you?"

Cassie nodded.

"She's not a very nice woman, is she?" he asked rhetorically, his face alight with a sympathetic smile.

Cassie laughed and blushed, but felt she had best not answer.

"It's all right," he said mildly. "I know she's not. But something about her . . ."

Cassie did not at all like the expression that came over him then. He looked starry-eyed, as though he were remembering Priscilla's silky black hair and shimmering violet eyes. Cassie self-consciously touched her own reddish locks, as a few strands fell sloppily from her bun. She glanced down at her small, practical body, mentally comparing it to Priscilla's long and lithe one.

"Why do I pursue her?" he asked aloud. "I can't think of anything I like about her, anything we have in common at all, and yet . . ." He shook his head speculatively. "I'm just drawn. I'm just drawn to her."

It seemed that there was going to be a lengthy silence. Malcolm was still thinking, and seemed as though he were preparing to say more, as though he did not expect Cassie to have anything to say on the matter, as though he expected her only to listen. Her crystal-clear voice nearly stunned him. "Sometimes," she said, her pink lips quivering, "sometimes we cherish those things which are far removed from us, things with which we cannot identify. Because secretly, we want something better than ourselves. We want to be loved by someone more perfect than we are."

Malcolm was so moved by the beauty of her words, and by the bell-like sound of her voice that it took him a moment to lick his lips and reply. "I don't think Priscilla is perfect by any means."

"No," agreed Cassie, folding and unfolding her hands, "but you think she is alien. She does not remind you of yourself, and therefore, you are drawn." She turned from him and faced the wall, clutching her waist, as though she feared her heart might sink and slither away if it were not held tight. "Someone who is nearer," she continued, her voice beginning to tremble, "someone who is less frightening, less haunting, not so . . . so inhumanly beautiful"—she took a deep breath to keep from sobbing—"may be overlooked, you see. No matter how much she may suit you, or . . . or how much she may . . . may care for you." She was trying so hard not to collapse into tears, concentrating so hard on the crisp white wall in front of her and all of its paint bubbles, that she did not feel him rise from his chair. She did not notice him at all until his breath tickled her hair.

He turned her around with gentle but firm hands. "Cassie," he whispered to the top of her bowed head, "Cassie." She did not reply, but stuck a fist in her mouth and shed tears all over it. He bent down so he could try to look her in the eye. "Cassie," he said gently, "what is it?"

Still, she could not answer.

So he studied her face carefully, and ventured, "My God. Have you fallen in love with me?"

She nodded, red-faced and still weeping all over her fist and arm. He tried to pry her hand from her mouth. When he'd succeeded, she said, "I'm sorry," so hoarsely that it was hard to recognize her voice.

Malcolm shook his head. "No," he said quietly, "no, don't say that." He kissed her. Tasting mostly salt, he pressed his lips into hers, and squeezed her in a firm embrace.

Cassie looked up at him, her green eyes like the jungle on a rainy day. Her face was desperately apologetic, and she started to speak. "I . . . I know I shouldn't . . ."

"Don't be sorry," he said, then leaned in for another kiss. Cassie melted in her relief, at his unspoken profession that he returned her feelings. She snuggled into his embrace with fierceness, a thousand lost hopes fading from her memory. She let him devour her mouth, in fact, encouraging him to do so. Her lips were but a toy at his disposal, to mold and move as he willed. Her mouth opened wide, beckoning to him, showing him that she held no secrets, that he could plunge as deeply as he wished, and find nothing to stand in his way. He stopped while he still found himself able. "I swore I wouldn't do this," he whispered, parting from her lips, still holding her jaw in his strong hand. "Cassie, I . . ."

"I'm so embarrassed," she frantically interrupted, "God, I . . ." She swallowed. "Look, Malcolm. I know there's . . . there's no hope. I know we can't . . ." She gritted her teeth to keep another sob from racking out. Her heart was full and heavy, aching and sliding within her breast. "Just . . . just don't tell me you hate me or I'm ugly or . . . Just don't walk out of here. Please." She dropped her head into his welcoming chest, receiving his kind strokes through her hair.

"Cassie," he breathed, squeezing her with all of his might. "Cassie, I can't . . ."

Her head was shaking against him before he finished the words. "Don't," she begged, "Don't talk that way. Please. Not after I told you how I feel."

"But you don't know what I am, Cassie. You don't know me as well as you think you do. Cassie, there are things you should . . ."

"Don't!" she spat out, shaking the tears from her face. "Don't tell me I don't know what I'm saying. Don't tell me what I feel."

His nod was slow and respectful. "Fair enough," he agreed, marveling at the brilliance of her emerald eyes in their passion. "Fair enough."

"You came to me because you wanted me to talk you out of marrying Priscilla," she challenged him. "Don't deny it."

He smiled as one who'd been caught. "You're right," he said quietly. "That's why I came."

"Then don't tell me that I'm the one getting carried away."

Malcolm's eyelids grew heavy, his head bowed low. "You're right. I shouldn't have come."

Cassie turned her head bitterly away from him. He didn't know what he was doing to her, how much he was toying with her hopes. He could not come to her, make her confess her love like an abandoned child begging for a home, and then walk away. Not when he was her only bright light, and the hope that he might care for her the only thing opening her eyes each morning. "Listen, I've been a convict for a while now," she said bravely. "I know what I must look like. If you don't fancy me . . ."

"Cassie," he nearly chuckled, "God, it isn't that."

"Then what?" she asked, showing her teeth, squinting back the tears. "What is it?"

"Cassie," he warned, grabbing hold of her clenched hand, "You don't understand. You can't understand. I'm not what you think I am. I . . ."

She shook her head at the sound of his discouragement. "Just say it if you don't care for me. Just say it!"

Malcolm took a deep breath. How could she think that? How could a man live with such a warm, attractive woman for weeks on end without caring for her? "I am your gaoler," he said at last. "It wouldn't be right." But his hands were still flowing through her red locks.

"You don't care about what's right," she challenged him. "You think I don't know you, but I do." She met his eyes squarely. "You despise righteousness."

Malcolm was so uncomfortable within his breeches that he had to shift his weight and grind his teeth. This was perfectly awful for him. He was a good man in so many ways, and yet, she was right. He had a glaring weakness for sin. The mind that told him it was wrong to touch his convict servant, that she should at least know of his secret first, was doing great battle with the darkness that told him this was a golden opportunity for delicious pleasure with a woman he had long admired. "Cassie," he warned shakily, "I . . . I am not a gentleman."

She was well aware of that. She'd overheard enough shocking banter in his study to know exactly what sort of a lover he was.

He kissed her with a ragged breath, his heart beating frantically in his gut as he tried not to do what he so desperately wanted to. "Cassie," he swallowed, his eyes clouded, "send me away now before I do something you will regret."

Cassie shook her head emphatically. "I will not."

Malcolm was touched by her determination. He looked endearingly into her eyes, stroking her lips with his thumb. Why had he come to her tonight? Just to talk about Priscilla? Or had he hoped all along that it would come to this? Her eyes were so beautiful. He loved red hair. God, how he loved red hair. "You have one last chance," he whispered, "to send me from this bed chamber."

Cassie did nothing as he brushed her freckled cheek with his broad knuckles.

So it was decided. With shocking strength, he carried her to the bed. Cassie flopped in his arms like a rag doll who was tired of being beaten and just wanted to be loved.

"Do you still think it's wrong?" she asked, her breath ragged as he lowered her to the feather mattress.

"Terribly wrong," he replied, "unforgivably wrong."

He eased her into a recline, and gently spread her coppery hair across the pillow. He took care with his task, curiously examining each strand as though it might tell him more about her. He liked studying his partners in sin. For him, the companionship to hell was part of the glory. He snuggled his lips into her soft mouth once more, pinning her wrists above her head. Cassie opened wide and gave in. She loved the feel of his breath against her cheek, of his warm body completely covering her own. She had lain on this bed many times before, wondering how it would feel if he came to her in the night. And now she knew. It was joyous. His hand reached under her skirt, making her shiver at the touch of her bare knee. His navy eyes flashed brightly down at her. "Am I going too fast?" he asked pensively.

Cassie shook her head, too overwhelmed by emotion to say anything out loud.

Satisfied by the amorously confused look in her eyes, he smiled and backed away so he could get a better look at the leg he was caressing. It was a soft, pale thigh, absolutely perfect in shape. He squeezed it gently, and examined it with love, completely ignoring the rest of her for the time being. Cassie had to close her eyes against the small voice that reminded her how shameful this was. To think that she had once been a strong and prudish woman! That she had tended to her family's affairs as though their honor was her very own. And now, she was a prisoner, her body being stroked and examined by the man she was supposed to call "master." She should have felt humiliated, and yet, she did not. It was her world which had humiliated her, which had made her an outcast and sent her to this island. She could feel no further shame by giving herself willingly to a man she so adored. "I am no longer afraid to be called a sinner," she whispered absently. "I no longer care what anyone thinks of me."

Malcolm turned his attention from her leg to her lightly freckled face, which shone white in the darkness. "Welcome to Australia," he said pointedly, then moved his lips to her thigh.

"Malcolm," she whispered, placing a frantic hand on his sturdy shoulder, "I've . . . I've never done this before."

Malcolm wasn't sure what to say about that. His eyes shifted leftward and then lowered. He paused, thought hard, then asked, "Should I stop?"

"No," she replied desperately, "just go slowly."

Malcolm smiled at her, and thought her face looked positively girlish. With her reddish hair all tangled and her face still fresh from tears, she looked like a wet kitten. The notion that she was a maiden aroused him beyond reason. He had never taken a maiden before. There was something dark and wretched about ravaging an untouched woman. Malcolm became so stiff that he could barely contain himself. He massaged both of her thighs, and then spread them. His eyes fell upon virgin flesh, glittering pink in the moonlight. His mouth fell upon her, desperate for this feast which had been saved just for him. His tongue slid deep inside her while his lips quivered against her tender bud. Cassie's eyes rolled, and her head fell back. Her breath came in ragged gasps that made her breasts rise and fall.

Malcolm pulled away, and kissed the feast he'd enjoyed so well. He stroked its curls in gratitude, as though saying good-bye to something sacred. He studied it, and used a finger to play with it. He wanted to know all about it before he broke it open. "Tell me what you love," he whispered to Cassie.

She was perspiring, and unable to speak. Her private flesh was tingling under his touch, wanting to know him as badly as he wanted to know it.

"What do you love?" he repeated, looking up from his treasure to see Cassie's youthful, emotional face.

"I . . . I believe I love you," she rasped out.

He didn't like that answer. It was too calculated, too prescribed. "What else?" he asked impatiently.

"I . . . I don't know." Cassie wanted him to touch her more, and talk a great deal less.

"Do you love your family?" he asked.

"I . . . I don't know, I . . ."

"Flowers? Birds? What do you love, Cassie?"

"Why . . . why are you tormenting me?" she asked lustfully.

His answer was as frank as it was mysterious. "I just want to know. I just need to know."

"Why, Malcolm?"

He shrugged. "It excites me."

"Very well," she sniffed, trying to contain her swelling feelings of desire, "I love the diary you gave me."

"Why?" he demanded, his eyes aglow with intrigue.

"Because it's the only thing that will listen to me."

Malcolm liked that response, for it was an honest one. He rewarded her with a flick of his tongue that made her shriek in excitement. He raised her gown farther and farther up until he could see her white belly, her strong ribs, and at last, her perfectly shaped bosom. He had her sit up so he could remove all of her clothing, sparse though it was. The gaolers had not given her proper undergarments. "What did you want to be?" he asked, stroking her smooth sides with both hands.

"What . . . what do you mean?"

"What did you used to want to be?" he asked, gazing at her breasts, trying to make them jiggle with the flats of his hands.

"A . . . a spinster, I suppose. A well-respected spinster."

He wrapped his lips around her pink-tipped breast, rewarding her for another honest answer. He suckled with expertise, neither hurting her nor failing to arouse her sensitive peak. She touched the top of his head and let out a soft moan. She wanted him to swallow her breast, to take it harder, to make it sting. Her thighs were jealous now, remembering how he had once kissed them with the same fervor. She grew wet and yearned to rub herself against him. "What . . . what do *you* love?" she cried, trying to speak his own language.

Malcolm did not reply right away, but finished his task. Then he looked up frankly, with that handsome face of his, and said, "I love sin."

"Why?" she asked breathlessly.

"Because it is righteousness that sent me to this island." He grabbed her roughly into a passionate embrace, lifting her from the bed and bending her backward at the same time. Cassie's legs began to open instinctively. She loved Malcolm's mysteriousness. It gave him such power. It gave him the power to intrigue her, and that, in turn, gave him the power to hold her hostage.

"Imprisonment has been hard on me," she confessed in a whisper. "Sometimes I'm not sure I'm still alive."

Malcolm knew exactly what she meant. "Let me awaken you," he offered, "You're still alive, you're only fading." He kissed the hollow of her neck. "I can help you," he whispered.

Cassie's legs opened wide, the delicious night air breathing into her bare, secret skin. "Help me, Malcolm," she said, holding on to his neck, "help me come alive."

"Are you sure you're ready?" he asked.

She nodded.

So he moved a hand to his breeches, and conducted what he considered to be the tediously mundane task of removing his clothes so he could return to the glorious task of taking a woman. Cassie breathed rapidly as she watched his neckcloth yanked away, revealing skin that was both soft and sturdy. The coat and the shirt went, too, revealing a collarbone that was pronounced, and a masculine chest that smelled warm and cozy. His arms were long, slender, yet deceptively powerful. And then she saw hipbones protruding beneath a flat stomach. He was lowering his breeches. "Stop," she said nervously, putting out a hand.

"What's the matter?"

She giggled at her own ridiculous shyness. "I'm . . . I'm a little . . . uncertain," she confessed, not wanting to admit she was scared.

Malcolm thought that was both touching and intriguing. He glided his knuckles along her cheek, and stared intently into her eyes, trying to imagine how it felt to be so vulnerable and feminine. "There's nothing to be scared of," he assured her, "I won't do you any harm." Some confusion crossed his face, for he had never been with a nervous woman before. He wondered whether all virgins were this way. Something about her fear was positively delicious, absolutely enticing to a man who enjoyed flirting with darkness.

"I know," she apologized, "I know you won't hurt me. I just . . ."

"Shhh," he said, pecking her on the lips, reaching for her hand. "See?" he asked gently, wrapping her fingers around his manhood. "Do you see?" He smiled. She felt him swelling within her palm, and her eyes widened boldly. She saw that he was still smiling, completely at ease with the intimacy they now shared. "That's all it is," he told her softly. "There's nothing to be afraid of."

Cassie took his lips this time, devouring them in a renewed fit of passion. Malcolm let her do this, though he preferred to be in charge. He let her part his lips and thrust her tongue past their border. Then, with a palm on her breast, he readied her for penetration. He pressed himself deeply into her fresh, young flesh, closing his eyes at the glory of the tight squeeze. He felt her break open and bleed, bathing him in delicious guilt.

Cassie cried out, the feel of a man breaking into her suddenly becoming too much for a woman who had spent her life pushing people away. She felt resistant; she felt torn. She could feel him swelling within her, and knew she did not have the power to drive him out again. "Malcolm . . ."

"Open your heart," he interrupted her, "give yourself to me."

The moment she met his hypnotic eyes, those words lingering in her head, she found herself stretching, relaxing, opening. The swelling within her grew. Malcolm kissed her without mercy. He was demanding. He wanted more than her body, she could tell. He wanted to know her secrets; he wanted to devour her. As he greedily took of her mouth and her loins, she knew that this was what she had expected of him. This was why she had come to him. She loved his kindness, was intrigued by his strangeness, but most of all, was drawn to his darkness. He thrust into her over and over, without mercy. Once her body grew accustomed to his, it took his battering without pain. She felt that he was searching within her, trying to find something that she herself had never found.

Malcolm grew more and more distant from her. His forehead sparkling with moisture, his beautiful eyes averted into the darkness, an expression crossed his face that was not joyous, but sorrowful. For him, lovemaking was an exploration of his own deep sadness, and a study of a beautiful woman with whom he would share the journey. He relished the feeling of opening Cassie wider with each thrust, of forcing her to reveal herself to his probing manhood. She could not hide from him, and she could not escape his seeking. He squeezed and released her wrists, holding them high over her head, wanting her to feel helpless, to feel that resisting his feverish curiosity would be futile. He liked playing the captor. He enjoyed watching a woman struggle in vain beneath his surprisingly strong grasp. "How does it feel, not being able to get away?" he asked her.

"I . . . I don't want to get away," she replied, a thrill building in her belly as he slipped in and out of her with slickness and speed.

"I know you don't," he smiled, "but how does it feel to know that you can't?"

"I don't believe you would hold me," she panted, thrusting her fingers into his thick, dark hair, "if I told you to stop, and I meant it."

"But you don't know that for certain, do you?" he challenged, an evil glint in his eye, a gentle smile on his lips.

Cassie grew wetter and weaker as she writhed to see whether she could get out from under him. She could not. His eyes were fixed and strong, his face partly hidden in shadow.

"How does it feel?" he demanded.

She raised her mouth to his and sucked hard on his lip. He let her do this, then withdrew and repeated the question. "I . . . I kind of like it," she said, wrapping her legs all the way around him so that he could pierce her without any interference.

Malcolm rewarded her gesture with a comforting peck on the lips. "That's the way," he said. "If you keep being so good, I'll reward you."

Cassie smiled, thinking it must be a joke. But she saw no trace of humor in his face. His strangeness drove her wild. "How will you reward me?" she asked, unable to keep her mouth closed, unable to keep her lips away from his ear, from his skin, from his lips.

"I'll make you scream," he promised.

Cassie rubbed her tender nipples against his chest, hardening them, feeling that she might break into a cry if she were not released from this delicious torment. "And if I'm not good?" she asked breathily.

He liked that question. It made his face darken, and

he let out a sigh. "I'll let you wonder," he said, devouring her mouth with a fierce kiss. His thrusts hardened and quickened, the muscles in his back flexing powerfully beneath Cassie's trembling hands.

"Mmmm, too hard," she said, feeling ravaged by his demanding pushes into her center.

"Are you afraid?" he asked, gritting his teeth, trying to keep himself from losing control too soon.

"A . . . a little," she confessed.

"Let me see your fear," he said hoarsely. "Let me see it." He raised himself with both arms, just enough to see her trembling weakly beneath him. She was trying to smile, and she was excited beyond measure, but she was afraid. And in her sharp, brilliant eyes he saw the face of fear itself, alive in its purest state, breeding in her soul, multiplying before his very eyes. He grinned his recognition at one of darkness's many incarnations. The electrifying light of fright winked at him through Cassie's loveliness, and drove him over the edge of excitement. He breathed wildly into her ear, moaning deeply, slickening the inside of her body with his liquid passion.

Cassie wanted it to flow all the way into her heart. She wanted to feel his hot juices spilling even into her head and hands. But there were places he could not touch, and things he could not give. Their joining could only be partial, no matter how desperately Malcolm strived to consume her. Cassie gasped. "Malcolm," she pleaded, reaching for him as he withdrew, "I need . . ."

"I know," he said gently, "I'm not going anywhere." He kissed the tip of her breast, making it tingle, and then he pressed his tongue firmly against it, making her grab anxiously at his shoulders, ready to explode. But he withdrew his mouth and whispered, "Not yet." He left her hungry as he slid his face between her knees. "This is the way to do it," he explained, studying his favorite feast, fondling it with a careful finger as he examined its reaction. He cupped her with his mouth, still looking at her face to observe her virgin reactions. He began to flutter his tongue, and watched eagerly as her face flushed and contorted in the moonlight.

Cassie felt her emotions collecting in solid form. They were thickening and growing within her gut, and she could not stop them. With every rapid slap of Malcolm's tongue, she was pushed closer to embarrassment. And there was nothing she could do to stop Malcolm's tongue. Her knees bent and her eyes squeezed shut. "Yes!" she cried, grabbing Malcolm by the hair. Still appeasing her, he pried away her fingers, and pinned her hands to the bed as she melted in seizure. He did not allow women to grab him. It was simply one of his rules. Cassie's entire being exploded into tremors, and her glistening, moist body was finally limp, her face weak and confused.

Malcolm got on his elbows and kissed her. She looked tender and in need of affection. He studied that look for a good long time; then, satisfied that he understood it fully, rolled to her side, and gathered her into his arms. It had been a long time since he'd finished his lovemaking like this. Priscilla didn't like to be held. She liked to be sent on her way just as soon as it was over, for she hated to linger with the feeling of having been conquered. She wanted to disappear and come back once she'd regained her strength. But Malcolm had had lovers before who liked to be cuddled. He really didn't mind doing it. In fact, he rather enjoyed the contrast between a woman in the heat of passion, and five minutes later, the same woman, so still and tender. "Are you all right?" he asked, kissing her warm forehead. His arm wrapped around her, he squeezed her affectionately against his side.

"I feel fine," she assured him. She took a deep breath, and basked in the glory of being alive again, of being a woman for the first time in her life. "Malcolm?" she asked, her eyes closed peacefully. "Why do you enjoy power? I mean, why does it excite you?"

He was absently stroking her, gazing at the ceiling. It was not having power that excited him. It was watching people respond to power. That the power came from him was irrelevant. But he did not explain that. He didn't want to talk about this now. "Was it all right for you?" he asked, "Do you feel all right . . . about what we did?"

"Yes," she said without hesitation. "I adore you Malcolm. I have no regrets."

He replied with a kiss on top of her head.

"Malcolm?" she asked daringly.

He sniffed. "Yes?"

"Will you open up to me now?"

Malcolm was silent for a long moment. "What is it?" he asked at last, hoping that perhaps she would ask something simple, something he could answer right now and appease her.

"Tell me about the man you killed," she requested boldly. "Tell me what happened in the barracks." Cassie knew it was a deeply personal question, but how could anything be more personal than what they had just done?

She felt Malcolm stiffen. The arm under her shoulders grew tight, and the chest under her head grew hard. This did not surprise her, as she knew it was a delicate subject which undoubtedly made him tense. But his words completely stole her breath. "You've been eavesdropping?"

Cassie's eyes flung wide. Something in his tone of voice told her that he was accusing her of a crime he found unforgivable. And she was guilty. "Malcolm, I . . . I wasn't eavesdropping exactly. I just . . . overheard."

He was no longer stroking her, no longer squeezing her. His eyes remained fixed on the ceiling, his body turned to stone. "That isn't possible," he said, so casually that Cassie could barely hear the simmering rage at the back of his throat, "The door to my study is fairly thick. Your ear had to be against it."

Cassie sat up. His arm had grown so hard beneath her that it was no longer comfortable. "Malcolm . . ." But that's all she could say. His eyes turned on her, and in them, she saw cold rage. It was the worst kind of anger, for it was not the type which blew out like flame. It was rock solid, and sometimes permanent. "Malcolm." She made a weak attempt at smiling, but the grin would not come. She had made a terrible mistake. She didn't know why her offense had been so serious in his eyes, but she could feel his scorn. His affection for her had been new, not yet stable. And she had nipped its bud. "Malcolm . . . why do you look at me with such hatred? It was not so terrible. I . . . I was only on my way to my room."

"How would you feel if I had read your diary?" he asked sharply, dispassionately.

Cassie's heart sank. She would be devastated if someone read her diary. "I . . . I would be furious. I would be embarrassed," she admitted.

"Then you know how I feel."

Cassie's eyes pleaded with him. "Malcolm, I . . . I didn't overhear anything shameful."

He raised a dark eyebrow. "That I killed a man is not shameful?"

"I . . . I'm sure I would understand. If only you explain it to me, I'm sure I would be on your side. I . . ."

His head shook coldly from side to side. "No," he said stonily, "that's not the point." Cassie gulped as she waited for him to finish. "The point is that I wasn't ready to tell you about that. You've violated my privacy."

"I've violated you?!" she cried, rising from the bed, her bare feet falling on a soft rug. "I gave you my virginity, but if I learn a secret of yours, I am violating you?"

His response was steady. "You *gave* me your virginity," he countered, "Just as you said. I did not *give* you my secret—you took it from me against my will. Makes it different, wouldn't you say?"

Cassie's head bowed in shame. "Malcolm," she pleaded, shaking her repentant head, "please forgive me."

He scowled at the ceiling and chewed on his cheek. He gave the matter some cynical thought, and then made a callous and angry decision. "I'm sorry, Cassie," he said, getting up. "I'm a little disheartened."

"Malcolm, don't leave," she pleaded, arms tensely crossed. "I didn't mean to hurt you."

"Well, you did!" he bellowed, just before reaching the door. His navy eyes were wild with intensity and rage. "That was the worst thing that ever happened to me! Do you understand?" He didn't wait for the answer. "I would have gladly told you, I would have gladly opened up to you—some day. But you robbed me of the chance! You stole my privacy, and didn't even think enough of it to hide it! Just . . ." He rubbed his hair in anguish. "Just let me go to sleep."

He stormed from the room, leaving Cassie to her shock and shame. In his wake, she felt empty except for the threat of tears. The room was dark and silent. Her lips were parted and her eyes unnaturally wide. Her last hope for joy was gone. She had no friends, no family, no dignity, no future . . . and no love. Her head turned to the window just in time to see a shadow move between the trees. It was back. Whatever it was, it was back. She raced to yank open the panes. "Come get me!" she shouted to the darkness, her hair and her voice completely wild. "What do you want?! Why don't you just break into the house and kill me! Come on! Are you a coward?!" She picked up a paperweight and chucked it into the yard. "Just get it over with and kill me!" The shadow vanished into the jungle, and Cassie collapsed into a fit of ragged tears. She crumpled against the wall, where she would remain all night, weeping into her fiery hair.

Fifteen

Egbert Madison smoked a green-leafed cigar as he basked in the aftermath of lovemaking. Unfortunately, his wife Sarah was nowhere to be found. He turned to his more regular lover. "You are spectacular, my dear."

A chestnut-haired beauty curled up beside him, having too little shame to cover her lusciously bared skin. "I know I am," she grinned, her wide brown eyes gleaming at him.

Egbert had never considered himself a disreputable man. He loved his wife and enjoyed their life together. He was not at all as callous as his brother, Wilbert, who left his family for weeks at a time without so much as an explanation. His personal excursions were short ones, and he held their secrecy to be of the utmost importance. He would never want to hurt Sarah by allowing her to find out he was unfaithful. That would be perfectly cruel. That he had affairs was not wrong in his mind, for he did not believe it unusual. Normality was his measure of morality, but for his wife to learn of it would be unthinkable. That's why he worried about Emma, his most recent lover. She was not well known for her discretion. "Emma, darling, you have a most mischievous light in your eyes this evening. Won't you tell me what's on your little mind?"

There was nothing little about Emma's mind. "I was just thinking," she sighed.

"Well, I didn't doubt that," he chuckled, "I merely asked what your thoughts were about."

She was on her stomach now, propped on her elbows and playing with some gray hairs on his chest. "I was thinking how very much you are like your brother."

Egbert frowned mightily. "I beg your pardon."

"It's true," she smiled, masking the evil intent of her words, "you two have so very much in common."

Egbert did not like to be reminded that he was sharing his brother's mistress. He had rationalized their acquaintance by recalling that his brother had abandoned the woman. It was just like his brother. No woman could satisfy him for very long. He always craved someone new, as though women were like feasts—useless once devoured. He found such notions barbaric. And yet, it troubled him that Emma had once shared his brother's bed. Something about it seemed so . . . incestuous. "We have nothing in common," he retorted. "My brother is irresponsible and reprehensible. Why, I recently met with his son, Samuel, and was not surprised to discover that the boy is growing to be exactly like him. Entirely without grace and charm."

"Ah, yes," she sighed, "that's right. He has a family."

"If you want to call it that," he grumbled.

"I suppose that's why he left me, don't you think? Or did he merely tire of me?"

Egbert cast her a suspicious glance. This was a most unusual turn of the conversation. Why on earth would she want to bring up something as degrading as her relationship with Wilbert? "I wouldn't take offense," he muttered. "He doesn't treat anyone well."

"And neither do you."

Egbert stiffened. "What are you saying, woman?"

"*Woman?*" she asked drowsily. "Is that what you call me now? Not *love?* Not *sweetness?* Not even *Emma?*"

He was taken aback by her calm anger. She did not

seem hysterical or enraged. She seemed cool and murderous. "Emma, darling? What is all of this?"

"I was going to ask you the same thing," she smiled darkly. "What exactly is going on between us?"

He was baffled. Did he really need to explain the nature of an extramarital affair? Surely, they had a quiet understanding. "Emma, what do you mean?"

"I mean," she said through gritted teeth, "that I'm tired of being used."

"Used?" he asked innocently.

"Yes, used. Or what do *you* call it? What do you call it when a man ruins me, leaves me without a husband or a shilling, because 'Oh, did I forget to mention? I already have a family.'"

"My brother is a cruel man," he consoled her. "I do not condone what he did, you poor thing."

"You're no different," she spat.

"But that's not true," he insisted. "I'm entirely different. Why, I . . . I buy you lovely things. Do I not? And I will hardly leave you a pauper when I go."

"No, of course not," she laughed, "because thanks to me, you're very wealthy. Isn't that right?"

Egbert stamped out his cigar with some edginess. If the fact that she once belonged to his brother disturbed him, it was nothing compared to what she was now recalling. "Umm, yes, yes. That's quite right. So you see that I am not at all like him."

"But you framed an innocent girl to secure your fortune," she drawled. "Wasn't that a bit Wilbert-like?"

Egbert nearly lost his composure. But rather than letting her disarm him, he took a grab at her ammunition. "You wanted me to," he reminded her. "You're the one who warned me."

"Warned you, yes," she chuckled. "Warned you that Cassandra was on the verge of discovering your little secret. But I didn't tell you to frame her. That was your own idea."

Egbert licked his lips furiously. "That money was rightfully mine. Wilbert never did anything to earn it. He did not assist our mother in her failing health, and was not even there at her deathbed! The first time he'd anything to do with her in ten years was to hear the reading of the will."

"But obviously, your mother forgave him. Obviously, she really didn't mind his marrying an Irish woman so much as you think, nor was she troubled by his long absences."

"She was a kindhearted woman," he said both frantically and with love. "She would forgive her sons anything. That doesn't mean she was right in doing so."

"She wanted your brother to have half of her money."

"He didn't deserve it!"

"What would you have done," she asked lightly, "if Cassandra Madison had stumbled upon your mother's real will? What would you have done?"

"I don't know," he replied stiffly. "I . . . I can't afford to part with it anymore, even if I wanted to. I've run up too much debt."

"Then it's a good thing I warned you, isn't it? She was such an organized young thing."

He didn't like to think about her. He'd met her only once, and then she had been a child. When he thought about the "deed," he liked to think about his brother, how much he deserved to be cheated of his inheritance. But he did not like to think about the girl. "The man I killed was just a beggar," he said defensively. "He'd nothing to live for anyway."

"But I didn't ask about the deceased, did I?" she challenged. "I asked about Cassandra Madison."

He closed his eyes with a sigh. "I had to do it," he said. "I had to do it for Sarah."

Emma clucked her tongue. "How touching," she drawled. "Suddenly so concerned about poor, abandoned Sarah."

"She isn't abandoned," he remarked uncomfortably. "I take good care of her."

"But I thought you were going to take good care of *me.*" she said with feigned innocence. "Are you really going to provide for us both?"

"Certainly. I care for you both . . . in . . . in different ways."

"I see," breathed Emma. "We each get half a man then, while you get two whole women." She clucked her tongue, and shook her head. "That doesn't sound very fair, does it?"

Egbert let out a false cough. "If you're having doubts about our . . . uh . . . situation, then by all means, tell me."

"I think that's what I'm doing, Egbert."

He rose sharply from the bed and reached for his clothes. "Fine," he said, not even looking in her direction. "If that's how you feel . . ."

"Are you so surprised," she asked, "that I wouldn't be attracted to a man twice my age?"

He stopped midway through the act of dressing. Not attracted? What on earth? "Emma," he scolded, "what is the matter with you tonight?"

"The matter with *me?*" she scoffed. "You've bedded your brother's forsaken mistress for nearly a year, and then dared to call yourself more noble than he, and something is the matter with *me?*"

"Emma," he snapped, turning very red in the face, "I thought we had an understanding. I thought . . . I thought we were rather fond of one another."

"Fond of one another?" she laughed. "Your name is *Egbert,* for Christ's sake! I can't even say it in the heat of passion without laughing! And *Wilbert* wasn't much better, mind you. You say your mother loved you, but I'm not so sure!"

His cheeks were ballooning now in his rage. "Well, if I am such a tremendous joke in your eyes, then why, dare

I ask, have you fallen so eagerly into my bed all of these months?"

"Isn't it obvious?" she asked darkly, and something in her face made Egbert's heart sink.

"No, it isn't," he lied. But he was already getting an inkling.

Emma stood up and met his eyes frankly, frighteningly. "I hate you," she said, barely above a whisper. "I hate you and your brother both. You've used me, and you've spat on your wives, and neither of you is worth the mud on my slippers."

"I see," said Egbert pompously. "Then you've used me to get back at my brother. Fine." He was wrestling desperately with his pride, for he had never been so insulted. "But I daresay he wasn't so offended as you'd planned," he added coldly, "for as I see it, he was quite done with you."

Emma shook her head with pity for the man who could not comprehend the depth of her revenge. "I knew he wouldn't care," she explained. "Believe me, I knew he wouldn't care. If, after six years of bedding him, I couldn't get him to care about my broken heart or my lost virtue, then I certainly knew he wouldn't care that I bedded his brother."

Egbert looked confused. His simple mind was not yet able to decipher her scheme.

"I wanted him to lose his daughter," she explained at last. "The only person keeping him from bankruptcy, the only person holding his family together."

Egbert scratched his chin. "Oh, I see, uh . . . then . . ."

He was still thinking about it while Emma got dressed. "Poor Cassandra," she mused, yanking on her girdle, "the victim of a philandering father and an unscrupulous uncle. I hope this teaches her that she will always be battered by men."

Egbert was still thinking. No matter how hard he tried,

he couldn't put the pieces together. His eyes rolled up and then down again, his fingers scratching more and more furiously at his beard. His thoughts were so painful that he almost didn't catch a glimpse of Emma as she prepared to walk out the door.

"Let me help you," she suggested, tossing her hair over her shoulder. "Cassandra wasn't going to find out about that will. I lied to you," she explained, tapping him on the nose. "Have a good evening, Egbert."

He was huffing and puffing, afraid he might fall over.

"Yes," she agreed, studying his whitening face with disinterest, "it's a shame, isn't it? You had her sent to Australia for no reason. Some uncle *you* are. What was it you were saying about being a great family man?" She swung open the door. "Oh, wait!" she cried, turning around one last time. "That's right. I heard that transportation didn't turn out to be stiff enough punishment in your eyes." She smiled mockingly. "I heard that you've hired someone to kill her. Oh, dear," she drawled with false sympathy, "I suppose it's too late to undo that, isn't it? Yes, I suppose it is. Poor, poor Cassandra."

He was loosening his collar, perspiring heavily and trying not to pass out.

"*Now* don't you wish you'd really been a good family man?"

Sixteen

Cassie could hardly bring herself to face Malcolm. All night, she had asked herself how she could do it, how she could show her face before the man who had taken her maidenhood and then abandoned her, rightfully scolding her for her thoughtless, wretched behavior. Being hated was always disconcerting. Being hated when she had done something to deserve it was even worse. But to be hated by a man who knew her more intimately than anyone had known her before made her feel worthless to the very core. More than once during the long and painful night, she had made the resolve never to go downstairs, but to remain in this room until someone dragged her from it. But with the dawn had come reason, and a reminder that she had faced embarrassment before. Gone were the spirits and fears of the night as the sun shone upon the solid, mundane earth. She would face Malcolm as though he were one of her family's creditors, and she were asking for a third extension on a loan. She would lift her chin, she would pretend to be in the right, and she would shut down the part of her that always wanted to know, *What does everyone think of me?*

Malcolm was having breakfast with a colleague. Cassie, descending the stairs, took note of this coldly. This was his defense against her, she decided. He would hide in the company of a friend—he would not even have the courage to face the woman he had scorned, but force her into mundane civilities by creating a social occasion. She relished being able to shun him with her thoughts. He was not so noble, this man who called her an eavesdropper. He was a coward. Her eyes were hard and narrow as she strolled into the dining room. Her hair was pinned neatly behind her head, for she had not wanted Malcolm to think she was trying to win his affections with glamour. Her demeanor was modest and controlled as she brought out the tea tray, but it was not shy. It was the stiff demeanor of someone who was not afraid to share herself, but simply didn't want to.

"Tea, sir?" she asked Malcolm with tight lips.

When he looked at her, she met his eyes firmly, with an unreadably strong expression. "Tea?" she repeated.

Malcolm fumbled with his cup. "Umm, yes, yes. Please." He had not wanted to have company this morning. His colleague's visit had been both unexpected and unwelcome. In fact, Malcolm had desperately wanted to speak with Cassie before he did anything else today. He needed to apologize. He had been upset last night, not only by feeling he'd been spied upon, but more importantly, he had been taken by surprise, forced to think about a day in his life that he normally tried to forget. It was not Cassie who had made him so angry, but himself. He still could not bear to think of himself as a murderer. "Cassie," he began gently, but her cold eyes stopped him, warning him that nothing he could say in front of polite company would be enough to undo the terrible wrong he had committed. He had abandoned her on the night she'd needed him most. This apology would have to be profound, and conducted in private. It would have to wait. "Nothing," he muttered. "Thank you for the tea." Then he tried to bury his face in it as his colleague chattered on.

"The convicts need to be returned promptly," the man was explaining. "We mustn't keep them at the hospital longer than is absolutely necessary. The fact is that this city thrives on convict labor, and when too many are taken out of commission for too long, our economy suffers. Now, I know that you are only doing what you think is best as a doctor, but you must remember that there are greater issues to consider. When you do what is right in the name of health, you may also be doing what is wrong in the name of prosperity. Nothing you or any of the rest of us have could exist without the help of prisoners. This house was not built by paid laborers, nor was the road paved by them. You cannot simultaneously depend on convict labor and inhibit it."

Malcolm peered at his colleague from over his teacup. He looked surprised, as though he'd never expected the gentleman to stop talking. Realizing that there was silence and that he was expected to break it, he cleared his throat. "If they want them out of the hospital faster, why don't they beat them a little less?" He asked it rhetorically and softly, as one who did not intend to listen to the answer, but intended to sit patiently through it.

The answer did, indeed, go on endlessly. "How do you expect them to work hard if there isn't a threat of punishment? Do you think these are the sorts of people who maintain a work ethic? They won't do anything, I assure you, unless they are bullied into it. And without punishment . . ." He was still talking when Cassie brought out the breakfast platter. Malcolm's attention immediately shifted to her.

"Thank you, Cassie," he said, trying to tell her something with his eyes. He knew he could not straighten out the mess he had created until they got a chance to really talk, but he hoped that he could communicate something to her just by casting an affectionate look her way.

It didn't work. Cassie's back was stiff, as was her voice when she asked, "Will that be all, sir?"

Malcolm dropped his eyes, frustrated by his failure. "Yes, thank you."

His annoying colleague was still jabbering, as though Cassie had never visited the table. "If it'd been up to me, I never would have troubled you with this crisis," he was explaining as Malcolm rubbed his weary eyes, "but there have been complaints. From people who really matter, if you know what I mean." He glanced upward, as though to indicate people with tremendous social status.

Malcolm, in turn, squinted at the ceiling, as though expecting to find someone hanging from it. "Which people?" he asked, by way of a private joke.

"Important people," griped his guest. "You know, the people up there."

Malcolm couldn't help smiling. "Oh, *those* people," but that didn't stop his colleague from continuing on. In fact, by the time Malcolm was able to rise from the breakfast table and fetch his coat, he was already terribly late for work, and frantic over how many people may have been taken to the hospital in his absence.

"Really, I have a bit more to say," said his guest, though Malcolm had given him more than an hour in which to vent.

"Yes, yes," said Malcolm, yanking his arms through his coat sleeves, "but perhaps we could finish up on the way to the hospital." One time, someone had died from a simple wound ten minutes before his arrival. There were other doctors, of course, but not enough of them, and many were not licensed to practice in England, so pitiful was their training. Malcolm knew that he could not be at the hospital twenty-four hours a day, but he would not forgive himself if he stayed away any longer because of this chatterbox.

"Well, it's more difficult to talk in transit," objected the man.

"But I'm sure you can do it," said Malcolm, swinging open the front door. "Cassie! Cassie, where are you?"

She appeared modestly and stiffly before him. "Yes, sir?" she asked as though bored to tears.

"Cassie," he pleaded, "I must talk to you when I return home. All right?"

She looked at him steadily, clear disinterest in her eyes. "Will there be anything else?"

Malcolm was frustrated that she would not take his meaning, that she would not understand that he meant to apologize. But with a wary glance at his colleague, he shook his head. "No, that's all."

Cassie was relieved when he had gone. The hardest part was over. She had faced him after that humiliating night, she had established the nature of their future relationship. It would be cordial. She swept the floor and dusted the shelves. For the first time since she'd arrived in Australia, she felt she would rather be at the Female Factory. The work would be harder, no doubt, and the punishments would be brutal, but there would be no Malcolm, no regret, no embarrassment. There, she could be seen as a workhorse without a heart, and right now that was more appealing than being seen as a stupid, childish girl who had fallen in love too quickly, and then robbed of all hope of love on the same disastrous evening.

Faith knew something was the matter, but she could never have guessed what. "Feeling homesick?" was all she could come up with.

"A little," Cassie lied. In fact, she never thought about home. Her life in England had been a determined struggle to gain respect for her family. Now that all she'd built had crumbled, she didn't have even the smallest longing to return. After the way her character had been assassinated in the courtroom, she wasn't sure she'd be able to hold her head up before respectable folk ever again. And trying it certainly didn't sound like much fun.

"Well, that's natural, I s'pose," said Faith, her dark eyes shiny as those of one who had gotten plenty of sleep last night. Cassie envied her. "We all came a long ways to get here. It's never easy leaving family behind."

Cassie was puzzled. "Were you also a con—" She remembered not to use the word. "A . . . transportee?"

"Heavens, no," chuckled Faith. "No, my husband and I moved here with hope of a better life. We didn't have much in England, you know. Heard things were different here. Heard anybody could make good, no matter where he came from."

"And is it true?"

"Goodness, no. Look at me," she smiled. "Still a servant. Traveled halfway around the world just to bake bread in a warmer climate." Her chuckle held good humor. "But that's all right. You don't find out unless you take a chance, right?"

Cassie studied the large, handsome woman with interest. Mounds of salt-and-pepper hair were spiraled around her head, making her look like an aging queen. It occurred to Cassie that though she had seen Faith every day since her arrival, she had never really wondered who Faith was, or what it would be like to be her. How strange to think that if fate had willed it, she could have been born into Faith's body and circumstances, and her concerns would not be Malcolm and prison, but whatever it was that Faith worried about. Somehow, the thought comforted her and made her feel that her own life was not so very important. "What does your husband do?" she asked, wanting to get deeper into Faith's mind.

"Oh, he hasn't been able to find any regular work," she confessed with some embarrassment. "You see, around here, there are prisoners to do all of the common man's jobs. Unless you have some special skill or education, like Dr. Rutherford, it's hard to see why anyone would pay you a fair wage when they can pay the gaolers a laughable wage and get the prisoners to do the same work."

"You'll call them *prisoners* but you won't call them *convicts,*" observed Cassie.

Faith lowered her gaze warily. "Love, this is an unfair world," she began cautiously. "A lot of people get worse than they deserve, and a lot of people get better. Since I don't know who's who, I just stick to what I know. That some are in prison."

"But what's wrong with calling us *convicts?*"

Faith thrust her hands nervously into her apron pockets. "Words like that have a way of sticking, even after you go free. Let's face it," she added kindly, "none of us here are the cream of society. I think it's best we all just get along and don't hold too many grudges. This won't be a prison colony forever, you know."

Cassie tried to return her warmth. "Faith, I already feel better, just talking to you."

Faith patted the girl's shoulder affectionately. "There, now. I know it's hard, losing your family and coming to this strange place. But you're just about a grown woman now. You'll get through it. And who knows? Maybe it's not too late to find your life's path."

Cassie lifted an eyebrow.

"People have done more with less," Faith scolded her. "You mustn't give up. Twenty years may seem a long time at your age, but you'll be younger than I when you're free. From where I stand, twenty years isn't even a raindrop in the ocean."

Cassie sighed, relieving mounds of tension. "You may be right, Faith. There may be a way for me to survive. But I tell you," she added softly, "all of my life I've fought to survive. I suppose I'd always hoped for a little something extra, something besides breath in my lungs and bread on the table. Secretly, I think I've always wanted to find a rose in my path, something unnecessary, and more beautiful than survival."

Faith smiled understandingly. She, too, had been handed little in the way of life's frills. Of gowns and balls and jewels, she knew nothing. And yes, she had always wanted those things. But there were other luxuries in life. There were more of those non-necessities that made it all worthwhile. Faith had known more than a dozen merry Christmases in which everyone had spent money they didn't have to buy gifts no one needed. There had been punch that didn't nourish, but only intoxicated. Senseless laughter, pointless singing, and, of course, that mother of all useless essentials: love. She gazed fondly at the auburn-haired girl before her. Undoubtedly, the poor thing hated her red hair. All Irish did. And undoubtedly, she thought that life would be over twenty years from now. All young people did. But there was depth and passion in Cassie's lovely green eyes. There was beauty in her striking face. And there was heat burning through her freckled skin. "I think you'll find a rose someday," Faith assured her in a tone beyond appeasement. "But you'll have to keep walking if you're going to stumble across it. So don't give up."

Cassie sighed again. Faith's words meant a great deal to her, and yet, there was something the older woman did not know, something that would critically sway her advice. Cassie had already found a rose, and dropped it. She didn't know if she could bear to search for a new one. Ever.

Seventeen

Cassie was writing in her journal, and it was growing late. Malcolm was still not home, though this was not unusual. Cassie had the sense that he had to all but tear himself away from the hospital each night. Normally, she awaited him anxiously, feeling a flutter of excitement when she heard footsteps in the front hall. But tonight, she dreaded his arrival, and prayed that she could make it through the night without finding herself alone with him even once. One more night, she told herself. *If I can get through one more night with dignity, he will understand that I don't want to talk about it. He will leave me be from then on.* But suddenly, her eyes jerked toward the open window. It was not just a shadow this time, it was a noise.

Cassie was frantic. Faith was downstairs in the kitchen, but the two of them were alone. Why hadn't she told Malcolm she'd thought there might be a prowler? Somehow, she'd been distracted. And besides, the first time she saw the shadow, Priscilla came in right behind it. It may only have been she all along. And last night, she'd not gotten a good look at it before it scurried away. Then, it might only have been an animal. Cassie grabbed a lantern. She didn't know exactly what use a lantern would be against a prowler, but she summoned her anger, narrowing her eyes and clutching the lantern as though it were a deadly weapon. If need be, she knew she could do something with it, something that would at least let the prowler know he had come to the wrong house. Cassie had never been a woman who took battery lying down. This place may have squelched some of her fire, but not all. She might be murdered tonight, but at least she would make her attacker pay with a cut or a bruise or an eye.

The shuffling grew louder, and it was with horror that Cassie realized the prowler was trying to climb to her own bedroom window. Whoever it was, he was not here to rob Malcolm. He was here for her. Her breathing was heavy and her teeth were bared. At last, she saw a face in the window, and it made her scream and lurch forward at the same time. Lantern held high over head, she was just about to send it smashing on the skull of the intruder, when she realized that her assailant was actually a very pretty young woman. In fact, her assailant was no assailant at all. She tossed the lantern onto the cushiony bed and clutched both hands over her own mouth, as though this were the only way to stop the screaming.

"Don't they believe in trellises around here?" asked Sheena, plunging headfirst into the room. "Ouch. That really hurt."

Cassie fumbled quickly to her friend's rescue. "My God," was all she could think to whisper, as she helped the girl to her feet. "How did you . . ."

"Find you? Had to bribe a gaoler to tell me where they'd sent you." Sheena said this with some pride, as though bribery were a fine art, and she had mastered it.

"Not that," said Cassie, "I mean, how did you . . ."

"Escape?" Sheena interrupted again.

Cassie nodded emphatically.

"Well, I haven't," explained Sheena, brushing herself off. "That is, not all the way yet. Getting out of the factory was the easy part. It's getting off this stinking island that's going to be the real challenge. Fortunately," she grinned, showing that none of her ordeal had stolen her youthful sense of mischief and confidence, "there are two of us. With only one, I'd never make it out of the line of fire. But together, I'll bet we can do it just fine. Now, quick. There are some things we're going to need. I couldn't bring anything, of course, so I'm counting on you to rummage supplies. Is your master home?"

Cassie was blinking rapidly. It was all too much. Seeing her friend, hearing her lovely Irish accent again after all these weeks, and now this urgent request. Escape. "Uh . . . I uh . . ."

"Don't mean to hurry you," said Sheena, "but we are sort of running for our lives. Could you answer a little faster?"

"No," she said. "That is, he's not home."

"Good," Sheena sighed, "excellent. That means you can go get the supplies on my list while I wait here. Hmm, nice bedroom, by the way. Now, all we need to do is find some merchants to sail us home. They won't do it at Botany Bay, of course, because they know they'll get caught and get hanged for helping us. We need to get to another port, somewhere that convicts don't often go. They'll still know what we are, of course, but at least they won't be so scared of getting caught. I have it all mapped out. Now, once we get there, we'll need to bribe them. If you can't find any money around the house, we'll just do it the old-fashioned way. You know, use our feminine charms," she laughed, "but most importantly, we just need to survive the journey. Very few ever have, I understand. So we'll need at least a good hunting knife, preferably a rifle . . . are you listening?"

Cassie was breaking out of her daze. This was all beginning to sound so real. "Sheena," she began, "if we are caught . . . if we are caught, we'll be hanged?"

"Probably," she shrugged. "Why? Is that some sort of problem for you?" She laughed at her own joke, then punched her friend affectionately in the arm. "Come on, Cassie. This is no time for cold feet. We've got to get going before daybreak. When it's time for work again, they'll notice I'm gone, and they'll start the hunt. We've got to make our break right now."

Cassie was feeling strangely pressured. She wanted to go for Sheena's sake, but not for her own. Why not for her own? "Sheena, I . . ." she swallowed, fearful of seeming cowardly, fearful of sounding like an unfaithful friend, "Sheena, I . . . I'm only here for twenty years. It isn't worth risking my life."

Sheena took no offense. "Cassie, I'm not asking you to come just to save my hide. If it were that, I'd just ask you for the supplies and be on my way." She met her friend's eyes with frankness. "But I don't believe you want to stay here for twenty more years. Do you?" When she got no reply, her voice grew more pleading. "Cassie, they're killing you here. Can't you see that? I can see it. When you first got on the ship, you wouldn't even give up your maidenhood, even though you knew it could buy you a better life. And now, look at you. Your face is sallow, you don't even want your freedom, and I'll bet a week's ration you're not even a maiden anymore." Cassie's lowered gaze confirmed it. "You see?" asked Sheena. "They've broken your spirit. Imagine what they'll do to you in twenty years. Sure, you'll probably still be alive. But will you want to be?"

Cassie thrust her chin into the air, a new determination in her gaze. Everything Sheena had said rang true. The old Cassandra Madison would never have humiliated herself the way she did last night with Malcolm. It was despair that had made her crave love. And captivity was the source of all despair. "Give me that list," she said to Sheena, stretching out a firm palm. "We're making a run for it."

Eighteen

The cold, blue mountains loomed in the west, like iron gaol bars. They were beautiful the way a jeweled sword can be beautiful. Their deadliness only added to their charm. "Can we make it over them?" asked Cassie, fearing their shimmering heights.

"No," said Sheena, the hot night wind whipping her raven hair into her mouth as she spoke. "Our only hope is to head along the shoreline."

"But we'll be so open! Anyone can see us."

"How do you walk so fast?" Sheena cried, panting to keep up with her redheaded friend.

"I'm sorry," said Cassie, "but I think we should cover as much ground as we can."

Sheena smiled to herself. She knew Cassie was a fighter at heart. She'd believed it the first time she met her, and was glad to see that some of what prison had taken from her was returning. "My legs aren't as long as yours," she said, but did her best to jog along.

"I think we should walk through the night," said Cassie. "If we're going to get caught, it will most likely be in the first few hours. So let's stay close to the trees and keep moving until tomorrow night."

"I'm going to have to eat, though," said Sheena. "They don't feed us well enough at the factory to build up strength for a twenty-four-hour bolt."

"Our supplies won't last long," said Cassie. "If we see

an edible plant, we should grab it. It'll stretch out what we have. Do you know anything about which plants are edible?"

"No," said Sheena, "but I know that crocodiles make good meals."

Cassie stopped walking and cast her companion a humorous glare. "You're planning to eat a crocodile?"

"Sure," shrugged Sheena boastfully. "Why not? We've got a knife."

Cassie rolled her eyes. "I'll leave that task to you."

"It's not that hard!" insisted her friend. "I heard that if you flip them onto their backs, they just freeze and let you slice their bellies."

"Like I said," chuckled Cassie, "I'll leave that task to you."

The moon was an eerie yellow. The ocean's waves grew loud beneath its madness, but the women moved so deeply into the forest that they could see nothing. There may as well not have been a moon or an ocean, for the trees towered overhead, creating an ominous mask for the sky. Even the chilly, blue mountains were hidden by the forest's false darkness. "Hold my hand," said Sheena. "I don't want to lose you."

Cassie did so, and found her friend's hand to be soft and plump in her grip. "Do you have a hand out in front of you?" she asked.

"Yes," said Sheena, "but it's not doing me much good. The trees are scraping me from the side."

"Me, too," said Cassie with a trembling sigh.

They were no longer moving quickly. The trees created a maze which they had to navigate with care. They couldn't even be certain they were going in the right direction, save the sound of the ocean's waves, which they carefully kept to the right of them. "Stomp heavily," said Sheena. "Snakes can feel vibrations in the earth. We don't need to walk loudly, just with pounding steps."

Sheena tried to adjust her footsteps accordingly. There was a dense moisture in the air. It was not only the darkness which felt thick, but the breeze itself seemed as heavy as wet sand. Everything felt wrong. Cassie did not feel as though she were on her way to freedom, but on her way to disaster. She didn't know how to express that to Sheena. But there was such a closeness between them, that she felt compelled to try. "I don't feel as I'd expected to during an escape," she said with a nervous swallow.

There was silence. Sheena was feeling it, too. The wind was not driving them on, but holding them back with its thickness. They were not running, but shuffling. She could not hear freedom's call. "I'm sure it'll be all right," she said in a husky voice. "Anyone following us will have just as much trouble navigating these trees as we are. And guessing which path we took will be nearly impossible, when we don't know ourselves."

This incited a nervous laugh from Cassie. "Yes, you're right." Her toe hit something, and she plunged to the ground, nearly yanking Sheena down with her. "Ouch!"

"Are you all right?" asked Sheena, kneeling beside her fallen friend.

Cassie was holding her leg and rocking.

"Are you all right?" Sheena repeated.

Cassie sucked some air through her teeth. "Damn it, why didn't we bring a lantern?"

"I'm sorry," said Sheena. "I thought the moon would guide us, that a lantern would draw attention. I . . . I didn't think about the branches overhead."

"It's all right," said Cassie, waving her hand. "I didn't mean to gripe. It's just my leg . . ."

"I can't see it," said Sheena frantically. "Is it twisted?"

"No." Cassie paused to suck in hard against the pain. "I just sliced it against something. A root or something, when I fell."

"Sliced?" asked Sheena. "Is it bad?"

Cassie held up a moist hand. "It's bleeding like mad."

"Oh, no," gasped Sheena. "Oh, no. This is bad. We need to tie it, to cut off the flow. Is it still bleeding?"

"Yes!" cried Cassie irritably.

Sheena tore off a piece of her apron and placed it in Cassie's hand. "Wrap it just above the wound," she instructed.

"I know," griped Cassie, "I know." She tied it as tightly as she could around her calf, wincing when this not only increased her pain, but brought a disconcerting falling-asleep sensation to her foot. Cassie moaned, dropping her head into both hands.

Sheena felt bad for Cassie, who had obviously suffered a painful wound, and was undoubtedly having second thoughts about the journey. On the other hand, she felt bad for herself, too. This escape was a matter of life and death to a convict who had been sentenced to permanent imprisonment. Whatever happened to Cassie, she herself must go on. She feared that Cassie, wounded and suffering doubts, would hold her back and ruin her chance of escape. She tried to keep both factors in mind as she took her friend's hand from her face and held it affectionately. "Cassie," she said, her dark eyes alight, even in the blackness. "Cassie, are you having second thoughts about running? Will the wound make it too difficult?" She hoped her tone had held as much compassion as selfishness, for truly, she felt both.

Cassie looked up from her leg. "I'm not having second thoughts," she said. "I'm just sorry I'm going to have to go on with this bad leg."

Sheena looked doubtful. "Are you sure? Because I would understand. I would understand perfectly if you wanted to go back."

"No," said Cassie, though she sounded uncertain, and even she herself could hear that. The truth was that she'd had doubts from the moment Sheena had climbed into her room. And though she wanted desperately to be free, she also had a very bad feeling about this haphazard escape.

"You're sure about that?" asked Sheena gently, as though she had already decided to send Cassie home. "Because I know I talked you into this, and I know it's dangerous. And I know," she said with a certain amount of pain, "that your sentence is not for life, like mine. You can still go back. It's only twenty years."

"Only twenty years," Cassie repeated miserably. That seemed like the rest of her life.

"Yes," said Sheena, "it's only twenty years. And if you sneak back now, while it's still night, nobody will know you tried to escape."

"Sheena," whispered Cassie as her eyes, adjusting to the darkness, began to comprehend the outlines of her friend's soft, pale face surrounded by bushy hair, blacker than the night. "Are you wanting me to leave you?"

Sheena's head bowed in shame. She glanced at Cassie's wounded leg, still bleeding slowly, despite the tied rag. "You should tie that tighter," she suggested.

"Answer me," pleaded Cassie, stunning her friend by combing a hand through her thick, dark tresses. "I can still walk, I promise," she added, fingering Sheena's coarse hair with affection, "but it's true I may limp. Do you want me to let you run ahead?"

Sheena met her eyes with regret. No one had ever played with her hair before. An unwanted child from the poorest of families, she had never meant anything to anyone. Men had bedded her, but she was too smart to think it had had anything to do with affection. Her parents had never liked her, and thought awfully much of themselves for doing the right thing and turning her in to the police. They had valued the law more than they had her. When at last, in her rage at a lifetime of abandonment and abuse, she had gone mad and tried to take her parents' very lives in a burst of anger, she thought it was official now, that she was no longer human and had no heart or soul. Yet, here she was, nearly a year after she'd given up all hope of deserving compassion, looking into the eyes of a true friend, someone who actually cared what became of her. "Cassie, you're welcome to follow me, and you needn't worry about slowing me down. I don't mind."

Cassie was already shaking her head. "No," she said gently. "No, this is too important. You run on without me."

Sheena felt guilty in her relief. "But will you make it back all right? Our path has been crooked."

"I'll be fine," said Cassie. "I'll just keep the ocean to my left this time, and I'm sure I'll reach the clearing."

"Cassie, I . . ." Sheena swallowed hard.

"I know," said Cassie, caressing her friend's pale cheek, "I know everything you're going to say. Now run. Quickly."

"If I make it," suggested Sheena with care, "is there anything you want me to do? Anyone you'd like me to check on?"

"My brothers," said Cassie, "check on my brothers. The oldest is named Samuel Madison. He's a rotten kid," she grinned, "but I love him, and if you could make sure he's all right . . ."

"I will," said Sheena, knowing well that they were speaking of fantasy. "And if I . . . if I don't make it?" she asked, deciding that the time for illusion was now over.

Cassie squeezed her hand with painful strength. "Then wait for me in heaven," she said frantically. The women hugged with all of their might.

"Cassie, I didn't mean it," Sheena whispered into her hair, "I didn't mean what I said about how captivity is changing you. I only said those things so you would come. You haven't changed, and you never will. You'll always be my first and only friend."

"Not your only one," said Cassie in a motherly tone. "You just haven't met the rest of them yet."

Sheena laughed, and her laugh had a nice sound. Cassie wondered whether she'd had many opportunities to laugh before. "Don't let them catch you on your way into the house," she warned, backing out of the embrace, "and if they do see you, tell them you heard something and were out looking to see what it was. They might be mad, but remember, they're not allowed to whip you, so it's all right."

Cassie nodded. "Godspeed, Sheena."

Sheena planted a kiss on her freckled forehead and then sped away, as only someone who'd said a thousand good-byes and didn't care much for them could. Cassie feared the moment she could no longer hear Sheena's footsteps weaving their way through the trees. It was then that she would be alone, completely at the mercy of the darkness. And only if she were lucky would she make it home, where she would then be at the mercy of Malcolm. He was surely home, but may not have noticed her absence at this late hour. On the other hand, he may have. The police could be looking for her at this very moment. But the same wind that had been blowing against her was now shoving her in the back. It felt right. Returning home felt like the right thing to do somehow. She wondered whether Sheena, now that she was alone, was also getting the sense that fate was on her side. She wondered whether her feet were moving with more speed, unhindered by the company of someone who was not meant to join her.

Cassie felt a pinch in her leg every time she dropped her foot. It was a good thing she lived with a doctor, she thought with some amusement. Likely, if she had continued her journey, she would have wound up with gangrene or worse. It was the sheer fear of being alone in these dark woods that kept her hobbling forth on that bad leg. She didn't know whether it was her terror-stricken imagination or the truth, but it seemed as though the wound was making her light-headed. Perhaps, she told herself, perhaps it was only her worst fear that she would lose consciousness from the blood loss. Perhaps it was the fear that made her light-headed. She thought so much about her leg, that she scarcely thought of the distance she had traveled. Whether she had another ten or another billion steps to go, she did not know. Her fear made time freeze in her mind. But at last, she saw the yellow moon through a clearing ahead and knew she had made it. But just as she stepped out of the woods and onto the edge of a road, she noticed a shadow. At first, she'd thought it belonged to one of the trees, swaying under the moonlight. But then, the shadow moved. And before she could gasp, she was grabbed by the arm.

Nineteen

She was so stunned, she lost her breath. When she lifted her chin and saw that she was looking right into the eyes of Malcolm, she was still too startled to be relieved. His grip on her elbow was rough, his eyes murderous. His bright hair and sideburns glistened beautifully under the yellow moon, but his face was hard and hateful. "Get in the wagon," he ordered through clenched teeth. His jaw was tight, and Cassie could tell it took a great deal of restraint to refrain from tossing her into the wagon more roughly than he did. As it was, she was hurled unkindly, and caught herself painfully with her bad leg. "Ouch," she cried, clutching the wounded calf.

Malcolm looked at her with disdain. "I said, get in."

Cassie reacted to his anger with her own, tightening her lips and crossing her arms as she climbed into the wagon seat. But truly, she knew she was lucky. Lucky it was he who had come for her, and not the law.

As though reading her mind, he leaped into the driver's seat and grabbed the reins. But rather than urging on the horses, he turned to her and asked, "Do you know how lucky you are?"

Cassie tried to stay angry. He had grabbed her roughly and shoved her toward the wagon without concern for her leg. She dwelled upon that in order to keep her face hard, her voice void of apology. "I can't believe someone is calling me lucky," she retorted miserably.

"Well, you are this time," he said. His voice was louder and deeper than usual. If Cassie hadn't known better, she'd have thought him dangerous. "What would you have done if the law had caught you? Do you know you could've been hanged?"

"What do you care?" she asked, turning cold, narrow eyes upon him. Memories of his cruel rejection began to swell in her breast. "So what if I'd been caught and hanged?"

"Oh, you think I wouldn't care?" he asked angrily, as though it were the stupidest suggestion he'd ever heard. "We had one argument, and now you think I want to see you dead? This is ridiculous." He snapped the reins and made the horses lurch forward.

There was a moment's silence as Cassie basked in the relief of going home, her head turned away from Malcolm and toward the blue mountains which had warned her not to escape. It was a beautiful, hot, breezy night, but Cassie could not let the silence continue. She wanted resolution. She wanted to know what he meant when he said he would have cared. "How did you find me?" she asked, by way of reopening the conversation.

To her surprise, Malcolm stopped the horses. Clearly, he was not in the mood to have a casual chat. If they were going to talk, they were going to have it out. He turned to her with bitter sarcasm. "I knew where you'd go because all ignorant runaway convicts head north for other ports. If you'd asked me, I'd have told you to go south to get around the mountains, but I knew you didn't know what the hell you were doing, so I followed you north."

Cassie was humbled by his temper and his sharp words. "Why did you follow me?"

"Why do you think I followed you?" he yelled. "I didn't want you to get killed. I don't care how much of my stuff you stole, you weren't going to make it off the island. Believe me. I've tried."

Cassie had forgotten that. But she now remembered Malcolm's friend chiding him about a "heroic" attempt at escape. "I might have made it," she said, sending hope to Sheena's heels.

Malcolm shook his head in exasperation. "Nobody makes it off this island, Cassie. Listen to me. Do you know what they did when they caught me?"

Cassie looked into his navy eyes with surprise. He was staring at her frankly, as though he were planning to tell her absolutely everything. She had never seen him so open. It was as though in his anger, he was no longer trying to protect her from the truth. "What?" she asked, eager for a taste of his story.

"They flogged me. Do you know what it is to be flogged?"

Cassie shook her head.

"You're tied to a triangle. The other prisoners are lined up to watch the spectacle. Every lash takes with it a piece of skin. Every lost sliver of skin leaves a raw opening for the next lash. You're beaten until you pass out, and then water is thrown on your face to awaken you. If you accidentally die, nobody cares. But if you're still alive when it's over—and it isn't over for hours—you're left dangling from your bound wrists. You're thirsty and naked and sunburned. They never tell you how long you'll be left bound. When they finally let you down, they expect you to go back to work. And if you can't, you'll get another beating."

Cassie's hands were shaking. "Malcolm, I . . ." She shook her bowed head. "How did you survive it?"

"How did I survive it?" he asked sharply. "My heart kept beating. That's all. You don't get to die until your heart stops doing that."

"But I mean . . ."

"Emotionally?" He shook his head, a blank look in his eye. "I didn't. Everything that was good and Christian in me is dead. Cassie, listen to me." He grabbed her elbow roughly and looked her right in the eye. "I killed a man that week. I killed him because I thought he was the one who led them to me. I thought he told them which way I went, as if it really mattered. As if they wouldn't have caught me anyway. But I needed someone to blame. And there he was. The gaolers had asked whether anyone knew anything, and he had stepped forward, said I'd gone south. When they let me down from the triangle, and I saw him shoveling alongside the others, pretending he hadn't watched my twenty-four-hour thrash-and-hang, trying not to look me in the eye," Malcolm swallowed hard, his breath so heavy it moved his shoulders, "I just went after him. I just killed him. And not with a weapon, mind you. I did it with my bare hands. I hadn't even known it was possible to kill a person by punching and clawing," he added distantly. "But apparently, it's not that hard."

Cassie was in awe. How could such a kind and gentle man have once been so ruthless? Yet, she could see that he had paid dearly for his brutality. He had paid by giving up all hope, and forever falling into a spiral of self-condemnation. She could see it so plainly now. His kindness was a repentance for his sins. A shadow had been born on that dark, murderous day, and had followed Malcolm ever since, asking to be fed with torment and burning sins of flesh in exchange for staying at bay long enough to let Malcolm exhibit kindness during his waking hours. Cassie bowed her head in shame. That she could feel sorry for herself when she was serving her sentence, not in the barracks as Malcolm had, but in the company of a man who treated her so well, was outrageous. "I'm sorry," she said calmly.

"For what?" he scowled.

"I'm sorry that I ran off and made you worry, and made you remember."

His faced softened. "Well, you should be," he grumbled gently. "If you'd been caught by the law, you'd have been sent to the factory at best, and there's nothing I could have done to stop it."

Cassie said nothing. Her back was stiff and her gaze sternly distant.

Malcolm gave up and reached for the reins. It had been a long night, to say the least. And he didn't know what else he could do to press upon her how stupid it had been to run. Giving the reins a snap, he urged the horses forward, and retreated into his thoughts. Yes, he still thought about what they had done last night. He had grown to love Cassie, and nothing would change that. He was still sorry about their spat, and still sorry he hadn't gotten the chance to straighten things out. But this matter was much more pressing. If Cassie ran off again, it could be the death of her. He wasn't sure whether any of his words had reached her, whether she understood that she must never try that again. "I'm trying to decide how I should punish you," he said matter-of-factly, his face in the hot wind, his hair catching the ocean's salt.

Cassie positively glared at him. "What?!"

He did not reply, but continued to think.

"You're not allowed to beat me," she informed him. "I know you're not allowed to, so don't even try it."

He let out a dark chuckle in his surprise. "Who the hell told you that?"

Cassie froze. "You mean it's not true?"

"Of course not," he laughed dryly. "What did you think? They sent a convict to my house that I'm not allowed to discipline?"

Cassie's head dropped. It was true. It made absolutely no sense. And how on earth would Sheena have known such a thing? It seemed possible that her friend did a little more in the way of relating information than in gathering it.

Malcolm took pity on Cassie in her newfound anxiety. He cast her a gentle glance and said, "But of course, I wasn't thinking about whipping you. Not sure I even own anything that would do well for that," he smiled, rubbing his chin.

Cassie took a deep breath in her relief. "Then what . . ."

"I don't know," he said. "I'm trying to think."

The thinking seemed to take an awfully long time, as the couple was already home before Malcolm spoke another word. Cassie was relieved to see the golden lanterns beaming through the windows of the white house. This prison of hers really was beginning to seem like home. Malcolm helped her out of the wagon and told her to go inside while he stabled the horses. She obeyed him. This really had been a humiliating attempt at escape.

When she ventured inside the front door, she found Faith there, waiting anxiously in the bright entrance. "Oh, good, you're back," said the cook, feigning a look of unconcern. It was clear she had been worried. "Well, then," she said kindly, "I'll just be on my way."

"Faith," said Cassie to the woman's turned back, "Faith, I'm sorry if I worried you."

Faith dismissed her with a wave of the hand. "I'll see you in the morning."

Cassie watched the old cook go with a heaviness in her heart.

Malcolm returned with a new coolness in his stride and calmness on his face. Clearly, he had stayed in the stables until his temper had faded. "Faith gone?" he asked gently.

"Yes," whispered Cassie, "Left just a moment ago."

"I see. Well, then . . ." He shrugged. "I guess I should just . . . have a look at that." He gestured toward the wound he had pretended in his anger not to notice.

Cassie twisted her lips. "I would prefer you didn't."

Malcolm proceeded with caution, knowing this was a delicate matter. He knew well that women never liked revealing their legs to a doctor. It had taken him years to rehearse his gentle coaxing. But this time would be, if anything, more difficult. For with strangers, he could pretend that as a doctor, he was incapable of noticing the seductive shape and feel of a woman's calf. But with Cassie, his guise was well spoiled. She knew he was a man, and saw her as a woman. Convincing her that he could set that aside while examining her would be no easy feat. His voice was as soft and gentle as he could make it. "I'll only clean and bandage it," he said. "I'll do it as quickly as I'm able." His eyes quietly pleaded with her.

Cassie swallowed hard. "Couldn't you have a nurse do it?"

He laughed softly and threw out his arms. "No nurses on hand, I'm afraid. I'm it." When she did not return his smile, he reached coaxingly for her hand. "Come," he said with a gentle nod, "if Faith were here, I'd have her stay in the room with us, but as it is," he shrugged, "you'll just have to trust me."

For some reason, Cassie didn't have any trouble doing that. She didn't like the idea of his looking at her bare leg, especially not after last night, but . . . somehow, she knew he wouldn't try anything. She let him lead her into his study and settle her into his favorite chair. She trembled as he knelt at her feet, and let out a nervous giggle when he removed her shoe. But Malcolm remained serious and handled her calf as though it were made of fine bone china. He gazed only at the wound, as though it did not have a woman attached to it. And he gave no reaction to the severity of the wound. He had decided a long time ago that patients didn't like that. Cassie grew so curious about his thoughts as he tested the tenderness of her skin, wiped away old blood, and tore away the sliver of Sheena's dress that had been so clumsily wrapped about her knee, that she could not help asking, "Is it bad?"

"Fairly bad," he replied mildly, then continued his work.

She looked down to see what he was doing, but could not get a glimpse past his shoulders. "Will you have to sew it?"

Malcolm grunted a little as he tore off a piece of clean bandaging. "Don't plan to," he said. "Looks like it was bleeding pretty badly at one point, but it's stopped. I'm going to wrap pretty tightly, though," he warned, flashing her a quick glimpse at his eyes.

Cassie nodded her understanding, and waited patiently as he went to work. She still felt terribly awkward, sitting so erect as he kneeled at her feet and touched her naked leg. She felt she ought to have something to do with her hands, or have something at which to stare. But at last, he lowered the hem of her dress and rose. "Finished," he announced, carefully putting away his tools without looking at her.

Cassie whispered, "Thank you," and rose to her feet. Her leg really did feel much better now as she tested it by placing some weight on the heel. She hurried toward the door, wanting to get to bed before any of this became more awkward.

But Malcolm stopped her. "Cassie?"

She did not turn around, but stopped walking.

He took a few steps toward her, but did not touch her. "Cassie, I . . . I'm sorry I . . . well, that I pushed you into the wagon." He rubbed his hair distractedly. "I . . . it wasn't right of me. I was angry, but . . . well, I should have been more sympathetic. Your life isn't exactly . . . bright, I know." He swallowed loudly. "I, of all people, should have understood why you ran."

But he did not understand. He did not understand that her running had more to do with her love for him than with any judge's sentencing. But how could she tell him that? She had told him once, and that had led to a most humiliating rejection in the end. If he still didn't understand the depth of her love, perhaps he never would. "You didn't shove me," was all she said. "It was more of a push, and there is no need to apologize."

Malcolm shook his head at himself. "No, Cassie. There's no excuse for a man's pushing a woman. I've never believed in that sort of thing. It was wrong. I'm sorry."

If Cassie didn't leave soon, she knew she would cry. He was being wonderful again. He was reminding her of all she loved about him, of why she had given herself in such an embarrassing fashion. "You're a good man, Malcolm," she said, pursing her lips against tears.

There was silence behind her. Malcolm did not think himself a good man, and she knew it. He said nothing.

"I accept your apology," she said at last, then made to leave before she said it again. Before she let him see her eyes, and see that he could have her again if he wanted to.

"Wait." He touched her shoulder to turn her around. And when he caught her eye, he was softened by her vulnerability. Unable to stop himself, he reached out and combed back a strand of her auburn hair. Cassie's eyes closed under the gentleness of his strong hand. "Promise me you won't run away again?" he whispered.

Eyes still closed, Cassie nodded. But his masculine touch cast a spell on her, and her lips parted, as though hoping there might be one more gesture of forgiveness between them. Malcolm thought it best not to indulge in a good-night kiss. There was just too much to think about. He had told her of his darkest hour, but had she had time to absorb it? Did she understand what he was? And what on earth could be done about the fact that she was his servant? They had rushed into their intimacies too quickly. He adored the woman whose freckled cheek he now stroked with his thumb. He had grown so fond of her so quickly. Yet, his wild yearnings for a woman's flesh had caused him to pull her into his arms before the path could be cleared for their joining. There might be a way for them to be together, but he had not yet found it. If only he had given it some more thought first . . . And he did blame himself. An emotionally shattered girl living in a convict's despair could not be blamed for melting under his kindness. That his kindness had turned into lust was his own fault. He was the one who had power, the power of freedom. So he was the one with responsibility.

He let her go without a kiss. "It's over between Priscilla and me," was all he gave her in the way of a promise. "I saw her tonight," he emphasized with a nod, "and I ended it."

Shame-faced, Cassie turned away. "I don't want to talk about this."

"Cassie," he pleaded, refraining from reaching out and grabbing her arm, "we really should talk about . . ."

"No," she said, moving toward the stairs, "no, just leave me alone."

"Cassie, are you ashamed about last night? Please don't be. I—"

"Just leave me alone!" she cried, and fled to her room.

Malcolm closed his eyes and sighed. It was his fault, he knew. It was all his fault. And worst of all, it was not Cassie for whom he felt sorry. It was himself. For he feared she now thought him a brute, and he felt that she may well be right. "Damn it," was his last thought before turning to his bedchamber, "I forgot to punish her." He sighed. "Or maybe I've already punished her too much."

Twenty

"It's over," said a stony-faced Priscilla, standing stiffly by the fire, her cloak still wrapped tightly about her shoulders.

"What do you mean, it's over?" snarled Miles, his silver hair alight with red from the burning embers.

"What do you *think* I mean?" she asked coldly, her violet eyes showing no sign of the tears she had shed only minutes ago. "He's called off the engagement. He's sent me away. He doesn't want to see me anymore. Do you understand yet?"

"What did you do?" he demanded. "How did you ruin it?"

"I did nothing," she replied coldly, refusing to meet the volume of his own voice. "I believe he has merely fallen in love with another woman."

"Who?!" he demanded.

"Cassandra," she replied. "I believe he loves her."

Miles scowled in disbelief. "How is that? She was described to me as being plain and half Irish."

"Half Irish, yes," nodded Priscilla, "but not plain. She's a man's woman. The sort women think are ordinary but men find appealing."

Miles wore a deep, thoughtful frown, but the rage in his black eyes was biting. "Why should his fondness for her cause him to end your engagement?" he demanded. "Why doesn't he just have you both?"

"Malcolm doesn't enjoy philandering," she replied. "It

isn't his way. He's excited by the depths of darkness that can be explored by one man and one woman. Having many women at once makes the experience shallow."

"If you understand him so damned well, then why couldn't you hold him?" he cried.

Priscilla could not remain calm in the face of that accusation. "You forced me to make him hate me!" she cried. "You forced me to deceive him, and I tell you he sensed it. He may not have the thoughts or the words to explain his repulsion to me, but somewhere inside him he knows! He knows that it has all been trickery, and it's your fault!"

"You told me he loves to be tormented!" Miles bellowed in return.

"Tormented, yes. But not deceived! Didn't I tell you he demands complete honesty from his lovers?"

Miles couldn't resist chuckling. "Well, he is certainly a twisted man," he mused.

Priscilla came readily to Malcolm's defense. "He is a kind and decent man," she spat. "I have yet to meet a truly good man without eccentricity, for how could a kind man live in a world like this without going mad? But you wouldn't know anything about kindness or decency, would you?"

"No, I wouldn't," Miles grinned, "but I do know that I have paid you well for a job you have spoiled."

Priscilla took a deep, regretful breath.

"There now," he said in a tone half-mocking, "you needn't be so worried. I don't intend to deprive you of your pay, so long as you, of course, remedy the disaster you have wrought."

Priscilla cast him a suspicious squint. "How can I do that? I told you he sent me away."

"Then we must have her sent away as well."

Strangely, Priscilla found she liked that idea. A slight smiled curved her lips. "But how?"

"Angel," he smiled, placing a sturdy hand upon her shoulder.

"Don't call me an angel. Just tell me your plan."

He removed the sturdy hand. "Very well. We begin by considering your other lovers. And don't tell me there aren't any. I know that I haven't paid you enough to buy your independence. I know there are other men supporting you."

Priscilla's silence was her answer.

"Good," he said. "Now tell me which of them might suddenly be in need of a new servant."

"None of them," replied Priscilla honestly. "There is no shortage of servants, of which I am aware."

"Then tell me which of them," said Miles darkly, "might be in need of a . . . what did you call it? A man's woman? A young redhead who might make a fine replacement for an older, less comely housemaid?"

Priscilla scoffed. "What do you want me to do? Tell one of them that I know of an attractive convict who could be transferred if enough money were put in the right gaoler's pocket?"

"No, of course not," he drawled. "I want you also to mention that she is insatiably lustful."

They both laughed. "Very well," said Priscilla, "but under one condition."

He raised a grizzly eyebrow.

"Now that we no longer need Malcolm, now that the girl will be living elsewhere . . ."

Miles already knew what she was going to ask. "I don't care what you do," he said gruffly. "Dr. Rutherford is no longer our concern. Once Cassandra is removed from his home, you need only stay close to her new master."

"And when I am not doing that?" she asked anxiously.

Miles shrugged. "If you can win him back, then as far as I'm concerned, Malcolm is all yours."

Twenty-one

There was a knock on the door. Malcolm stood up irritably from his breakfast, setting aside a book he'd been reading at the table. Cassie and Faith were in the kitchen, getting an early start on washing the dishes, so he served as his own butler. He clutched the door handle and chewed quickly, trying to swallow before opening it. "Yes?" he asked, then cleared his throat when he found his voice. "Sorry. Yes? May I help you?" The stern stranger on his front porch handed him a rolled parchment. "What is it?" shrugged Malcolm with disinterest.

The message bearer was a tall and slender middle-aged man, though not as tall as Malcolm. His hair was shiny black and his sideburns sleek. "Orders from the lieutenant," said the man. "Cassandra Madison is being reassigned. The lieutenant apologizes for any inconvenience, and promises that your new servant will arrive on the next shipment from England."

"Tell him I don't want her reassigned," Malcolm replied calmly. "Tell him she's needed here, and if he has a problem with that, he can come talk to me himself. Good day."

The stranger prevented him from closing the door. "Doctor," he said sternly, "I'm afraid I cannot accept your refusal." He nodded toward the front gate, where several armed gaolers were waiting to escort the prisoner from the premises.

Malcolm narrowed his eyes at them all. "What is this about?" he asked fearfully. "Why is she being reassigned?" He worried they would take her to the factory, a fate Malcolm understood to be worse than death.

"She is needed in another household."

"Whose household? And why is his need more important than mine?"

The messenger bowed his head, for he deeply regretted confessing the relevant matter. "Sir, with all due respect, you are an emancipated convict, and by law, do not have the same rights as men who are sent here in the line of duty. The gentleman who has requested her is an employee of the British government, and . . ."

"And why does he want *my* servant?" Malcolm interrupted brashly.

The messenger's head bowed even lower. "He . . . he fancies redheads, sir." He smiled as though hoping Malcolm would take his meaning, and appreciate the humor in it.

Malcolm's blue eyes grew absolutely murderous. "What do you mean?" he asked slowly, his eyes narrowed into deadly slits. "What do you mean, he fancies redheads? Answer me!" The man would not. Malcolm would not release the messenger from his outraged gaze. "She is not a concubine!" he spat. "What the hell is the matter with you?!" And to this, he truly wanted an answer, for he could not fathom how anyone could be so casual about something as unconscionable as what the man was suggesting.

"Yes, of course you're right, sir," said the messenger, unable to hide a snicker. "Of course she isn't a concubine." He looked at Malcolm as though he of all people should know what pleasures a female convict could bring to a lonely bachelor.

Malcolm had sworn he would never hit anyone again. Not after what had happened so long ago. He had pledged himself to a life of pacifism. But his hatred ran so deep, not only on Cassie's behalf, but also on behalf of all those who had been labeled *convicts* for life, and were living at the mercy of minds like his. Including himself. His mind made no effort to stop his fist, which landed squarely on the messenger's nose. The other guards rushed forward in defense of their own, and the ruckus which followed was enough to summon both Cassie and a very worried Faith.

"Dear God!" cried Faith. "What is it?!"

Cassie wiped her hands on her apron, eyes agape at the sight of so much violence. She tried to retreat, hoping to avoid getting caught by the random blows. But as soon as she was spotted by a guard, she was grabbed. "Hey!" she called, not knowing what she could possibly have done wrong. "Let me go. I had nothing to do with it! What are you doing?"

Faith was quick to rush to the girl's defense. "Unhand her! Doctor!" She looked around frantically, but saw that he had been outnumbered and restrained. His mouth bleeding from one corner, his hair fallen in his eyes, he had stopped trying to break free of the man who held his arms behind his back. Faith looked from him to Cassie, who was now screaming not to be taken. "Won't somebody help us?" she asked quietly.

Cassie, believing she was being sent to the factory, called out in an inhumanly hoarse voice, "No!" When she caught the cook's eye, she changed her plea to, "Faith!" And when she saw Malcolm watching her, glassy-eyed, arms pinned back, she called, "Malcolm!" But all was wasted breath. And her would-be saviors had to watch helplessly as she was manacled like an animal and pulled by her hair into the wagon.

"Lucky I don't arrest you," said a guard, spitting in Malcolm's face. Malcolm didn't care. He was still watching Cassie.

Her screaming could still be heard as the wagon rattled down the dirt road, and she gradually lost sight of the tasteful white house surrounded by tropical trees and lush landscaping. The little house with no servants' quarters, and the bedroom through which a soft, hot breeze always blew. Her desk overlooking the trees, her very own diary, her cozy canopy bed. All of these things were lost to Cassie now. And before her, she was sure, were twenty years of hard labor and sorrow.

Twenty-two

Cassie was not taken where she feared. She knew when the wagon stopped so soon that she could not be at the Female Factory. But she felt no hope. For no matter where she was being taken, it was not Malcolm's house. And all hope of serving an easy twenty years was gone.

"Get up," said the gaoler, as though she were resisting. He pulled her by the elbow, scarcely giving her the chance to scramble to her feet without a stumble. "Why the long face?" he mocked. "Don't like your new assignment? Aw, that's too bad. Isn't that too bad, Roy?"

"Just a crying shame," replied his sarcastic companion. "All she did was break the laws," he sneered. "You'd think we ought to be sending her on a pleasant holiday."

Cassie closed her eyes and ears against their mockery. They expected her to believe that they cared about the law, when all they cared about was their own power—the power to belittle her even as they stripped her of her life. Her face was bland and cold as she was dragged, stumbling, toward the modest, unpainted shack before them. Her ankles were chained, as though she could have run from them if she'd tried. *Such brave men,* she thought, finding dignity in a private joke. *There are four of them, and yet they chain my legs.*

"Not as fancy as you're used to, eh?" asked a guard, chuckling as the shack grew nearer. It was a handsome home, elegant in its simplicity. The ocean waves smacked against the rocks and a small fishing boat parked outside the shack like a carriage. Fishing nets were laid out to dry in the yard, shells caught in their tangles. The house itself looked loved, though worn. Its plain brown roof was lopsided, and there could not have been more than two or three rooms indoors.

"A convict ought to be glad to have a roof overhead," said another, as though Cassie had been the one to call the shack pitiful.

"Is Robin home?" asked a gaoler, rapping on the front door, which did not quite fit in its frame.

"Should be."

It was only a moment before they all knew for certain. For appearing in the doorway, his hair disheveled from the ocean wind, his shirt crudely unbuttoned, was none other than Robin Carthage, the very gaoler who had betrayed Sheena in the newcomers' barracks. Cassie couldn't help smiling. In her madness, she wanted to laugh out loud. Life could be a very cruel joke, and if she were watching rather than participating, she might have been having a grand time of it. It was ludicrous. Of all the people to whom she could have been reassigned, it had to be the one person on this island whom she already knew to be malicious. Cassie shook her head. There seemed to be no dealer in this game, deciding which person deserved which card. Life was nothing more than an unthinking spiral, always traveling either up or down, depending on some intangible source of momentum.

"Oh, it's her?" asked Robin, grinning. "I know her. She was on my last transport."

Cassie got the distinct impression that he expected her to say hello. But she could not bring herself to do it. She stared at him as though he were the death of her.

"You know this one?" asked a guard. "Well, good. Then she ought to feel right at home." He chuckled menacingly.

Robin was still gazing at her, inspecting her from head to toe, trying to remember whether he had bedded her. Cassie cowered under his stare, bowing her head against his examination of her assets. He was not an unattractive man. His coal black hair and sideburns were shiny and sleek. His face was well chiseled, and his body long and lean. But he could not be called handsome by anyone who had ever known him. His conscience was too ugly, stained by a hundred pleading convicts who had been ravaged by him. "She's as pretty as I remember, too," he winked, as though Cassie should have been flattered by the compliment. She was sickened.

"Why did you decide to get a servant, anyway?" asked the guard. "I didn't know you liked to have your house cleaned."

Robin looked laughingly around at the shambles that was his living room. "When I can't walk from one end of the house to the other without tripping, that's when I think it's time to get a maid."

The men all joined in his laughter. "Well, I for one am just glad you've decided to stay in Australia for a while. Doing the transports must get tiring."

Robin rolled his eyes in exasperation. "*Tiring* isn't the word for it. I hate those trips. You have no idea what kind of conditions they have us living in on those ships." Cassie glared at him. "I'm sure I'll go back to doing them," he went on. "The money's good. But for a while I'm just going to watch the barracks and fish." He smiled mildly, as though a gentle way of life really suited him.

"Well, maybe this here will give you something else to do," laughed the guard, slapping Cassie on the backside. She blinked so long, it was as though she were in prayer.

"Maybe," he grinned, "maybe. Thanks for bringing her."

The guards all nodded in departure, and Cassie smiled as she watched them go. No fewer than four male guards had been needed to escort her. They were all such terrible cowards. She wondered how they lived with themselves. As soon as the men were gone, Robin's expression changed. He dropped his smile, and tossed out his friendly demeanor with a slam of the wobbly front door. He unfastened Cassie's manacles with the speed of a man who had devoted much of his life to freeing enchained maidens for his pleasure. When he had finished, and Cassie rubbed her stinging wrists, he did not look into her eyes, but only at the cluttered room around him. "Well," he said, pointing aimlessly, "go clean."

Cassie started laughing. "Clean what?" she couldn't help asking. "Is there something under the filth which needs to be cleaned?" The dark living quarters had pieces of stained cloth strewn over the windows as curtains. There was no furniture, save a stack of blankets that seemed to serve as a sofa. The black cooking stove was in plain view, and perfectly grotesque with its splotchings of dried, spilled food. The splintered floor was covered with clothes, dirty dishes, half-eaten food, and fishing accessories.

Cassie was Robin's first servant, for he could never have afforded one in England. For that reason, he did not think to strike her, as a more experienced master with his callous tendencies would have. Instead, he adopted a look of bewilderment. "Well, isn't there something you can do?" he asked, considering the logistics of cleaning a home for the very first time in his life. "Surely, maids have . . . tricks or something."

Cassie wiped a tear of laughter from her eyes. She was aware that her senses were slipping from her. "Well, do you have a broom?" she asked, thinking that would be a nice start.

"A broom? Uhh, yes. Yes, a broom. I think I have one." He disappeared momentarily, and Cassie heard a great deal of clanging and clattering in his absence. "Damn it!" she heard him yell twice, each time after something seemed to have fallen and broken. At last, he returned to the living quarters with a broom. "Here." He thrust it into her hands.

Cassie looked at the instrument with uncertainty. She would have to clean it before she could clean anything else. "Thank you," she said, her nose wrinkled in disgust.

"I like my supper ready by five," he announced sternly, "and I get angry if it's late."

Cassie looked warily at the splotched stove. "I'm to cook your meals as well?"

He seemed to take offense at that question, for it made him feel as though he had asked too much. And nothing made him angrier than feeling he had made a mistake. "Yes!" he bellowed. "What did you think? This was some sort of a holiday?" In his dark eyes, he did not look so much a menacing master as an insecure child. But it didn't matter what he was, so long as he held complete power over Cassie, which he did.

She bowed her head obediently. "And what do you like to eat?" she asked by way of distracting him from his anger.

"Fish."

She nodded complacently. It had been a stupid question. "And for breakfast?"

"Fish."

"Fish," she repeated, her nodding becoming rhythmic. Again, a stupid question.

"And you'd better not eat much, either," he warned with an unattractive squint. "I can't waste all of my fish on greedy-mouthed convicts."

"Of course not," she muttered.

He made a painful grab at her jaw and squeezed tight. Forcing her lips into a circle, pinching her cheeks into redness, he lifted her chin. He studied her emerald eyes with vicious scrutiny, as though something were beginning to return to his memory. "Oh, yes," he said at last, still squeezing her throbbing jaw, "I do remember you now. I knew you were on the boat, but I couldn't remember how well we knew each other." He bared some teeth by curling his lip. "I never bedded you, did I?"

She could not shake her head in his clutch.

"What's the matter? Can't talk?"

As a matter of fact, she couldn't.

"Well, we'll take care of that tonight," he promised her, not referring to the talking. "Are you looking forward to that? Do you want to be in my bed?" He grinned as though knowing well she was frightened, but believing she would secretly enjoy it.

Cassie's stomach lurched in fear. She tried to pull away from his hand.

"Yes, you'll like it," he mocked, setting her free. He reached for a cup of water and guzzled it, his back turned to her. Clearly, he was not as frightened of convicts as his gaoler friends had been. Cassie imagined he was more experienced.

She touched her raw cheeks, where his fingers had bruised her. She looked at the broom, and thought about cleaning. But then she looked at his turned back, and knew she had to say something. She could not get through the day, believing that it would end in his cruel arms. "Mr. Carthage!" she called frantically.

He turned with a sinister and pleased look in his squinted eyes. He had just removed his shirt for comfort, revealing a well muscled pair of arms. But his soul was so ugly that Cassie wanted him to cover himself. "What?" he snarled, as though she had disturbed him from an important task.

"I . . ." Cassie could not think of anything to say to a man like this. What would make someone like him change his mind? She could not appeal to his sense of decency, or his pity, or his kindness. "I have a venereal disease," she announced.

A horrible silence ensued. Robin stared at her as though trying to digest the full import of her words. His face was confused as his weak mind tried to comprehend why she had told him this bit of gloomy information and how it was relevant to himself. At last, he burst into a brief chuckle. "Oh, that's all right," he called, "so do I." And Cassie was quite sure he wasn't joking.

She began the sickening task of sweeping Robin's floor with a painful ache in her heart. Only days ago, she had been so full of bread and water that she had greedily wished for a rose. And now, she was reminded of just how beautiful bread and water could be to someone who had none.

Twenty-three

Samuel Madison missed his sister. It had taken some time for the missing to settle into his heart. His had never been a close family. In fact, all of its members usually rejoiced in one another's absence. When Father was gone, there was more food on the table for the rest of them. When Mother was at one of her soirées, there was one less chattering mouth to hear. Samuel, like the others, had never had anything in particular against Cassie. But the thought of missing a family member was alien to him. After all, didn't the whole family share a secret ambition to slip away and never see the others again? When Cassie was arrested, Samuel's first thought was, *Drat. I can't believe she got out before I did.* That other families would have mourned the parting occurred to him, but did not affect his apathy over losing a sister. Until now.

Cassie had been his only friend. He didn't realize that she was a friend, didn't call her a friend, and didn't treat her as a friend. But now that she was gone, and her absence had settled in, he realized that he had been left in the madhouse without a nurse. All of his life, he had been able to joke with Cassie, commiserate with her over the unfortunate time and place of their births. She had run the house without his noticing it, leaving the rest of them free to carry on ungratefully. And she had been an anchor among all of the madness. Now, there was absolutely no one to whom he could turn. And there was a matter even more pressing than the loss of the sanity she had radiated, and the bills she had managed to pay. She had been kind. How she had learned kindness in a family which had never heard the term, he wasn't sure. But Cassie had been born with a deep and true heart. Without her, there was absolutely no love left in the family. And no love in Samuel's life.

"Samuel!" cried his mother, "Samuel, have you seen my brooch?!"

He had quietly sold a great number of the family's possessions. His Uncle Egbert's money would help some, but in order to waylay a few of the more righteously embittered debt collectors, he'd had to part with a few useless-looking items around the house. "Haven't seen it," he said to his mother, "but if you just keep looking, I'm sure you'll find it." He hoped this would keep her busy for a while.

"Oh, this is disastrous!" she cried, her heavy golden gown rustling around her. "I am expected to be ready in an hour!"

Samuel turned his chocolate eyes in her direction, looking very much like a puppy as he was often told he did. "Why don't you wear something else?" he asked, in a rare show of mercy.

"Something besides my brooch?" she asked, aghast. "Oh, I couldn't! No, no. I planned this entire outfit around that brooch. If I were to wear another piece, I'd have to change my gown!"

"I really don't think that's necessary," he drawled. "If you can't find the brooch, why don't you just wear your pearls?" There was a crash somewhere in the distance. Mrs. Madison looked at her son with a startle. "Just the kids," he shrugged. "Probably got into the china cabinet."

Mrs. Madison was relieved that it was nothing out of the ordinary. "Well, then," she sighed, "isn't anyone looking after them?"

"No."

"Oh." She thought about this for a moment, an index finger draped daintily across her chin. "Hmm. It does seem we ought to hire someone."

"Can't afford it."

"Oh, well then," she shrugged, "if we can't, we can't. Now about my brooch. I know I left it on the buffet table not more than a week ago. I've tried and I've tried to think where I might have moved it, but . . ."

Samuel could take no more. Wincing against the oncoming storm he was about to create, he blurted out, "Mother."

She chattered on a bit more before he interrupted again.

"Mother," he said more loudly.

She stopped talking and looked at him with a startle. "Yes?"

Samuel met her eyes with bravery. He would have done anything not to tell her about this, but it seemed she simply wasn't going to forget about the brooch. "I sold it."

A gust of wind outdoors filled the silence.

"I sold it," he repeated.

His mother's eyes grew murderous. "You *what?!*" she screamed, loudly enough to make Samuel cover his ears. Her cheeks had grown bulbous and red. Her normally dull green eyes grew livid.

"Now, Mother, hear me out. I—"

"Hear you out?!" she cried. "Hear you out?!" Her slipper stomped the floor with a thunderous weight. "Do you know what that brooch meant to me?"

Samuel felt awful. He never would have sold it if he'd known it was something important. But honestly, he had never seen her wear it before. "Was it a family heirloom?"

"Of course not." she snapped, "My family didn't have

any money or jewels. But it had an emerald that exactly matched my eyes!"

"That's what it meant to you?" he asked with a humorously raised eyebrow. "It matched your eyes? That's it? Well, honestly, Mother. I'll go find you a piece of glass that can do that."

"You expect me to wear glass jewelry?!" she shouted. "Oh, my word! This is awful. First, I have a murderess for a daughter, and now a thief for a son!"

"Don't forget the two small vandals in the kitchen."

"Yes, them, too. I . . . wait a minute!" She placed both fists on her broad hips. "Do not change the subject! I want to know where you sold that brooch, and then I want you to buy it back."

"With what money, Mother?" he groaned.

This caused her a moment's pause. She didn't know exactly how much money she had or where it was located. In fact, she had never given the matter much thought at all. But at last, she replied, "Well, with whatever money we have. Now, go get it."

"Mother," said Samuel, rising to his feet. He was still boyishly slim, but had grown to tower over both of his parents. "We have no money," he said as gently as he could. "Not anywhere."

"But . . . but that simply isn't true!"

"Mother, this is not about your pride," he said. "I know you like to think we are wealthy, but in truth, our funds have been spent. There is nothing left of them, and if we do nothing, we will have to leave our home."

He watched carefully to see whether the news was absorbed properly. His mother's eyes grew puzzled for just a moment, and then returned to their stubborn glare. "I don't believe that. What about the money you said you received from your uncle?"

Samuel shook his head. "It will help us, but it will not save us. Mother, we need to cut back on our spending."

"But my brooch!" she cried, touching her bare dress.

"I'm sorry I took it," he replied, without complete honesty, "but what would you have said if I'd asked whether I might have something to sell?"

"Naturally, I would have said no!" she cried.

"Exactly. That's why I had to take matters into my own hands. I thought you would never miss the brooch. I'm sorry." He had never felt so adult in all of his life. With Cassie at home, there had never been reason to be adult. But now, more and more, he was feeling responsible for his family, and gradually becoming a man.

"You get that brooch back," she snarled.

"Mother, if you think you miss a piece of jewelry, imagine how you'll feel when they take the house."

"Impossible!" she cried. "If things were that bad, your father would have told me. He would have done something!"

Samuel could not help laughing at that. "Do I have a father?" he asked, chuckling.

His mother glared, so he took it back.

"All right, all right," he relented, "I do have a father. But surely you know that he is not home enough to look after our affairs."

"He keeps an eye on them," she protested defensively. "He's just busy is all."

Samuel furrowed his brow. "Yes, he's busy. I'll give him that. But he does not keep an eye on anything, Mother. If he comes home one day and finds that the house has been reoccupied, I daresay he'll just turn the horses around and find another bed to sleep in."

Mrs. Madison gasped.

"Well, it's true, Mother. All of us children know it. He doesn't care about you, he doesn't care about us, and none of us care about him."

She struck his face.

Samuel accepted this with closed eyes and a patient

expression. He was learning what Cassie had learned long ago—that leadership sometimes meant fighting, and sometimes meant standing still, stoically holding one's ground. "I'm sorry," he was able to say, even after having been slapped, "but if we wait for our father to become a family man, we shall all live in the poorhouse. I'm trying to make up for his absence, Mother, and I'm doing the best I can." He took her hand gingerly in his, trying to stir up love in his heart the way Cassie had always been able to do. The feeling didn't come, but the words did. "Now go to your soirée, Mother. And have a good time." His boyish humor kicked in, and he could not resist adding, "Perhaps you'll meet a nice man there, and we can all live happily ever after."

Her eyes were ablaze with anger, but she did not want to hear any more about their poverty or her failed marriage. So in hopes of escaping any further brushes with reality, she fled. She did it with a head held indignantly high, of course, and feet that stomped angrily. But nonetheless, she fled. Samuel sighed heavily in her wake, collapsing onto a velvet loveseat. A loveseat. What would he ever know about love? He'd never even courted. He'd never even exchanged flirtatious glances with a woman. His life had been about frolicking about on the family's isolated estate, until now. And now, it was about trying to save all of their skins. Now he understood why Cassie had never had a suitor. He'd always thought it was because she was too strong to attract men. But now he knew the truth. She had given her life to this family, as he was about to do.

It really was discouraging to know that he would never know the sweetness of love. For he believed he would not grow to be like his father, callous and ungrateful. He believed that if he ever were blessed with a wife, he would adore her and cherish her and never indulge in the greediness of pursuing others. He really wanted to try kissing. In fact, he was at the age of wanting desperately to try much more than that. But he would settle for a kiss. Just one kiss upon a pair of cherry-red lips would do so much to brighten his spirits. It was a terrible thing to be young, restless, and completely isolated from a world full of women. If only he could send the word out to all of those soft, warm creatures out there that he was available, and interested, and that he would treat a woman so well! Then it wouldn't matter that he was stuck in this house, doomed to a life of managing tedious financial affairs. Some youthful beauty would just come prancing up to the door and knock, saying, "Hello, I'm here to meet the young gentleman who is looking for someone to adore." He laughed out loud at the image. It was not easy being sixteen.

A few months later, there was a knock on the door. "Hello," said the most beautiful, raven-haired woman Samuel had ever seen, "I'm a friend of Cassie's from Australia. I'm looking for Samuel Madison."

Twenty-four

Malcolm did not know where Cassie had been taken. He paced back and forth in his living room, and when that grew dull, he paced back in forth in his study. Faith could offer no consolation. She felt just as miserable as he did. It was a dangerous thing when a girl was given assignment. Who knew to what evils she was being subjected at this very moment? Her new family might beat her, or starve her, or the man of the house might use her. It was a well-known fact that these things went on regularly in households all over Australia. But it was so different when the convict involved was someone they both knew. "May I get you some tea, Doctor?" was all Faith could bring herself to say, for it was a useless lie to say everything would be all right.

Malcolm shook his head, unable even to speak. He paced like a wild animal, his eyes deep in circular thought. There was nothing he could do. Absolutely nothing. If no one would tell him where she was . . . she could be anywhere. He had not been to the hospital all day, and Faith knew that said a great deal about his feelings for the girl. Within the privacy of her mind, she could not help wondering whether he had fallen in love. She certainly hoped so. Cassie was a fine girl, not at all like the sadistic beauties he normally preferred. The thought that Cassie may have helped save the doctor from Priscilla made it all that much harder to bear that she was gone. "It isn't right," Faith said, "treating a girl like a slave who can just be passed from one owner to the next. It isn't right."

Malcolm looked over the fist at his jaw to cast Faith a look of agreement. Then he continued to pace. A knock at the door caused Faith to take her leave. "Hello?" she began, swinging the front door wide—then she saw it was Priscilla. "Oh." She cast the violet eyed vixen a look of humble disdain. "Is the doctor expecting you?"

"No," replied Priscilla, thrusting her fine-boned chin into the air, a gesture she had learned from a lifetime of being scoffed at. "But I wish to see him." Her tone left no room for debate.

Faith obediently opened the door wider and granted her entrance. "Right this way."

"I know the way," Priscilla announced coldly.

"No matter," said Faith slowly and stubbornly. "It wouldn't be right for you to make the trip on your own." She led the woman to Malcolm's study at an annoyingly slow pace. She knew that the last thing Dr. Rutherford needed right now was a visit from this wretched woman. When she reached the study, she cast him a look of regret. "Doctor?" she announced warily. "Seems you have a guest." Then, without further ado, she bowed her head and retreated, closing the door gingerly behind her. She shook her head with a sigh. Why, tonight of all nights, did that woman have to pay a visit? She sluggishly walked away, determined to get at least a little dusting done on this very dark day.

"Priscilla," said Malcolm imploringly, "this is not a good time."

Priscilla removed her cloak seductively, revealing a black dress that was low in front and falling gracefully from her slender, lightly golden shoulders. Her black hair was glossy and sleek, left intentionally free from its bun so that Malcolm could see it in all of its silken glory.

Her violet eyes were striking, as always, as they shimmered from within her delicate face. "I wanted to talk to you," she told him, closing the distance between them.

"Not now, please," he begged. "Priscilla, I've had a wretched day, and . . ."

She reached out and touched his cut lip. She caressed it with care, as though soothing her warrior's battle wounds.

"And I thought I'd made it clear it was over between us," he finished, causing her to remove her dainty hand from his face.

"I don't know what I could have done to anger you so," she retorted, arms defensively crossed.

Malcolm grimaced. This was the last thing he needed tonight. He did not believe in breaking women's hearts, though admittedly, he had done an awful lot of it lately. He would have been happy to console Priscilla, and to reiterate his gentle breaking of their engagement. But not at this moment. Right now, all he could think of was Cassie. With a sigh, he did the best he could. "Priscilla, you have done nothing to anger me. As I said, I have merely decided against a marriage of convenience. I know I said I would grant you the respectability of being my wife, and I am a cad to break a promise. But I have decided that it would be doing us both a disservice to give up on finding a genuine marriage. You are a . . . a beautiful woman. And I know that you will meet someone. I . . . I care for you. But you know there has never been love between us."

Priscilla could hear the unspoken words in his speech. Cassie. This was all about Cassie. Deciding she had a better chance of fighting the bull than evading it, she ventured to say, "I was sorry to hear that your servant was reassigned."

Malcolm looked upon her with suspicion. "How did you know about that?"

"Faith told me," she lied.

"Oh. Well, then, I uh . . ." He hardly trusted himself to speak of it, for fear his voice would break. "Thank you," he said at last, "thanks for your concern."

"She really was a pretty thing, wasn't she, Malcolm?" she asked, leaning into one hip to exaggerate her own considerable assets.

Malcolm noticed the posture, and the beautiful line it created, but did not feel any longing. "Yes," he replied, "Yes, she was pretty." How could he explain to Priscilla that it was not her auburn hair that drew him, nor her exotic green eyes? How could he explain that Cassie had made him feel like a virtuous man again? A man who could be comforting and strong, and—what had she called him? Kind. She had needed his kindness, and had made him feel powerful every time he delivered it. She believed in his kindness, that there was still something good in him, that it was not just an act. But Priscilla only liked him for the same reasons he liked her: he could be evil and fierce, and together, they could delve into darkness untamed. All of that was a great deal of fun, he admitted. But Cassie had made him feel that the light within him had not been wholly extinguished. She needed him, and needed him to be gentle. And the light he gave her had a magical way of shining back on himself. "Yes, she was very pretty," he repeated flatly.

"But she wasn't right for you," Priscilla challenged him.

"Priscilla, don't," he said quietly, "Please don't." He was in absolutely no mood to be seduced.

"Don't what?" she laughed, touching her breast as if she didn't know. "Don't what, Malcolm? I'm only trying to be reassuring."

"Well, don't be," he snapped. "Just . . . just leave me be." He turned toward his window, blackened by the night, and peered out of it, as though deep within him lay some outrageous hope that he might see Cassie strolling past his gardens. But in the darkness, he only saw darkness.

"I'm sure she's just fine," said Priscilla.

Just hearing those words made Malcolm's heart thud. He knew perfectly well that she was not fine. And neither was he.

"It's not the end of the world," said Priscilla, hoping desperately that it was true, that Malcolm did not love Cassie so much that her loss *was* the end of the world. "She's merely been reassigned. It's not as though she's been killed."

Malcolm had a vision that he had been trying to avoid all day. It was the image of Cassie trying to sleep in a strange bed somewhere, and being intruded upon. A heartless gaoler coming to her room and pinning her to the bed, holding her still, watching her tears, but feeling no remorse. Malcolm had never felt so needed as he did right now. Even the patients in the hospital did not need his assistance as much as Cassie did. For the worst thing that could befall them was death. Cassie could very well be suffering worse. He thought about her amusing declaration: *You're not allowed to beat me.* It had been amusing at the time because she'd been so confident, and she'd been so wrong. But it no longer amused him. The fact was that no one would protect Cassie from anything. She was out there somewhere, completely at the mercy of a stranger—and a gaoler, no less. If only Malcolm knew where. "You don't know what it's like to be a convict," he told Priscilla, voicing something he never had before. "You don't know how we're treated. You don't know the way people see us. Believe me, Cassie would welcome death on this night."

Priscilla felt he had tried to put a rift between them. It was true, she was not a convict. But she fell just shy of being a prostitute. Did he think she didn't know what it was to be treated like an animal? "How can you say that?!" she cried, for he really had hit a raw chord. "How can you say that . . . that girl, whom you know must have lived in the lap of luxury all of her life before she got arrested, understands more about pain and ostracism than I? How can you say it, Malcolm?"

There was an unusual amount of sincerity in her cry, and Malcolm was drawn to sincerity. His eyes grew more thoughtful and sympathetic. He took a step closer to her. "Priscilla," he said soothingly, "Priscilla, I didn't mean that." He blinked thoughtfully at her distressed face, trying to imagine what despair she must have known. "I know you've had a hard life," he said at last. "I didn't in any way mean to call you spoiled. I only mean to say that there are peculiarities about being a convict that are unlike the hardships experienced even by the downtrodden and the poor. For there is guilt when people spit upon the poor. They may hate them and fear them, but they do feel guilty about it. With us," he smiled, shaking his head, "they feel insanely righteous about seeing us battered. It's different. That's all I'm saying. It's just different."

Priscilla felt satiated by his words, but even more, she felt hope. He was looking right at her now, thinking not of Cassie, but of her. She loved him so that she could not resist grasping at this opportunity for his attention. "I just think that you and I have so much in common," she said desperately. "You underestimate our compatibility. When you say things like that, I don't understand—it just hurts me so much."

Malcolm observed that she had lost her sincerity, but he didn't know how to respond. The first question that came to mind was, "What compatibility?"

"The compatibility between us!" she cried. "Malcolm, don't tell me you haven't felt it." She draped a delicate hand across his sideburned cheek. He let her do this only because he was madly curious to see what she would say. "I know we haven't had a conventional courtship," she confessed, causing him to laugh shortly. "I know that ours has been a joining of passion, and that neither of us has ever been fond of formalities. But don't you remember how it feels when we're together?" she asked, lifting a seductively straight, black eyebrow. "Don't deny that there is something irrepressible between us," she begged. "When we make love, Malcolm, there's more to it than lust. You know there is," she added with hope.

Malcolm swallowed at being so near such a beautiful woman. Truly, she was enchanting. And truly, his body was already remembering all of the nights they had spent together in such ecstasy.

"What's wrong with indulging?" she asked. "You always say I broke your heart, and yet you took me back. I stir something in you, Malcolm, as you stir something in me. You say I torment you, and yet," she let a finger fall to his strong thigh, where it tickled and enticed his breeches, "doesn't a little gentle torment lead to the sweetest bliss?" She smiled as she observed him shifting uncomfortably. "You can have me now, Malcolm," she said. "You can take me right here." She blew hot breath into his ear, stroking his masculine jaw with her slender hands. "Anything you want to do," she offered, "I'll do it." She felt his hands take her hips, squeezing them as though he were about to lift her. In her excitement, she tickled his ear with her tongue.

"You're right," he said, in a strangely distant voice, "there is something between us. And I'm going to have to give the matter more thought."

She encouraged his delicious words by letting him feel her breasts against him.

"Just as soon as I find Cassie," he concluded, then gently pushed her away.

Priscilla was so angry that she spun around and grabbed her cloak. "Good night!" she called angrily behind her as she stormed from his presence. The fire in her eyes was so dangerous that Faith did not dare see her to the door. She watched Priscilla let herself out, then slam the door behind her with a bang. On the other side, she boiled in her anger, stomping away from Malcolm's tasteful little house in a burning rage. She nearly trampled his flowers, then slammed his iron gates behind her in disgust. The dirt road, dug by the labor of a hundred enslaved convicts, provided sturdy earth for her pounding steps. The air was hot and sweet, but she could scarcely enjoy breathing.

It wasn't fair. She loved Malcolm. She would never tell him so, never risk the rejection, but she loved him. He was the kindest, most decent man she had ever known. Of course, his competition wasn't overwhelming, but nonetheless, there it was. He was graceful and intelligent and gentle. Every other man in her life had been brutal and egotistical. Why couldn't she have a man like Malcolm? What was wrong with her that she could capture his body, but never his heart? It wasn't fair. She had been trying to make him love her for ages. True, she had made some mistakes along the way. But she had never stopped trying. And Cassandra Madison won his heart in a few short weeks. It made her ill. What did that freckled convict have that she didn't? She had to know. She had to learn the secret of how to win a man's heart. She only hoped Cassie Madison would be alive long enough to tell her. It would be a shame if she were murdered before being able to share that secret.

Twenty-five

Cassie had cleaned Robin's shack well enough so a path through the living quarters could be navigated without stumbling. She could have done a better job, she reasoned, but then again, her motivation was weak. She had done as much as she thought she needed to do to avoid a beating, and no more. "It looks great!" he cried, never having seen his shack in such a gleaming state before.

Cassie repressed a snicker. "I'm glad you're pleased."

He didn't want to seem too pleased. It wasn't good, he decided, for a servant to feel she was doing well enough. It would squelch her motivation to try harder. So he eagerly added, "But your cooking needs some work. The fish was tough. Don't cook it so long."

Cassie nodded with a great show of complacency, for someone who was sure she would take any opportunity to slice this man's throat.

Robin was looking at her strangely, so strangely that it made Cassie tense. On this day, he had spoken more to a convict than he ever had in his life. It was odd, given that he was a gaoler. But his swift interactions with Cassie on this day had marked the closest he'd ever come to knowing a convict. Somehow, that made it more difficult for him to drag her to his bed. He was looking at her now as one who was trying to convince himself that he had not seen what he saw. He studied her face, trying to believe once again that she was not human. He reached out and caressed her cheek, causing her to quiver, and bow her head low. That didn't help. She was responding to him as a regular woman would have. And he needed her to respond like a wild animal, trying to break free. He swallowed. "You have strange eyes," he said.

Cassie was shaking so hard, she had to fold her hands to steady them. Her knees were knocking together, and she feared they might give way. She took a deep, quivering breath but did not reply.

"How did you get such strange eyes?" he asked. "I've never seen their like."

Cassie cut her eyes to the side in an expression of exasperation. Then she lowered them. Again, she did not reply.

Robin was gradually hardening himself against her. Her silence was helping. It was easy for him to imagine that she was unable to speak, that she was not smart enough to say a word. Just a frightened animal, he told himself. Not a woman at all. He leaned in for a kiss, which she did not receive. But that was all right. He hadn't expected her to. He had only wanted to press his lips against hers in a show of power. To prove to her that she could not refuse him a kiss. "What was your crime?" he asked her in a low voice. "Why were you sent here?"

Cassie turned her face away. She did not want to tell him.

"Answer me!" he demanded.

His shouting had been so close to her ear that she was startled into attention. "Mur . . . murder," she whispered.

He grinned triumphantly. "Then it's murder for which you will pay tonight." He made a crude grab at her hips, squeezing them with brutal force, pressing her shaking body against his firm one. His eyes were dangerous, his lips were curled, and his kiss was insincere.

As soon as Cassie was let up for breath, she cried out,

"You are not God! You are not my judge! And you are not my rightful executioner!" She pushed at him with all of her might. At first, he watched her struggles with amusement, keeping his arms wrapped firmly about her, but then, she nearly broke free. That made him angry.

He took hold of her elbows, pinching them into redness as he shook her. "You are nothing! Do you hear me?" he growled, his face growing hot. "You are filth! You are disgusting! You are a disgrace!"

"I am human!" she cried, still pulling against his grip, no matter how sore it made her arms.

"You are a murderess!"

"And still human!" she cried.

"You had no mercy on those you killed."

"You don't care about those I'm said to have killed! You care only for an excuse to belittle me! You're glad there are killers out there! For without them, you'd have no job and no one at whom to sneer."

The truth made him so angry that he backed her against a wall, allowing her head to hit the wood with a bang. "The judge may have let you off easily by sending you here," he sneered, "but I will not." He ravaged her mouth with an angry, suffocating kiss. She was plastered against the wall, his hand climbing under her dress. No amount of slapping it away did any good. It only encouraged him. She tried to shift and twist within his cruel embrace, but it was all of no use. His kiss grew fiercer, and it had been so long since she was able to breathe, she thought she would choke. She grew frantic under his rising fingers, which threatened to slide between her thighs. Her eyes wide open, her arms aching from the struggle, she thought it was all over for her.

There was a knock at the door. Cassie looked heavenward in her relief as she found herself suddenly free. She was able to take a deep breath and straighten her gown as Robin moved abruptly to answer the door. She had never been so grateful for the use of her arms and legs. She saw that Robin was buttoning his shirt and rolling his shoulders to ease his tension and make himself presentable. After rubbing his face and taking a quick swig of whiskey, he did his best to plaster on an amicable facial expression. He swung open the door expectantly, and Cassie could not believe her eyes. It was Priscilla.

Twenty-six

"Did I interrupt something?" asked Priscilla with a look of amusement. She took note of Cassie's frazzled hair and crooked dress. And she knew well the look of a man on his way to the bedroom. Robin had that look all over him.

"Not at all," he greeted suavely, lifting her slender hand to his moist mouth.

Priscilla scoffed. "I'm glad to see your new servant is settling in," she teased, looking right into Cassie's frightened eyes.

"Never mind her," said Robin. "Come, let us have some privacy." He led her to the bedroom, shouting over his shoulder, "Cassie! Finish cleaning this house, and don't disturb us."

Cassie could not understand what Priscilla was doing here. She supposed it was possible that she had merely taken a new lover, now that Malcolm had broken off their engagement. But how could she go so easily from Malcolm to Robin? Didn't that seem a bit of a step downward? And it seemed too much of a coincidence that the same woman would be involved with both her first and second assignor. Unless, she supposed, Priscilla slept with everyone. In that case, there would be no coincidence involved. In fact, the more Cassie pondered it, the more this seemed the best explanation. But she could not completely cast aside her sense of unease. Was Priscilla following her? Why would she do that?

Cassie went to the task of cleaning, her mind still deep in thought. At the moment, she did not mind the filth under her scrubbing rag, for no matter how dirty Robin's house was, the task of cleaning it was far more pleasant than what had nearly befallen her. While hours ago, the cleaning had seemed an unbearable chore, she now thought she could almost enjoy the safety of cleaning house every day, so long as she could avoid Robin's advances. It was amazing how relative happiness was. For now, this cleaning rag seemed to be her friend. It could keep her from Robin, and if she focused on it enough, it could keep her from thinking of Malcolm. And how greedily she had asked for his love, when she had already received his kindness.

Priscilla had always enjoyed Robin as a lover. He had a rough and straightforward sort of touch, not nearly as enticing as Malcolm's. But he was in fine shape and had a handsome face. And in the right mood, she could enjoy his rough tossing. "Have you missed me?" she asked sulkily.

"Wildly," he replied. "It's been too long since you've paid me a visit."

"I've been busy," she drawled, stretching out across his bed, propping herself on her elbows.

Robin thought himself a very handsome man. He had not been born into a high station—had, in fact, been very poor as a boy, but he had been given one gift. He had always been able to have most any woman he wanted, within his station. He knew that women fancied his dark, rugged looks, and he took it completely for granted. He neither relished it nor wondered about it. He had always just known that they liked him. But Priscilla was such a beauty that when he first saw her, he thought he finally understood how women must feel when they saw him. If they were as attracted to him as he was to Priscilla, then it was no wonder they took so well to his advances. Of course, he knew what Priscilla was. He knew that she bedded half the men in Sydney. But that didn't matter to him, so long as he was one of them. "Well, let's see if we can't make you even busier," he winked. He sat on the edge of his bed and pulled her against his chest. "Come here," he grinned, "I've missed you." Then he dove in for a powerful kiss, much kinder than the one he'd given Cassie.

When she was let up for air, Priscilla smiled. He had such a tight embrace that it was nearly uncomfortable, and his kissing was direct, as though it were not a seduction but a practiced formality. She knew that Robin only enjoyed one part of lovemaking, and they hadn't gotten to it yet. But she touched his jaw and marveled at his dark, handsome face. His narrow eyes were smiling at her, waiting to see what she would do. When she opened her mouth, he expected to hear one of her famously enticing lines. He waited expectantly, for he loved aggressive women. But her words were a disappointment, to say the least. "What do you think of Cassie?" she asked.

"Who?" Robin really had forgotten all about her for a moment. But now that he was forced to recall, he broke out of his puzzled expression and said, "Oh, yes, Cassie. Uh . . . I don't know," he shrugged. "What do you mean?" And why must we talk about this? was going to be his next question. But he dared not ask it, for Priscilla's temper was notorious. Any man with a little generosity could borrow her beauty, but there was no way to win her back once she'd been angered.

"I mean," asked Priscilla, playing with a piece of his black hair, a gesture he did not particularly like, "what do you think of her? Is she . . . is she pretty?"

"Not as pretty as you," he said.

She narrowed her eyes skeptically. "Do you mean that?"

He nodded, gazing mesmerized at her exotic violet eyes.

Priscilla believed he was telling the truth. "Then what is it about her?" she thought she asked herself, but when he looked puzzled, she realized she had spoken out loud. Quickly, she thought of another question to cover the awkward one she had blurted out. "Do you find her intoxicating or seductive?"

Robin looked incredulous. "She's a convict," he explained, his nose wrinkled. "I see her as a convict. That's all."

Priscilla frustrated him further by rising to her feet in a swift motion. She paced to the far side of his bedroom as he watched her enticing silhouette. "I know of a man who is madly in love with her," she announced.

"Really?" scoffed Robin. "You're joking, right? Here in Sydney? How could she have met someone here in Sydney?"

"The details aren't important," she snapped, "but I will go mad if I don't discover his reason." She tapped her fist against her chin several times.

Robin's mind gave some dull thought to the matter. "I don't know," he shrugged. "Maybe it's a redheaded issue. Men are funny about red hair. We either love it or we hate it, and can't be persuaded to change our stance. Maybe he loves it."

Priscilla was shaking her head. "No, no. It's nothing so simple as that. This man is . . . he's too strange for that."

Robin was now on his feet, trying to change the subject by slipping his hands around her tiny waist. "Maybe he likes his women in chains," he jested, nibbling on her ear.

Priscilla's eyes flew wide. "What did you just say?"

"Sorry," he whispered. "It was a crude joke."

Priscilla shook her head. "No. No, you may be right. Of course you're right. It's her vulnerability, isn't it? It's the fact that she is a lost kitten, so to speak?"

"Whatever you say," he whispered, drawing her closer to his anxious flesh.

"It makes sense," she concluded aloud, ignoring his pawing. It really did make perfect sense, given all she knew about Malcolm and his obsession with the balance of power. And yet, her heart would not agree with what seemed so right. From deep within, her fears were not allayed. She still believed that Malcolm loved Cassie for reasons she could never fathom, and for virtues she could never possess. It was a pleasant notion that he had merely grown tired of playing with Priscilla and had found a new, more enticing game with Cassie, in which he could play master and gaoler. But she had seen the look in his eyes when he spoke of her. She knew he loved her.

There was a crash outside the door. Robin, whose face had been buried deeply in his lover's neck, looked up with a startle. Impatience narrowing his dark eyes, he flung open the bedroom door and ran out to get a look at the culprit. Dazedly, Priscilla followed him, though she had been so deep in her own thoughts, it took her a long time to realize what had happened. But now she saw it. Really, it was nothing. Cassie had been cleaning, and accidentally broke a very inexpensive glass. Priscilla had just turned away in disinterest when she heard Cassie shriek. Robin was shaking her brutally, and demanding, "How could you be so stupid?"

Priscilla cast a look of distaste upon him. "Is it really so important, Robin?" It was growing late, and she wanted to finish their lovemaking so she could return home at a seemly hour. She never stayed the night in any man's arms. Sleeping in her own bed was her favorite luxury.

Robin did not seem to hear her objection. He was red

in the face and violent in the eyes. He shook Cassie with such force that her head hit the wall at least twice. "Do you know what that cost me? Do you know what it's worth? Huh? Well, it's worth a hell of a lot more than you are, that's what. So how are you going to pay me back, huh? What are you going to do? Is this worth some money?" he asked, yanking the fabric of her skirt. "No. It doesn't look like it. How about this?" He tugged at her hair. "Should I cut this off and sell it? Will that pay me back?"

Cassie looked as though she were trying to remain proud. She looked like a martyr, accepting that she was going to be beaten, and merely praying that it would be over soon. She was trembling, her lips were dry, her breathing ragged. But impressively, she shed no tears. She allowed herself to be shaken, closing her eyes against Robin's hot energy as though she were waiting for it to pass. Robin, in the meantime, was working himself into a louder and louder bellow. The more he yelled and the less he was challenged, the more confident he grew that he was right. And the more he wanted to indulge in this moment of unconditional power. But when he lifted his hand and prepared to pound the back of it onto Cassie's raw cheek, he found he was being restrained. It was not a powerful restraint, but somehow, the hand on his elbow caused him to lose his resolve.

He turned to see Priscilla's eyes, glaring at him in the dim light. Her voice was slow and positively spooky as she asked, "What is the matter with you?"

He looked at the hand which had been so close to striking Cassie. He looked at the freckled girl, closing her eyes as though still expecting to be hit. Then he looked at Priscilla, whose stoic face told him he had better not do it. He let Cassie go and turned immediately to the woman he adored. "Priscilla, I'm sorry. I forgot you were here. I didn't mean for you to see such a thing."

Priscilla smiled darkly, her head shaking from side to

side in a slow rhythm. "You fool," she chuckled. "Do you realize you're apologizing to me for nearly killing someone else?"

He didn't get it. "Yes, yes, I'm sorry," he said, wrapping his arms tightly around her. "I'm so sorry. You were a guest in my home, and you had to see this. It was not chivalrous of me."

Priscilla laughed once more. "Chivalrous? Why, I believe you're the first man I've met who's heard the term. Too bad you mock it."

"I don't mock it," he swore. "I . . . I don't usually behave this way. Not in front of a lady."

Priscilla sighed, and for the very first time, cast Cassie a look of understanding. "Dull knives are more dangerous than sharp ones, aren't they?" she joked. And Cassie, taking her meaning loud and clear, had to repress the strong urge to smile. Robin didn't get it.

"What? What do you mean?" He tried to join in their grinning, but after a while, gave up and reached for his whiskey.

Priscilla went home with an ache in her back. All of the lanterns were out, and for one blissful moment, she thought she was completely alone. She put her hands on the small of her back and stretched, moaning at the release of tension. She stretched her arms way overhead and rocked from side to side, trying to get the kinks out of her ribs. Then, just as she began to lower her gown, preparing herself for a night of delicious, private sleep, she heard a voice. "Did you see her?"

Priscilla jumped, then scowled at being forced to do so. "Miles," she groaned, "why didn't you light a lantern? At least then I'd have known I had company."

"I was trying to sleep," he explained gruffly. "Now answer my question. Was she there?"

Priscilla sighed audibly. "Yes, Miles. Where else would she be?"

"Well, what was the situation?" he asked, trespassing deeper into her privacy. "Is she protected?"

Priscilla, tremendously disinterested in having this conversation, began to look around for her hairbrush. She preferred to sleep *au naturel,* but she absolutely couldn't rest without first brushing her hair. "I suppose Robin provides some protection," she muttered. "I can't see killing her while he's standing right there, worried over how he'll get his house cleaned without her."

"Is he always there?"

"Yes, Miles," she drawled sarcastically, "he's always there. He doesn't need supplies or food like the rest of us."

"Stop being smart," he snapped. "I put up with your wise mouth often enough—I don't need to do it when we're talking business. Now tell me. When does he leave?"

Priscilla took a deep breath, thinking hard. "Well, he works at the barracks," she said at last, "and he's an avid fisherman. Between the two, I'd say he's gone for most of the daylight hours except on Sunday. When he drinks," she added with a roll of her eyes. She didn't want to give Miles any indication that this was a church-going man with morals.

"Fine," he said gruffly. "Will he be gone tomorrow?"

"I imagine so."

Miles nodded gravely. "Then tomorrow, I want you to pay her a visit. Do you understand?"

Priscilla crossed her arms pensively. Head bent in thought, she suggested, "Wouldn't you be better for the job?"

"Don't tell me you're getting scared," he said.

Priscilla shook her head.

He dropped a coin crudely down the front of her dress. "Maybe this will grant you some courage."

She spat at his gesture, then turned and stormed to her bedroom.

"You're going tomorrow?" he double-checked.

Priscilla sighed on the other side of the closed door. "Yes!" she cried irritably. "Yes, I'll go! Just leave me be. I said I'll go!"

Twenty-seven

Cassie spent a miserable night in the living room, tossing and turning on a pile of blankets. Somehow, she had thought Robin would force her to sleep in his bed. But apparently, unless he had use for her there, she was not welcome. She worried horribly over the incident with the broken glass. What troubled her most was not that he had shaken her and spoken so brutally, but that she knew it would happen again. She could not go through life without making mistakes. Someday, she would drop another glass. And she now knew what to expect from him when she did. It was a blessing that Priscilla had been there this time to distract him, but she could not always count on such luck.

She stared up at the dark ceiling, feeling completely alone. And she thought about making love. Robin would never leave her alone on the matter, she knew. She could fight him off all she wanted, but someday he would take her. And she wondered how it would feel. With Malcolm, it had been so exciting. She had felt more alive than she ever had before, her heart swelling with conflicting emotions that made her body tremble. But Malcolm had been so gentle. And Robin would not. She could hardly bear to think about Malcolm. Her breath grew ragged in the dark. Every time she remembered that night when she told him she loved him, she felt so embarrassed, she couldn't stand herself. She still loved him, of this she was sure. And she mourned his loss as she had never mourned even the loss of her family. But she swore she would never again, so long as she lived, tell anyone *I love you*. If only she had not told him, if only she had kept her distance and continued to admire him from afar, then she could have remembered her days with him fondly. The memories would not be tainted by her shame.

Robin woke up much too early for her taste. It wasn't that she minded an early rising, but somehow, he had decided that the best time for fishing was before sunrise. And that pushed her limit. It was in a half-daze that she cooked his breakfast that morning. And it was with fog in her eyes that she watched him leave. When he returned with fish on the line, she received the unfortunate news that she was expected to scale them. The night before, he had cut off the heads. But she'd known this would happen. The longer she stayed, the more he would use her. The more she did, the more he would expect her to do. It was only a matter of time before he would ask her to drive him to work.

Cassie seemed to have sand in her head as she scaled the fish that morning. She could not do with so little sleep and so little food. Robin had been stingy with her portions at meals. She made a mental note that in the future, she must eat while she cooked, before he could see how much there was and divide it so brutally unevenly. She knelt outside of the shack and watched the sun shine on the hot, blue ocean. She hated scaling fish. It seemed so cruel to slice them when they were struggling and unable to breathe. She kept her eyes on the bright sun sparkling on the water to distract her from the gory task. Then, suddenly, she caught a glimpse of her knife, glimmering in the sunlight, as though it offered some strange hope. She closed her eyes and breathed hard, gathering her courage. She knew what she had to do. Her heart swelled with the freedom of being able to control her own destiny once again. But her hands trembled in miserable anticipation of what she would have to do to exercise that freedom. She would wait until Robin was nearly home. And she would use not the knife, but a rope. A rope and a tree was all she would need, and she would be free.

When Robin arrived, he heard a scream. Cassie lay in an uncharacteristically dramatic pose, sprawled across the rocky shore, one leg twisted, her face contorted in agony. "Help!" she called.

He scowled as a callous gentleman will when asked for help. "What did you do?"

"My leg!" she cried, touching it with a wince. "It's broken! I . . . I need to go the hospital!"

Robin was in no mood to turn his wagon around. He had just returned and was immensely looking forward to a hot meal and bath. "Maybe it can be sort of pulled back into place," he suggested, though he had never done such a thing before, and wasn't sure how to go about it.

"No!" she cried, her face rosy and moist with salt water. "It won't heal properly if it isn't done right!" She gasped as she tried to move the leg. "Ahh!" she cried, "if we don't have a doctor fix it, I may not be able to work again."

This caused Robin some alarm. He looked longingly at his fishing poles, which he had so desperately wanted to put to good use. Then he looked mournfully at his little house, which offered such luxurious protection from the winds. A hot meal and a soft bed would not be his yet. He looked angrily at Cassie. "Very well," he snapped, "get in the wagon. I'll take you to the hospital."

Cassie licked her lips with a look of forced patience. "Robin, I can't walk."

He groaned. He couldn't believe that not only was she not going to fix his supper or draw his bath, but he, as

master, would be forced to chauffeur her. And if all that
weren't enough, she wanted to be carried. He lifted her
with absolutely no care for her injured leg and tossed
her into the wagon as though it didn't matter how she
landed. Cassie groaned at being handled so roughly, and
with a broken leg, no less. She'd underestimated how
much it would hurt to inflict such an injury upon herself. But as the horses lurched forward, she felt no
regret. She tossed her head back and let the wind catch
her hair. She had done it. She had saved herself. And
there was nothing so freeing to a captive as finding the
courage to make a choice.

It was a blessing to Cassie that her pain had rendered
her nearly unconscious by the time they reached the Sydney hospital. If Robin had been a kinder man, he would
have warned her of what was to come. But as it was, it did
not even occur to him to make certain Cassie was at ease
as the screams came into hearing. The screams were from
those being dragged and carried into the hospital. They
were the screams of those who were not ready to die. For
a broken leg might be easy enough to fix, but everyone
knew that to come to Sydney's hospital with illness meant
never to leave. It may well have been the worst hospital of
its time. Its rate of cure was so pitifully below its rate of failure that corpses cluttered the entrance. It was impossible
to bury them fast enough.

Cassie could vaguely hear the weak pleas of those
around her. "Take me home. I'm not ready to die!" She
could not see who'd said that, whether it was the elderly
lady with panic in her brown eyes, or the little boy whose
parents were on their way out the door. But it was the
smell, and not the voices, which overwhelmed her. The
stench of death and human remains was all around her.
It was so overpowering that she forced herself to breathe
through her mouth, worrying that as she did so, sickness
would pour down her throat. Robin was carrying her

down an echoing, gray hallway. The ceilings were so high, the building seemed to be a mockery of a church. Cassie absently waved to a rat which scurried by, wondering how it would feel to be so small.

She was placed on a hard cot, soiled by the blood of the last patient. She watched vaguely as Robin turned away, his footsteps echoing above the screams of children. She had a distant notion that it was wrong of him to leave her, that to leave somebody in this place was the epitome of abandonment. But she was too groggy to care. Her leg had stopped hurting, but she knew it was an illusion. She knew that the pain was still there, and that it was she who had departed. A sour-faced doctor asked whether she could hear him. And then he asked someone else, "Has she gone into shock?" Cassie observed his questioning with curiosity, studying the deep wrinkles on his face. But she had forgotten how to reply.

Her mouth began to move, though. No voice emerged at first, but she kept moving her lips, as though quite certain something would spring forth if she only kept them in motion. At last, she heard herself whisper, "Malcolm." The doctor did not seem to hear it, so she said it louder, "Malcolm." He heard her this time, but looked at her as though she were babbling nonsense. He reached for her foot. "Doctor Rutherford!" she managed to cry out. "I need Doctor Rutherford!"

This caused the sour-faced doctor to take notice. "What did you say, child?"

Cassie was perspiring fiercely, unaware of her head turning from side to side. "Doctor . . . Doctor Malcolm Rutherford," she said. "He . . . he's my doctor."

The man scowled. "That doesn't make sense, child. He doesn't make house calls."

"I must speak to him!" she cried. "I must . . ." She was panting now, and couldn't keep talking. She just kept repeating, "Malcolm."

The heavily wrinkled doctor looked to his nurse. "Is Doctor Rutherford in surgery?"

"Yes."

He sighed. "Well then, I'm just going to have to set this leg myself." He reached again for her foot.

"No!" cried Cassie. "I need Doctor Rutherford!"

"Quiet," scolded the old man. "I'll tell him you've been asking for him. Now hold still." He lifted her skirt most ungraciously, baring her contorted limb. As he began to pull, Cassie gave out a yell which echoed throughout the gray, cathedral-ceilinged hallways. And then she knew no more.

Twenty-eight

When she awoke, it was to the most beautiful pair of eyes she had ever seen. Navy blue and warmed over with kindness, the eyes fell upon her with concern. Cassie could not resist reaching up to touch the face which held them. Malcolm kissed the hand that touched him, then lowered it to her side. She realized that although she was under blankets, she was strangely cold. The ceilings seemed so far away that it was as though the sky itself were a dull gray, and the whole world an echoing tomb. In the other beds, there were dying patients, and doctors scurrying about to save them. But Cassie felt quite alone and safe under the caring gaze of Dr. Rutherford. "Malcolm," she whispered, her voice coming out in a mere squeak.

"Tell me what happened," he demanded. "Where did they take you?" He tried to sound as though he had not spent his days trying to track her and his nights mourning his failure.

"Malcolm," she squeaked, a tear coming to her eye, "Robin . . . Robin Carthage. They brought me to his house, and . . ."

Malcolm anxiously wiped the tear from her face with expertly gentle hands. "Is he the one who broke your leg?"

Cassie shook her head, and sniffed back her tears. "I

broke my own leg. Malcolm, I had to see you. I had to ask for your help."

He stopped her before she broke down crying. He couldn't stand to watch that. He took her in his arms as unthreateningly as he could, refraining from squeezing her against him. He created a firm cradle for her shaking body, and said, "Don't cry, Cassie. Please. Just tell me what happened."

"Malcolm," she sobbed into his stiff shoulder, "he . . . he shook me, and I just broke a glass. I didn't really hurt anything, but he was so angry. And I know it will happen again, and . . ." She sniffed. "He tried to . . . well, to do something to me. I can't tell you what. I'm too ashamed. I . . ."

Malcolm listened to her fragmented sentences with a dark gleam in his eye. Inside, he was raging. He didn't know who Robin Carthage was, or exactly what had happened. But he had hurt Cassie badly enough to make her think that a broken leg and a trip to Sydney's hospital would be less painful. He wanted to kill the man. And the more he listened, the stiffer he grew. He was hardening against his own fury, trying to shield Cassie from it. "It'll be all right now," he said, though he desperately wanted to know more details. He wanted to know what had been done to her so that when he killed Mr. Carthage, he would know exactly why. But he could not press Cassie for information. He would not ask a trembling lady whether she had been raped. He would not force her to tell of her own degradation. "No one can hurt you here." Her sniffing subsided a little, so he pushed some moist hair from her forehead with a smile. "Well, except the lousy medical service, of course," he teased, "but I'll make sure none of us doctors gets our hands on you."

She grinned. "Malcolm, I heard you're the best doctor in the whole country."

"Yes," he smiled back, "but I had to move to Australia before anyone could say that."

She took a heavy breath with some relief, and found enough bravery to part from his brotherly embrace. She sat upright on her cot and moved the blankets to examine the splints on her leg.

"Don't do that," ordered Malcolm, wrapping the blankets firmly back around her. "You were in shock. You've still got chills. I don't want to see that blanket off of you. I'm your doctor now, remember?"

She returned his kind smile, but still did not feel at ease. "Is there anything you can do to help me, Malcolm? I mean, after . . . after I get out of here?"

"Well, one thing I know I can do for certain," he replied, "is make sure you don't get out of here anytime soon. I'll take over your case, so you won't be able to leave until I release you. I don't know what to do from there, but this much I promise," he said, combing her hair firmly from her forehead. "I won't release you until I'm certain you'll be safe."

Cassie closed her eyes in relief. "Then you . . . you think I did the right thing?"

"As your doctor?" he smiled. "As your doctor, I would have to urge people not to break their own legs."

She found the strength to laugh.

"But as a man," he said, his eyes mellowing, "I would have to commend your bravery."

Cassie bowed her head. "I'm always coming to you as some sort of a helpless child," she said shamefully. "You have rescued me more times than I can count. And while I am deeply indebted to you, I also feel rather . . . pitiful."

"I used to be helpless, too," he said firmly, his eyes sternly sympathetic. "Captivity breeds helplessness. You did the right thing to come find me."

Cassie appreciated his reassurance, but it did not alleviate her sorrow. "I have never been helpless before, you know," she told him with vulnerably open eyes. "I was always the strong one at home."

He studied her thoughtfully. "Somehow, I don't have trouble believing that," he said. "There's a lot of courage in you."

She wanted to say something else. She had feared she might never see him again, and had imagined a thousand times what she would say at this moment, when his ruggedly handsome face was once more within her reach. It was a frightening thing to say. Frightening because it could be taken as an overture for romance, when naturally, she planned never to make such an overture again. She knew her love was unrequited, and that Malcolm's kindness was simply that: kindness. But she thought perhaps there was a way to say it which would not make her sound like a love-struck child. And he deserved to hear it. "Malcolm," she said, her eyes brave and frank, "if I'd known I would some day be reduced to begging for charity and kindness," she swallowed emotionally, "you are the person I would have wanted to beg. I have never met a finer man."

This hit Malcolm in a tender spot she could never have seen. He would not let himself be called a fine man. He knew he was a villain and a sinner, and he could not see himself otherwise. Yet, when he was with Cassie, he felt that he was indeed a gentleman. He knew it wasn't so, but it felt like the truth. Only when he was with her. Something inside him began to melt, and he thought he would be reduced to tears if he did not walk away at that moment. He wanted to be Cassie's cry for help; he wanted to be her rescuer. But he didn't deserve it. If she'd seen him that night, if she'd watched him as he tried to tear another human being apart . . . she would know it was all an act. He was himself that night. Now, he was just forcing himself, against all instinct, to walk the straight and narrow. "Thank you," he managed to say.

"I mean it, Malcolm."

He saw in her eyes that she meant it. And he wanted to believe right along with her that he was good and virtuous. He nearly said it. He nearly said, *I am only a good person when I'm with you, and I love you for it,* but he did not. Instead, he rose awkwardly to his feet and stammered, "Well, I . . . I've got to go to the waiting room to see who else needs help. I . . . I'll come back as soon as I can."

Cassie crossed her arms as he left her. She had said too much again, she was sure. She had repelled him just as she always repelled him. Her heart and her mouth were far too big for her own good. She dropped her head miserably against her hard pillow and tried to get some sleep.

It was late that night that her eyes opened again and she saw the shadow. It was right outside the hospital window. A shiver crept up her legs. There could be no doubt about it now. Someone was out there, following her.

Twenty-nine

"She's gone!" Priscilla cried, storming into her modest home, anger all over her face. "I've just been to Robin's, and they're both gone! Miles, it isn't my fault. I had planned to do everything, just as you told me. But the wagon was gone, she was gone, he was gone!" She was furious at Cassie for getting her into trouble with Miles. At that moment, she didn't care whether the girl was murdered or not.

"It's all right," said Miles mildly.

"I can't believe I lost sight of her!" Priscilla continued, trying to impress Miles with her own anger, in hopes it would cool his own. "I was sure he would never take her from the house! You should see . . . what did you say?"

"I said it's all right," replied Miles, flicking the ashes from his cigar. His pale eyes glistened mischievously in the dim light. His deeply wrinkled face broke into a grin. "I have learned that the poor thing suffered an injury this afternoon. She is at the hospital."

"Is that so?" asked Priscilla warily. "Then I assume she is well guarded?"

"At the moment," he assured her, "but she won't be tonight. At night, most of the staff goes home."

"Then we'd better get there by dusk," said Priscilla sternly.

"I'll make sure the coast is clear," he confirmed, "and you run in."

A nod sealed the agreement.

Cassie found it hard to slumber, for she had seen the shadow once more, and could no longer imagine it belonged to a wild animal or to her imagination. Someone was following her. Her hands and knees shook under the blankets, and it was not only from chill. The moaning of dying patients became eerie in the darkness. Malcolm had obviously been kept a good while with his next appointment, because he had not come back. The hospital was understaffed, and the nurses were scarce. Most of the doctors had gone home. It was true that she was surrounded by people, but what could a dying man do if she was attacked? The rapid flurry of mice and rats echoed through the empty hallways, and made her pull the blankets to her chin. She hoped none would get in her bed.

She had to sleep. There was no sense in this, she told herself. There was no use in worrying over something she could not control. If someone was out there, waiting to pounce, there was nothing she could do to prevent it. She expected to occupy this hospital bed for a very long time. Surely, she could not go night after night without rest. It didn't make sense. She would have to force herself to sleep. She closed her eyes and tried to think peaceful thoughts. Waterfalls. Rose gardens. Her brother Samuel's antics. The smell of grass in the rain. Silvery snow on Christmas morning. Her favorite childhood doll. Anna, that had been her name. Anna with the porcelain face and the yellow curls. Misty days in the city, when even the puddles under one's boots felt romantic. Chocolate. Oh, how she had always loved chocolate! Sunsets in the forest. Strong winds that blew her skirts in summer.

"There you are," said a merciless voice.

Cassie's eyes flung wide, and she found herself staring into Priscilla's cold face. "What are you . . ."

Priscilla did not let her finish. She stuffed a rag in Cassie's mouth before it could be stopped and then shoved her into the arms of a silver-haired gentleman. He lifted Cassie cruelly over his shoulder after Priscilla had bound her wrists. Cassie struggled with all of her might, but with her leg in a splint, there was little she could do without feeling a shock of pain. She found herself being carried out of the hospital, unable to scream, unable to resist. But she made the loudest noise in her muffled throat that she could. This caused Priscilla to snap at her. "Shut up!" she said, her eyes murderously stern. "Don't you understand? We've been hired to save your life."

Thirty

Cassie was unbound once she'd been thrown into a wagon. Her mouth was free, but she hardly knew where to begin asking questions. "How did you . . . Save my life from what? I mean, why . . ."

"Can't we put the gag back in her mouth?" asked Priscilla irritably.

"Be nice," said Miles. "Cassandra, we didn't mean to startle you that way, but we couldn't risk your screaming as we carted you away, and we couldn't stay long enough to engage in a lengthy explanation."

Cassie's leg was killing her. She was so terribly cold as the wind whipped through her hair on this eerie night. "Where are we going?" she asked.

"To my home," said Miles.

"It's *my* home," Priscilla corrected him bitterly. "You just treat it as though it were yours."

Miles chuckled as though delighted to be contradicted. He was being unusually cordial. Clearly, he wanted to make a good impression on Cassie. "I stand corrected," he announced. "We are going to Priscilla's fine abode."

"There's nothing fine about it," she warned, fearing that Cassie would scoff.

But Cassie had slightly more important things on her mind. "Why did you take me from the hospital?"

Priscilla and Miles exchanged looks, as though deciding which of them would venture into the long story behind their kidnapping. It seemed Miles, being the diplomat of the duo, would be the natural candidate. "Well, we honestly don't have time to delve into all of the details," he began. "I fear Priscilla and I have not yet had our rest for the night. Your being taken to the hospital rather threw us for a curve."

Cassie waited patiently for him to continue.

"But the gist of it is something like this," he began with a sigh. "You are being hunted."

"I guessed that," she interrupted. "I keep seeing a shadow."

Miles and Priscilla exchanged wary looks. "I see," said Miles at last. "That isn't good. In fact, we had rather hoped that the assassin had never made it to Australia. It isn't easy, after all, to hire a killer in England and expect him to come this far in search of his victim, no matter how much of his pay is withheld."

Cassie could bear the slowness of this explanation no more. "What killer?!" she cried. "In England? Who hired a killer in England?"

"I know this must be difficult for you," he said. "It is rather startling to learn one has enemies, but surely, you had already guessed as much. Surely," he said with a twinkle in his eye, "you knew that you had been framed."

Cassie's heart lurched with a hope she had not felt since her trial. "You know who committed the murder?" she cried. "You know who made it look as though I did it?"

"Actually, I don't," he said, to her great disappointment. Cassie sank into her seat. "But I do know a lady named Emma Crane, who did *not* have you framed. It is she who hired me to protect you."

"Emma Crane?" asked Cassie confusedly. "I'm sure I've never met her."

"That's because you're not a man," Priscilla chimed in coldly. "She's a prostitute."

"And she's Priscilla's sister," added Miles.

Priscilla shot Cassie a look of humor. "And my parents are just so proud."

"Of you both, I'm sure," Miles chimed in brutally.

Priscilla glared at him with pursed lips, but could not argue. She crossed her arms tightly, and stiffened her back.

"Apparently," said Miles to Cassie, "Emma knows who framed you, and knows that he also hired an assassin to kill you. For some reason, she has taken it upon herself to rescue you from your otherwise certain doom."

Priscilla yawned. "She's probably the one who arranged the whole thing in the first place. No doubt that's how she knows about it."

"Why would she do that?" he snapped.

"I don't know. But I wouldn't put it past her."

Cassie was having trouble absorbing all of this. "You mean," she asked, "that someone hates me enough to have me sent to this island and then have me murdered?"

"Oh, now, I told you she's smart," drawled Priscilla. "Listen to that. She managed to repeat everything we already said in one try."

"Be quiet," snapped Miles, then turned to Cassie with a patient grin. "I don't know that anyone hates you," Miles assured her. "It may merely have been that you were in someone's way or that someone wanted you out of your parents' will."

"My parents won't likely *have* a will," she scoffed. "I wouldn't be surprised to learn they'd spent all their money by now."

"Well, I'm sure that whatever it is, it's something very impersonal," said Miles. "I can't believe that anyone would hold a true grudge against someone so lovely."

"Oh, please, Miles," Priscilla broke in. "You don't want me to get sick in your carriage, do you?"

He shot her an angry look, but Cassie wasn't paying attention to any of it. "Who is this Emma person?" she wondered aloud, "and why would she want to save me?"

"All we know is that she hired us to do it," said Miles.

"She hired *him,*" Priscilla corrected, "then she generously offered her sister as an accomplice. Since I lived here anyway, she didn't think it would be any trouble." She rolled her eyes.

"Of course, I doubt your sister expected you to charge the high fees you've demanded from me," said Miles scornfully. "In fact, I rather think she expected you'd help for free."

Priscilla turned to Cassie in confidence, as there was no one else to whom she could turn. "Miles adores my sister. Just as every other man in London adores her. Pretty sad, isn't it? She was going to be the good girl of the family. You should have met her ten years ago. We all thought she would be a princess until the rumors started going around." She grinned triumphantly. "I'm glad not to be the only black sheep."

"Stop speaking ill of Emma!" cried Miles. But the carriage had pulled to a halt, and the conversation was mercifully ended.

Priscilla's house was modest, but compared to Robin's, it was a palace. It seemed Priscilla took great pride in pruning her flowers and keeping her shutters well painted. It was a charming little white abode with a tiny picket fence between the forest and the garden. Cassie felt as though she were entering a very private place as the wooden gate was unlatched before her. It seemed like Priscilla's own little magic hideaway from the world.

"Miles," Cassie pleaded, as she was admitted into the warm, cozy cottage, "we must tell Malcolm where I am. He saw me this afternoon. He thinks I'm still at the hospital—he'll panic when he finds I'm gone."

"Stop worrying about Malcolm!" Priscilla snapped.

"Why don't you keep your mind on what matters? There is someone trying to kill you!"

Something about the urgency of her remark made Cassie think Priscilla was jealous of her and Malcolm. But how could she know what had transpired between them? "I am worried about the killer," said Cassie in a re-assuring voice, "but I am also worried that should I be found missing, someone will think I have run. They will think I am an escaped convict."

"It is true, Miles," Priscilla said, "We mustn't keep her here."

"Then where do you suggest we put her?" he demanded. "The hospital isn't well guarded at night. She'll be killed if we leave her there. And if she's found anywhere else, she'll look like an escapee."

"Except Robin's house," said Priscilla in a sober tone. "If we bring her back to Robin's, she'll be safe and legal."

"No!" cried Cassie, her eyes rounding in her panic. "No, I will not go back there! I won't! I would rather be caught here by the law."

Priscilla had very little tolerance for emotionalism. "That's ridiculous," she scolded calmly. "You can't tell me you'd rather be flogged and sent to the factory than live with Robin."

Cassie took a deep, quivering breath, her eyes still filled with determination. She couldn't, in perfect honesty, disagree with Priscilla. Her two options were equally unthinkable. So as much as she wanted to argue, she could not. "It is possible, however," she said, "that I would rather die than face either fate."

Priscilla shrugged indifferently. "That's up to you. Just don't make it look like a murder or else Miles won't get his money, and he'll make me return mine."

"Priscilla!" Miles shouted, placing an arm around Cassandra. "Where is your compassion?!"

"At least it's not in my breeches," she snickered.

Miles scowled, but feared that a reply would only draw more attention to the remark. Instead, he turned politely to Cassie. "Please, sit down on the rug. I fear there is no sofa, for Priscilla finds them much too civilized." He cast her an evil glance.

"The rug is comfortable," she retorted, "and if you don't like my accommodations, Miles, feel free to leave."

Miles knew he had been defeated again, for his home was in England, and Priscilla's cottage was one of the few places he had to stay in Sydney.

Cassie eased herself onto the bearskin rug, using the wall for stability as she could not bend her splinted leg. She landed on the floor with a little bang, her hips cushioned only slightly by fur. When he saw her wince, Miles said, "Oh, you poor dear. Shall we get you some hot tea?"

"No, no, thank you," said Cassie, rubbing her thigh. "I think it will take something stronger than that to ease my suffering." She offered a weak smile.

"I'll get her some brandy," said Miles.

As Miles went to the liquor cabinet, Priscilla found herself feeling rather awkward all of a sudden, alone with Cassie. She looked down at the freckled redhead who was rubbing her leg and taking deep breaths against the pain, her back erect against the cold wall. Priscilla did not know what to say to someone who had been so central to her life for so long, and yet, whom she really did not know. She had a strong dislike for Cassie, but at the moment, she could not remember why. Looking at her now, it seemed that Cassie was just a stranger, and not an enemy at all. Then she sighed in relief as Miles returned with two shots of brandy, one for himself and one for Cassie. "No, thank you, I didn't want one anyway," said Priscilla sharply.

"I don't recall asking," he said, handing Cassie hers with such gentleness, it was as though he thought her a sick child.

Priscilla suddenly remembered why she hated Cassie. It was because men treated her with tenderness. It was because Malcolm gave her compassion, while showing Priscilla only his darkest impulses.

"I'm still so confused," said Cassie, taking the brandy in both hands. "Miles, you were in England? And a woman hired you?"

"Yes," he said, "Priscilla's sister, Emma. She told me there was a young lady here in the underworld whose life was in danger, and that she would pay me hand-somely to protect you. She offered Priscilla here as an accomplice, thinking she would help out her own sister without expecting anything in return," he sneered.

"I've never known my sister to do anything out of the kindness of her heart," she declared.

Miles went on. "When I got here, I found that I really did need Priscilla's help, for I had no way to get inside Dr. Rutherford's estate. It cost me a pretty penny of my own earnings," he sneered again, "but I managed to per-suade our mercenary friend here to reacquaint herself with Malcolm Rutherford so that she might keep a close eye on you, and tell me when or if the assailant ever ar-rived. You see," he added viciously, "Priscilla had broken the doctor's heart, and run off with a more dashing suitor."

"Not more dashing," Priscilla breathed, squeezing her-self in her crossed arms, "just wealthier. It was the biggest mistake of my life!" she cried. "I was a fool to leave Mal-colm! Do not mock me!"

Miles was clearly unconcerned by her remorse. "In any case," he went on mildly, "we knew it would not be diffi-cult to woo the doctor back into her arms, given her obvious appeal and his equally obvious weakness for women. So I had her check on you regularly while I snooped about the perimeters of the house. But frankly, we could see no sign that any assassin was on your trail.

We had begun to think the villain had never made it to Australia."

"No," said Cassie, "someone has definitely been following me."

"Then I'm glad we had sense enough to get you out of that unguarded hospital."

Priscilla was feeling humiliated and hot. She turned an evil glare on Miles and said, "Haven't you forgotten to tell her something?"

"What?" he asked innocently.

She smiled coldly. "About how Malcolm banned me from his home? About how you feared we could no longer keep an eye on her? About how you decided to fix it?"

Miles blanched. And Priscilla loved the sight of it. He did not want to tell that adorable little mouse of a redhead that he had forced her into the arms of Robin Carthage. "Well, I . . ." Mercifully, Miles's words were interrupted by the sound of wagon wheels. "What is that?" he demanded.

Priscilla raced to the window. Squinting into the dusk, she paused, trying to make out the details of what she saw.

"Has someone pulled off the road here?" asked Miles frantically. "Are you expecting anyone?"

"Shush, Miles!" she snapped, then continued to peer. "Well, for the love of . . ."

"What is it?!" he demanded.

Priscilla spun around. "Hide Cassie. It's Malcolm Rutherford."

Thirty-one

Some men might have knocked angrily upon the door, but Malcolm, in an unusual show of bitter restraint, knocked with politeness. In fact, his rapping was so steady that Priscilla answered the door with a smile, thinking for just an instant that perhaps he was merely coming for a visit. As soon as she saw his face, she knew that wasn't so. He nearly toppled her on his way through the door. "Where is she?" he demanded, turning disgusted eyes upon Priscilla after scanning the empty room. "What the hell is going on?"

Priscilla was too frank a woman to ask what he meant. She could see in Malcolm's narrowed blue eyes that he knew Cassie was here, and she would only make a fool of herself by stalling. "How did you find us?" she asked, crossing her arms defensively.

Malcolm looked truly repulsed. "I asked you, where is she!" he cried. "Answer me!"

"In the bedroom," she said, pointing. She could hear Miles's angry groan. The stupid oaf, she thought. He didn't even know when a game was finished. He honestly believed that stalling would send Malcolm away.

Malcolm wasted no time in moving toward the closed door, and when he thrust the door open, it was with a loud bang. "Cassie?"

Cassie was still being restrained by Miles, her arms

pinned to her sides, her body crushed against his, but she managed to beam at the doctor.

"For godsake, let her go," said Malcolm, reaching out to rip one of Miles's arms from the injured girl. "What is the matter with you?" He heard Priscilla stroll up behind him just as he'd roughly wrenched Cassie from Miles. "What's going on here?" he demanded of Priscilla. "I followed your wagon from the hospital. What are you doing?"

"Why didn't you call the authorities?" asked Miles stupidly.

Malcolm cast him a reluctant glance, as though annoyed he was still in the room. "I didn't know whether Cassie was coming voluntarily or not. All I saw was the wagon pull away, and that she was missing. If she were escaping, I didn't want to turn her in. But this doesn't look very voluntary. What's going on?"

"We are saving Cassie's life," Priscilla informed him.

"No, that's what I was doing," he retorted. "Remember? I work at a hospital."

"I'm not talking about her leg," said Priscilla calmly. "Someone is trying to kill her."

Malcolm looked disbelievingly and almost angrily at Cassie. "What is this?"

"That's what they tell me," shrugged Cassie.

Priscilla moved closer to Malcolm so he could see the sincerity in her sharp features. "Miles and I were hired to protect Cassie. But unfortunately, at the hospital, we were unable to do so."

"Hired?" he scowled, "What do you mean, *hired*? By whom?"

Priscilla raised her eyebrows at Miles, clearly hoping he would explain.

"All we know," he grumbled, "is that someone's been sent from England to kill the girl, and we're not supposed to let it happen."

Malcolm cast narrowed eyes upon Priscilla once more. "How long ago?" he asked suspiciously.

Priscilla lowered her gaze, an expression so uncharacteristic that Malcolm was taken aback. She looked humble. She looked guilty. Malcolm had never felt so foolish in all of his life, as he nodded his head up and down slowly, as though to say, *I see. I see.* He turned his head away and began to pace the room aimlessly.

"Malcolm," Priscilla began, surprised that he allowed her so much silence, enabling her to go on. "It isn't the reason I returned to you. You must believe me. It is true that Miles and I were hired, but . . ." She took a deep breath, her heart beating rapidly. This was her one and only chance to explain herself. If she failed now, she could never have him back. So, of course, this was the one time she could think of no intelligent words. "I . . . I came back to you because I . . . I love you. I . . . I know it sounds ridiculous now, but . . ."

"Yes," he interrupted at last, turning toward her, his hand rubbing his sideburn, "it sounds ridiculous."

Priscilla was silenced by his reprimand. For though he spoke steadily, and in a melodious, not gruff, voice, no one could give a scolding as effectively as Malcolm. It was something about his face. The look in his eyes told her that she would never be pardoned, and that in his strange, complex inner world, she had just become a villain forever. "Malcolm—"

"No matter," he said, meaning exactly the opposite, "I didn't come here to patch things up with you. I came here to see why you've kidnapped one of my patients."

"And now you know," said Miles.

"So what?" demanded Malcolm, recovering from shock well enough to be angry once again, "This is your plan? To keep her here?"

"We hadn't finished discussing that," griped Miles.

"But we think she should return her to Robin's," said Priscilla bravely. "We think she will be safest there."

"Like bloody hell," said Malcolm. "She's not going back there."

"But the hospital doesn't have security all night long," she pointed out. "You know there isn't enough staff to keep watch. And if she goes anywhere else, she'll be charged as a runaway."

Malcolm knew only one thing, and he said it again with a swift shake of his head. "She's not going back to Robin Carthage's."

"Then what do you suggest?" asked Miles harshly, believing he was competing for male dominance in the room.

Malcolm kept forgetting he was there. Every time he looked at Miles, it was with some combination of surprise and disgust. "I suggest I might have been informed of this sooner," he said.

"We were supposed to keep it all very quiet," Miles explained. "The lady who hired us didn't want word of this getting out. We weren't even supposed to tell Cassandra. We certainly weren't supposed to involve anyone else."

"Oh, I wasn't involved?" asked Malcolm, looking sharply at the shame-faced Priscilla.

"Malcolm," she pleaded, as she would plead with no one else, "please listen to us. Taking Cassie was our only course of action. We couldn't leave her alone in that hospital room!"

"And if we don't return her to Robin quickly," Miles added, "she'll be called an escapee."

Malcolm closed his eyes for a pause. The one thing out of all of this which disturbed him most was the prospect that Cassie could be declared an escapee. He knew too well what would come of that. "Get me a drink," he ordered Priscilla in a voice too smooth, given his distress. When she did not move, he opened his eyes and said again, "Go on. Get me a drink."

This time, she left to do his bidding, for there was something about the gentle way he gave commands which left no room for discussion. When she returned with a goblet of cognac, he sniffed and swirled it for several long seconds as though planning to savor its thick texture. Then he guzzled it in one breath. "Thank you," he said to Priscilla, then placed the goblet gently on the bedroom mantel. He had never been in this bedroom before. It was strange. He had been Priscilla's lover off and on for more than a year, and had never seen her bedroom. Even when he'd come to her cottage, they'd made love by the firelight in the front room. She had never invited him into this room, in her quiet, personal space filled with feminine treasures. He noticed a china angel on the mantel, which seemed to be praying toward the bed. He never would have suspected that Priscilla had a religious streak.

Cassie was feeling strangely forgotten. Though in the abstract she was the center of everyone's attention, her presence was being quite ignored. Leaning against the bedroom wall, favoring her unsplinted leg, she thought that perhaps it was time for her to offer a suggestion. Bravely, she suggested the very thing she feared most. "Malcolm, I think I should go back to Robin's." When he looked at her with wide eyes, she continued. "I don't want to do it. I hate him. I hate it there. But they're right. What choice do I have? I don't think I should risk being missing any longer. In the morning, he may come to pick me up at the hospital." Cassie hated herself for being so practical, but it was in her nature. Initially, she'd thought she would rather be killed than returned to Robin. But time had mellowed her emotions, and given her mind time to break through.

"You're not going back," said Malcolm firmly. And

somehow, Cassie was relieved. Even though she knew he was stating the impossible, there was something about the way he said it that made her quite certain that she would not have to go back. Somehow, she was not going back.

"But I must," she said, eager for him to argue.

"It's out of the question," he replied, staring at the mantel, thinking hard. "You're not going."

"She must," said Priscilla.

"It's out of the question!" he bellowed, his face turning red. Everyone was so shocked to hear him yell, that all eyes grew wide and all lips grew tight. Malcolm turned away from their frightened stares and returned to his deliberation. All of this talk was distracting him. A plan was beginning to form in his mind, but he needed complete silence before it would solidify.

After a long pause, Miles finally broke the silence. "Well, it seems to me we're all sitting around gabbing about nothing. We all know what must be done—none of us likes it, but that's just too bad. The fact is, at least she won't be dead. At the hospital, you don't have time to watch her, and Priscilla and I have to sneak in. We need her somewhere she won't be left alone, and we can visit"

Malcolm muttered something, rubbing his eyes, that nobody quite heard.

Only Priscilla caught a word or two of it. Her eyes narrowed into purple slits. "What did you say?"

He looked up. "I said," he replied exhaustedly, "that I believe it's better if she dies."

Despite their quizzical looks, no one would say anything as they tried to make sense of Malcolm's remark. Then Miles spoke. "You mean we should just let her get killed?"

"No," said Malcolm briskly, "I thought we should just kill her ourselves."

Miles was startled at first, then intrigued.

"I'm joking," Malcolm informed him, "but I do have a plan."

Priscilla suspected she knew what it was.

"I shall pronounce her dead," he said thoughtfully, as though still working it out in his own mind.

"From a broken leg?" asked Priscilla worriedly.

"It can happen," he replied, "and in a hospital as poor as ours, no one will question it. I shall pronounce her dead from . . . infection or complication, I don't know. I'll decide later. I can claim that her corpse has been tossed in the hallway with the others, and no one will be any the wiser."

Cassie cleared her throat, but no one paid her any mind.

"*Then* where will she go?" asked Priscilla.

"She could stay here!" Miles was quick to volunteer.

"No!" cried Malcolm and Priscilla simultaneously.

"She will stay with me," said Malcolm. "I'll make sure she isn't seen."

"Malcolm," Priscilla implored, "do you understand the risk? Do you know what would happen to you if you were caught doing any of this? The fake pronouncement, hiding a fugitive . . . all of it. Do you know what could happen to you?"

His features were fixed and unresponsive. Priscilla's heart sank. Obviously, he did know the risks. And obviously, he was willing to take them. For Cassie. Always for Cassie. Was there anything anyone wouldn't do for Cassie? She shot the red-haired girl a look of disdain, wondering that any man could find beauty in her freckled face and ridiculously broad mouth. Cassie, realizing she was being given notice for the first time in quite a while, took this opportunity to speak. "Does anyone care what *I* think?"

In truth, no one did. But Malcolm was the one person who felt obliged at least to feign interest. "What is it?" he asked.

"*What is it?!*" she cried passionately. "How can you ask

what is it? Maybe I don't *want* to be dead! Maybe I don't *want* to be hidden in your attic."

He couldn't resist a gentle smile. "Well, I thought I'd at least put a blanket up there for you."

She knew perfectly well that he had no attic, and was only teasing, but still, she felt aggravated. "You know what I mean! Maybe I don't want to hide indoors for the rest of my life. Maybe I'd rather serve twenty years with Robin, then go free. Your plan has no deadline! Once I'm pronounced dead, it will be so forever. I'll never have a normal life."

"But it's perfect," argued Priscilla. "Don't you see? The killer will think you're dead, the law will think you're dead . . ."

"I don't want to be dead!"

"Malcolm is making a pretty big sacrifice for you," Priscilla scolded.

"Who asked him?!"

Malcolm felt he'd had a long night to say the least. But still, he found it in himself to offer Cassie some comfort. Wrapping an arm about her shoulders, he tried to give her a friendly squeeze. But he found himself pushed away by a surprisingly powerful shove. "Don't coddle me!" Cassie cried. She looked around the room accusingly. "Now, I know that everyone here has reason to protect me, but I have some news for you all. I never asked *anyone* to protect me! So all of you, just mind your own business, and let me do what I must!"

"Which is?" asked Priscilla mockingly.

"Return to my assignment."

"You won't do that," said Malcolm calmly. When Cassie glared at him, he met her eyes steadily. "You won't do that," he repeated. "If I have to, I'll carry you out of here and lock you in my house, but you're not going back to that place." He shrugged as though his words were so obvious, there was no sense in repeating them. "Come on," he said softly, "let's go. How's your leg?"

Cassie resisted his examination of the splint. "Leave me be."

"Can you walk if I lend you my shoulder?" he asked, as though she had not just spat at him, "or do you need me to carry you?"

"I don't want to go with you," she replied, though her voice had grown softer. "I'm not agreeing to this."

Carefully, he lifted her into his arms and asked Priscilla, "Would you open the door for us?"

"Certainly."

"I don't want to go," repeated Cassie, though she was beginning to realize that she wanted very much to go. She hated everyone for making this decision on her behalf, and she hated herself for letting them. But she wanted to go home with Malcolm more than anything else in the world. "I should return to Robin," she said weakly.

"Can't let you do that," whispered Malcolm, turning sideways so he could take her from the bedroom.

"I used to be in charge of my own life," groaned Cassie, so softly that only Malcolm could hear.

"Captivity breeds humility," he whispered in turn.

Thirty-two

When they arrived at Malcolm's home, Cassie expected to see the dawn breaking through the darkness, but the midnight sky had only lightened to charcoal in its starless stretch to the horizon. Cassie slapped a mosquito off her arm. She could smell the ocean in the hot wind, and wondered whether she would ever smell it again. She might never go outdoors again, if all went according to plan. She might become a wraith in Malcolm's cellar. It all seemed so unthinkable that she had not spoken a word for the duration of the carriage ride. She was officially a fugitive now. Her heart would grow slow in dull captivity, then it would race in panic at every close call, but it would never beat steadily and naturally again. Could this really be her fate?

Malcolm helped her from the carriage, and offered his elbow as a crutch. His thoughts were unreadable. He seemed concerned over her leg, for he watched it carefully as they hobbled along. But if he had any thoughts besides that, Cassie could not see them. "Where shall I hide during the day?" she asked, as they stepped quietly into the threshold of Malcolm's house. They were walking with softened footsteps, as though her captors might be waiting at the top of the stairwell. The first ray of gray morning light suddenly broke into the clean entry, allowing the carpet to brighten from maroon to red.

"I don't know," said Malcolm tiredly, shutting the door behind them.

Cassie showed him her own weary eyes. "Well, you'll have to do better than that," she told him softly, and without anger,

He was startled by her eyes. They were so sad. "Yes, you're quite right," he told her. "I've insisted on this much. I'll sort out the details."

Cassie turned to hobble up the stairs. She was so scared that she felt empty inside. The thought that in a few hours she would be discovered missing—and she *would* be sought—was terrifying. But she did not show her fear to Malcolm. She held her shawl tightly about her and leaned into the banister, fully prepared to inch herself up the stairs, one at a time. She had learned long ago that there was no point in sharing fear. Sharing it only spread it. It did not heal it.

"Let me help you up the stairs."

"I don't want you showing me to my room. I can manage."

"Cassie, wait." Malcolm clutched the banister, looking up at her as though he wanted something desperately. She faced him calmly and waited. But he could not find the words. "I just," he licked his lips, "I just . . . just wanted to tell you that I . . . I've missed you."

Cassie replied with a cold turn of her head. He was torturing her. She was tired of loving someone who did not share her feelings. His stammering attempts at friendship were not making her feel more loved. They were making her feel that he was trying to soothe her battered heart. She would hear none of it. Of all times to patronize her with words about missing her and liking her and being so darned glad she was back, this was the worst. Hadn't she suffered enough? "Thank you," she said so abruptly that Malcolm felt he'd been slapped. "Thank you. That's nice. Good night."

Malcolm didn't understand her sharpness. With no other explanation on hand, he decided she was just angry that he'd brought her here. He bowed his head. It wasn't like him to make a decision for someone else. It wasn't like him at all. He prided himself on his ability to quietly tend his own business. But he just couldn't do that when it came to Cassie. The thought of her living with Robin Carthage . . . was enough to turn him into a tyrant. This, he supposed, was what she now thought him to be. "Good night," he replied softly, and then let her hobble away.

It was hard to watch her struggle with the stairs, but somehow, he knew he had to let her do it. He had to let her feel a moment of independence. When he could no longer see her, he felt so alone, he was tempted to follow her. But he didn't. Instead, he went to his study, the room brightening in the morning light, and lit himself a pipe full of tobacco. The sweet taste helped him gaze out the window without hatred. It was true, Malcolm felt hatred for the world around him. But the painful feeling was always softened by the deepest sense that everyone living in it was the victim of a terribly amusing joke. But where was the humor in Cassie's life being in danger? What good could possibly come of her spending her precious youth in hiding? He smiled uneasily, for he already knew the answer. At least, he mused distantly and guiltily, at least she would be here, with him. And perhaps that had been the key to his plan all along. Now he truly felt like a selfish tyrant.

Thirty-three

Samuel was standing in the threshold of what he now considered his very own home, as he was the only one looking after it. He could not believe what stood before him. He never got to see young women. His family was too strange. He had given up all hope of courtship. And now, he looked thankfully toward the heavens, mouthing, "Thank you, thank you. I'm sorry I never believed in you before." He had never seen a woman with such flawlessly raven hair, so dark that it was frightening in its loveliness. He had never seen such porcelain skin, so void of the freckles and scars which plagued even the most handsome members of his family. He had never laid eyes upon a figure so lush and curving. It was all he could do to resist embracing this tender maiden. Surely, she would be the most fragile and vulnerable of creatures. Surely, if he so much as brushed a finger across her ivory cheek, she would tremble. He had no doubt that such a beautiful woman must be the most tender and chaste of flowers.

"Why are you just standing there, you idiot?" she snarled. "Aren't you going to let me in? It's raining out here, for godsake!"

Samuel did a double take. She had an awfully sharp Irish accent, and a bit of a scratchy voice for such an angel.

"Do you speak?" she demanded. "I didn't think I had come all this way for a moron!"

Samuel looked over each shoulder. "Are you sure you have the right house?"

"We're not in the middle of London, you know! There aren't any other houses out here. Of course, I have the right house. Let me in! I've something important to tell you. I am a friend of your sister!"

Samuel smiled oddly. "Now I know you have the wrong house," he observed. "My sister didn't have friends. She's never even been to a dance."

"Why do you speak as though she is dead?!" Sheena cried.

"Well, she might as well be, hadn't she?"

Sheena rolled her eyes and growled, "Look! I've just come from Australia. I've just seen your sister. Now, will you let me in?"

Samuel broke into a broad grin. "Well, of course," he answered amusedly. "Now that I know you're an escaped felon, please, by all means, my home is yours." He widened the door so she could enter.

Sheena did not catch his sarcasm, and didn't feel the least bit awkward about making herself right at home. She settled into a velvet love seat, wringing the water from her long, loose hair, creating something of a puddle beside her. She tore off an overcoat which was far too large for her, and did her best to strike a civilized pose. "Aren't you going to offer me tea?" she asked. She had never been in an elegant home before, but was certain that tea was the usual welcoming gesture.

"Oh, I uh . . ." Samuel's hands were in his pockets, and his squinted gaze was still fixed rather firmly upon the beautiful monster who had invaded his property.

"Don't you have any?" she demanded.

He glanced toward the kitchen. "Probably," he shrugged after a pause.

"Well, have your servant fetch me some."

"We don't have any servants," he objected. "Well, not anymore. We sort of . . . kept forgetting to pay them, and, well," he shrugged again, "they're rather fussy about that as a lot."

Sheena crossed her arms. "Well, that is a fine way to welcome a guest. No tea."

"I thought you were an escaped Australian," he reminded her with some puzzlement.

"Well, does that make me any less of a guest?"

"Well, you also weren't invited."

"Look, do you want to hear about your sister, or not?" she challenged him with piercing eyes.

Samuel wasn't sure how to answer that. He supposed he did, though he couldn't believe there was anything uplifting to learn. He couldn't stop looking at Sheena's blue eyes. They were gorgeous. When she'd come to the door, he'd thought they were black eyes, dark as her hair. But now he could see that they were a magnificent, glimmering blue. "I . . . I trust Cassie is doing well?" he suggested with a certain trepidation.

"Is that what you think?" asked Sheena.

"Well, no," he confessed. "Quite the contrary, I suppose. But, I'm not sure why you would want to tell me about it. I can't imagine what I could do to help."

Sheena patted the love seat, inviting him to sit near enough to smell the rain in her tresses. This was an invitation Samuel could not resist. Instinctively, he glanced at the stairway, making certain that his mother was not planning to break away from her newest illness to come pay a rare visit to the home's lower level. It appeared safe. He sat as near as he dared, remembering with some awkwardness why they were called *love seats*. The shape of the cushion forced him to lean nearer to Sheena than, as an insecure young man, he would have liked. He apologized as he pulled himself away from her, using the arm of the chair.

He couldn't decide whether to turn his head all the way to face her, thereby being nearly close enough to kiss, or to stare straight ahead while he spoke to her. The two possibilities seemed equally awkward.

"My name is Sheena," she began, for she had a very important message to relay, and was tired of wasting time.

"Hello," he greeted, staring straight ahead as he spoke to the woman at his side. It had been at least a minute since he'd blinked.

"And you are Samuel, are you not?" she asked. "Cassie told me all about you."

Samuel nodded. "Mmm-hmm. Yes."

"Am I making you feel awkward?" she suggested. "Because I don't mean to—I just want us to talk. I've come a long way, and I have something very important to tell you."

"No, no, not awkward," he replied, tapping his fingers rhythmically against his knees.

"Good," she said, "because I'm going to need your help. I cannot do this alone. We're going to have to be partners in this, and . . . you're sure I'm not making you uncomfortable?"

A few droplets of rain were still sparkling like ice in her midnight hair. She smelled like a clean, rainy night. "Not uncomfortable," he said in an unnaturally high voice.

Sheena rolled her eyes. In all of her life of bedding filthy, despicable men, she had never met one who was too nervous to look her in the eye. It seemed ludicrous. And to think they were the same age! "If it will make you feel better, I shall move," she announced, and dragged an armchair to the other side of the coffee table. "Is that better?" she asked mockingly.

It really was much better. Samuel was now able to compose himself, regaining his usual slouching demeanor to some degree. He relaxed his elbows on his knees and leaned into them, trying to fix his eyes on her lovely face without appearing bewitched. He lowered his eyebrows, thinking this would make him look more as though he were in a listening mode. "Please," he said, "I'm listening." At first, this was a lie. But when the first sentence sprang from her mouth, he found himself at full attention.

"Now we both know that Cassie is innocent of murder," she began.

Samuel was startled into a jolt. "We do?"

Now Sheena was the startled one. "Well, of course we do! You don't mean that you . . . you mean you actually thought . . . you thought . . . your own sister!"

Samuel shrugged indifferently. And it was only then that Sheena realized that she was up against the strangest family she had ever encountered . Not only had he assumed that his own sister was guilty of murder, but he didn't really care!

"Didn't you think it was a little odd?" demanded Sheena, trying to control her temper. For she had come to love Cassie in the brief time they had been friends. And she was outraged that Cassie's own family would betray her. "Did Cassie really strike you as a murderer?"

"Well," Samuel grinned slyly, "you don't strike me as a murdereress, either." He still was not certain that Sheena's story was true. To say that it was rare for someone to escape Australia and swim to England would be a gross understatement. He wasn't sure who this woman really was, or why she was there. But he was so thankful that she had floated in, he was willing to treat the entire visit like one of his restless dreams come true.

Sheena was only slightly humbled by the remark about her not looking like a murderess. "I had my reasons," she replied awkwardly. And something about the way she said that made Samuel do a double take. She'd sounded as though she really had killed someone. "Anyhow," she

said, changing the subject abruptly, "I'm not here to talk
about myself. We need to do something about Cassie.
We have to get her out of there! You see," she began, but
then had to pause. She had waited so long for this meeting, had rehearsed her words so many times, that she
suddenly felt as though a spotlight were upon her. She
took several deep breaths and then proceeded.

"I escaped on a merchant vessel," she explained, finding it easier to rise to her feet and pace while she spoke.
Samuel now had the pleasure of examining all of the
rich, soft curves of her figure. "I traveled far from Sydney by foot, far enough that the gaolers were not so
prevalent. And then I bribed a merchant vessel to take
me home. Oh, they knew what I was, of course. They
took one look at me, and could tell I had been running
for days. I must have looked like a drowned rat! But they
also knew that they were too far from Sydney to be in-
spected for convicts. There really was no danger in
helping me. And, of course, I was willing to . . ." She
smirked at her comically innocent listener. "Well, let's
just say I was willing to pay them. It can be a long journey from Australia to England without any company."

Samuel didn't get it, but was enjoying watching her
story. That was, listening to her story, he reminded himself. Listening. He was supposed to be listening.

"It was on the ship that I learned of Cassie's innocence," she explained. "Oh, of course, I had already
known she didn't do it. Any fool could see that. Well . . ."
she cocked her head at Samuel, "*almost* any fool. But I'd
never imagined there would be proof! I never dreamed
that there was any way to show without a doubt that a
person was innocent. But on that ship, I learned." She
shook her head in disbelief. "Some blithering idiot had
gone around to all of the Australian-bound ports, privately asking men how much it would cost to have
someone done away with. Can you imagine anyone

being so stupid? He actually approached strangers, knowing only that they were heading for Australia, and having heard rumors that they were mercenary men! And he told them that he wanted someone killed. One of the men he'd approached was on my ship, and he was giving everyone a jolly laugh over it. I was laughing, too, until I heard that it was a red-haired girl the bloke had wanted to kill. I knew it was Cassie. Something told me. And the first thing I did was start asking questions."

Samuel, confused by his difficulty in paying attention combined with the outrageousness of her story, could only shake his head. "Why would somebody wanting to kill her prove her innocence?"

"Don't you see?!" she cried, tossing her dark hair impatiently over her shoulder as she glared at him. "He wants to kill her because she knows something! And that's the very reason he framed her! Look." She retrieved a crumpled piece of paper from her bosom and spread it upon the coffee table. "I had the sailor draw a sketch. Do you recognize this man?"

Samuel was still staring at her bosom. What else was she keeping in there? But then his eyes casually dropped to the smoothed sheet of parchment. And what he saw made him recoil. "This is my Uncle Egbert. Where did you get this?"

"You don't listen, do you?" she cried. "What have I been talking about this whole time? It's a sketch of the man who framed your sister!"

Samuel shook his head. "No, no. That can't be. I mean, he doesn't like us any more than we like him, but surely he doesn't despise us enough to go to all that trouble."

"I'm telling you he does!" she cried. "He's trying to kill Cassie! Don't you see? If we find him, we find out what it is she knows. And if we find out what it is she knows, then we have evidence that she was framed."

Samuel was very impressed by the sketch. Its concrete existence almost convinced him that Sheena wasn't completely out of her mind. Yet, this made no sense at all. "Even if we were to find out that there was a motivation," he said, "that isn't proof. Cassie has already been sentenced. We would need to prove beyond all doubt that she had been framed, and I don't see how . . ."

"Can you give up so easily on your own sister?!" Sheena cried.

"Who's down there?" came a weak call from upstairs.

"No one, Mother!" yelled Samuel. "It's just another bill collector. Go back to sleep. Sorry," he nodded at Sheena, "please go on."

"I may not know much about the law," she whispered hoarsely, her eyes forbidding him to look away, "but at least I don't give up so easily on my friends. This may not mean much to you, with your . . . your fancy house and your nonchalant hatefulness." She glanced about the mansion with some disgust and envy. "But I haven't had very many friends in my life. And when I get the chance to help one, I do it. Now are you with me? Or are you going to turn your back on your own sister, as though she were a common tramp?"

Samuel had to think about that one. All of this seemed terribly farfetched. But if there was any way to bring Cassie home . . . He really did miss her. He really did need her. Though he would never say so, deep within his breast, he really did love her. "All right," he said, "we'll look into it."

"Together?" she challenged him.

"Yes, together," he promised.

Sheena clasped her hands triumphantly. "Excellent! Now there's just one other little thing."

Samuel raised an eyebrow.

"Well, I . . . I don't have anywhere to stay. I had just rather assumed that, well, once we became partners, I

would naturally . . . well, you people have guest bed-
rooms and such, don't you?"

Samuel turned his eyes once more toward the heavens. "Thank you, thank you," he mouthed.

Thirty-four

Cassie had never felt so lonely as she did in the weeks and then months following her imaginary death. At first, she was frightened. Frightened of pretending, frightened of hiding, frightened of being caught. Every time she thought about what would happen to her if ever a guard stormed the house, she found herself overcome. She might be flogged and sent back to Robin, her sentence might be extended, she might be hanged. But as the weeks passed, and no such thing occurred, her panic gave way to a new sensation—boredom. There was nowhere she could go, now or ever. She wondered whether Malcolm had thought about that before pressing this maddening scheme upon her. She wondered if he cared.

Even the holidays had passed unnoticed. She heard carolers and had to hide beneath the window so they would not peer in and see her. She heard Malcolm entertain a small group of friends, she heard them laugh and she heard their glasses clinking, and it made her feel like a monster, something wretched that could never be shown to the civilized world, nor be exposed to joy. Christmas. She worried that her family had not been able to afford gifts for the holiday without her help. Then she broke from such thoughts. It was not her problem anymore, not her concern. She was nothing but a ghost in the attic.

Cassie's leg had healed, but she scarcely cared, for she had no use for it. Every morning, she awoke in her bed, but did not rise, for Faith was not to know of her presence. To tell her would be to put her in danger as an accomplice, so Cassie hid in the room which Malcolm now mysteriously locked, keeping the key from Faith without explanation. Every time she asked about it, he pretended merely to have forgotten once again to open it, and then sent her on her way for the night. Cassie had only her books and her diary to keep her company, but she did not write in her journal. There was nothing to tell it, except that she was terribly bored.

Malcolm had no difficulty convincing his colleagues and the law that Cassie had died quite painfully from infection. What were they to do? Sort through the corpses which cluttered the hospital hallway, and search for the one that looked Irish? It didn't strike anyone as an appealing task, and it wasn't as though the death of a prisoner was uncommon. Malcolm was delighted that his plan had come off so well, and yet, when he returned home late at night, opened Cassie's bedroom door, and invited her to supper, he had the distinct sense that she was feeling anything but delight. He didn't blame her. Though he had bought her books and puzzles to occupy her mind, he knew that her existence was bleak. He knew that she was bored and sad. But he couldn't blame himself, either. The alternative had been unthinkable.

Cassie always picked at her food when they shared their supper. Normally, this would not have troubled Malcolm, for he had the ungentlemanly habit of reading at the table, and silence made that so much easier to do. But because he knew that Cassie was repressing her misery, he found that he could think of nothing else but drawing her out. "I uh . . ." Malcolm put both elbows on the table one evening, and leaned forward a bit, "I've been . . . thinking. And," he swallowed, "I think we can get you out of here. That is, I think we can send you back to England after a while, after everyone forgets. I . . ." He checked her for eye contact, but found that she was pushing her food around with a fork, barely listening. Nonetheless, he continued. "I don't think it's safe yet. It won't be for a while. People will recognize you if we try to ship you off. We'll need some more time to pass, but . . ."

Cassie glanced up at him with eyes that were positively drooping with the weariness of stagnation. Their sharp green color had cooled to a dark olive, and her face had grown pale enough to make her freckles fade. She had not bothered to brush her unbound hair. "When will that be?" she asked tiredly.

Malcolm heard something in her voice that made him lose his train of thought. He cocked his head. "When will . . . what be?"

"The day I'm shipped off," she replied, and the anger in her weak voice was unmistakable. "Do you suppose that will be tomorrow? Next week?"

Malcolm froze in the onslaught of her bitterness. He did what he always did when confronted with hostility. He stepped away and studied it, his eyes growing strange and distant.

"I didn't think so," she said. "Somehow, I think it will be many years before you think it's safe enough for me to leave. And by the way—what will I do once I return to England? I will be a fugitive there, too, will I not? Everyone will recognize me. I'll have to hide. I could go somewhere else, of course, to another country, but then how would I earn my living? Where would I sleep?"

Malcolm was not inclined to reply. He wasn't thinking about her question, but about the accusation beneath the question. He leaned back in his chair, squinting his navy eyes at her as though she had become some strange specimen. He wanted her to say more. He didn't want to interrupt. But when she did not speak up, he started his cautious reply. It was then that she chose to speak.

"No, don't," she ordered, pushing her full plate aside

and rising to her feet. "Don't tell me any more of your plans for me. Just let me go rot in my room."

Malcolm did not get up, but stopped her by grabbing hold of her elbow. "Cassie." It was all he said. The rest he spoke with his eyes. He wanted her to be honest with him, to tell him exactly what was on her mind. Her arm felt tender beneath his clutch. Her gaze was frozen by his intelligent eyes, so narrow in their upset. There was something so magnificent about him, so unusual and awkwardly gallant, that she wanted to stay with him, angry as she was. "I don't like being your puppet," she said, though her voice was softer than she'd wanted it to be.

Malcolm cocked his head and said gently, "Puppet? That doesn't make any sense." A little smile crossed his face at the same time that it crossed hers. "Come," he begged her, "wasn't it the right thing, coming here?" He ducked his head, trying to get her to look at him. "Wasn't it?"

She did not answer, but only shook her head defeatedly, gazing at the floor as though she could not bear to look at him. Secretly, her heart was feeling full. She loved him. She had loved him forever.

"Come on," he begged her, "talk to me. I know you don't like being a ghost here, but would you really have liked staying at Robin's? Even if I'd been able to let you go? Honestly, Cassie. Think about it before you answer. I know you didn't want to go back there."

She shook her head and tried to move to the stairway once more.

His grip prevented it. "Don't leave," he groaned softly. "Cassie, talk to me."

When she turned her eyes on him this time, she looked suddenly possessed by a demon. Her eyes were emerald green again, and sharp as a slivered edge. Her face was burning red. "What do you want from me?!" she cried in a voice much too loud for such a weary soul.

Malcolm was so taken aback that his eyebrows lifted and his pupils widened, but he did not move. He just listened.

Cassie tossed her arms about as though wanting either to strike out or grab onto something. "You saved me as though you treasure me!" she cried. "As though you loved me or wanted me. But you don't!" And suddenly, tears filled her eyes and made her chest shake. For she had just spoken the truth, and summoned forth its pain. "What do you want from me?" she sobbed.

Malcolm tried to absorb her words. They didn't make sense to him. He could see she was hysterical, and couldn't blame her for being so, after so many weeks of captivity. But how did he know whether she spoke from her heart or from her madness? He stood up, but didn't know what to do after that. He didn't dare embrace her. "Cassie," he began, for he loved her name. He had always loved her name. "Cassie, you're not making sense."

"Stop being my bloody doctor!" she screamed, making both of their ears sting from the high pitch of her voice. "Stop telling me that I mustn't be listened to. And start listening!"

Malcolm felt properly humbled, and silenced himself with ease.

"I promised myself I wouldn't do this," she muttered, beginning to pace, "I promised myself I wouldn't open up to you again, but I must!" she cried frantically. "I must! What else can I do? You want to be my savior, my captor, and my protector, but nothing else! Why are you torturing me? Why won't you let me go?"

She looked so desperate, that Malcolm really wanted to console her. But he was just too shocked. He watched her tears fall for many long moments before confessing in a low voice, "I'm sorry about what I did, Cassie." She didn't know what he meant until she looked up and saw the regret and embarrassment on his face. He nodded, as though to tell her that her guess was right, that he was talking about their one and only night together. It seemed as though it was difficult for him to mention it, as though he was having to brace himself for the words which followed. "I know that what we did was wrong," he said with a nod, "and it was entirely my fault. I've never thought it otherwise." He would not let Cassie interrupt. "No, it's true," he continued, "I was not the prisoner. I am the one who should have kept my senses. I remember how I walked out," he added with a mortified shake of his head. "It was awful. It was unforgivable. I just panicked. But . . . but I've never . . ." He was struck by the way the light was catching her eyes. It made him stare, and blink rapidly. "I've never felt so close to someone," he breathed, as though a piece of him hoped she would not hear, "and when I learned you had gotten even closer than I knew, that you had . . . well, overheard me . . . I panicked."

Cassie shook her head violently. "These are lies," she moaned, though she was also not immune to the romanticism of the low light, and the way Malcolm's voice had softened to a deliciously deep whisper. "I don't believe that's why you left me," she said, for she'd had weeks of misery in which to give thought to the matter. "I think I know what it is." She broke into a sad smile.

Malcolm didn't want to hear her theory. He was enchanted by her auburn hair. Red was such an unnatural color, so inhuman. It had never failed to draw him to a woman. His hand started to move toward her.

"It's because I'm not Priscilla," Cassie quietly announced, breaking the soft love spell she had inadvertently cast upon his soul. "I am not beautiful," she explained boldly, "and I am not intriguing or mysterious." She ran a hand through her tangled hair. "I have much reason to find you handsome," she said. "You have been dear to me, and kind, and you are . . ." She shook her head at the sight of his chiseled features as though in awe of a magnificent natural wonder. "You are beautiful," she finished quietly. Then she bowed her head. "But no matter how many times I go over it in my mind," she confessed sadly, "I cannot think of any reason that you should be drawn to me."

Malcolm actually laughed. It was a soft laugh, and a natural laugh, the kind that would come from someone who'd just heard something too silly to discuss. "What?" he asked, as though he wanted to hear the rest of the joke.

She didn't want to repeat herself. She didn't want to seem as though she were asking to be corrected. "Let's . . . let's not talk about it anymore," she pleaded. "Let us just retire. I'm sure we are both exhausted."

"Not in the middle of this," he said firmly, clutching her elbow once more. "Do you really believe you're not lovely?"

She tried to smile kindly, but managed to look more sad than ever. "I didn't say that," she answered softly, "I just . . . I just don't see that a man would want a woman who makes him feel comfortable, when he has a woman who makes him feel sinful."

Malcolm was stunned by both the wisdom and the error of her words. She had come so near to understanding him, and yet, a centimeter away from the truth was as good as a world away. She did not know his heart. "Cassie, I want to touch you," he said, and a fierceness was moving in his eyes.

"No," she insisted, "don't pity me. I know I am dull." She winced at the memory of all the days of her youth she had spent keeping accounts rather than attending dances, fighting bill collectors instead of flirting with boys. She had always known that love was not for women like her. "Just leave me be," she said, nearly closing her eyes from the pain. For though she had believed she would never find love, she had truly hoped. God, how she had hoped.

"You aren't listening," he said softly, strangely. "I asked whether I could touch you." He lifted one of her freckled hands and studied it, stroking the tips of her fingers.

"Stop it," she begged.

"If you want me to," he shrugged, but made no attempt to stop. He bit his lip as he stroked the inside of her wrist.

"Let me go," she whispered heavily, and she was not talking about the hold he had on her wrist. "Just let me live my own life."

"At Robin's house?" he asked with a raised eyebrow, then returned to the study of her slender arm.

"If necessary," she spat. "What happens to me is not your concern."

"I care for you," he said.

"That isn't strong enough!" Her scream was worse than jarring—it was enough to make his ears sting.

"I adore you."

She met his eyes hotly. "Well, that's closer."

Their eyes were locked, and neither could look away. A ray of heat was holding them each hostage. "Cassie, don't tell me you love me or you will regret it," said Malcolm. "Don't make professions in the darkness which will shame you when morning comes. Some day, you will be free from here. Don't say something which will embarrass us both when that day comes."

"You're a good person," said Cassie. "I'm not ashamed to love you."

"I'm not a good person. I'm only a cautious one. I keep my rage in check."

"No, I know the difference," said Cassie. "You are a good man."

"That's where you're wrong!" he shouted, and though there was no violence in his handling of her, an unmistakable evil crossed his face. "You don't know me."

"That's what you tell yourself! You pretend to punish

yourself for what you did in the barracks, but in truth, you simply do not want the kind of love I can give. The truth is you just don't want me. You hate yourself for wanting Priscilla more, but you cannot help it!"

"Is that what you think?" he nearly laughed, as though he had forgotten all about his anger. "Is that what you really think?"

"It's what I'm sure of."

A light twinkled in his eye as he grabbed her second elbow and pushed her gently against a wall. His handsome face leaned over her pale one, threatening to kiss her, as his hands squeezed and kneaded her arms. "You're arousing me," he whispered breathlessly.

"I don't believe you."

"Do you need me to prove it?" he asked, his eyes sparkling angrily in the darkness where a candle had just been quieted by the wind. "Is this what it will take to prove that I find you exciting? Is this what you have wanted me to do?" he asked, gently fingering a breast.

Cassie closed her eyes, for she was feeling rather frightened in her abandon. "I don't want you to pretend you feel something you don't."

"If you catch me pretending, let me know," he whispered, and lowered himself to suckle on her breast. He removed it from its gown while leaving the rest of her fully modest. He took it in both hands and turned it, gently rolling it between his palms.

"Stop it," she whispered, touching his soft chestnut hair, "you will only make me love you more."

Malcolm didn't believe in Cassie's love. She was only a prisoner, grateful for any kindness. He had been there. He knew. It was wrong to take advantage of her willingness once more, this willingness which came from gratitude and not true love. But Malcolm was Malcolm. And the wrongness of it was fueling the fires in his loins. He was weak for women, and he had let his excitement go too far. "Stay still," he demanded quietly, as he further studied the warm breast in his hands. He did not even look at her eyes. He was intrigued only by her body, studying the pink crest which tickled his thumb, and the pale flesh which he could mold so easily in his palms. "Please hold still." He wet his tongue before pressing it against her peak.

Cassie felt as though a trickle of water were rising from the tip of her breast to her heart. She began to rub his hair fiercely, gripping it nearly to the point of causing him pain. Malcolm stopped suckling and smiled up at her. "I don't think I said you could touch me, did I?" he asked, with a reassuring expression that let her know he was being mischievous.

Cassie sighed deeply. "Why do you like to play games, Malcolm?" But she was smiling, too. She liked his games. She liked everything about him.

"They aren't games," he said quietly, lifting her hands from his hair and placing them at her sides. "I take it very seriously." And his handsome but twisted smile left a lot of questions as to whether he spoke the truth. "I want to see the rest," he said, putting his lips so near hers that his words blew air against her. His hands began to fumble with her gown. "Show me the rest," he said softly. Cassie went after his lips hungrily, even as she tore at her own gown. She knew she was going to get hurt again. She knew she was giving herself to a man who wanted her only once more. But she couldn't convince herself to care. There was so little life left in her. And she had thought of him for so long.

He was stiff against her kiss at first, as though he considered retreating. He preferred to kiss, rather than to be kissed. But after a moment, either he or his masculine urges told him to let the kiss happen. So he returned her hunger with his own devouring of her lush lips. Cassie found herself being lifted onto the dining table, but she scarcely cared. When she felt wood under her backside, she relaxed into this new support and continued her ravenous kiss. His mouth tasted sweet, and she found herself squeezing him with both arms and legs. He pulled away from the kiss and played with a tiny strand of her fiery hair, a soft piece just above her ear. He gently twirled that one lucky strand around his fingers, and studied it as though it were a golden ring. "Unbelievable," he said of the color, and tucked it behind her ear, making her feel ticklish and tender.

Her gown was already unfastened, but Malcolm stepped back for a moment to lower her sleeves and view her bare shoulders and neck as though he were examining a work of art. He pushed her hair away from her face. "What are you doing?" she whispered.

Malcolm was squinting quizzically. "I'm just trying to imagine you as a painting." Her hair color was so subtle, with its random, shimmering strands of fire. Her neck was slender, and her shoulders porcelain. Her face was beautifully and widely sculpted, freckled as though sprayed with drops of gold. And then of course, there were her eyes. Had they not been of the brightest green, their exotic shape would have fooled him into thinking she was from the Far East. You're magnificent, he thought. But he did not say it. Instead he asked her to, lie down, in that way of his—so soft that it was completely inoffensive, but so firm that it should have been an outrage. Cassie leaned back along the table. She watched him only vaguely through foggy eyes as he stripped off his shirt. "Sturdy table," he remarked, patting its shining surface with a grin.

"Strong enough to support us both?" she asked dreamily, returning his smile.

"I daresay we're about to find out." He slid off what was left of her gown, letting it fall to the floor, leaving her bare and ashamed.

"No, please, I need . . . something," she begged him, trying to sit up and cover herself.

He put out a strong arm to keep her from rising. "No," he said dreamily, taking a seat as though he were simply waiting for a meal, "no, you're fine."

"I'm *not* fine," she blushed furiously. "At least lie near me so you're not just staring."

He smiled, for it was such an odd request. Lie near her so he couldn't see? She wanted him closer so he would seem farther away. "Don't be embarrassed," he whispered, running the gentlest of fingers along her side. This small, sensitive touch ignited Cassie's passion in a way that even lovemaking could not. He was gazing at her as though she were beautiful, as though she were a treasure. And he was touching her as though she would break under the slightest pressure. He touched her belly, her hips, and her shoulders, studying them, enjoying their curves, enjoying the way she was spread before him, vulnerable and willing. He did not touch her breasts, or any of her most womanly spots. It was as though he were saving them, as though he wanted to work up an appetite before enjoying his feast.

At last, he stood up, but rather than covering her bare skin with his own, he knelt between her dangling legs. Cassie could feel his hot breath on her womanhood, and found herself gripping the edge of the table in her longing. He pursed his lips and breathed lightly on her. This sent shudders up her hips, and made her legs tremble. Again, he breathed. "Malcolm," she whispered, tears filling her eyes, "Malcolm, I love you." She could not see the ceiling, for it was too dark. And she could not see him, because of where he crouched. All she was aware of was her own mind.

"Why?" he asked gently. Cassie went wild, for he had moved his mouth from her in order to speak, and she now desperately wanted him to put it back where it belonged.

"Keep . . . keep doing it!" she ordered through gritted teeth.

Malcolm grinned. "Sorry." He put a finger where his mouth had been, knowing that this would ease some of the frustration while he waited for her reply. "Why do you love me?" he repeated.

And as he'd hoped, he got the reply that could come only from a woman whose mind had shut down, and whose spirit had come forth for the act of lovemaking. "Because you make my knees weak," she said.

Malcolm smiled in anticipation. "Why do I make your knees weak?" he asked, fingering her harder, his eyes glowing with brilliance.

"Because you're so strange."

"Then it's the distance," he decided, pecking her thigh with his soft, warm lips. "It's the distance that makes me attractive."

"You're wrong," she rasped. "I love you more the more I know you."

He decided to put his tongue to better use. He slid it in circles around her hottest swelling, without quite touching its tip, without quite letting her feel she'd been fulfilled. Cassie was weeping silently in her ecstasy. She felt that this was one of her last chances to enjoy herself. She felt like a dying woman. This moment was one of life's last and only gifts to her. She didn't think she had a future. "Don't let this end," she whispered, and she was not certain whether Malcolm heard. He just kept gliding his tongue in all of her most private places, avoiding the spots which would drive her to ecstasy. He was helping to make it last. She suspected he was doing it because he simply enjoyed lovemaking, but she pretended that he understood. She pretended that he knew how it felt to grasp at one last chance at love before it was all over. To pluck one last rose.

He moved his tongue from her womanhood to her

navel and to the crevice between her breasts. At last, he was covering her tingling skin with his own. Cassie hugged him and tried to squeeze him close. Her hands clutched his warm, soft skin, which hid such hard muscles. She pressed her breasts into his chest, and kissed his firm shoulders. He felt her tears fall down his back, but he did not ask about them. Instead, he just clasped the back of her fiery head with a big hand and held her there. He tried to feel what she was feeling. He tried to let her soft sobs make his own chest move. But he could not get inside her. He could make guesses about her pain, but he could not see its face. "Do you want me to stop?" he asked.

Cassie shook her head vigorously against his neck. "No, I . . . I want it to last forever."

"Anything that you remember, lasts forever," he said at last.

And Cassie knew this was true. Somehow, her weeping softened.

Malcolm pulled her away, just slightly, so she could see the humor in his eyes. "And as I'm only a mortal, I'm afraid that's the closest I can come to making something like this last forever." He nodded at his manhood, "I mean, I do what I can, but . . ."

Cassie started laughing, and soon he joined her, his blue eyes sparkling into hers, making her feel light and silly inside. The smile left her only when she felt him against her, ready to penetrate. He tried to keep his own smile, as difficult as it was in his intense state of need. He brushed the hair from her forehead, and said, "Don't stop smiling, Cassie. It won't hurt."

She nodded, swallowed hard, and tried to reanimate her smile. It was difficult. She was nervous. He pressed into her, making her feel full and strangely violated. There was a part of Cassie which never wanted to be this close to anyone, which wanted to push him away. And that part instinctively put a hand on his chest. Malcolm lifted the protesting hand and kissed it. "I like your resistance," he said dreamily, his thrusting beginning to take on a rhythm. "It's so honest."

"I don't mean to resist," she said. "I don't want you to stop."

"I know," he replied. "That's what I like. The uncertainty, the contradiction."

"Why?" she asked breathlessly, finding that her body was trembling from this delicious violation. "Why do you need to find darkness in making love?"

Malcolm watched her move beneath him, loving the sight of her breasts jiggling under his commanding thrusts. "That's what excites me," he replied.

"You're fascinated by evil because you're such a good man! It's foreign to you. That is why you find it so interesting."

Now he was just angry. Now he knew that she didn't understand him, didn't know him. How could someone as bright as Cassie mistake him for a good man? She knew what he had done in the barracks. She knew he was a killer. Was there anyone in the world who could see through his false, polite ways? It seemed there was not. And it made him angry. He wanted people to recognize him for what he was. He wanted them to be smart enough to see through the lie. Especially Cassie. He had really hoped that Cassie, of all people, would know what he truly was. He thrust into her violently now, no longer trying to be gentle. Cassie gasped in alternating surges of pleasure and pain. A big smile was growing across her face as the silence between them thickened, and the wood under her back rubbed her skin raw. "Harder," she whispered, but Malcolm was not taking commands. He thrust exactly as hard as he wanted to, pushing them both nearer and nearer to explosion, a tight expression on his face.

At last, he exploded inside her, his anger flowing from him, leaving him light and suddenly comfortable. Cassie had only just begun to find her own release, so he did what he could to stay inside her, using his fingers to help sustain her ecstasy. He watched her face break into a crazy smile, a beautiful glow shimmering on her moist cheeks. They could both see in the dark now, and looked at one another in amazement. How could mere mortals bring such pleasure to one another? Surely, at that moment, neither thought of the other as purely mortal. They kissed in such a way as to feel that their lips were connected, that they could feel the pressure of one another's weight. But they did not open their mouths, for it was not a lustful kiss. It was a kiss of joining, and of trying to savor every part of the moment.

Malcolm relaxed, wrapping an arm around her lazily. "Ouch," he said, shifting against the table, "this isn't very comfortable."

"You noticed that, too?" she asked sharply, but still smiling. "It's a fine time for you to think of that."

Malcolm chuckled apologetically, stretching his arm out, searching for something. "Where is my tobacco pipe?"

"It's in your study," said Cassie, closing her eyes peacefully, "and it wouldn't be good form for you to ask me to go fetch it right now. Men who bed their servants have to fetch their own pipes. It's the price you pay."

Malcolm grinned broadly. "Gain a lover, lose a servant, eh?"

"It seems a sensible rule."

He urged her to snuggle closer with a squeeze of his arm. Cassie was still a little new at cuddling, and wasn't sure she liked it. But soon, she felt warm and safe by his strong, naked side. *For a woman who thought she would never fall in love,* she thought, *I certainly fell hard when it finally happened.* She looked at Malcolm's pensive face.

"And I certainly picked a strange one," she added to her-self with a loving grin.

A look of mischief came over Malcolm's eyes. He spared her a glance, biting his lip deliciously. "Do you want to do something absolutely dangerous?" he asked her, rolling to his side.

Cassie lifted an eyebrow. "Does it in any way involve getting out of this stuffy house?"

"Yes."

"Then I'm dying to hear."

He combed her hair with his fingers, still grinning brightly. "How would you like to go to a party with me?"

"You're joking."

He shook his head. "No. It's a masquerade. You can hide your face."

"Oh, Malcolm! That is so dangerous! I couldn't."

"Well, you don't have to," he challenged her, "if you'd be too scared."

She scowled. "Daring people to do stupid things only works on children. I know you won't really think me a coward for refusing to do something so blatantly care-less. And if you do, then you're the foolish one."

Malcolm stopped smiling and shook his head. "No, no. I really didn't mean to pressure you. You're right, it's too dangerous. I just wanted to show you that I heard what you said, and that I shouldn't protect you against your will. It is, as you say, your life." He waited mischie-vously for the expected reply. But his face was completely straight. He looked as though he had already forgotten about the masquerade, had given up on it as a foolish thought.

Cassie thought about her chances of living to old age, and believed they were slim. She thought about the chances that she would either be stuck in this house for-ever, or caught and hanged, and believed those odds were looking much better. She imagined the sparkling lights of a masquerade, of being the woman on Malcolm's arm. "All right," she snapped, causing him to break into a grin, "I'll go. But what about my hair? They can all see its color."

"We'll get you a wig. It'll be fun." He was biting his lip as he smiled, thoroughly anticipating the danger and excitement of their outing. The only thing more fun than breaking the law was flaunting it. He knew that he would be even more nervous than she was, but he loved feeling extreme emotions like fear and then conquering them. It was what made life worthwhile.

Cassie, on the other hand, absolutely hated doing things that she knew were stupid. If she got caught on account of wanting to go to a party, if this soirée cost her her life, she would feel like the world's biggest idiot. But she had been sensible all her life, and it had gotten her nowhere. She was ready to get out of this house and into a party dress. A piece of her just didn't care that it might be the last thing she ever did. "I want a golden wig," she said impulsively, "I have always wanted to have long, golden hair." And she realized ashamedly, that this was so. How petty!

Malcolm tried to picture it. "Yes," he said, "I think that would be quite fetching." He kissed her wickedly. "Come, we'd better get started. The party's next week. I'll need your measurements." He pulled her upright by the hand.

"Wait!" she cried. "You're not going to look at my measurements, are you?"

"Of course," he replied with a squint of failed comprehension. "I'm going to measure you myself. I'll have to, if I'm going to have a dress made."

"But wait!" she cried, as he led her toward the hall, "I don't want you to see the numbers! My waist is rather wide for my hips, and . . ."

"Cassie," he interrupted, "I'm a doctor. I don't notice things like that. I'm simply collecting facts."

"Oh, please!" she cried, as he whisked her away. "You've got to be joking!"

"Of course, we'll get a better measurement if you're not wearing anything," he observed.

She rolled her eyes heavenward. "All this for a party," she mused, sickened with herself, "a ridiculous, frivolous party." She couldn't stop smiling at the thought of it. It would be her first one.

Thirty-five

"What we need is a plan." Sheena leaned into Samuel, as though prepared to share some deep, dark secret. But in truth, her mind was blank.

Samuel had never been so close to a woman who was not his own sister. He debated over how much to move toward her, how close to let their faces get. "Yes, a plan," he replied stupidly. He let his head bob in mock thought.

"I say," began Sheena, sensing that it was her duty to take charge, "that we drive into London. You do have carriages, don't you?"

Samuel nodded.

"Then we drive into London and we face your uncle and get him to confess everything!"

Samuel furrowed his brow. His narrow eyes moved to the left and then to the right, and then at his companion, a small grimace crossing his lips. "That's your plan?"

Sheena shrugged.

"That's your plan?" he repeated. "Get him to confess?"

"Well, it's only a start," she replied defensively.

"Get him to confess," he said again, in amused disbelief. "Why don't you just make our plan, get them to let Cassie go? I mean, without an idea on how to do it, we might as well make our plan to get him to flog himself. I mean . . ."

"All right, I get your point!" she snapped, rising to her feet with crossed arms. "It was only the beginning of a plan. I'm sure I can think of a way to get him to confess. Do you have anything to hold over him? Anything embarrassing he wouldn't want anyone to know?"

"No, everyone already knows his name is Egbert. I don't think we can hold that over him." He shook his head impatiently. "Anyway, you're missing the point. We don't need him to confess to us. We need him to confess to a judge or . . . or a magistrate or something. What good is a confession to us?"

"Then we'll need to find evidence!"

Samuel feigned collapse. "Another well-thought-out plan," he announced.

"Well, I see you're awfully grand at finding fault with my suggestions," she spat bitterly, "but where are yours? Are you just going to sit there and criticize while your sister toils in Australia for a crime she did not commit?"

Samuel sighed. "All right, all right," he mumbled, rising to his feet. "Give me a moment." He paced for several long minutes while Sheena glared at him, challenging him with stern eyes to come up with something that could not be criticized. "All right, I've got it," he announced, punching his own hand. "Here's what we'll do. First, we pretend we've become engaged. We go to my uncle's and . . ."

"Engaged?"

Samuel was careful not to look at her. "Yes, engaged. Now, hear me out. We pretend we've been engaged and that we must visit him to announce our elation."

"Do we need such an elaborate excuse just to pay him a simple visit?"

"Yes," he assured her, "we really do. He would never believe I was visiting just to be kind."

"But why an engagement? Couldn't we tell him some other monumental news, like . . . oh, I don't know . . . you are starting a business venture, or . . ."

"But that wouldn't explain your presence."

"Perhaps I could be your long-lost cousin."

"Is it so bad to be betrothed to me?" he asked indignantly, trying not to laugh at himself. "You know, I'm not such a bad fellow. I'm sure there are women out there who would be more than happy to become my imaginary bride."

"Name one," she challenged him, just for the fun of it.

"Well, I . . ." Samuel squinted as though peering into his own past. He tried to recall whether any young women had ever expressed any serious interest in him. It was true he hardly ever had the chance to meet new women, but hadn't there been a few back when Cassie was running the household, and he was free? No, there really hadn't. Although he had imagined from time to time that he was receiving a flirtatious glance, and had been struck brutally more than once for returning it with a wink. "I couldn't begin to name them all," he announced bashfully. "Now, back to our plan . . ."

Sheena grinned knowingly. She could tell he had never courted a lady, and found it rather endearing. She had never met such an innocent before. She had never known there was such a thing as an innocent man.

"We're engaged," he continued, "if that's all right with you." He gave her a comically bitter glance. "Unless I need to get on bended knee and ask for your hand in marriage before you'll agree to it." Sheena shook her head, repressing a laugh. "Very well then, we're engaged, and we must tell my uncle because . . . because . . ."

"Because we want him to come to the wedding?"

"No, he'd never believe that. We need to tell him because—"

"I can see the two of you have quite a rapport."

"You haven't met the rest of my family yet," he warned her. "You haven't even begun to see strange family relations. Now, let's see . . . Ah! I've got it!" He snapped his fingers. "We want an expensive wedding gift."

"Charming."

"Yes, indeed. We'll have to think of something specific to ask for, something my parents would never give us."

"Nor mine."

He cast her a quick glance. "Well, you're going to be from a poor family."

"What?!"

"Well, it's the only way it makes sense. Why else would they not have heard of the betrothal? Obviously, my parents disapprove."

"And why would they disapprove of me?" she asked furiously, fists on hips.

"Well, obviously, because we're going to make you poor to suit our story."

"But I don't want to be poor!" she cried. "Perhaps it is my family which doesn't approve of you! Had you thought of that? Perhaps we're the rich ones, and you are the ones who can't even afford to pay your servants."

"Ouch, that hurt."

"Well?" she demanded, "it makes just as much sense, doesn't it?"

Samuel frowned. "I don't want to be the one who's disapproved of."

"Well, neither do I!"

"But you're a convict."

"Your uncle doesn't know that."

"Yes, but I do. And now I have to imagine that the family of a convicted murderess thinks that I am not worthy of their daughter. That's pretty insulting, even for me."

Sheena literally spat, which was a gesture that both stunned and delighted Samuel. As sheltered a life as he had led, he hadn't known women could spit. "Then let's just say that everyone hates everyone!" she declared. "Your family hates me, my family hates you, your family hates my family, and we hate each other too!"

Samuel shrugged. "That sounds reasonable."

Sheena was gearing up to spit out a slew of insults, but upon hearing his amicable reply, she stopped herself. She looked at him with some puzzlement. And when she saw the light of fun in his eyes, she broke into a smile. She hadn't noticed before, but he was mildly handsome, in a slouchy sort of a way. "Then we're ready to go?" she asked brightly.

"Certainly. Just allow me to pack."

"But what will your parents say?"

Samuel frowned. "I don't know. I hadn't thought of asking them."

"Well, surely they'll notice your absence."

"You don't know my family very well," he observed, "but if it will make you feel better, I'll leave them a note."

"It won't make me feel better," she assured him. "Remember? Your parents don't approve of me. I just as soon leave them in the dark."

Samuel grinned. "Serves them right, doesn't it?" And with a wink, he began his climb up the stairway, two casual steps at a time. "I'll get you some of Cassie's old clothes, too!" he called. "They may be a little small, though."

"Are you calling me fat?" she yelled after him.

"Irresistibly buxom," he corrected her. "Stunningly curvaceous. Now try not to murder anyone on our little trip," he added in a mutter.

"What?!"

"Nothing, dearest."

Thirty-six

Cassie had never been so afraid in all her life. And fear had never been so delicious. Malcolm had bought her a black velvet dress. Black was not ordinarily her best color, but with the wig of platinum curls, tied up high and then falling in a cascade of ringlets, the black dress was positively striking. Its skirt was straight, its sleeves cheerfully puffed. The high waist met the fringe of a tiny, matching velvet jacket. The sleekness of the dress made her look taller and thinner than she really was. When she removed the little jacket and spun before the looking glass, she thought she looked like a very erotic queen. Her small breasts were mashed into perfect balls, straining at the fabric of her dress and nearly escaping its low cut. She slid around her bedroom in dainty black satin slippers. She tossed her head from side to side, feeling her new blond hair fall over one shoulder and then the other.

A knock at the door made her rush for the little velvet jacket. Buttoning it carefully over her plumped breasts, she cleared her throat. Properly straightening her back, she welcomed Malcolm with a widening of the door. "Hello," she said gently.

It was not yet dark outside. The sun was only beginning to grow dim. The party would not begin for a few more hours, so there was plenty of time for Cassie's hands and knees to tremble in anticipation and terror. Malcolm had not yet dressed. But he was looking at her rather strangely. There was an intensity in his navy eyes, and an expression of repressed awe. He was biting his lip. "You look beautiful," he said, crossing his arms as though to contain himself.

What flattered Cassie was not his words, but the fact that he meant them. She could see that in his face and in his posture. He was genuinely impressed, and something about that made her blush. "Well, I suppose blond hair must suit me," she replied, drawing attention to the phoniness of her attire. It was her way of telling him that he was admiring something which was not real.

"Anything would suit you," he answered quickly. "You're lovely."

And that was enough to melt Cassie. She couldn't even look at him, she was feeling so tender. "I have never been to a party," she told him.

Malcolm cast her a quizzical look. "Why?"

"I was always . . . busy," she said, eyes cast down. Then suddenly, she feared he would believe her unpopular. "It's not that I hadn't been asked," she added hurriedly, "I just . . . well, I thought parties were silly."

"They are," he smiled, "that's what's so fascinating about them. Nobody really wants to throw them, because it's too much expense. Then no one really wants to go, because it's too much fuss. Yet somehow, the soirées still occur, and when all is said and done, everyone seems to have a good time. Whatever that means," he added whimsically, but with a spark in his eye.

Cassie smoothed her gown against her legs. "I'll feel a fool if I'm caught tonight."

Malcolm's reply startled her. "You won't be caught," he announced.

She looked up at him as though she must have misunderstood. "What do you mean?" she laughed nervously, "I could easily be caught."

"I won't let you be," he told her, and she could tell that

he really meant it. He leaned away from the wall and strode toward her with his hands in his pockets. He did not remove them until he was close enough to touch her. He tenderly brushed her chin with his thumb, a strange confidence in his eyes. He liked the way her lips quivered, and the fact that she did not pull away, though he sensed she wanted to. "I wouldn't let them take you," he said. "They'd have to kill us both." He said it so calmly, yet Cassie believed him more thoroughly than if he had shouted it with indignation. It was not love he had declared. But it certainly was passion.

"I wouldn't let anyone take you, either," she said. And though it had been a spontaneous remark, she found, once the words had left her lips, that they were true. She would put herself in the line of fire if Malcolm's life were at stake.

Malcolm bit his lip as he took one last moment to examine her tempting lips. "Well," he said, not wanting to spoil the conversation by overextending it, "I suppose I should dress."

"You look fine as you are," gulped Cassie.

"Thank you," he smiled, "but this isn't nearly uncomfortable enough to be proper. Besides, no one would believe I'm your escort, you look so pretty."

Cassie flushed, even as she hated herself for doing so. "Well, you'd better change, then," she agreed. "I don't want people thinking you're my servant."

Malcolm chuckled as he made to depart. "By the way," he said over his shoulder, "have you thought of a name?"

"A name?"

"Yes, a name. A way to be introduced."

"Oh, I . . . I suppose it doesn't matter. Anything but Cassie ought to do."

His eyes smiled. "Choose one," he urged in a soft voice, "choose a name you like."

"Oh, no," she shook her head as though her sensibilities had been insulted, "any name will do. Just call me Jane or something."

"Jane?" he asked. "Is that a name you like?"

"It's fine."

He approached her once more, sending chills down her spine by touching her shoulder. "Choose one you like," he urged her. "Tonight, you have golden hair, after all. You can be anyone you wish. What's your favorite name? What do wish yours had been?"

"Malcolm," she giggled, "I do believe you're encouraging me to play make-believe like a little girl."

"Play make-believe," he urged her with a soft, seductive breath upon her forehead, "play make-believe like a little girl."

Cassie's eyes closed at the gentle, masculine sound of his voice. She didn't want to tell him. She didn't want to tell him her favorite name, because to do so would be to admit she had thought of it.

"What is it?" he asked. "Who do you want to be?"

He was the only man in the world to whom she could reply. He was the only man in the world she trusted. "Deborah," she answered bashfully.

"Deborah?"

"Yes," she flushed. "I want to be Deborah."

He replied with a kiss on her forehead. The softness of his lips drove her wild. Still, it was not a passionate kiss, but a gentle kiss to seal an understanding. He would never tell anyone that she had long fancied the name Deborah. A girl's dreams and imaginings were sacred and private. Malcolm knew this, and would not betray her trust. "I'll meet you downstairs in a few minutes," he said, then turned on his heel, leaving her alone with the realization that she had always wanted to play a game of make-believe. Just like all the other girls had. She took a deep, seductive breath as she touched the velvet at her bosom. It was delicious to be a sinner at last.

* * *

The house which hosted the masquerade was neither large nor elegant. It was a wooden home of average size, and its inhabitants were probably not rich. But they were determined to throw a masquerade as grand as any in old England. Orange lantern light poured through the windows, robbing the night of all its mystery and fright. No one on the road that night could have been scared of the dark when such gay laughter was chiming in the wind, and so many happy people were standing in brightly lit windows, unable to see out but eager to be seen. Outdoor lanterns lined the pathway from the road to the open front door. To be left shivering under the stars when there was so much warmth and wine within the house was unthinkable. Cassie wanted to rush in.

Malcolm was looking dashing as he led her to the entrance. His brown tailcoat, tight-fitting breeches, and tall, sleek boots showed off his height and his slender masculinity. His neck sash was of black, to match Cassie's gown. The color did much to exaggerate the striking beauty of his dark sapphire eyes, barely concealed by his elegant black eye mask. His short brown hair glittered with hints of gold in the hot lantern light, and his sideburns accentuated the clear angle of his jaw. For the first time, it occurred to Cassie to worry that other women might envy her acquaintance with him. She wondered how it would feel if another woman at the party challenged her right to be at his side.

Reassurance came immediately. A slender beauty in a white dress and glittering white mask positively beamed at Malcolm as she greeted the couple at the door. Her chocolate hair was shiny, her bright smile absolutely contagious. But Cassie learned something about her escort at the very moment in which the graceful bird squeezed his elbow. Malcolm did not flirt. He would not embarrass the lady at his side, no matter how much he was tempted. "It's a pleasure to see you as well," he replied kindly to the woman's gushing. His nod was formal, his smile shy. "May I introduce my guest, Deborah Whittaker."

Cassie smiled. Whittaker? How had he come up with that?

"Charmed, I'm sure," said the woman. "Where on earth are you from?"

"England," said Cassie, causing the woman to laugh gaily at the obviousness of her reply.

"But what part?" she asked.

"London," she said, hoping that enough people lived there that she could not be traced.

"Well, how marvelous! What brings you to our dreary island?"

"I would hardly call it dreary," replied Cassie in earnest, her eyes peering past the intrusive form which blocked her way to the delightful masquerade. Everyone inside seemed to be having such fun. She wondered how long it would be before she would be permitted to pass and join them. "As a matter of fact, I find Australia to be rich, fertile, and cheerful. I try to holiday here as often as possible."

"Really?" asked the woman, gazing suspiciously at Malcolm. "And do you always enjoy Dr. Rutherford's company while you're here?"

Malcolm opened his mouth to defend his lady, but Cassie interrupted. "Always," she broke in, without a hint of remorse. "Why, the holiday just wouldn't be the same without the doctor to serve as my guide."

Cassie could tell that the lady wanted to ask where Cassie was staying, for surely it would be a huge scandal if she was residing with the unwed doctor. But she did not give her hostess the opportunity to ask the invasive question. She clutched Malcolm's firm arm and said, "Thank you for having us to your soirée," to which her hostess was required to nod gracefully and invite them in, biting her tongue all the while. Cassie now had no doubt. That woman had designs on Malcolm. She realized that her handsome, soft-spoken young doctor was probably the target of nearly every marriage-minded woman on the island. After all, with whom was he competing? Convicts? She squeezed his arm with affection, having to remind herself that Malcolm, too, had once been a convict.

The party felt warm and dizzying. There was so much gentle intoxication all about, that it seemed troubles were very far away, indeed. There was so much life and pleasure in all of the glowing, masked faces and loud laughter that it seemed as though no one there would ever die. Plush rugs, more cozy than elegant, brushed under Cassie's slippers. The lantern light all around was a warm orange. Tiny chandeliers specked the guests with glitter. The food was ample rather than dainty, tasty rather than elegant. The glasses were not of fine crystal, and the wine was not the best quality, but nobody seemed to know it or care. They had all been middle class in England, and believed that this was the life of the aristocracy, save a few harmless details. No one seemed to be talking about anything, yet they were all talking. Champagne glasses held high, they were laughing and using their lips to make words. But the words were not meant to create discussion. They were just another way of touching and being touched.

"Where is the dancing?" Cassie whispered to Malcolm.

"There's no ballroom," he told her with a sly grin. "Nobody here is wealthy enough to have a proper masquerade. We just wear masks and pretend we're at one."

If Cassie had had a drink, she would have spit it out in her laughter. "Oh, Malcolm," she chuckled, "I'm so glad we came. I really am."

He liked the way her eyes sparkled behind her black,

feathered mask. He thought she looked alive again. "Let me get you some spirits," he suggested. "Maybe it'll help take your mind off a few things."

"Like what?" she laughed. "Like prison, and being hunted by both the law and a murderer?"

"Little things like that, yes. Stay here." With a gentle smile, he bowed and backed away from her, steering his way toward the punch bowl.

Cassie could not stop smiling. She felt as though she were floating through the room like the phantom she was. No one could recognize her, she was sure of it. For on that night, she was not Cassie, but a blond vixen named Deborah. While most women held their masks to their faces by a stick, Cassie's was strapped on like a man's. She had been too fearful of dropping it. The satin sash tied around her temple was unusual, but not enough so to cause much staring. What caused staring was her captivating beauty. She was a small, well-shaped blonde with perfect ringlets tossed over one shoulder and black velvet clinging to her firm frame. The plume-feathered mask concealed the slant of her eyes, but not their magnificent emerald color. Even her freckles seemed paler against her light wig, like gentle golden highlights in her skin.

Cassie did not stop to talk to anyone. She moved about the room like a ghost who could not be seen. She listened to one conversation, and then another, but only smiled and moved on when her presence became observed. Everyone was too intoxicated to wonder at her fleeting behavior. She was trying to soak in the vibrant life all around her, like a leaf absorbing light after withering in the darkness. She breathed deep the smells of perfumes and pipes. She widened her eyes to the dim, warm light. She opened her ears to the clinking of glasses, and the silly laughter. She did not know whether she would ever know these things again, so she would have to store them in her memory for all time.

Malcolm returned with two glasses of red punch. He handed one to her and said, "Be careful. I hear it's strong," then he sipped from his own round cup.

"I handle spirits rather well," she warned him with a flashing smile. "It may take a great deal of this before you're able to take advantage of me."

Rather than laughing, Malcolm looked thoughtful for a moment, swirling his punch in his hand. Biting his lip, he said quietly, "I really don't like bedding intoxicated women."

Cassie would have rolled her eyes, had she not been in such a good mood. "It isn't really necessary," she scolded, "to remind me that you've devoted half of your life to experiments in lovemaking. You could at least pretend that I am the only one." A swig of her fruity drink showed him that she was not as upset as she sounded.

"You're the only one now," he promised her, with faithfulness in his eyes.

She met his gaze bravely. "Yes, but not forever. There's no future for us."

Malcolm did not move his gaze. He wanted to say something to her about that. He could not say that she was wrong. He could not say that there was promise of a bright future, when she was forced to live in shadow and was being hunted all around. He could not even tell her that he had no doubts as to whether he was really the best man for her. He was not as pure a soul as she was. But still, there was something he wanted to say, if only he could have found the words in time. He wanted to tell her something about not giving up hope, about not closing a door just to prevent the wind from doing it first. He wanted to tell her that he didn't think it was impossible—just unlikely. Nothing was impossible. But he saw the practical glint in her eye, and did not know how to soften it. Before he could say a word, she had emptied her cup and said, "More, please," with a broad smile that showed she was not going to have her mood spoiled on this night.

With a gentleman's obedience, Malcolm cast her a friendly grin and bowed low. "As you wish," he replied, shaking her empty cup, clearly impressed with the speed at which she had drunk. He chuckled, then departed with a courteous nod.

Malcolm and Cassie had thought that they'd anticipated everything which could possibly go wrong at this event. Cassie's costume was secure and concealing. Malcolm's behavior was unsuspicious. Her story made sense, and all should have been well. But there was one impending disaster which they had not foreseen. Priscilla was attending the masquerade. Dressed in a brilliant bloodred gown, which flattered her charcoal hair beyond reason, she was standing by the punch bowl, looking at Malcolm with hungry eyes, feeling fragile and regretful in a way that was quite unlike her. Her violet eyes, usually so worldly and bitter, were nearly wide with girlish glee as he drew near. Self-consciously, she smoothed her gown against her luscious hips and tiny waist. She stood up as straight as she could. There was no doubt that she was the most fetching woman at the party, even compared to Cassie. But not in Malcolm's eyes.

He stiffened when he saw her, and nearly changed his mind about getting Cassie's punch. But it was too late. She had seen him, so he proceeded. "Malcolm," she began in a sultry but trembling voice.

"Don't trouble me," he said firmly, keeping his eyes fixed on the heavy crystal punch bowl, carved ornately with flowers and vines.

"Malcolm," she pleaded, ignoring his frigidity, "I've wanted to say I'm sorry, but Faith has been sending me away. Malcolm, please. I want you to know that my feelings for you were sincere. I'm sorry I couldn't tell you that I was keeping an eye on Cassie, but they wouldn't let me tell anyone. That really has nothing to do with you and me. I really meant everything that happened between us."

"You're a liar, and I don't wish to know you anymore." His words were biting, but his posture was casual.

Priscilla was wounded, and for once in her life, was not ashamed to show it. "Malcolm, you've got to understand."

"I do understand," he said, filling his cup to the brim. "That's the problem. I understand who you are, and I don't like it." And with that, he spun on his heel and returned to Cassie. Priscilla watched him go, first with misery, and then with intrigue. She squinted her violet eyes. Was that Cassie? Of course it was. Who else could it be? A smile curved her lips. She'd never have suspected the little mouse would have such courage. To come to a party in disguise, knowing that being caught could mean her execution? Very impressive. But it was too dangerous. If anything happened to her, Priscilla and Miles would both have to forfeit their pay. She hated to return to business, especially with Malcolm's cruel rejection still burning. But this did seem to be an emergency.

Malcolm returned to Cassie with all of the affection and warmth he had denied Priscilla, as though he'd been storing it until he could see her gentle face again. "Enjoying the party?" he asked, having caught her floating around the carpet with an ethereal smile.

Cassie was startled, but returned his adoring grin with her own, gracefully accepting the cup of punch. "It's fun not to be me, not to be real," she said. "Everyone should have the opportunity to experience life this way for just one night."

"You're beginning to sound like me," he chuckled self-effacingly. "I fear I've been a bad influence on you. Pretty soon you'll be musing about darkness and pleasure."

"Shoot me if I get that bad," she remarked, causing him nearly to spit out his punch with a laugh.

Suddenly there was the sound of commotion outside. Malcolm got a strange look on his face, a look of intense concentration, even while his lips were still on his cup. He was listening intently. Someone shouted, "Brawl!" and Malcolm scowled.

"Not exactly the high society of London, is it?" he remarked with a wry grin. "As hard as they try . . ."

A crowd was gathering at the front door to watch the fight. Cassie could not see the brawling on the lawn, but could see the winces on the spectators' faces whenever a fist hit its mark, and the forced smiles and chuckling remarks they used to ease the tension. Malcolm peered at the spectators for a moment, and then shook his head with a frown. "Aren't any of them going to stop it?" he asked himself aloud. Another moment of waiting answered his question. The crowd was enjoying the fight. "Oh, for the love of . . ." He put down his cup and glanced apologetically at Cassie. "Pardon me," he bowed, then spun around and excused his way through the crowd at the doorway.

Cassie followed behind him, though she knew she should not. She worked her way to the very edge of the crowd, just close enough to see what was happening. There were three or four men involved in the fight. It was hard to tell the number, for the spectators and the actual aggressors were rapidly melding. There was so much shoving and rolling on the ground that it seemed one of the beautiful black wrought iron lanterns might be toppled to set the grass on fire. Cassie saw her hostess looking frantically out the window, undoubtedly fretting that her party had been ruined but not feeling brave enough to step outside. There was yelling and cursing such as Cassie had never heard. And then there was Malcolm.

His tailcoat thrown off and his sleeves rolled up, he was making his way to the most dangerous part of the commotion. "Break it up!" he called, his hair falling over his forehead. When his shout was not heeded, he wrapped his arm around the neck of one of the largest assailants. The huge brawler clutched the arm as it choked him, but could not remove it. His opponent used the opportunity to take a swing. But Malcolm stretched out his free arm to keep the other man at a distance. "Take it somewhere else!" he yelled. And the spectators began to listen. It seemed this was a sentiment which had not occurred to them until now.

"He's the one who punched me!" yelled the opponent in his gruffest voice. He pointed a thick, accusing finger at the man in Malcolm's clutch. He was breathing heavily, and bleeding from the lip.

"Then beat the hell out of him," shouted Malcolm, "but do it somewhere else!" He loosened his grip on his victim so that both men could catch their breath. The other fighters stopped pounding each other as well. Seeing that the central two were taking a rest, they used this new turn of events as an excuse to pause and listen.

"He," the man Malcolm had choked gasped for air, "he called me a convict," he said, pointing at his bleeding opponent. "He's nothing but working trash, come here to pretend he's noble. And he spits on me because I served my time."

"Just take it somewhere else!" yelled Malcolm. Then, softening his voice, he added, "There are women here." Both men looked at him now, as though he had spoken some very obscure truth. They peered around at the crowd, lowering their eyes in shame when they saw women standing in the windows.

"Well, I'll go somewhere else if he will," said the convict.

"I didn't even want to fight to begin with," said the other, throwing up his hands.

Malcolm turned and walked away. He didn't really care how this resolved itself. He just couldn't believe that there hadn't been a single other man willing to stick up for the women's right to spend days looking forward to a party, and not have it ruined by a couple of brawling idiots. When he saw Cassie, he put his hand on her back. "I'm sorry," he said, leading her back toward the house, "I hope that didn't ruin your evening."

"Not at all," she smiled, loving the way he looked with his chestnut hair all awry, and his muscles bursting from use. She flushed as they crossed the threshold, for she was almost too shy to say what she really felt. But somehow, the intoxication of the night enabled her to speak. "Actually," she said with a big, nervous grin and a bow of the head, "I thought you were very brave."

Malcolm did not reply, as he was still rather annoyed. He seemed in a hurry to get her inside and forget all of this. He was leading her rather forcefully through the crowd.

Cassie ventured further. "In fact," she said, "I thought the way you handled that was rather . . . well, attractive."

"Attractive?" he asked, grinning for the first time since the fight had broken out. "I like the sound of that." He squeezed her affectionately against him, causing Cassie to feel warm and excited.

She looked quickly into his smiling eyes as he continued to lead her carefully through the dispersing crowd. "It's very appealing," she laughed, delighted that he did not mind her boldness, "when a man defends the honor of ladies."

"Oh, well now," he teased casually, "did I ever tell you about the time I rescued a litter of kittens from a burning house?"

"Really?" she laughed. "I don't recall."

"Oh, yes, it was brutal, but anything for those kittens, you know." He spotted a cozy chair before a blazing fireplace and thought that would be a nice place to settle her. He pulled her gently by the hand. "Then there was, of course, that little skirmish I had with those highway robbers. I couldn't let them steal from that carriage full of orphans." He gestured for her to take rest in the soft, velvet chair.

"My," gasped Cassie with delightful sarcasm, "I never knew you were such a daring and violent man."

Malcolm couldn't keep from cracking a smile. "Well, I never knew it would arouse you so much to think me so."

Cassie crossed her arms indignantly as she sat. "Malcolm," she scolded in all earnest, "I did not use the word *arouse*, and I would thank you not to use it, either."

Malcolm knelt by her chair and nodded humbly. "I'm sorry," he said, "that was very rude."

It would have been impossible for Cassie to remain angry. There was always such honesty in his eyes. When he said he was sorry, she knew it was so. And that was a rare attribute.

"I'm sorry to intrude."

Malcolm turned his head with a start, and then bent it as though to groan, *What else could go wrong?* It was Priscilla.

"Cassie," she said stiffly, looking like a queen in her royal red gown, "or Deborah, as I understand you're being called tonight, I do apologize, but I need to speak with your escort in private."

Cassie froze for a moment, feeling terrified that she had been discovered, but then she relaxed as her senses took over and she remembered that Priscilla was on her side. "It's quite all right," she replied.

"No, it's not all right," moaned Malcolm, rubbing his disheveled hair. "Priscilla, I'm busy."

"I'm afraid I must demand that you speak to me at once."

"You can't demand that," he nearly laughed. "You can't demand *anything* of me. Be gone."

Priscilla did not budge. And Cassie was looking awkward. Observing the tenseness of the moment, Malcolm let out a heavy sigh. He knew there would be no peace to this evening until he had settled matters with Priscilla, and gotten her to leave him be, once and for all. "Fine," he breathed, "Cassie, I'll be back in a moment." He gave her a gentle kiss on the lips, a gesture which was more affectionate than was required of him. He wanted Priscilla to see it.

The straight-backed Priscilla led him to a private study. "I don't think anyone's using this," she announced, closing the door behind them. "We probably shouldn't be in here, but we'll only be a moment."

Malcolm did not even sit. He rested his back against the wall and crossed his arms impatiently. "What do you want?" he asked sharply, glancing at a clock as though timing the duration of his agony.

"Malcolm," she said softly, approaching him tenderly and with proper remorse, "I am truly sorry about this, all of it, but . . ."

"But what?" he interrupted impatiently, "What?"

Priscilla was wounded, but only enough to sharpen her tone. She lifted her chin even higher. "It is too dangerous to bring her here," she said curtly. "We've trusted her to your care, but we thought you would be careful. We—"

"*You* trusted her to my care?" he asked with annoyance bordering on indignation. "*You* didn't trust her to my care. *I took her!* And I would have taken her regardless of whether you trusted me or not!"

"Malcolm . . ." she began.

But he did not let her finish. "Look, just leave us alone," he demanded. "It's only one night out. It'll be over soon, and then she can go on hiding. But instead of scolding me for letting her breathe, I wish you would help me to think of a way to get her out of here."

"It's impossible," said Priscilla, who did not care whether Cassie ever saw the light of day again. "Miles and I have discussed it. The only way out of Australia is by ship, and she won't be allowed on a ship, even disguised, without some means of proving she is not a convict."

"What about over the mountains?" he suggested desperately.

"There's hardly any civilization over there," she laughed, "and she would never survive the journey."

"It's been done," he reminded her. "Men have escaped the barracks through the wilderness."

"You don't know for certain that any of them survived. Those are only rumors."

Malcolm knew she was right, but could not bear to give up. "She can't just stay in her bedroom for the rest of her life," he said, feeling the pain of Cassie's torturous confinement.

"In her bedroom?" A horrible smile came over Priscilla's face. "You mean to say you aren't sharing a bedroom?"

"That's none of your business," he spat, not at all liking her vindictive expression.

"Really, I'm surprised, Malcolm. I would have thought the idea of ravaging a helpless outlaw would excite you beyond reason. Have you really resisted the opportunity?"

Malcolm would not be goaded. He replied to her evil eye with a look of absolute condescension. "Are you finished, Priscilla?"

Priscilla's head dropped with a sigh. "No, Malcolm," she said, sweetness making its way into her voice. "I was hoping that I am not finished. That *we* are not finished." She took a step nearer to him, knowing that he could not step away, with his back against the wall.

"Well, we are," he told her calmly, not reacting to her nearness.

"Malcolm," she pleaded, wrapping her arms around

his neck, a gesture he allowed only because he was so far from being moved by her seduction. "Malcolm, I want you back."

"You used me," he reminded her, hands in pockets.

"No, Malcolm, I swear it. It's the mission that I used—not you. I used it to get close to you again, because I could not bear being apart. Jilting you was a mistake I knew I had to remedy. Malcolm, you're the only man I have ever loved."

"Love?" he smirked. "Where did you learn a word like that?"

"Do you think I have no heart?"

"That's exactly what I think."

She moved her face toward his, smelling the warmth of his stubbled jaw, loving the shape of his lips, longing for his touch. It had been so long. She had lain in bed each night, imagining that he was there, holding her, saying erotic things and touching her with tenderness and savagery. She could only pray that her violet eyes would entrance him, and that the feel of her lips on his mouth would remind him of what he really was—not the dull and respectable lover of a girl like Cassie, but a wicked and dark angel to the likes of herself. She forced a kiss upon his hard, unresponsive lips.

The door flew open, and Cassie, in her golden ringlets, stood in its wake, her face frozen by the sight of her betrayal, her lips parted but motionless. There was a sudden jading of her jewel-like eyes. It was as though she had expected this, expected that the world was too cruel to let her have love. And without astonishment, rage, or hysteria, she turned calmly on her heel and left the party. "Cassie!" Malcolm cried, nearly toppling Priscilla in his effort to rid himself of her embrace. "Cassie, wait!" He darted from the room, leaving Priscilla alone and nearly in tears. She thought about running after him, but did not. She crossed her arms miserably. He really didn't love her.

Malcolm caught up easily with Cassie, but it was no use. "Cassie, please listen to me," he said, keeping up with her fast pace through the door and onto the road. "It wasn't what it looked like. There is nothing going on between Priscilla and me. Not anymore." Cassie placed her hands over both ears and continued walking. "She forced that kiss upon me," he continued, and he knew she heard, because an amused smile crossed her lips, though her pace did not slow down. "Listen to me," he begged, reaching for her arm, but she shook him off. "I was trying to get rid of her. I have absolutely no interest in . . ."

Cassie stopped walking, and turned to him. Snatching off her wig, she let her own fiery hair sparkle against the black sky. "I want no more of your games," she told him, placing the wig in his hands. "I don't care what you do or who you kiss. But it's not going to be me anymore." Then she calmly turned around and continued her stride down the road.

"Cassie," he pleaded, letting out a nervous chuckle of disbelief, "where are you going? You can't just wander around at night. It isn't safe. At least let me take you home, and we can argue there."

"I don't want to argue," she told him, still walking, "I want to be rid of you. I want to be rid of you and your twisted heart, your obsessive soul, and your strange mind. You're not good for me, Malcolm. You're not good for anyone, except maybe Priscilla."

"I don't want Priscilla!"

"Tell that to your . . . your body!"

Malcolm grabbed her angrily by the arm. Spinning her to face him, he yelled, "Listen to me!"

Cassie was not immune to the nearness of his strong body, and the handsomeness of the face that looked down at her with such passion. But her reply was clear. "I will not listen to you, Malcolm," she said calmly, "and if you don't unhand me, I'll be forced to scream. I am not wearing my wig, so I will be arrested, and you will be arrested for assisting me. Screaming would be a stupid thing to do, I admit. But right now, I'm prepared to do it."

Malcolm looked at the wig in his hand and slammed it to the ground. Then he looked in her eyes and saw that she was not bluffing. She was defeated enough to do it. He had killed her faith in him. Stiffly, he let her go. He was still trying to think of some last point to make, some last utterance that might make her come back, when she fled down the dark road, out of his sight. He raced to his carriage, prepared to follow her.

But following her would do him no good. For half a mile down the road, a hand flew over Cassie's mouth, and she was dragged into the carriage of a stranger. Her luck had finally run out.

Thirty-seven

"Dearest? Dearest, where are you?" Mrs. Madison shuffled awkwardly through the parlour in her cumbersome gold satin gown. "Oh, there you are, Wilbert, I've been looking everywhere."

Mr. Madison closed his book and gave his wife a look of false concern. "Darling, you shouldn't be out of bed. Not in your health." In truth, he had simply been enjoying his privacy. He knew as well as the rest of his family that there was nothing wrong with the mistress's health.

"Well, I know, dear," she said, placing a concerned hand on her own forehead, "but this does seem rather important. Have you seen this?" She handed him a sloppily penned note, which her husband observed through a narrow spectacle.

"Hmmm, can't say as I have," he answered in a most fatherly fashion. He handed back the note and re-opened his book.

"Well, doesn't that seem a bit odd?" she asked him, with an expression that kept wavering as she tried to decide how concerned she ought to be.

"What?" he asked with a yawn. "That Samuel has decided to tell my brother about his betrothal? I should say it's a little odd. I'd never known they were so close. But it seems a friendly enough gesture."

"Not that!" she scolded him. "I mean the fact that we didn't know he was betrothed."

"We didn't?"

"Well, I didn't!" She tapped on her chin in attempted remembrance while batting the note against the side of her gown. "No, I really don't recall any mention of a fiancée," she declared. "I think he may have had a friend once, but that was a boy. I think. Oh, dearest," she cried mournfully, "you don't suppose he told us and we simply forgot, do you? Oh, my. Does this make me a bad mother?"

"Don't be ridiculous!" He slammed his book down and rose to his feet. "You are a wonderful mother! Why, you might as well call me a bad father, if you're going to start that."

"Oh, you're right," she sighed into her husband's chest, "it isn't our fault. It's just that boy—he's so . . . so . . . so sarcastic and obstinate."

"He certainly is," he said, stroking her broad back.

"And our daughter . . . oh, I can't even speak of her. Oh, Wilbert, I only pray that our youngest two will turn out all right."

"Where are they, by the way?"

"Oh, heavens, how would I know? Please pass me that handkerchief."

Doing her bidding, he watched as she blew her nose noisily into the cloth. "There, there. It'll be all right, my love. I'm sure that when Samuel told us of his engagement, we were merely preoccupied. With all of our responsibilities, well . . . a young man like that just doesn't understand what we go through to put a roof over his head. I'm sure he would forgive our absent-mindedness."

"Yes," she sniffed, "yes, you're right, of course. Just remember when we see him that we mustn't let on our surprise. We must appear in every way to be nonchalant. He must not know that his betrothal slipped our minds."

"Of course, my dear. Of course."

She tilted her head with a wrinkled brow. "Whom do you suppose he is marrying?"

Her husband shrugged.

"Oh, well," she sighed, "at least she will take him off our hands, whoever she is."

"Indeed, my dear. Indeed." He headed upstairs to get his trunk.

"Darling?" she asked. "You're not going out again, are you?"

Mr. Madison froze on the stairwell. "Well, I . . . I have very important business to attend to, my dear. Very important."

"What sort of business?"

"The usual."

"I would think the perfumery could go a week without you." She said this scoldingly, but then melted into a smile. "Though I am awfully proud of you," she admitted. "Who would have known that you have such a fine nose that they should summon you over and over throughout the year to seek your advice?" She positively beamed with pride.

"Well, dear," he said, brightly, "there is a lot of money to be had in perfume. They want to get it just right."

She nodded understandingly. "Yes, dear. We shall miss you, as always." He beamed at her and then continued to ascend the stairs. As an afterthought, his wife called out behind him, "But, darling, do tell them to stop spilling it all over your clothing. You know the servants haven't shown up in weeks, and I don't know how we'll get it out this time!"

"Yes, dear."

Thirty-eight

The happy couple was now arriving at the home of Uncle Egbert, both horses and humans soaked to the skin by a rain which had not ceased since their departure. Sheena was sniffling and crossing her arms defensively across her chest, her thick hair dripping water upon her freezing forehead and cheeks. "I am probably going to die now," she announced. "Of course, the way you drive, it's a miracle I've made it this far."

Samuel knew that he was something of a reckless driver. But he truly had been doing his best to lead the horses carefully. This had been the smoothest journey he had ever taken, as far as galloping was concerned. It was certainly disappointing to hear that even his most cautious navigating was too rough to make an ordinary person feel safe. An ordinary person, of course, being someone who was not a member of his family. "I drove the best I could," he replied soberly, with a shrug. "I didn't think it was so bad, really." He leaped from his seat in a very athletic but juvenile manner, then strolled to her side of the carriage, offering assistance.

"No, it really wasn't so bad," she agreed sarcastically. "We only came close to tipping over about six times. Why, if there had been no turns in the road, it probably would have been a smooth ride. Who would have guessed that there would be turns in the road?" She rejected the hand he offered with an annoyed slap upon its palm, then hoisted herself down. "I don't see why you wouldn't just let me drive," she grumbled. "I may not have been born with my own team of horses, but at least I can manage one."

"I'd be too embarrassed," he answered with youthful candor. "People would stare at us if you were the one handling the team."

"And they weren't staring at us as it was?" she asked before sneezing.

"I didn't notice anyone staring."

"You were going too fast to notice!"

Samuel felt a little dejected by her scolding. She looked so pretty with her hair dripping all over her borrowed cloak. Her eyes were so vibrantly blue against the gray fog, which hid their feet from view. He really wanted her to like him. But he resigned himself to the idea that it might take some time. After all, he didn't know how to court. And she didn't know how to be courted. That would probably slow things down a bit. "I'll let you drive on the way home," he relented.

Sheena couldn't believe it. Despite all of her griping, she never dreamed a man would let her have the reins. "What?"

"You can drive on the way home," he repeated. "I suppose I don't care that much what people think of me. Just don't drive so slowly that it takes us a week."

"I do not drive slowly," she informed him hotly, but she accepted the arm he offered, for she was most impressed by his liberal state of mind. "I shall drive in every way more competently than the likes of any man could."

"Very well," he shrugged. "Good. I suppose." Had he just been insulted? Probably, he reasoned. But somehow, he didn't mind being insulted by Sheena. Gentle hostility seemed to be her way of relating.

There was a beauty in the drabness of the day. The fog was the kind which could hide werewolves. Both the people strolling and the horses trotting seemed to be deep in introspection. It was weather for imagination and remembrance, not excitement. There was a gracefulness to everyone on foot, a self-consciousness in their faces. The stone of Uncle Egbert's town house was as gray as the rest of the world. It was difficult to see where the rain ended and the building began. But through one rectangular window, a warm fire could be seen. It illuminated a sofa and a soft chair, promising a colorful warmth and brightness denied by the outdoors.

It was Mrs. Madison who answered the brass knocker. Her pretty face and soft brown hair were welcoming, though her expression was not. She looked surprised to see Samuel, and she seemed to be struggling to give the impression it was a good surprise, instead of the kind of surprise it really was. She forced a smile which did not hide the upset in her round eyes. If Samuel had been a more sensitive soul, he would have wanted to creep away immediately, for the words of welcome which escaped her lips were not convincing. "Oh, my! What are you doing here?" Several blinks later, she realized how terrible that had sounded, and tried to improve it. "I mean, are you lost?" She knew that hadn't helped, but she was just so taken aback.

"No, nothing like that," Samuel announced jovially. "I'm just here to visit my favorite aunt and uncle."

Egbert's large, grizzled face appeared behind his wife's. "We've already given you money."

Samuel laughed. "Oh, Uncle, what a sense of humor you have. No, no. I'm here to announce my engagement to this lovely lady." He gently pushed Sheena forth so they could get a good look at her.

Mrs. Madison managed to look a little bit happy for them, though there was still the remainder of an unpleasant startle upon her face. "Oh, how nice," she said weakly, arching her lips into what was technically a smile. "That's very nice."

It took Uncle Egbert only half of a second to guess that this visit had nothing to do with sharing jolly news, and everything to do with wedding gifts. But he did not want to be rude to the raven-haired young lady, whom he did not know. So he, too, managed to grumble, "Well, congratulations," and it sounded somewhat jovial.

Both aunt and uncle were staring at the girl, wondering what sort of a woman would marry their nephew. They would have guessed it was a farce, except that the young lady had been standing right there when Samuel said they were engaged, and had not corrected him. She appeared to be somewhat disheveled, but this could have been caused by the rain and the November chill. She was awfully comely—plump, milky-skinned, with hair like midnight. Had he compromised her? They both lowered their gazes to the stranger's stomach. But they could not see anything through her wet cloak.

"May we come in?" asked Samuel, as rain was still dripping on them from the ledge above.

There was a distinct hesitation on behalf of the hosts, but after the awkward pause had lingered for some time, the door widened. "Of course," said Mrs. Madison, "please do." She glanced warily at her husband as the couple carelessly stepped over the welcome mat and adorned the fine Asian rug with wet footprints. My God, they realized. The fiancée was just as vulgar as their nephew.

"What's for supper?" asked Samuel, steering his way to the kitchen.

"We've already eaten!" cried Mrs. Madison. "We . . . we dine rather early here."

"But I'm sure we can find you some bread and honey," Egbert chimed in, carefully eyeing Sheena's hourglass figure as she removed her cloak.

"Yes, yes, of course," said his wife nervously. "Let me see what I can fetch you." She hastily disappeared.

"Well now," said Egbert, "please have a seat." He invited them to make themselves comfortable on a large, emerald sofa. Sheena did her best to sit properly, or, at least, as she had always observed proper ladies sitting. She held her back awkwardly straight, crossed her ankles, and folded her hands tightly in her lap. Egbert was still staring. "So, when did this exciting event take place?" he asked, once they were all seated.

"Oh, a long time ago," said Sheena, "a very long time ago. We've been engaged for ages."

It was the first time Egbert had heard her speak, and he now realized how Samuel had won her. She was Irish. Just like his father, he had chosen an Irish woman for his wife. Egbert would have been ashamed, but for the fact that his shame about Samuel was already so deep, it could not be worsened. At least, he thought, at least the boy is getting married. "I have not heard of it," said Egbert.

"Well, you see," Samuel explained, "my parents don't approve, and . . ."

"Nor do mine!" Sheena interrupted fiercely. "They're so embarrassed by him, they won't even attend the wedding."

Samuel scowled. "Mine aren't coming, either. They say it's all a horrible mistake, and . . ."

"But at least they didn't call me an ogre. My parents called *you* an ogre," Sheena said.

"I don't remember that," said Samuel in a warning tone of voice, trying to let her know she had gone too far.

"In fact, I'm thinking of not attending the wedding myself," said Sheena. "I'm thinking of boycotting it, too."

"Well, so am I," growled Samuel.

Mrs. Madison had just walked in with a plate full of

warm, sliced bread, and struggled not to drop it. "Well," she said uneasily, "it is so delightful to have you both here. There is so much for us to talk about. Would you like tea?"

They both eagerly held out their cups.

Mrs. Madison glanced at her husband as she poured. "Darling, you look exhausted."

"Hmmm?" Egbert was still eyeing Sheena. "Ah . . . oh, yes, dear." He gave her an understanding nod. "Yes, yes, I am. Very exhausted. I fear it's nearly time for us to retire."

"But it's only seven o'clock," said Samuel disinterestedly, as he was scoffing down the piping hot fare laid before him.

"Oh, that's . . . that's normal retirement hour for us," he assured them. "We uh . . . we sleep a lot here."

"Well, don't worry about us," said Sheena, eating at the same rapid pace as Samuel, "we're good at entertaining ourselves."

"Good, good." The husband and wife exchanged horrified glances. "Umm, you know I do plan to go on a trip sometime over the next few days. Do you uh . . . do you have somewhere you'll be going after this?"

"No," shrugged Samuel, "this is our only stop."

"Oh, that's . . . that's wonderful."

In fact, not even his wife could have guessed how deeply inconvenienced Egbert was by his nephew's untimely visit. There could not have been a worse night for him to impose. For on this night, Egbert had promised to meet Emma. Sneaking out of the house without Sarah's notice was difficult enough, but to avoid the prying ears of three would be a fantastic feat. He could only hope that they were all very sound sleepers. And he could only wish that his appointment were later in the night, to insure that his guests would have time to fall into deep slumber. But he could not change the time of his meeting, for to do so, he would first have to meet her and explain.

Weeks ago, it would have seemed preposterous that Egbert would even be trying to arrange a meeting with Emma, who had betrayed him so brutally and scolded him so viciously. Indeed, he had planned to abandon her—not because he wanted to, but because he felt required to. She had told him plainly that she had always despised men, most of all himself. And she had fooled him into framing his own niece, just for spite. As hard as he had tried, there was no way he could scramble her confessions in his mind to make them seem less horrendous. And he had felt the imaginary eyes of the world upon him, judging him, and instructing him that he must never return to her, lest they lose all respect for his manhood.

But as days and weeks had passed, he had grown lonely for her silken hair and slender figure. He found that shunning her gave him no relief from the pain of her betrayal, and from what she had caused him to do. Indeed, he felt that touching her youthful flesh, shaking her wildly in the moonlight, and kissing her lips with brutality was the only way to relieve the suffering she had caused him. When he looked at his dear wife, he adored her, but did not want her. And when he looked at other potential mistresses, he was dismayed by the thought of how much work it would take to break them in, to get to know them, to teach them how to please him, to feel at ease with them. He still wanted Emma. And when he thought about the eyes of the world judging him a weakling for returning to her viciously laughing heart, he suddenly realized that there were no eyes. The eyes were a figment of his imagination. Nobody knew his weakness except for himself and Emma. And so he returned to her, promising that he no longer loved her but could not stay away. And she, in turn, promised that she had lost even more respect for him at seeing him return, but that she would have him anyway. She wanted the gifts and the jewels that often fall into the hands of mistresses.

It was too early, and Egbert knew it. He and his wife had been in bed for some time, his wife softly snoring, himself wide awake, listening intently, his nightcap clinging to his skull, his hands frantically gripping a blanket. The young couple had stayed awake until a very unseemly hour. And they had only just retired when Egbert knew he could wait no longer. If he were late, Emma would have already left, just to punish him for his tardiness. He would have to be quieter than he had ever been before. He would have to ready an excuse, should he be caught. His heart was pounding and his hands were shaking as he made to open his wardrobe. The only thing more deliciously and frighteningly exciting than seeing Emma, was risking getting caught.

Samuel had just fallen into the lightest of slumbers when he noticed the sweet smell of rain on a woman's hair. His eyes opened just a little, and he saw the soft, white, hazy hourglass shape of some sort of seductive ghost. It floated nearer, and he instinctively reached out to welcome it. "So beautiful," he murmured with a yawn, pulling it near him with a strong but slender bare arm. "Come here, angel, I won't hurt you." He nuzzled her thick, sweet-smelling hair with his nose and tried to wrap her in a firm embrace, pulling her alongside him in the bed.

A fist landed in his gut. He was suddenly very wide awake. "Get your hands off of me," growled Sheena. "I didn't come in here to be your first love. Something important has come up."

Samuel did not hear her second sentence. "First love?"

he asked defensively. "What would make you think I've never . . ."

"Just a wild guess," she said with a roll of her eyes. "Now, come. You've got to get dressed."

"Get dressed?" he asked groggily, reaching out to stroke her dark hair once more. Somehow, in his young man's mind, he had not yet given up hope that his first lovemaking might occur. After all, he wasn't wearing much, she wasn't wearing much, and there was a bed in the room. It seemed that they might as well. "Can't we wait until morning to get dressed?" he asked, brushing her silken cheek with his knuckles. Before she could move away, he tried for a kiss, lunging into her with strength and passion.

"Oh, for the love of . . ." She held him at bay with both arms and shook her head with annoyance. "Will you just listen to me? Your Uncle Egbert has sneaked out of the house."

Samuel blinked at her dazedly. "What?" he asked lazily, putting his head on her shoulder, like a little boy asking for comfort.

"Stop it," she snapped, pushing him away. "You're not listening to me. I said that your uncle is gone. He's run off!"

Samuel shrugged. "So?"

"So he's got to be up to no good!" she cried in a loud whisper. "Don't you see? We came here looking for suspicious behavior, and we've found it! Your uncle has no doubt gone off to some secret meeting with his fellow conspirators. The ones who framed Cassie!"

"What makes you think that?" he asked with squinted eyes. He was still frustrated over her rejection.

"Well, I don't know it for certain," she backtracked, "but I do know he's going somewhere in secret, else he would not have departed under cover of night. Now, hurry. We must follow him! Oh, hurry, you idiot."

"It's not that I don't like pet names," he said, reluctantly sitting upright and planting his weary feet on the floor, "but couldn't you have chosen *honey* or *peaches* or something? You're probably not aware of this, but some people think *idiot* has sort of a negative connotation." He stretched his arms overhead as though he were in no hurry to go on this goose chase.

"Hurry up!" she cried. "If you don't hurry, we're going to lose sight of him! Come on!"

"All right," Samuel grumbled, "let's go. Let's go find out whether Uncle Egbert really framed my sister."

"He did!" cried Sheena. "You'll see, all I've told you is true! And tonight, we shall have our proof!"

Thirty-nine

Cassie fought her captor like a wild animal. She had not felt so trapped or so savage since she had been nearly ravaged on the convict ship. She knew from what Priscilla and Miles had told her that her captor meant to take her life. And believing that her own death was imminent did something very strange to her. It made her crazed and powerful. She kicked and punched, and nearly overcame the strength of her captor's arms more than once. He was struggling so fiercely against her newly found power that he feared he would lose her. His arms were bruised, his lip was cut, and his eye was now swollen. Cassie would not be an easy victim. And for this reason, once he finally overpowered her, he gagged her and secured her brutally with rope.

The carriage ride was terrifying. Cassie could see her would-be assassin, but she did not know him. He was a stout man with graying hair and a large, flat nose which had been broken more than once. His square hands were rough from a lifetime of hard work. And his face was strangely normal. He did not look like a killer. He did not look angry or vengeful, or even coldly business-minded. He looked like an honest man with a worried face and a nervous habit of swallowing hard. Cassie would have spoken to him, had she not been gagged. But as it was, she could only be bounced around by the roughness of the road, unable to steady herself because of her bound hands. She could only wonder in horror where they were going, and why she was not yet dead.

"I'm sorry we have to meet this way," said Cassie's captor, having led her to a run-down, windowless shack in the middle of a forest. It was a perfect place for a killing, Cassie observed. No one would ever find her there. She was so scared, she feared her heavy breathing would make her pass out. She wished he would get it over with. She wished she could just die before she had to think any more about it.

"Who are you?" she asked, as though it mattered.

"Well, I can't really tell you that," he reasoned, "but I'll give you a hint. You know my wife very well."

"Why can't you tell me?" she asked. "You're going to kill me anyway."

"Not necessarily," he replied with a twinkle in his eye. His words were like a comforting squeeze on the shoulder. Cassie could not believe she had heard them. He might not kill her? She looked again at his aging but once gentle face. He did not look like a killer. Her first impression had been right. He was not a hardened criminal.

"Why not?" she was brave enough to ask. "Weren't you hired to take my life?"

That question visibly troubled him. "You know about that?" he asked, turning from the fire he was stoking.

"Yes, I know about that," she replied with an icy bite in her eye. "I know that someone framed me and is now trying to kill me."

A sudden feeling of weakness softened his features before he shook it off. He had not known about the framing—only that he'd been hired to kill her. He knew nothing of what she had done to deserve such a cruel enemy as the proper gentleman who had paid him. "How did you know?" he asked, as though fearing he had done a poor job as an assassin, having been detected so easily.

"It's none of your concern," she answered. "Just tell me why you haven't done it yet."

He found a black iron cooking pot and hung it in the hearth. Cassie noted that he was filling it with enough broth for two people. Two people. He expected her to live long enough to eat with him. This was good news. "Well, I'm going to explain that to you," he said, "but first, let me fix our supper."

Cassie did not want to argue that it was too late for supper, being nearly midnight. If he wanted her to eat, she would eat. She would do whatever it took to make it out of that shack alive. She looked about at its darkness. Even the hearth was not enough to lighten its gloominess. It smelled dank, as though all of its logs had been soaking in scummy water. It had only one room, and it looked as though the room had never been furnished. No one had ever lived here. It was a place for young couples to make love on the sly, a place for dark minds to commit dark crimes. But it had never been a home to anyone. She and her captor sat on the splintered wood floor as he tended the pot. "Have you been living here?" she asked. She knew that the more she spoke, the more human she would seem, and the more difficult it would be for him to kill her.

"Only the past few days," he grumbled, but did not seem interested in continuing that line of talk. Cassie could guess that he had been hiding there to make sure no one ever came by, to make sure it was a safe place to bring her. He untied her wrists and handed her a ladle of poorly made soup. It was nothing but a dirty-smelling broth with some sunken chunks of meat. But she thanked him and took the bowl. She waited for him to take his first bite before she took hers. Good. It was not poison.

She began to eat, though she was not hungry. She watched him blow on his spoon and swallow his chunks of meat with only the slightest of chews. He seemed accustomed to his own bad cooking. Yet, he had a wife? "Who is your wife?" she asked. "This woman I know so well."

He blew hard into his spoon, then answered, "I can't tell you."

Cassie had anticipated that answer, but had asked the question in hopes of getting him to speak. The silence was killing her. She watched him carefully for any more clues about his character. He had not once glanced at her breasts. That was very good. He was not interested in her as a woman. "Who hired you to kill me?" she asked, knowing well that no assassin would answer such a question. She was asking only to get him talking again.

But he shocked her by replying in a most candid manner. "Some fellow named Egbert Madison. Never met him before."

Cassie nearly spit out her soup. A wry smile crossed her lips, and her eyes grew evil. She could not believe what an idiot this man was for telling her the name of his employer. And she could not believe the name he had just given her. "What?" she asked, trying not to let out a little laugh of cynical disbelief.

"I know—it's a terrible name, isn't it?" He chuckled a little as he drank down the last of his supper.

"It's my uncle," she told him flatly. "What's going on? Why did he want me dead?" But something was already starting to make sense to her. Her eyes squinted thoughtfully as images of her life began to come together into one sensible picture. Uncle Egbert. Why would he do it? And more importantly, why wasn't this news more surprising?

"I don't know," said the clumsy assassin, "he didn't tell me why. He only told me what he was offering for the job. More than I've seen in a lifetime of wages. Digging roads," he scowled, with a weary shake of the head, "that's my usual lot in life." A dark chuckle followed. "Before the bloody convicts took all my work."

Cassie was in no mood to argue, though with a jerk of the knee, she wanted to point out that the convicts had never wanted his work—they were just slaves. But she was not about to allow a change of topic. "When did he hire you?" she asked, trying not to sound frantic.

"About six months ago," he shrugged.

That was right after her sentencing. The moment he'd learned that she would not be killed for her alleged crime, he had hired someone to make sure that she was. Why? Lord, she had never liked that man. He had lived in luxury while her family had struggled, never offering to share more than a few crumbs of his lavish inheritance. She knew that there was animosity between the two brothers; she knew that Egbert looked down on her father for being a philanderer and for having married an Irish woman—the same things which had kept him out of his mother's will. But still, when Cassie was running her household, she had hoped that Egbert would share some of his fortune, if not for the sake of his fallen brother, then for the sake of the children, who had done no wrong. Egbert had never been willing to help. And when he would toss a morsel of assistance their way, he would expect to be thanked as profusely as if he had sacrificed his home and carriage for them. There was something about the way he hoarded that wealth which had never sat right with Cassie. She knew this had something to do with the money. Somehow, this was about money.

"Did he give you any other instructions?" she asked him. "Did he say anything besides just to kill me."

"Yes," said the older man with some thoughtfulness, "he said to make it look like an accident. But I told him I'm no assassin. I told him I don't know how to make things look like accidents or how to cover my tracks or anything. I told him that for the money he's paying me, I'll cut a woman's throat. But if he wants someone to do it more cleverly than that, he'd better hire someone who knows what he's doing. I'm just a working man."

"Then why didn't he hire someone else?"

"Don't know," he shrugged. "He was asking everyone who was at port that day. I was unloading a ship in London because I'd run out of work back here. Agreed to take a journey, and help out on the ship. I'll never do that again—it was horrible work. But when I was unloading at port, he started asking everyone about the job. They were all laughing at him—even the dirtiest men on board were saying they'd never take a job from someone stupid enough to ask right out in the open. I was the only one who said I don't care. So I got the job."

"Then why aren't I dead?"

He answered this one rather cautiously. "Well," he began, almost embarrassedly, "I uh . . ." He squeezed his lips together, making something of a sympathetic frown. "I don't really want to kill someone."

Cassie swallowed.

"I have a better idea," he continued. "I don't want to get your hopes up, because I will kill you if I have to," he insisted, as though convincing himself rather than her. "But uh . . . but I thought there might be another way. I thought . . ."

Cassie was so scared, she could not urge him on through the pause. For as bumbling and pathetic a crook as he was, her life depended on him, and her chances of breathing for another day seemed to flutter up and down with each of his words.

"I thought there might be someone who would pay me even more than what Madison paid me," he explained, almost kindly, "someone who wants you alive even more than he wants you dead."

Cassie's expression was frozen, her eyes round.

"Malcolm Rutherford," he said. "I think he might pay something to get you home alive. Maybe he would pay a lot."

"I'm not sure he has that much," she said breathlessly. "Are you sure he has that kind of money?"

"Yes, I think so. It'll be close," he shrugged, "but I think he has it if he digs deep."

"How do you know he will pay?"

"I don't know for sure, but I'm going to try."

And Cassie had an amazing feeling about that. A feeling that felt like honey melting over her bones. Of course Malcolm would pay. No matter what his feeling for Priscilla, no matter what angry words had passed between them, he would pay. She had never trusted anyone so much in her life. "Faith is your wife," said Cassie stonily, "isn't she?"

Her captor looked at her as though she possessed some sort of magic. "What? Who told you?"

Cassie shook her head slowly, patronizingly. "How else would you know how much money Malcolm has, or that he loves me enough to sacrifice everything for me?"

The assassin flushed. He knew he was a very, very bad assassin.

"Does Faith know?" asked Cassie, with merciless intent. "Does she know what you've been hired to do?"

He nodded.

Cassie lowered her gaze. She thought of Sheena, who didn't trust anyone. Maybe Sheena was right. "I see," was all she could say.

"Well, I'd better tie your arms again," he said. "I can't have you running off." He said it as though it were a line he'd heard from another, more experienced assassin. Cassie did not flinch or resist as he retied her wrists behind her back. Her eyes were distantly hateful, her breathing slow. She thought she would rather die than have learned that both her uncle and Faith had betrayed her. She thought she would rather die than stay days in this foul-smelling shack. And she thought she would rather die than ask for Malcolm's help once more, knowing as she did that he, too, had betrayed her. Memories of Priscilla's lustful violet eyes tormented her throughout the sleepless night, during which she suffered an itch she was unable to scratch.

Forty

The night Cassie was taken, Malcolm had parked his carriage and jogged in and out of the buildings of Sydney. In each brothel, he turned down the offers of prostitutes with a "No, thank you, love" and darted his eyes frantically about. Where could she be? The truth was that she could be anywhere, and that was more frightening a thought than he could bear. If she were not on the open road, and she were not in a building, then she had to be in the wilderness. And there was just no way to find her in all of that maddening outdoors. He simply could not give up, when Cassie's safety could be at stake. The thought of just leaving her out there was unthinkable. And yet, what else could he do? What good was it to wander day and night, without any sense of which direction to head? No, his best bet was to go home and hope that she found him there. But in the morning, he had awakened with a jolt, for there had still been no sign of her. And he had never felt so utterly helpless in his life.

Faith had been less reliable of late. She had always been such a punctual and hard-working employee, but recently, Malcolm had not been able to predict her arrivals and departures. It seemed she was badly preoccupied, and Malcolm was too grateful for her years of good service to say anything. He would let her have a period of distraction. Goodness knows, he was suffering from a similar condition himself. "Hello, Faith," he greeted her, holding a cup of tea that he'd been forced to brew himself, because she was very late.

There were bags under her eyes and a gray hue to her usually rosy face. "Good morning, Doctor." She did not take notice of his frantic pacing, and Malcolm found that odd. He usually couldn't suffer so much as a bad mood without her trying to counsel him. But on that day, she walked sullenly past him to the kitchen without saying another word.

Malcolm returned to his pacing in the hallway. He wasn't going to work. There was no way he could perform surgery in his frame of mind. It would be better for the patients to be assigned a different doctor. Given the selection of doctors, he never thought he'd be thinking such a thing, but in this case, it was true. He was unfit to work. And what's more, he just didn't know what to do about it. Where could he go? Where could he look? He had already searched every corner of the town. He had already skimmed the edge of the wilderness. And then the thing which would help him least occurred. There was a knock on the door.

For a moment, Malcolm imagined that Faith was going to answer it. But a minute passed, and another knock followed. So he slouched over to the door, and flung it open. It was Priscilla, wearing a black cape and looking as fetching as she did wicked, her violet eyes sparkling beneath the hood. "Oh, God," Malcolm groaned, "what is it?"

"Is that any way to greet a guest?" she asked, pushing her way past him and hanging up her cape in the hallway. Malcolm was relieved that at least, her beige dress was modest.

"What do you want?" he asked, his navy eyes fuming with resentment.

"I've come to see Cassie."

"Cassie is gone."

Priscilla looked aghast, her eyes widening and her lips tightening. "What?"

"You heard me. She's gone. And I might go so far as to say it's your fault," he added, moving close enough to make her uncomfortable. He was intentionally towering over her, trying to make her feel small. His eyes were squinting scornfully and his chiseled jaw was twitching.

"Well, where did she go?" she stammered, finding herself retreating just a little toward the wall, but not all the way.

"That's a good question," he drawled spitefully. "Where *did* she go? I don't know, Priscilla. Where would you go if your man was being unfaithful?"

"Unfaithful?" she smirked. "Malcolm, it isn't as though you were married. You don't mean to tell me that she believed you would always be true."

"Cassie believed it," he said confidently, turning his back on the woman he was sure meant nothing to him.

"Why?"

"Because it would never occur to her to think otherwise," he reflected, gazing out the front window through myriad white crisscrosses. "She never asked me to be faithful, she never asked about our future, but she expected," he said with certainty, "she expected that for the time being, I would keep our promise. She pretends to be practical, but she's not. She is a romantic. Love is the one thing she conducts with innocence."

"Then she picked the wrong man," snickered Priscilla, sauntering toward his turned back. "You're quite a lover, Malcolm. But the one thing you are not, is innocent. Especially when it comes to making love."

Malcolm could not argue, and yet, he did not quite agree. He was devilish when it came to making love. But was he devilish about love itself? Or did he, like Cassie, long for someone he could trust with complete innocence. He wasn't so sure. "I suppose you're right," he admitted uncertainly, "but it doesn't matter now. I can't find her."

"Did you check the inn?"

He cast her an irritable glance. "Don't you suppose I checked everywhere?"

Priscilla supposed he did. "Perhaps she's run off into the wilderness then."

"Probably," he replied with dry, uncomfortable lips.

"Well, we must find her."

His expression darkened even further. "Which way do you suppose we search, Priscilla? I've been in that wilderness once before, as you recall." Memories of his failed escape from the barracks no longer tortured him, but they did make him angry. "I was barely alive when they recaptured me. Which direction shall we head?"

"Well, you and I must stay here, and continue to comb the town," she agreed. "It's most likely that she'll give up and turn back. We must be here to get her back to the house and hide her if she shows her face anywhere. But we'll send Miles to search the wilderness."

"Why is that?" he half-smiled. "Because we don't care whether Miles survives?"

"That's about the size of it," she shrugged.

Malcolm couldn't help laughing, despite his grief. "Well, you'll have to be the one to send him. I'm not suggesting that a man run off to his death."

"Fine." But she was not ready to leave, and Malcolm could see that. She was walking slowly toward him, the way she did when she wanted to play. And Malcolm took a deep breath, with eyes closed, expecting to feel her arms wrapped around his waist at any moment, and her breasts pressed against his back.

"Leave me alone, Priscilla," was all he could say when

it happened. But his voice was low, and his will was weakened by despair.

"Malcolm," she said gently in his ear, "when this is all over, I want us to be friends again."

He was still looking at the window, flitting his eyes left and right in hopes of seeing Cassie. He tried to pretend there was no one pressing against his back. "I didn't know we had ever been friends," he said softly and mercilessly. "I thought we had been bed partners."

"Do you enjoy tormenting me, Malcolm?"

He felt himself stiffen. "Yes," he replied, in complete candor.

"I enjoy it, too," she said, and he felt her cool tongue on his ear. "That's why we need each other." Her tongue began to move in circles. "Torment me, Malcolm," she said, lifting his strong hands to her breasts. "You don't want love. You want darkness. Let's go play in the darkness, Malcolm."

"Behave yourself," he warned, removing his hands from her breasts.

"Or you'll give me a spanking?" she asked seductively.

Malcolm couldn't help smiling at her. "Stop arousing me," he ordered. "I told you. I'm set on Cassie."

"Cassie's no fun," she promised him, trying to tickle his belly through his shirt. "Cassie wants you to take care of her. She wants you to be faithful and good. I'm the one who wants you wicked, Malcolm. I'm the one sees you as you are—strong and brilliant and completely unholy. Cassie thinks you're a savior. I know that you're the devil."

He was glancing around for his tobacco. He couldn't think of anything else that would calm him down and get him out of this fix. When he couldn't see where it was, and knew that Faith, in her state of mind, would not remember, he decided to settle for a drink. "Get me a drink," he told Priscilla.

She studied his expression. He wouldn't normally order her about unless he was aroused, and wanting to play a game of domination. She saw that dark light in his eyes that made him look so deliciously handsome. This was the Malcolm she loved. It was the fine and decent man who was so shockingly unafraid of sin. "Shall I serve your drink in a glass?" she asked. "Or shall I drip it somewhere more enticing?"

"Just get me a drink," he told her, "and make sure there's nothing under your dress when you get back." He nearly winced at himself as he spoke, but that did not keep his heart from pounding, or his manhood from hardening. Priscilla had been right. This was what he was, and Cassie could never understand that. Cassie deserved better. She deserved a love full of light, not a mind full of darkness. It was better that she had left. Curse the stars if she were hurt or injured or worse, but bless them if she had found freedom from the likes of him.

A smile of triumph crossed Priscilla's lips even as she lifted her gown to show him there was nothing underneath. Malcolm nodded approvingly, and, finishing his Scotch in one swig, slammed the glass on a table and pulled her roughly into his arms. So roughly that she could stand of her own accord, but was forced to hold the exact position in which he placed her, back bent and feet barely touching the ground. Her lips, too, were at his mercy, for he left her no freedom to reciprocate or invite actions of her own. But Priscilla was the one who had beaten him, and they both knew it.

Forty-one

Malcolm stopped sleeping. He took up coffee, and spent his nights staring out the window of his study. In the daytime, he searched, but he had no hope. It no longer seemed real that he might turn a corner and see Cassie's red hair. Searching for her was only a ritual, something he did to ward off the pain. He didn't believe he would ever see her fresh, youthful face again. He didn't believe he would ever smell her sweetness or watch her luscious mouth move in speech. He believed she was gone, or had never existed. What he would have done to get back a few precious moments with her! If he had known that she would soon be gone, he would have treasured her more; he would have told her things he'd never told her; he would have taken more time from work, just to show her that special valley to the northwest where the flowers bloomed all year long. And he would have made love to her every day, no matter what problems lay ahead.

But as it was, he had stolen only a few kisses, and enjoyed her womanly flesh only a few wicked times. He had held himself back from her, as though the less she knew of him, the stronger her love would be. He had loved with hesitation, and he had faltered when it came to Priscilla. It was true that Priscilla had thrown herself at him on that regrettable night. But it was also true that he had allowed himself to be alone with her. He had never fully forsaken her. He had always wondered whether she might be better for him than Cassie was. And it was because Priscilla was crafty and perceptive that she sensed his doubts, and thus, had not given up her pursuit. It was Malcolm's own weakness which had driven Cassie away.

Priscilla would still not sleep at his house. He had urged her to make herself comfortable, and to stay the night. He remembered with pain how Cassie had yearned not to be left alone after he'd taken her the first time. He never wanted to do that to anyone again. So he had kissed Priscilla's forehead, pulled her into an embrace, and said, "Stay. Stay with me tonight." But Priscilla was not Cassie. Miles had gone in search of their ward, and Priscilla was anxious to get home and enjoy the silence. There was nothing she loved so much as sleeping alone in her own little cottage. She would not waste any of these precious nights in Malcolm's bed.

In the daytime, she was always around, though. With Malcolm taking a "holiday" from work, Priscilla was able to enjoy his company all the day through. Sometimes they searched Sydney for Cassie, a task Priscilla was finding rather useless and mildly insulting. The look on Malcolm's face as he searched told her that Priscilla herself was still not number one. But she joined in the daily ritual nonetheless, and enjoyed taking delightful breaks from it in his study. Strangely, Faith did not complain or even remark on Priscilla's increased presence. It was odd, given how much she disliked her for all the times she'd broken the poor doctor's heart. But Faith had grown so sullen and silent of late, that even her acceptance of Priscilla did not startle Malcolm.

The slender beauty was sitting on Malcolm's lap when the message arrived. "Who's at the door?" she asked, pulling away from a kiss.

"Who cares?" said Malcolm, catching her skull in the palm of his hand, and pressing her back to his lips.

"Doesn't Faith answer the door anymore?" she asked haughtily.

"Why should you care? You're not paying her." He tried to kiss her again.

Laughingly, she pushed him away. "Answer the door, Malcolm."

He scowled. He did not like being interrupted when he was aroused. But as the knocking increased, he grudgingly lifted Priscilla from his lap and rose to answer the call. "What is it?" he asked with annoyance, flinging open the white door. But there was nobody there. On the ground before him was a scroll, tied with a ribbon. He chuckled sardonically. Whatever the visitor had to say, he was certainly cowardly about it. Malcolm picked up the scroll and began rolling the ribbon off with impatient hands.

"What is it?" asked Priscilla, creeping up behind him to touch his waist.

Malcolm's expression was unreadable as he stared at the sloppy writing in his hand. He did not reply.

"Malcolm?" she asked more urgently. "What is it?"

At last, he broke from his thoughts and folded the message into his vest. "Cassie's alive," he said, then spun on his heel.

Priscilla followed frantically behind. "Where are you going? Malcolm, what does it say?"

He went into his study and opened a desk drawer. "It says he wants money. Some sod has Cassie, and he thinks I'm going to give up my life's earning to get her back."

"Well . . . well, are you?" she asked, wide-eyed.

His eyes were positively murderous as he slipped something shiny into his pocket. "No way in hell."

Forty-two

Malcolm had not felt like an animal since that wild night in the barracks when he had shed the blood of the man who had cost him his escape and won him a flogging. Priscilla had heard of that night, and had always believed that Malcolm was capable of losing his reason. But she had never before seen such murder in his eyes. It looked as though the liquid in his eyes were boiling, His slouching walk remained eerily calm and steady. He tried to stop her from following him, but he did not try hard. "Stay here," he ordered, swinging himself onto an unsaddled mare.

"I will not," she replied stubbornly.

If she had been Cassie, he would have remained firm. But because she was Priscilla, and he did not think her very sensitive, he merely shrugged. "Suit yourself." And he neither resisted nor assisted as she hoisted herself behind him. He urged the mare forward with an inconsiderate jolt that nearly sent Priscilla flying from the rear, but she held fast.

Malcolm knew well the grove where he was supposed to meet with the kidnapper. It was a place he had often taken a book during his early days of freedom, when he could not bear to be indoors, could not bear to be reminded of how it felt to be contained. Back then, his house was still being built, and he had only just started at the hospital. Rather than return home to all of the hammering and sawing, he would merely grab a book and a packed supper that Faith would shove at him, and run to the grove. How strange that he would be summoned to that very spot to meet Cassie's captor. It could not be a coincidence, he knew. As the horse galloped forward, Malcolm's blue eyes were narrow with thought. The captor knew Faith. He had to. How else would he have known that Malcolm knew where this grove was?

He could see a short, squat form standing nervously in the distance, all wrapped in black. It looked ridiculous. Malcolm already knew this was a clumsy kidnapper. His invitation to meet had been far too dangerous, and now the moron had the gall to arrive alone? It would have been pitiful, if it had not been so vile. This miserable creature had kidnapped Cassie. And God only knew what he had done to her. Malcolm's jaw was clenched as he pulled his horse to a halt. He leaped from his mare, trusting Priscilla to follow behind him. He did not offer to help. His heart was full of Cassie.

"That's close enough," called an aging voice behind the black cloak. Only the kidnapper's eyes could be seen, and Malcolm could not place them.

Malcolm kept walking. He swaggered toward the loathsome captor as though he had not spoken.

"I said that's close enough!" called the man.

The warm wind blew through the sleeves of Malcolm's silken shirt, fanning them out. He did not slow down.

The captor grabbed something he'd been hiding behind a tree. It was a slender, writhing form, also wearing a cape. But in this case, the cape was wrapped only to the neck, and above it blew long, cherry strands of hair. The hair was beaten backward, and a freckled, heart-shaped face was revealed, capped with exotic emerald eyes. Malcolm stopped walking and put his hands in the air. "Don't hurt her," he said. "I won't come any closer." He watched uneasily as the man placed a sharp knife at

Cassie's throat, causing an indent but not a cut. Malcolm's jaw was flexing and relaxing, over and over. He was watching the knife. All he could look at was the rosy skin beneath that sharp point. He was watching for a bubble of blood that would tell him the knife had made its entrance. Thus far, he did not see one.

The sight of Cassie's bitterly proud face, in such stark contrast to her trembling hands, nearly made him soften. If there had ever been any doubt, there was none now. He loved her. He would never find another to be her equal. Could any man find this woman less than heart-achingly desirable? Could any man pass up the opportunity to save her? To soothe away her protests? He didn't think so. She was as rare as the red hair she hated so much. She was as strong as she was weak, and as comforting as she was exciting. Malcolm all but forgot that Priscilla was standing behind him, so royal in all of her fashionable beauty, and so plain of heart.

"Do you have the money?" asked Webber, as Malcolm tried not to show how much he cared for the lady in Webber's clutch. His skin was twitching over his grinding jaw.

"The amount you requested is more than the cost of my house," Malcolm replied calmly, his gaze still on Cassie. "I'd have to liquidate everything to bring you that amount. There wasn't time."

Webber had not thought of that, of course. He was so new at this criminal business, he rarely thought of anything. "Well, how much did you bring?" he asked impatiently.

Malcolm let his eyes cut sharply to the would-be assassin for just one bitter moment. "I brought enough."

"Well, how much is enough?" Webber whined. "I can't trust you for the rest. You'll never pay me once I let the girl go." As though this had only just occurred to him, he squeezed Cassie more tightly, making her wince at his closeness. "Unless you have most of it, we'll just have to come back another day."

"Why did you take her?" Malcolm called.

Webber was surprised by the change of subject, and it made him pause. "Why? Well, I . . . I was paid to. But . . . but now I want you to pay me more."

"And what makes you think I would?" he shouted into the wind. "What makes you think she's worth so much to me?"

Webber snorted. "Well, you're here, aren't you?"

Malcolm chewed pensively on his inner cheek. "But how did you know?"

Webber shrugged. "Makes no difference, does it? I've got the girl, and unless you bring the money next time, she'll be finished."

Malcolm's eyes hardened and narrowed. If the sight of Cassie had sweetened him, the words of her captor had sent him plunging back into red-hot memories of how it felt to be an animal. He watched coldly as Webber pulled Cassie toward his buggy. "Same time tomorrow!" he called. "If you bring the law, the girl dies. And if you don't have the money this time . . . well," the cloth over his mouth moved as he smiled, "it's your last chance."

Malcolm shook his head with condescension as he slipped his hand in his vest pocket. "Cassie!" he called. "Look over there!" Both the startled Cassie and her captor glanced first at Malcolm's expressionless face, and then in the direction in which he nodded. Just as Cassie turned to look toward the mountains, a bullet landed in her captor's chest. Webber crumpled to the ground in a heap of black cloth. Cassie found herself yelling, "No!" She knelt beside the dying human lump, but Malcolm had already run toward her, and was turning her away.

"Don't look," he told her, forcing her into a hug that would block her view. "Just don't look." Priscilla was already on her knees beside Webber, pulling off his wraps and making sure he was dead.

"Not dead yet," she announced. "Give me the pistol." She held out her hand expectantly.

"Put your hand away," Malcolm snapped. "There's no need to finish him off."

"Oh, my god," said Priscilla, biting her lip. "This is Faith's husband."

Malcolm didn't care. He was holding Cassie, enjoying the feel of her breath against his neck. He thought he might never let go. Her trembling made him tremble. Her strong grip made him squeeze back with breathtaking force. He thought he might crush her, he was so in love. But she did not seem to care. She was trying to crush him, too. "Did you hear me?" asked Priscilla. "I said this is Faith's husband."

"I heard you," he said in a loud whisper, "I heard you." He buried his face in Cassie's red hair. Was she real? He couldn't let go. He could never let go. "Cassie, I have longed for you," he heard himself say. "We'll get away from here—both of us. And I'll never let you go."

Just as Cassie was about to return his sentiments, her pride made her pull away. She looked pointedly at Priscilla, who was still marveling that she had never suspected Faith's involvement. And then she looked coldly at Malcolm. "It looks as though you have a patient, Doctor Rutherford." She nodded toward Webber. "You'd best get to work."

Malcolm wasn't feeling hurried. His decision not to finish Webber off was based solely on his desire to keep Cassie from witnessing a murder. "I love you," he repeated. But there was no reply in her stubborn face. "I just saved your life. Doesn't that count for something?"

Slowly and gravely, she shook her tangled head of hair. "Yes, Malcolm. I am once again in your debt. But I would be lying if I said I were pleased that it is so." She pursed her lips coldly at him. "Please go tend the patient."

Malcolm yanked her arm before she could wander off. "What's the matter with you?" he demanded. "I just said I love you."

"Words," she replied, "just words."

Malcolm turned his head to follow her gaze. When he saw it landing on Priscilla, with her capes and raven hair flapping about in the wind, he bowed his head with frustration. "Cassie, it's not . . ."

"It's not what I think?" she laughed. "Malcolm, it *is* what I think, and you know it."

"Cassie, it's you that I . . ."

"You already have a whore, Malcolm," she said cuttingly. His eyes widened, aghast and maybe just a little impressed. "You don't need me." She kissed him chastely upon the forehead and whispered, "You have been so good to me, Malcolm." There were faint traces of tears in her emerald eyes. "I should thank you a thousand times over. But not by being your concubine."

"My what?" he sneered, "What are you talking about? Cassie, listen to me . . ."

She pulled out of his grip. "I'm turning myself in, Malcolm." She glanced once again at the violet-eyed beauty in the wind. "I've hidden long enough. And I've done it at the expense of my dignity. I have loved you, and I have needed you, and I have relied upon you. But you have always returned to Priscilla. It's time for me to accept your kindness for what it has been—kindness, and nothing more." She fought against the temptation to cry. She looked at his handsome face, the intelligence of his blue eyes, and the strong shoulders she had once held in a wild attempt to find something greater than survival, something lovely that would last.

She would miss him so much. She would miss his warmth and his strange ways. But most of all, she would miss the hope. The hope that something lasting might happen between them that would sweep her away from the terror that her life had become. It had been a long time since she'd lived without that hope, and she didn't know how she would endure. But she knew that she could not accept charitable love. No more. Malcolm was not a saint—he was simply kind. He had a weakness for wanton women, and she really was not one. She was ordinary. And Priscilla was a goddess. So with an aching heart she knew what she had to tell him. "Good-bye."

Malcolm smiled darkly—he couldn't grasp the idea that she would think he'd let her walk away. "You can't turn yourself in," he said plainly. "They might hang you. Or, at least, they'll flog you. Come on, we'll talk about this at home."

But Cassie was beyond persuasion. She was already as good as gone. "I'm leaving, Malcolm. And if you try to force me to come with you, I'll escape, and you'll be caught for harboring a fugitive. You cannot hide me if I'm not willing to hide. It can't be done."

"Look, if I have to lock you up, I will."

"And I'll scream, and someone will come see what all the noise is."

"If I have to gag you . . ."

"Let her go, Malcolm." It was Priscilla this time, and for once, there was nothing mischievous or vindictive in her eyes. Both Cassie and Malcolm stared. "Let her go," she repeated, stepping nearer. "She'll go anyway, so why make her hate you before she does?" She looked respectfully at Cassie, as though for the first time; she admired the girl. Cassie nodded appreciatively, then began to walk.

"No!" Malcolm tried to go after her, but was stopped by Priscilla's grasp.

"She doesn't belong to you," she said. "Let her go." And somehow, with unblinking eyes and heavy breath, he paused. It was as though he were paralyzed, trapped in stone, and forced to watch life go on without being able to live it. Cassie was leaving. And he deserved it. He had always known that he deserved to lose her. It was as though he had made sure that this day would come.

Cassie walked across the windy grasses with her head held high and a proud, sad smile upon her lips. It was finally over, and she was finally doing the right thing. In her heart of hearts, she hoped they would hang her.

Forty-three

"Who is that woman?" Sheena was leaning into the well-lit window of Emma Crane, getting soaked by the cold rain, but too curious to care. It seemed that Uncle Egbert was up to the juicy kind of mischief that made standing in the rain worthwhile.

"I don't know," said Samuel, "but if you press your face any deeper into that glass, they're going to think a pig is spying on them."

She whipped her head around. "Did you call me a pig?"

"No," he recoiled regretfully, "I just meant that when you press your nose against a glass, it—"

"I'm not pressing it *that* hard," she spat, "and if you would step a little closer, maybe you could help me look."

"I can see from back here," he said, hands stuffed in his pockets.

"Not very well. Here, come stand where I am. Look."

Samuel squinted into the bedroom, watching his uncle's hands carefully. They were so close to Emma's breasts, he thought surely he was about to bare one of them. If he just stood there long enough, perhaps he would get to see the crest of one for the first time in his life. Emma's were round like perfect spheres, with the tips way up high. He could see that through her chemise. Samuel liked that kind. He also liked the kind that were more oval, and rose far out in front of a woman. But he could also see the beauty in a smaller, more subtle breast which rose like a firm mound, close to the bearer. He wondered at the color of the tip.

"Are you getting a good look?" asked Sheena.

"Pretty good."

"Can you hear what they're saying?"

"No."

"Well, move over, let me try again."

"Not yet," he said, extending an arm to stop her from pushing him out of the way.

"Why not? Are you seeing something crucial? Are you—" She followed his gaze carefully and then rolled her eyes. "Oh, get out of my way, you useless . . ." She gave him a mighty shove, nearly toppling him. "Oh, my goodness," she said before he even had a chance to recover. She was peering through the window, her eyes narrowed slits.

"What is it?" he asked, brushing himself off.

"It's your uncle," she whispered. "She's giving him something."

"Well, what's so odd about that?"

"It had blood on it."

"What? How do you know it's blood?"

"I know blood when I see it."

"You know, it really scares me when you say things like that."

"Hush," she snapped, "I'm trying to hear." She pressed her ear firmly against the glass.

"Are you hearing anything?"

"Not with all of your chatter. Now be quiet. I think I'm getting something."

Though the windows of the modest town house were cracked and rattling, it was hard to hear their low mutters. Uncle Egbert's voice was nothing but a low vibration, but Emma's higher voice was easier to make out. Sheena could not hear every word, but she caught bits. "You're the one who came back," cried the woman, speaking louder as she was becoming aroused. There was another low rumble from Uncle Egbert. "I do, too," protested Emma, "I most certainly do. How can you say that?" There was more muttering from him. "I never told you I love you"—muttering—"No, I did not. You are . . . Stop interrupting me. I told you I've had it with you and your brother and all of your kind, and—" She shook her head emphatically as the muttering continued. "No, I didn't. What I said was that I want you to have it because I'm finished. I just don't care anymore."—muttering— "You're pathetic! You're just pathetic!"

In response to her loud tone, Egbert finally raised his own deep voice. *"I'm* pathetic?" he roared, *"Me?* I forgave you! I'm the bigger person here!"

"Forgave *me?"* she scoffed loudly. "I never asked your forgiveness! You didn't forgive me because you're noble! You forgave me because you're weak, and you wanted to bed me again, and . . ."

"Don't talk to me that way after what you did!"

"After what *I* did?" This time, a cruel smile crossed her lips. "I'm not the one who framed her. I'm not the one who had that beggar killed. All I did was tell one little innocent lie."

"Innocent? Innocent?! Did you think that telling me she'd discovered the will was innocent?"

"Of course not," she spat, "I did it on purpose because I hate you, and I wanted to see you suffer. I never dreamed you'd be so pathetic as to continue to come and see me. I thought you had at least some self-respect."

"I haven't seen you try to expel me from the premises."

"That's because I like the money," she growled, "I let you come for the money. That's all. If it weren't for that, I'd never be seen with a spineless bastard like you."

He slapped her hard but she didn't care. She was used to it. "That's what I hate about your kind," she sneered, after rubbing her cheek for a stunned moment, "there's nothing you won't do when you're backed into a corner. You're spineless!"

"Cute couple," said Samuel.

"Did you hear what they said?" asked Sheena excitedly. "They said they had Cassie framed. I told you! I told you that's what happened. Now, what will could they be talking about?"

Samuel shrugged. "Must be my grandmother's. She's the only one in my family who's been kind enough to pass away."

"Then that's it!" cried Sheena in a loud whisper. "They've tried to hide her real will from you. Emma led your uncle to believe Cassie had discovered it, and so he had a beggar killed and framed her for the murder so she would be sent away."

Samuel scratched his head. He had to admit, that's what it sounded like. "But uh . . . but what do we do?"

The window slid open with a heavy, scratching sound. The two youngsters turned their heads, no longer breathing or blinking. And the sight of Egbert's red face was enough to make their hearts freeze as well. "Couldn't sleep?" he asked them menacingly.

Samuel forced a broad smile. "Why, hello, Uncle! What are *you* doing here?"

He wasn't amused. The look on his face told them that he knew exactly what they had done, and how much they had seen and heard. It also told them they were in a great deal of trouble. "I'll thank you to step inside," he told them, and they knew he had a gun. They couldn't see it, but they just knew it. He spoke as someone who was armed. "This is all your fault," Sheena mumbled, hiking herself up through the windowsill, "if you hadn't been so noisy . . ."

Samuel grudgingly assisted her, but retorted, "I think I did a great deal less chattering than you."

"Yes, but your voice is louder."

"Will you two stop arguing?" asked Egbert, reaching out his hand to help Samuel climb through. "We've some much more pressing matters to discuss."

"What is there to discuss?" asked Sheena hotly. Her fists were on both hips, and she had no fear. "You framed Cassie! We heard everything!"

"Oh, that's just great," moaned Samuel, dusting himself off from the climb. "Anytime you're captured by a murderer, it's a good idea to start off by telling him you saw and heard everything. That's sure to make him let you go, genius."

"He already knows that we know!" she argued. "I'm not going to play games. This horrible man framed the only friend I've got!" Her eyes were positively fiery. "And I won't pretend I don't hate him."

Egbert smiled condescendingly. "Such a bundle of personality, she is." He touched her chin with false affection, as though pinching the cheek of a child. "I admit," he told Emma, "I hesitate to kill my nephew. If I have learned anything, it's that one is never finished hiding from a murder. I hate to put myself through it again."

"I'm touched," said Samuel.

"Be quiet, you tiresome boy." Emma took Egbert's hand as though they were friends, and had not been quarreling at all. It seemed she had become distracted by a more interesting enemy. "What shall we do with them?"

Egbert shook his head at his nephew and sighed. "Whatever made you follow me tonight? If only you had not done this—"

"He's not afraid of you!" spat Sheena.

"Yes, I am," said Samuel weakly. "I really am, Uncle. I promise."

"I hate to kill you," Egbert said.

"He doesn't care if you kill him!" cried Sheena. "He

would rather die than sit idly by and let you get away with murder!"

"Sheena . . . do you mind?" pleaded Samuel.

"Tell me something," said Egbert. "What were you two planning to do after you finished spying?"

"We were going to turn you in!" said Sheena. "And we still are!"

Egbert chuckled. "Oh, really? Such a spirited young lady," he smiled at her. "Not too bright, though."

She spat at his feet.

"Uncle," Samuel pleaded, "listen to me. We really didn't hear that much. We don't have any way to incriminate you. Really, if you let us go, we won't tell anyone anything. And even if we did, they wouldn't believe us. We have no proof. So please . . . please, just let us go. You said yourself, you didn't want another murder on your hands."

All of that appealed to Egbert's sense of reason. He had just begun to deliberate, when Sheena cried out, "Yes, we do have evidence! That shirt!" she cried, pointing to the bloodstained cloth Emma had given him early in their encounter. "It must be the real bloodstain—not the false one with which you framed Cassie for the trial! You must have taken it from the killer so there'd be no conflicting evidence. She must have promised you she'd burn it, and then kept it to hold over you."

Egbert sighed at his nephew. "You know, you would have been a lot better off without her."

"Don't I know it."

Egbert sighed at the shirt. "It really is too bad that I'm going to have to do this," he said, revealing the pistol he'd held in his pocket.

"Uncle," cried Samuel frantically, "you can burn the shirt now. Then there will be no evidence, and nothing for us to tell anyone—nothing that they would believe."

"That's not true!" said Sheena. "I'll bet there's lots more evidence that they've tried to hide! There's got to be a murder weapon, a killer who'd be willing to talk . . ."

"Sheena!" cried Samuel.

"I'm afraid the girl is right," said Egbert, with a twinkle of regret in his eyes. "I simply can't have anyone pursuing this. Just having you out there searching for clues is too much of a risk. She's quite right. There is evidence to be found if someone is determined enough. I'm sorry."

He nearly pulled the trigger, but then hesitated. And before he could regain his courage, he was knocked to the ground. As the pistol misfired into the ceiling, Egbert was flattened by Emma. "Hurry!" she cried to the young ones, "Take the shirt. There's more, too. I'll show you."

Sheena did not hesitate. She grabbed what she could while Egbert still had the wind knocked out of him and could not throw off Emma's full weight on his back. But Samuel squinted his puzzlement. "Why?" he asked suspiciously, kicking the gun from his uncle's hand, "Why help us?"

"Because," she gasped, red-faced from the effort of holding him down, "it was never your sister I wanted. Never even met her. It was always him. It was always him I wanted to hurt. Now help me tie him down."

Samuel did so, adding a few lighthearted apologies to his fuming uncle. He tore off his vest and rolled it. Tying it around his uncle's wrists, he said, "So sorry. Is this too tight?" He yanked the knot as hard as he could, until it nearly dug into the old man's skin. "That's for Cassie." As his fear wore off, his outrage increased. Samuel was not prone to outrage. He had learned to mask his heartache with a casual coolness. But the more he thought about all the pain Egbert had caused his sister and, really, himself, the more he lost control. "This is for taking our money," he said, kicking him in the side. He bent down and tied his uncle's ankles. "And this," he said, "this is for me." He thought about it for a moment, chewing on his cheek, "Because I never realized it before, but my sister was all I had."

Forty-four

Cassie did not turn herself in. She'd had every intention of doing so, but it had been a spontaneous plan, and like so many spontaneous plans, it had been poorly thought out. She would get Malcolm in trouble if she turned herself in. He had lied, and proclaimed her dead. She was tired of owing him, but she knew that she owed him still. And at the very least, she must not have him arrested for aiding a convict. Relief filled her breast the moment she realized she could not turn herself in. Her steps took a sharp turn, and she found herself wandering toward the hut where she had recently been kept prisoner. She hoped Malcolm would put the clumsy assassin back together. She felt sorry for him and did not want to see him die. A one-way fare back to England with a couple of broken bones would be punishment enough. After all, he had shown her the hut which would now serve as her sanctuary.

Cassie let herself into the crumbling shack, feeling an emptiness in her limbs. She had no real plan. She didn't know how she would get food or where she would go after this. All she knew was that she would no longer be relying on Malcolm. She would live or die by her own wits. And it was about time. She reflected on Malcolm for one last moment and made a mental note. "Never ever," she told herself, "come to depend on the one you love, for nothing is less attractive in his eyes." It was a sad and cynical thought, but she believed it nonetheless. Malcolm could never have loved her so long as she needed him so desperately. It had only been a fantasy, bred of captivity and desperation. People didn't fall in love with those who needed them. They fell in love with those who had something they needed.

Forty-five

Malcolm found Faith standing in his doorway that evening, her cape blowing around her in the darkness, her eyes unblinking. He had not sought her out. He spent the day wandering aimlessly in search of Cassie, his mind too much on love to worry about his anger at Faith. He was returning home at a brisk pace, but when he saw her, he slowed down. It was his way of saying, *You can flee if you like. I'll give you every opportunity to be a coward.* But she waited for him like a soldier, like a faithful friend. When at last he reached his porch, he stopped and said nothing, one leg propped casually on a step. He waited.

"He's dead, isn't he?" It was all she said, her voice hauntingly low.

It wasn't the overture he'd expected, but he gave it the dignity of a reply. "I tried to save him," he told her, "but I had to do what I did. I have no regrets."

Faith's moist eyes turned on him with bite, but her words were not angry, they were repentant. "I didn't know in the beginning," she said. "I swear to you that I did everything I could to dissuade him once I learned."

Malcolm had stopped looking at her halfway through the sentence. "I can't accept that," he said, "I can't listen to that. Faith, I adored her and I . . . I feel that you betrayed me."

Faith's heart implored him. "Doctor, I would never

have betrayed you myself. I never wanted the girl hurt. I couldn't stop my husband."

"Yes, you could."

Her features sank in the face of his cutting interruption. When she was able to look at him again, all she said was, "Money is so precious when you don't have it."

His reply was tender. "I know."

"It wasn't money for jewels and horses, Doctor. It was money for survival."

"But I pay you well."

"Well, for one person, Doctor. Not for two. My husband couldn't find work anywhere on this island, and our cupboards were bare. We were in debt." She chewed her lip through his silence, then added, "I don't expect you to forgive me, but . . ."

"Good."

That stopped her from finishing the sentence. "Doctor, I know that I am an accomplice. What are you going to do with me?"

Moved by her downcast eyes and the shaking of her hands, Malcolm frowned. "What do you *want* me to do?"

She shook her head, unable to answer, unable to tell him that she wanted him to kill her and relieve her of her guilt. Her trembling hands grew worse as memories of her overbearing husband and all of the thankless years she had supported him flashed in her mind. "I . . . I wouldn't blame you if you . . . if you . . ."

"What? Killed you?" he guessed sternly.

She couldn't answer. Her lips began to quiver.

Malcolm kicked the stair, and groaned. "Damn you," he said, "you know you didn't have to come here. Damn you for making me do this. Just . . . just, damn you, Faith."

"I had to, Doctor. I had to face you, had to pay for what I did."

"Oh, *now* you're scrupulous? What remarkable timing you have!"

"Doctor, I . . ."

"No, don't say another word. You're coming with me."

The deed was done, and Malcolm had returned home. It didn't take him long at all to realize that Cassie had not turned herself in. If she had, the authorities would have been knocking on his door within the hour. Not that he would have cared. He was in the mood to be arrested. It had been a long time. A long time of pretending to be a well-adjusted member of society when he really, deeply hated everything about the world and those who dwelled in it. Especially right then. Cassie had left him. Faith had betrayed him. All he had left was . . . oh, dear God. As his eyes rested on her slender beauty, he felt ill. Priscilla was all he had left. "Will you stay the night?" he asked her, still worried that the authorities might come for him. It was for himself that he wanted her to stay, for his own comfort, so that he wouldn't be alone when they arrived.

"You know how I am," she replied lightly, "about sleeping in my own bed. I can't stand not to have kicking room."

His eyelids lowered, and he gently gritted his teeth. He said nothing. There was a long silence; no one knew how to make silence seem quite as loud as Malcolm did. His silences always stung.

Priscilla cleared her throat, just to hear a sound. "I'm still so surprised about Faith," she said brightly, anticipating the exchange of gossip. "It's hard to believe she knew all along, that she never warned us. I know she was desperate for funds, but I never . . ."

"I think she didn't believe it," said Malcolm in a milky voice.

"What?"

"I said she didn't believe it. I think she blocked it out.

When she was here, she imagined that her husband wouldn't really do it, that her persuasion would work, that she would stop him."

"But that's ridiculous," scoffed Priscilla. "If she'd really cared, she would have warned us."

"And seen her husband arrested?" he challenged with a raised brow. "No. She imagined that somehow she could dissuade him. And I think she hoped that somehow they could keep the money."

Priscilla sighed deeply. "Well, I'm just glad you turned her in. The factory will be just the thing for her." She rose from the sofa and began to pour herself a drink, but as the decanter touched the glass with a ding, something stopped her. "Malcolm?" He had a dreamy and distant look in his eyes. "Malcolm?" she repeated. Nothing, not a sound. "Malcolm," she said again, "you did turn her in, didn't you?" Nothing. "Malcolm?"

He rose suddenly to his feet as though in a rage, but then he only opened his desk drawer calmly and retrieved his smoking pipe. "No," he said softly, "no, I didn't."

"What?"

He stuffed it with tobacco.

"Malcolm?" she demanded, grabbing him by the elbow, "Malcolm, I know you feel bad that you weren't able to save her husband, and I know she has been a good servant for many years, but . . ."

"I sent her away," he announced. "Priscilla, listen to me." He turned to her and melted her with his beautiful navy eyes. "I don't ask the law to help me." His voice was smooth and kind, and his expression held no remorse. "The law and I lost our friendship years ago when I was arrested for stealing sheep. I have no love for it, and I ask no favors of it. And besides . . ." he held a flame to his long, elegantly carved pipe, "I thought it was poetic justice."

"How so?" she asked with a lift of a thin brow and a fist upon one hip.

He laughed softly at a private joke, blowing out some smoke in the process. "I have sent a criminal to England," he explained, then waited in silence for her to join in his gentle laughter. Soon, she did, and he went on. "They can call it a present from Australia."

Priscilla was laughing, but still thinking. "And she went willingly?"

"Of course. What choice did she have? I told her it was that or the law. I took her to the docks, made sure she got on the boat, then I gave her enough money to get by while she finds work in London. Though of course," he said, wiping a tear of laughter from his eye, "I warned her she could hardly use me as a reference."

Priscilla laughed again, though this time it was with a wondrous shake of her head. "Malcolm," she said, "you are a kind man."

"No, I'm not," he said stiffly.

"Yes, you are," she said. "You can laugh as you like about the irony of sending a criminal from here to England, and you can boast as you like about your rebelliousness against the law. But I know what you did," she said flatly. "You took mercy on a friend." She paused, watching him swallow hard. "You really are a gentleman."

Malcolm resisted the sentiment with an abrupt turn of his shoulders. "Cassie doesn't think so," he said, holding his back to her. "She would rather go to prison than spend another moment with me."

"She just knows she isn't right for you," said Priscilla, wrapping a slinky arm about his neck. The next words she whispered hotly in his ear. "She knows it was only a girlish fancy she had for you. She could see that your heart was mine."

"I don't love you, Priscilla." His words could not have

been crueler, nor could they have been received by
someone less vulnerable to cruelty.

"You will," she promised him, trying not to let the sudden ache in her heart come to the surface.

"Stay the night," he said. "The authorities may still
come for me."

"They won't come," she said. "Malcolm, if they're not
here by now, then Cassie has changed her mind and run
off."

"I want to search for her," he said, pained by the memory that it was Priscilla's doing that he had not run after
her.

"It is only your protective instincts," she said, "playing
tricks on your mind. You don't really want her, Malcolm." She circled his ear with a narrow finger. "It is
cruel of you not to let her go when you simply don't
want her."

"How do you know what I want?" he asked, his eyes
narrow and misty, his arms crossed.

"You always come back to me, don't you?" Her fingers
moved sensually from his neck to his strong shoulders,
and then along his arms. They rested at his hips, threatening to venture further, willing to arouse him beyond
imagining.

He bowed his head. He hardly cared where her hands
were, for he was feeling quite incapable of arousal. It was
true, what she had said. He was not good enough for
Cassie. Something in him always drove him back to
Priscilla. Because she, at least, was surely not too good
for him. In this, he could have faith. "I hate myself," he
whispered.

And that made Priscilla pull back. She withdrew from
his neck, stepped backward into the light of the study
window, and looked at his turned back. Something was
wrong. She had never, ever heard him say that before—
that he hated himself. Her heart sunk. Did he really hate

himself? Or did he hate himself only when he was with her. Priscilla fetched her cloak. "Where are you going?" he asked, spinning around.

"I uh . . . I have something I must tend to." She did not look him in the eye, but busied herself with the mechanics of putting on a cape.

"No you don't," he chuckled. "You've got nothing to do. Why are you going?"

"I . . . I'll be back in the morning," she said, "I just . . . just leave me be." And with that, she fled.

Forty-six

Sheena and Samuel fancied themselves to be quite the crime-fighting duo. They had outwitted and restrained the evil Uncle Egbert, and now needed only to arrange the formality of having him arrested, and Cassie set free. When they appeared before the magistrate with their new evidence in hand, they were halfway expecting to be granted some sort of medal of honor. After all, had they not solved a mystery that even the barrister and all the king's detectives failed to unravel? They could hardly wait to see the expression on the wigged man's face when he finished examining their discovery. They squeezed each other's hand in irrepressible excitement as the old man looked over their find. But when the magistrate looked up, he hardly seemed prepared to give them a medal. "So she's innocent," he announced. "Is that all you came to tell me?"

Samuel looked shiftily to his left and then his right, trying to absorb the question. But Sheena stepped forward with vigor. "Is that *all?*" she asked. "Of course that's all!"

He smiled condescendingly. "Well, then, I'll thank you for wasting my precious time." He rose from his desk and stood before a rain-soaked window. "I suggest you two refrain from telling my secretary something is an emergency unless it really is so. Next time, I'll have you arrested."

Sheena kicked his desk. "For what?" she demanded. "What would be the charges? Trying to obstruct injustice?"

Samuel slowed her with his hand. "Your Honor," he said, "we don't understand. Does this mean you won't let Cassie go?"

"Who? Oh . . . uh," he glanced down at his file, "Cassandra Madison. I see. Let her go?" he laughed. "For what reason?"

"Innocence?" he suggested.

The magistrate laughed. "Innocence." He forced himself to belt out another floor-shaking guffaw. "Young man, if a technicality like innocence were enough to set a man free, I daresay the streets would be crawling with ne'er-do-wells. Now I'll thank you to be on your way. My wife awaits me in the corridor."

Samuel looked nearly as angry as his companion. "We shall *not* be on our way!" he shouted, loudly enough to impress Sheena. She tossed her thick hair in his direction, casting him a look of support. "We shall know why you won't help my sister! We won't leave here until you explain! We—"

"Lower your voice," warned the magistrate.

"I will not," he said, lowering it. "You will have to have me arrested if you want me gone. I cannot walk out that door not knowing why I was unable to get my sister returned from Australia when the law knows she's innocent. I cannot." His face had broken into a little sweat, and Sheena couldn't help finding it a little handsome. She liked passion in a man. Well . . . if she liked anything in a man, which was uncertain, then it would have been passion.

The magistrate looked impatiently at the grandmother clock on his shelf, then sighed at the crime-fighting duo. "Very well," he relented, "sit down."

"I will not," said Samuel.

"Sit down," the old man warned, with both a scolding

and a promise in his eyes. A promise that there would be a reward for obedience. Samuel sat. The old man paced. Sheena glared at him as though she would never take a seat, but Samuel nearly forced her to do so with a tug at her arm. Still fuming, she relented, falling into a chair with an unladylike thud and a rude cross of her arms. The magistrate remained on his feet, as though it gave him great pleasure to look down upon them. He spoke as one who did not care how his words were received. "How dare you cry to me about the plight of one person," he scolded them in a shaky voice. "Have you any idea what this job is like?"

Sheena scowled. "Judging from your fancy office, I'd say it's a bloody picnic."

"Then you'd be wrong!" he sneered. "Let me tell you what I have to face every day. I have to face the responsibility of keeping an entire country at ease. An entire country! Son," he said, turning his black-eyed gaze upon Samuel, "have you any idea what the law is for? I mean, what it is really for?"

Samuel shrugged. "To keep people safe?"

The magistrate shook his head with violence. "Not to keep them safe, but to make them *think* they are safe," he corrected him. "Do you think we have it within our power to keep all of the criminals off the street? To keep anyone from harming anyone?"

Samuel looked warily at Sheena.

"Yes, now you see," said the old man, "I'm not in the business of delivering justice. I'm in the business of controlling hysteria. Now, I am deeply sorry about your sister. But look at this from a wider angle. A beggar was murdered that night. Not someone anyone cares about, mind you. It was only a beggar. But it frightens people to have murderers about. They want us to do something about it. They pay taxes, they worry for their children, and they want to know that all is well. Right now, that is what they believe. All is well. Why would you want to scare them by telling them we caught the wrong man? Just to help one girl?" He let out a scoffing laugh. "I suppose you think it will make them feel better that we've now caught the real criminal. Well, it won't. It will make them feel that we are prone to error, and we don't want them to have that fear. Do you understand?"

Unfortunately, he did. "But Cassie . . ."

"Look there," he interrupted, "look at all the happy, secure people who believe they are safe and protected. Do you see them? Look how many of them there are. Now, isn't happiness of the many more important than the happiness of one?"

"But you haven't protected them!" Sheena cried. "The killer is still at large!"

"Lots of them, I'm sure," he chuckled. "We'll never catch them all. Undoubtedly, there will be another murder today, and then another tomorrow. Shall we tell the people we've resigned ourselves to that?" he asked, with a twinkle in his eye. "I think not. I think we shall tell them that we are solving the problem, one Cassie Madison at a time. I'm sorry this particular one was an error. Good day."

"When did you lose your passion for this job?" asked Samuel with a curious squint.

Sheena rose to her feet. Pointing a warning finger in the face of the magistrate, she fumed, "Is this the game we're going to play? Well, let me tell you something. You can't beat me at the game of deceit. You like to go the easiest way? Well, let's see what the easiest way is now." She yanked both of her sleeves from her shoulders.

"Young lady," he exclaimed, "what on earth are you doing?"

She thrust herself against him. *"Why?"* she asked dramatically, *"why* can't you accept that it is our baby? It can be a blessing, not a curse, don't you see that?"

The magistrate backed away, but soon found himself against a wall.

"I love you!" she cried.

He tried to shush her, all too aware of his wife's presence in the corridor. But Sheena assaulted his shushing lips with a kiss. "We can be happy, I know we can! Tell me it wasn't just one night!"

"Young lady, will you—"

"Why do you send me away?" she asked, touching her belly. "I know it will be a boy, I know it will! And we can name him . . ." She glanced at his desk. "Charles Jr.!"

"If you think this is going to dissuade me . . ." he began.

But then there was a cry from beyond the door. "Charles!" cried a tender female voice. "Charles, is that you in there?"

"You're not married, are you?" gasped Sheena, clutching her mouth. "Oh, no, tell me it isn't so! Tell me our love was not a farce!"

"Charles?!" came the cry, and then a turn of the handle.

"No!" he shouted. "No, Bella, don't come in! Don't come in! I . . . it's a very private meeting in here. I—"

"Who is that woman I hear? Charles?"

Red-faced and frazzled, he choked out in a whisper, "Very well. Get off of me."

"Very well, what?" she asked.

"Very well, I . . . I'll have them arrested. I'll straighten this out." He tried to push her away, but to no avail. She was clutching his collar in a fist.

"And Cassie?"

"Fine, yes, yes. Just go away. Please, or I'll change my mind."

"I'm not leaving until I see you give the orders."

"Fine, fine, just . . ."

"Charles?" This time the door handle turned in full, and a plump woman emerged. Sheena released her victim just in time. "Charles?" The woman looked questioningly at Sheena. "What is this?"

"I just, I just . . ."

"He was just about to call the detective," said Sheena, causing him to melt in his relief. "Isn't that right?"

He nodded emphatically. "Why, yes. Yes, of course, I—"

"And there is no time like the present?"

He stared blankly at her. When he hesitated, she touched her belly tauntingly. "Yes, yes. Of course. Right away."

Sheena grinned triumphantly at Samuel, who slapped his palms silently together in applause, his eyebrows raised to show how deeply he was impressed. When the magistrate had turned his back, Sheena gave a dainty curtsy, followed by an exaggerated bow to Samuel and a flutter of an imaginary fan.

Samuel and Sheena laughed nearly all the way home. "You were incredible," he told her. "I've never seen anything like it. You should be an actress. Or a demon," he added with a wink.

Sheena laughed brightly. "Well, you were in rare form yourself," she said. "I've never seen you so angry. I would almost have thought you cared . . ." She cast him a goading look.

"I do care," he said, "I really do."

"Well, you don't always seem it," she pouted, crossing her arms. "Sometimes I would swear I love your sister more than you do."

"It isn't so," he said, calmly shaking the reins. "I just . . . I just don't say things like that. My family is very awkward about expressing our love for one another. Mainly, because we don't have much love for one another, but partly because we're reluctant to say it."

"Then you do love Cassie?" she asked.

Samuel nodded solemnly. "Yes," he said, "I really do."

Sheena seemed satisfied with that, and let her arms fall to her side. The rain had stopped, and the sun was threatening to make an appearance from beyond the gray clouds. She found that she was truly happy. She had saved a friend. For once in her life, she had done something good, something for which she could feel proud. It made her feel so warm inside that she decided she'd best think of something dark quickly, lest she become one of those sappy, cheery people she so hated. She thought about prison. When she glanced to her right, she noticed that Samuel also had a strange, thoughtful look on his face. "What are you thinking?" she asked.

"Something horrible," he replied. "I'm trying to clear my palate of all those gruesomely wholesome thoughts I was just having about loving my sister."

Sheena grinned brightly. "You know," she said, with a tilt of her head, "I'm starting to like you. In fact," she added with a squint, "you're really not as terribly ugly as I thought at first glance."

"Well, thank you," he said at last. Coming from her, he supposed this was a grand compliment.

"And aren't you going to return the favor?" she asked, lifting her head up high.

Samuel frowned. "I have the suspicion that if I gave you a compliment like that one, I'd soon find a fist in my gut."

"You would not."

Still, Samuel thought it best for his health that he offer something a little more flattering. "Very well, then," he said, "I . . ." He swallowed awkwardly, for he had never spoken words of love to a woman before. "I uh . . . I think you are the most beautiful woman I have ever met." He kept his eyes on the road.

Sheena studied him with scrutiny. "That sounds like

hogwash to me," she announced after a pause. "You went too far. If you had said I am pretty, I would have believed you. If you had said I am beautiful, I could have accepted it. But to say I am the most beautiful woman you have ever met . . ."

"You forget how little I get out," he interrupted. "I've only met known about a dozen women who aren't related to me, and six of them were old."

She stopped talking and glared. Then she saw a corner of his mouth lift, and realized it was a joke, and a funny one at that. She burst into laughter, and smiled for minutes on end, gently reaching for his hand without realizing it. They held hands until Samuel pulled back on the reins, a look of horror and astonishment on his face. "What the . . ."

The white estate was in sight, its cobblestone drive crowded with carriages. Music rang out from the parlour piano, and laughter and good cheer broke through the windows. The horses trotted forth without assistance. Samuel was too stunned to steer them, but they knew the way. His mother, stuffed brutally into a silver gown, raced to meet him wearing a big, rosy grin. "They're here!" she cried. "They're here!"

People Samuel had never seen before encircled the carriage. When he was able to speak, he said, "Mother, what . . ."

"It's your wedding party," she exclaimed. "We wanted to show you how happy we are, and how very interested we are in your life. When I got your note, I . . . well, I realized we should have celebrated your betrothal. Look, I've invited all of your friends."

"I don't have any friends."

"Well, I found some for you," she snapped. "Now, come greet them."

Sheena had already been helped down from the carriage by Mr. Madison, who gaily announced the arrival of his daughter-in-law. "Jean," he told everyone, "this is Jean."

"Sheena," she whispered, but her smile was bright.

"Why, yes, of course. Sheena," he said. "My daughter-in-law, Sheena."

Samuel mouthed the words, *I'm sorry,* at her, but she didn't react. She was having far too much fun, and couldn't stop grinning. She had never been to a party before, much less an expensive one. It was a good thing Uncle Egbert's estate would soon be theirs, else Samuel did not know how his parents would reimburse the caterers. "Mother, I . . . There's something I need to tell you."

"Yes? Yes? What is it?"

"I'm not, that is, we're not . . ." He looked to his right, at the snowy-skinned angel with dark tresses, and thought about her sharp, cynical ways. He gulped. "No, Mother," he began again, with a rough shake of the head. "We're not . . . you see, I . . ." This time he caught her eye, and she offered him a soft smile. His heart fluttered. "We're uh . . ."

Sheena grabbed hold of his elbow with a proud glint in her eye. "We're overcome," she announced. "We're simply overcome."

Samuel looked at her dumbfoundedly.

"Come," she winked at him, "let us entertain our guests."

"Sheena . . ."

"Samuel," she interrupted in reply. She stopped walking and grinned at him.

He shook his head in bafflement. Then he reached for her hand. Feeling its warmth, he gazed into her magnificent blue eyes. "Do you really mean . . ."

"Well, naturally, I don't want to do it," she said haughtily and teasingly, "but since they've already thrown the party . . ."

Her smile was so bright and pure that Samuel could

not help but smile back. "You really are a strange woman."

That set off a twinkle in her eye. "Would you have married anything else?" she asked.

He gave her hand a good squeeze and showed her the spark in his own eye. Their smiles were infectious. They had been so busy on their journey that they had failed to notice that they had fallen in love. But at that moment, they knew it. Their mission had brought them together, and neither could imagine parting ways. Samuel leaned forward, and for the first time in his life, kissed a woman. He grasped the back of her head, feeling the thickness of her hair, and somehow, his mouth seemed to know what to do. Their lips locked in warmth that quickly grew hot. They emerged from the kiss and looked at one another as strangers, as something called a husband, and something called a wife. They eloped in the morning.

Forty-seven

"Miles, I have excellent news for you," Priscilla announced bitterly. "Our job is finished, and we can keep our pay. And here's the really exciting part—are you ready? You can get the hell out of my house. You're free to go." She tossed an old shirt at him.

Miles was sitting by the window, soaking in the wintry sunshine, the hottest time of the year. Swigging brandy and spitting on the floor, he was feeling quite comfortable. "Just as soon as I find myself a place to go," he said, throwing the shirt over a chair. "I have to find just the right house to move into."

"Oh, no, you don't," she growled. "You've been living here for months, and I haven't seen you once search for a place to live—or a job, for that matter."

"I'm taking my time," he said groggily. "I have to find a job that pays well but isn't too difficult."

"Take your time," she said. "Just do it somewhere else!"

"I'm not going anywhere," he said in a deep voice with a threatening look. "I've told you I'll move out, and I will. But not right now!"

"Don't take that manly tone of voice with me!" she yelled, tossing her long, straight hair out of her face. "You lost your right to act like a man the minute you started leeching from me! You're nothing but a pathetic bum, and I won't have you in my house any longer!"

That made him so angry that he actually rose from his chair, a feat which required some effort, as he had barely moved in days. He gestured as though to strike her, but she thrust her chin into the air, telling him that she didn't care whether he did or not. That stopped him. "This is my house," she growled. "It might not look like much, but it's mine. The only thing I've ever asked from life is a little privacy, and I'm damn well going to have it!"

He grabbed her roughly by the shoulders. "Now, you listen to me," he began.

But she interrupted him. "You've nothing worth hearing! Get out!" The screech of her last exclamation was so piercing that Miles had to cover his ears. He sneered at her, his gruff, heavily lined face expressive of some unfounded notion that he should have the upper hand, that he had a right to the upper hand. But he saw no sign of relenting in her narrow-eyed face. If he didn't leave, she would keep screaming, and keep throwing things. He knew that. But how could he leave and still maintain his dignity as a man?

"You're not worth it, you whore." He picked up his old shirt, then raised his arm to defend himself against the onslaught of clothes being slung at him.

"Take this with you! And this! And this! And this!" she was yelling, as the bundle in his arms grew larger and larger.

"Damn you, woman," he griped. "I don't know how I put up with you as long as I did!"

"Good! Then you won't have to darken my doorway again!" With one last mighty shove, she expelled him from the premises, slamming the door against his back. Miles turned around and cursed at the little cottage, feeling that somehow he ought to go back in and have the last word. But with the door already shut, it seemed too embarrassing to reopen it. So he wandered away, grumbling, trying to reenact the scenario in his mind so

that somehow in the retelling, he would come away looking more manly.

On the other side of the door, Priscilla took a deep
breath and sighed, pressing her back against the splintered wall. Silence. It was a beautiful sound. She looked at
her fireplace, her chairs, the little door leading to her bedroom, and broke into a grin. Alone at last. It was all hers.
She started jumping around, basking in the knowledge
that no one could see her. She spun around and laughed,
then hopped into the bedroom and back out again. "Privacy!" she shouted as loud as she could, "All alone!" She
screeched and raced about until she was out of breath,
and panting, collapsed like a rag doll in her very own
chair. She would never have another houseguest, no matter how badly she needed the money. She closed her eyes
and thought about making some tea with a splash of
brandy. And not having to offer some to anyone else! She
felt so relaxed and so relieved that it put her in the spirit
to do something kind. She thought about Malcolm,
slaving away at work today. Perhaps he would enjoy a
home-baked dinner? She glanced about at her kitchen.
Yes, that would be a kind surprise for him. She was very
much in the mood to share her elation!

It did not occur to Priscilla until she had actually
stepped into the hospital that she had never before visited Malcolm's place of work during daylight hours. But
when she entered the echoing stone corridor, and
smelled the disease, so thick that she had to place a
handkerchief over her nose and mouth, she knew she
had never seen such a place in broad daylight. There
were actually dead bodies piled in the hallway, some of
them with eyes still open and limbs sprawled in awkward
positions. Yet, the high ceilings and strange, moaning
sounds made the hospital seem like a church. Some-

thing inside Priscilla was moved, and something in her heart lent sincerity to this place of suffering. She straightened her narrow back and proceeded forth as one who felt both proud and humbled by her reverence toward the dying and the deceased. Then she peered at Malcolm through a window at the end of the hall.

She had never seen him so active and alert. The cynical, distant thoughtfulness was gone from his eyes, and in its place was immediate concern for the here and now, and for the human beings whose lives he'd been entrusted to save. He spoke to the nurses with both firmness and respect. "Get me another bandage. I don't care, just get me . . . Ms. Sherbourne, please. Just bring it to me—now." His hands moved steadily across a gaping wound as he spoke. He was sewing! He was sewing together two sides of a person's skin, and without a flinch. His handiwork was steady and perfect, even though he was surrounded by commotion. Already, another patient was screaming from a bed, and a nurse was calling for Malcolm to come immediately. Malcolm looked up with gentle eyes and said, "One moment. Give her some morphine. I'll be there just as soon as I finish this." Then, in reply to insistence that it couldn't wait, he answered gently, "It has to. I have to finish." His hands sped up considerably, but did not grow sloppy. The moment he'd tied the knot, he literally ran to the other patient. "Hold her hands down," he instructed the nurse.

Priscilla was in awe. She had never seen him this way. And she had never really, really looked around to see suffering outside of her own. She waited outside the door for what felt like hours, just watching. People walked by, howling and limping. Some of them begged not to be taken inside. "Don't take me in there!" cried a convict, flanked by two gaolers. "I'm all right! I'm not going to die! Don't take me in there. Nobody comes back out! Let me go!" And as they literally dragged the man, his feet hanging behind, Priscilla felt a tear come to her eye.

After a while, she could no longer hear him yelling. She continued to wait, and to listen, and to feel.

At last, Malcolm emerged, scruffing up his own hair, and sighing from exhaustion. He saw her out of the corner of his eye, and said, "Oh, hello, Priscilla. What are you doing here?"

It took some effort for her to straighten up and look at him. It was as though she'd been in a trance. But after a short pause, she handed him a basket and said in a scratchy voice, "I . . . I made us some sandwiches."

"Oh, thank you," he replied casually, but did not take the basket. "I've, uh, I've got to wash my hands." He held up his bloodstained arms and smiled. He turned around to leave, but Priscilla called out to him.

"Wait! Malcolm!"

He faced her once more, this time with a raised eyebrow. "Yes?"

Priscilla forced a smile. It wasn't her usual smile—it held no mystery or mischief. It was her most sincere attempt at a smile of warmth. "I . . . I watched you in there. I . . . I was impressed."

Malcolm did not respect her enough to treasure her compliment. But he nodded gracefully and said, "Thanks. I'll be right back." And he departed with a little confused shake of his head. Priscilla waited breathlessly for his return.

"Malcolm!" she cried the moment he returned. "Malcolm, I . . . I wanted to ask you something."

He thought she was behaving rather strangely, but decided he didn't care, and simply replied, "Yes?" as he rolled up his sleeves and reached inside the dinner basket.

Priscilla looked around at the dead bodies. "We're not going to eat here, are we?"

Malcolm nearly spit out his first bite of sandwich with a laugh. "Sorry," he said, offering his elbow, "I'm afraid I'm rather used to the gore. I forget that some people can't eat in all of the stench. Come on, there's a lovely bench outside."

Priscilla took his elbow, feeling that she was on the arm of the most valiant man on earth. She tried to catch the eye of each passing nurse, to see whether she might see a glint of jealousy. There was definitely a little bit of it. Clearly, the nurses were impressed by her handsome escort, the best doctor in the hospital. "Have you ever bedded a nurse?" she asked.

He gave her a strange look. "Is that what you wanted to ask me?" He couldn't help developing a look of annoyed puzzlement. "Umm, no. No, I've never bedded a nurse."

"Why?" she asked, as one who really didn't value fidelity, and wasn't truly concerned with the details of his romantic history except where it satisfied her curiosity.

"Because it would hardly be fair to ask a young woman to work here if she thought she was also a candidate for courtship, now would it?"

"Oh, Malcolm, I'm sure some of them wouldn't mind."

"And some of them would," he replied. "I don't know which is which, so I think it's best to assume they've all come here just to work as I have." He settled her onto a lovely stone bench beneath a willow tree and handed her a sandwich. "Is that all you wanted to ask?"

"No," she said quietly, picking at the bread, "I . . . I wondered how someone might come to work in a place like this." She kept her face down, waiting for his reply. Malcolm noticed that and thought it was odd.

"Well," he laughed, "you might go to prison and get assigned to the task."

"I'm serious, Malcolm," she said with some irritability, "what if I wanted to work here?"

Malcolm couldn't believe it. The thought of Priscilla wanting to help people was frightening enough, but to think of her in the operating room, picking things up with the tips of her fingers so as not to get her hands dirty, was more than he could bear. "I'd say you'll change your mind when you sober up," he chuckled darkly. Then he took a bite of sandwich.

Priscilla fumed as she rose to her feet. "What did you say?"

He squinted at her as though she'd gone mad. "You heard me. You'd make a terrible nurse. Almost as bad as you are a cook." He looked at his sandwich unimpressedly.

Priscilla slapped his face, to which Malcolm only blinked in reply. It was a habit of some ladies which he did not like, but he didn't feel it was cause for retribution. So he stuck his tongue in his injured cheek and just gazed at her patiently. "Malcolm, you are the most despicable, heartless . . ."

He raised an eyebrow. "Are you really this angry or are you just misbehaving so I'll think of some amorous punishment to inflict upon you when we get home?"

Priscilla stormed away, and it was not until then that Malcolm realized he'd actually hurt her. He stood up and followed. "Priscilla, wait."

"What for?" she called over her shoulder. "I'll see you tonight. I'll see you in your bed. That's all you want from me, isn't it?" And she stomped away, leaving him with a basket and a pile of barely edible sandwiches. Malcolm dropped his head in his hands.

Forty-eight

Malcolm knew where Cassie was. He'd known for days. He didn't want her to think he was following her or trying to rescue her again, so he swore to himself he would never visit. But he'd had to know she was alive, and so he had hired a scout to search high and low, find her, and let him know that she still breathed. One day a fellow doctor wrapped his arm about Malcolm's shoulder and said, "Dr. Rutherford, the patient you lost some time ago, the one who had been assigned to you? I have just received word from the police—poor dear. I know this will be hard for you to hear, but she has been pardoned. Apparently, she was wrongly convicted."

When he heard this, he did not care that he would likely be tried for aiding her. He did not think even once of himself. He stated simply, "She is not dead. I lied. She is hiding in a cabin west of the Harrisons' lot. I'll have to send someone to deliver this."

His co-worker was dumbfounded. "Malcolm," he said, "You don't mean you—"

"Yes, I do," he replied disinterestedly. "I loved her and so I proclaimed her dead so she could escape. You can summon the law if you like—just make sure she gets this message. Never mind, I'll send someone myself." He hurried off to find a messenger.

His colleague felt frozen. Malcolm Rutherford was a fine man, and the best doctor in all of Sydney. There had been disagreements among the staff, disagreements during which Malcolm always seemed to be standing alone on one side of the fence. Should convicts be treated while free citizens wait? In that sort of thing, Malcolm had always been rather difficult, for all the staff knew that he himself had once been a convict and had irrational sympathies toward them. But no matter how much they argued, no one on the staff thought Malcolm to be anything other than the most valuable and genuinely gallant among them. The doctor had no trouble believing that Malcolm would assist a convict. That was exactly the sort of thing he would do. But he had trouble believing that Malcolm wouldn't trust his colleagues to remain at his side during such a critical moment. They all owed a great deal to him and his expertise. It was time to let him know just how much he meant to them.

Cassie had survived alone in the cabin quite well. The business of surviving had kept her thoughts away from a life that had slipped away from her. She made good use of the old pot that Faith's husband had kept over the hearth, though the heat from keeping a fire burning made the cabin nearly unbearable. The mosquitoes were eating her alive, as the walls were badly cracked and the boards had gaping holes between them. For food, she had been forced to gather plants, mostly guessing which ones were edible. And she was grateful for the small amount of food which had been left behind by the previous tenant, for unfortunately, she had discovered herself incapable of hunting. There was a rifle hanging over the cot, but even after she had talked herself into aiming and firing at something, she realized that aim was something that took practice, and practice was something she'd never had. She knew her days were

numbered. She couldn't survive forever by herself, and
she could never again turn to anyone for help. So she
knew she was only counting time now. She had saved
one shot in the rifle.

She had taken to sleeping very long hours. The
longer she slept, the less she had to eat. And besides,
there was nothing to mark the points in her day, no
reason to be up at any given hour. The constant over-
sleeping had changed her somewhat. It had made her
feet heavier and her freckles darker and her eyes
weaker. She had grown to associate awakeness with the
groggy feeling of shuffling around with her head in
thick turmoil. She wasn't sure anymore that she would
know what to do if she ever saw another human being.
It seemed she had forgotten how to talk, and how to
take interest in another. The very idea of trying to entertain someone seemed tiring. But strangely, when
she heard a knock on the door, her eyes flung wide.
What she'd thought would be a dreaded moment—
the moment she was caught, the moment she would
have to face the outside world—turned out to be an
exciting moment, one in which she was finally awakened from her sluggish dream of an existence.

She did not speak, but only wrapped her blanket
tighter about her chin. She cleared her throat with several soft, guttural noises.

The knocking continued until at last the flimsy door
squeaked open and let in a flood of shocking sunlight.
Cassie had to protect her eyes from its glare. "Are you
Cassandra Madison?" asked the youthful voice of a
nurse-in-training. Cassie could not believe her ears.
The voice was so pleasant and unfearsome that she
forced herself to open her eyes and see its bearer. It
was a golden-haired lady, dressed in a blood-covered
smock. She looked like an angel standing in a tunnel
of sunlight.

"I . . . why do you ask?" Cassie croaked, surprised that her voice came out at all, after so little use.

"I've been told to deliver a message to you," said the nurse with some uncertainty in her voice. It was clear she felt awkward about awakening Cassie, and about the strangeness of the message she'd been sent to deliver.

"Wh-what is it?" croaked Cassie.

The nurse let out a nervous half-laugh. "Well, you might want to sit up for this, love. It's quite a message."

Cassie sat upright, tossing her feet off the edge of the cot, but she still had to squint to look directly at the nurse. "Well?"

"You've a full pardon. A gentleman named Egbert Madison was arrested in your stead, and you are free."

"Is this a joke?"

The nurse handed her the document, signed by the magistrate himself. Cassie read it over and over, thinking that surely this was some sort of a trap. But if they knew where she was, they could have just arrested her. Why would they orchestrate an elaborate scheme? "What . . . what am I supposed to do?" she asked weakly.

"Go home," said the nurse, a smile brightening her face as she began to find joy in being the messenger of this grand news. "Go home and get back to life."

Cassie shook her head slowly. "Does my family know?"

"I don't know."

"Well . . . well, what do I do? Just get on a boat?"

"Just get on a boat," said the nurse brightly. "It's that simple."

"And all of this . . ." She looked around her at the shabby shack, and then through the open door to the wild woods beyond. "All of this is just gone? It never happened?"

The nurse didn't know how to answer that. She just shrugged.

"How did you find me here?" asked Cassie.

"I don't know," she answered. "Dr. Rutherford sent me. I don't know how he knew . . ."

"Doctor Rutherford?" asked Cassie.

"Yes, he . . . he said he didn't want to see you, but that he wanted you to know . . ."

Cassie closed her eyes in a long wince. "I see."

"Well, would you like to come back with me?" asked the nurse. "Your ship won't be leaving for a few days, but you could stay in town now. You're a free woman. The doctor gave me these coins to give you . . ."

"Tell him to keep them," snapped Cassie. "Tell him . . . no, don't tell him anything." She sighed heavily as she reached for her cape. "Just don't tell him anything about me at all. It can be as though we never met." She wrapped her cape around her, even though it was hot. It was the thought of returning to England that made her do it, the thought that she would soon be facing civilized society, where women always covered their shoulders.

She rode in the nurse's carriage, sucking in the salty air as though trying to hold on to it. She knew she must look a fright, her fiery hair all in tangles, her complexion ruined by too much sleep and not enough bathing. She had not once changed her clothes. But she didn't care. In a matter of weeks, she would be returning to the home which had shunned her and ruined her life. And she would be expected to forget all this, to become "normal" again. No one would want to hear her tales of the horrors she had seen, and the suffering she had endured, or even of the wild ocean and the fierce jungle, and especially not of her lost innocence to a man more strange than the country which surrounded him. A man like that could never have existed in England, she thought. Only a place as savage and as fundamentally deranged as this could produce a man like the one Malcolm Rutherford had become. She prayed she would not see him before her ship left port.

* * *

"I have something most urgent to report," said Malcolm, pushing his way through the crowded docks to meet with the captain of the British vessel sent to retrieve Cassie. "It is regarding Cassandra Madison."

"Yes, yes, I heard," said the captain. "You must be the doctor who tended to her. I'm so sorry. It's such a shame, her having come here in error, only to die of infection. Such a waste of a young life."

"She's not dead," said Malcolm without hesitation.

The local head gaoler, who had been standing by the captain apologizing for his wasted journey, scrunched up his face at Malcolm's bizarre words. "What?"

"She's not dead," said Malcolm, "and I have no regret. She—"

"Yes!" cried someone behind him. Malcolm turned around and saw something most peculiar. It was one of his fellow doctors, wandering toward him, flanked by a pair of nurses. As they neared, Malcolm saw that there were more doctors taking up the rear. In fact, it appeared as though the entire hospital was on its way. He hardly knew what to say. But his colleague did. "It was a miracle," he announced to the captain and gaoler, "rose from the dead, she did."

The gaoler started laughing. "What?" But when he saw their stern faces, he stopped. "What are you all saying?"

"We were witness to a miracle," said another doctor. "None of us has ever seen anything like it. She was dead one minute, then the next, she was running about. We were so overcome, it simply slipped our minds to revoke our pronouncement that she was dead."

"We really meant to tell you," added a nurse.

The captain just looked baffled, but the gaoler was starting to catch on. "Now, wait a moment," he warned them. "If I find out that Miss Madison is still alive, I shall have you all—"

"All of us?" asked a doctor skeptically. "Indeed?" He looked pointedly over his shoulders noting the impressive size of the crowd. "Every doctor and nurse in all of Sydney?"

The gaoler fumed, his face growing bright red. "You are all criminals," he said, "I could have you all . . ."

"We know," interrupted a nurse. "We know what you could do. You could deprive this entire town of a hospital, just to get revenge against one girl, who appears to be innocent in the first place."

The ship's captain shook his head to clear it. "What does all this mean?"

"It means," said a doctor, tossing his arm about Malcolm's shoulder, "that you shall have your cargo, after all. Tell us what time she's to be at the docks, and we'll bring her. Tell her family she's alive!"

Many cheered at this as the crowd marched away, leaving the grinning captain and the fuming but relenting gaoler in their wake. Malcolm gave his colleague a friendly squeeze on the shoulder that said more than he could have with words. He tried to meet the eyes of each and every doctor and nurse in the mob, to thank them individually, but they only grinned back at him as though they were having too much fun to accept his thanks. Malcolm had known it for some time, but had never really acknowledged it until now: he had found a home here, and he would never leave. Nothing his friends could have done would have earned his deep gratitude as much as helping him see Cassie safely home. For she was and always would be the love of his life.

Forty-nine

Priscilla watched Cassie from afar as she readied herself for her voyage. Cassie looked very serious, very businesslike, as though she were determined to face her ugly past and menacing future with dignity. She was trying to look cold, her lips pursed and dry, her eyes narrow in the face of all the chatter at the docks. But she could not hide the warmth that radiated from her, whether she liked it or not. It shone from her hot-colored hair and her golden freckles. It shone from her heart. Priscilla continued to watch, a black cloak beating ominously about her in the ocean air, her raven hair whipping about her in long, snakelike strands. Her cool violet eyes indulged in a long, thoughtful assessment of the convict girl who had caused her so much trouble—by first, throwing her into Miles's company for the duration of that well-paying-but-hardly-worth-it mission, and then by stealing Malcolm's heart. Malcolm, the one man Priscilla had ever admired, the one man she had ever considered decent and fine. He wanted Cassie, not her. And for the first time, that made her smile. In fact, it brought warm tears to her eyes, which she had to brush away before taking one last look at the red-haired troublemaker. Priscilla felt happy.

She walked briskly to Malcolm's house. She didn't run, for she was too rational to let emotion drive her into a sweat. But she walked as quickly as she was able.

When she arrived at his porch, her heart was pounding. Her hands were shaking with joy as she unclasped her cloak at her throat. It took a long time for Malcolm to answer the door, as he was still getting used to being without Faith. When he answered, he looked less than thrilled to see Priscilla, something she had grown accustomed to. But he was polite, and he welcomed her in. "I shan't stay long," she told him, letting her cloak slide from her shoulders into his hands. "We don't have much time."

"That's particularly crude," he remarked nonchalantly, hanging up her cloak, "even for you."

"Actually, I'm not talking about that," she replied, unfazed. "In fact, we won't even have time for a kiss." She faced him suddenly, her eyes open and honest. "Not with Cassie's ship leaving so soon."

It took him a moment to say, "What?"

"*You* don't have much time," she said.

Malcolm looked at her as though she were quite mad, but then forced himself to break from his astonishment and appear casual. "Ah," he said, "I see you've suffered amnesia. Let me catch you up, then. Cassie and I don't speak, and haven't for some time now. Would you like me to take a look at your head?"

Priscilla touched his face and looked in his eyes so frankly and so emotionally that it made it impossible for him to remain flip. "Go after her, Malcolm."

Malcolm tried to pull away and tried to laugh. "What?"

Priscilla offered him a weak smile—weak because her lips trembled, but not weak of spirit. "She's good for you, Malcolm," she said in a ghostly manner, "and I'm not."

As truer words had never been spoken, it was hard for Malcolm to reply. His jaw flexed a little, in something of a nervous reaction, but he could think of nothing to say except, "So?"

"So," she answered, "I'm letting you go."

"You never kept me here," he said. "What is this all about? I've stayed with you of my own accord."

"Because you thought you weren't good enough for the woman you really wanted," she said, "and Malcolm, I'm telling you that you are. You're good enough."

Malcolm crossed his arms defensively and studied her as though she had lost her mind.

But Priscilla knew he was still listening, and knew that her words were affecting him. "I saw you in that hospital, Malcolm. You're a hero in there. I see you. I see how you treat everyone, Malcolm, with dignity and respect. Even Cassie, when she was a convict, practically your slave. You were good to her, you were kind. You've been a hero to that girl, and—"

"I'm no hero!" he said louder than he'd meant to. His face was contorted up in anger and pain. He looked like he wanted to hit someone. "You have no idea!" he said desperately, though he was trying to remain gentle. "You have no idea who I am. Where do you even find the gall to stand there and tell me I'm good, when . . ." He combed back his hair with a frantic hand. "What is this even about? If you knew me, Priscilla, if you knew how much I hate. Oh, God, you don't know much I hate."

Priscilla was calm in the face of his wrath, and smiled at him stoically. "But you love Cassie," she said. "You love her, and so I know you can love."

Malcolm turned his head away.

Priscilla approached him and placed a hand on his shoulder. He shook it off and gave her a warning look, as though he very well might strike her. But she wasn't afraid and put the hand right back where it had been. "Malcolm, you only acknowledge one side of you. The other side is kind and decent and loving. We all have two sides, Malcolm. We all have lots of sides. But sometimes we have to choose among them. That's what makes us who we are. And this is your opportunity to choose. She'll be leaving in an hour."

Malcolm shrugged her off once more, but this time it was with less determination. "She doesn't want me," he said. "Even if it were true, even if I could . . . she doesn't want me to—"

"She wants you to," said Priscilla in a most confident tone of voice. "She wants you to."

He turned his head and looked at her with suspicion. "How do you know?" he asked, trying to remain unconvinced, trying not to get his hopes up. But there was hope growing in his breast, some in a part of him that had absorbed Priscilla's words.

"Because she's in love with you, imbecile," she said. "She wants you to stop her."

"What makes you so sure?" he asked. "She told me plainly that she doesn't want me to follow her. You see, she knows that I'm not good enough. She knows—"

"She wants you to prove her wrong," said Priscilla. "She didn't mean, 'Don't follow me.' She meant, 'If you're going to follow me, do it with a vengeance.'"

Malcolm smiled, though he didn't know why. "Why didn't you tell me that before?"

Priscilla laughed. "Because I wanted you for myself. Isn't it obvious?"

He squinted his puzzlement. "And now?"

"I have a new love," she told him.

For some reason, he wasn't surprised. "Who is it?"

"Me," she said, lifting her chin high. "I'm going to live for me."

"Haven't you always?"

She socked him affectionately with her dainty glove. "I'm serious, Malcolm. I'm going to live independently, as I always should have. I'm going to work at the hospital."

"You're joking," he pleaded, "tell me you're joking. You're not going to be a nurse."

"Well," she said brightly, "I am not joking, but neither am I going to be a nurse."

"Huh?"

She touched his nose with a finger. "I'm going to be a doctor."

His eyes flung wide. "A doctor?"

"Oh, good. You can hear. Yes, Malcolm, a doctor. I'm afraid you're going to have some competition." She turned haughtily away from him and reached for her cloak.

"But a woman—"

She turned to face him with piercing violet eyes, challenging him to say one more word. He thought better of it. "A doctor?" he repeated instead. "Really? A doctor?" Somehow, he was able to picture it. Somehow, he thought it really was going to happen. She would be a terrible nurse. But a doctor? She was certainly bright enough.

Priscilla handed him his coat. "Now, am I going to see you and the lovely wife at professional soirées, Malcolm? Or are you just going to stand there and be morbid."

Malcolm yanked the coat from her. His heart was pounding so furiously, it made him swallow. He was going to get Cassie. He was going to stop that ship. "Priscilla . . ." he began, "I've . . . I've been unfair to you. I . . . I know I've spoken callously."

"I'm glad to hear you say it," she confessed, "but maybe you can tell me about it at your wedding. You really are in a hurry, you know."

Malcolm wasted no time. He knew he would be a nervous wreck by the time he reached the docks. What if she rejected him? He couldn't let that happen. He just couldn't. "Thank you," he said, hugging Priscilla, giving her a strong but platonic squeeze. "Thank you." He kissed her softly on the cheek and then fled. Priscilla watched him go with a dazed expression. She would miss him. But at last, she would have what she had always truly wanted from him—respect. And she had really, really done something good. She knew it. She had made someone she loved believe in himself again. She walked home slowly, a cool breeze on her smiling face. It was a beautiful day. She wondered how many beautiful days she had missed in her life. No more. No more fighting—not for herself, anyway. Her smile brightened when she spotted her happy little cabin, secluded from the road by flowering bushes. She could hardly wait to begin her new life with her true self.

Fifty

Cassie felt bitter. There was no doubt about that. She stood patiently at the docks, waiting to be invited to board, her cloak flapping all around her. But her hair stayed in place, for she had tied it securely into the most perfect of buns. She wanted to look stern because she felt stern. She felt like an angry mother going home to scold the children who had betrayed her. Her parents would say they'd known all along she was innocent. They would be liars. The magistrate might say he was sorry. He, too, would be a liar. She might have hoped that after all she'd suffered, a luxurious vessel might have been sent to retrieve her from this prison of an island. But the ship was plain and sturdy, and her quarters would be cramped. There would be no attempt to make amends for the crimes committed against her. Surely, she would be lucky even to get an apology from anyone besides the sea captain, who did not even owe her one.

Cassie expected to return home to unpaid bills, angry creditors, and a family who expected her to save them. She had no funds of her own, so she would try to save them, or else she herself would go to the poorhouse. But she would conduct her family tasks with bitterness in her heart, for she knew well that not one soul in that house had ever believed in her. They had not even seen her off. It would have made her cry if she'd been of a mind to, but she wasn't. It had taken months for her to transform from a practical-minded spinster to an emotional idiot, pleading for mercy at every turn. But it had taken only hours for her to swing back. She was her old self again, already.

It did occur to Cassie, as she noticed signs that the ship was nearly ready to be boarded, that it might be a fine idea for her to get married once she was back in England. That would be one way to be freed from her parents' financial straits. But there were two problems with that plan. One, it would leave her family in the dust, and she wasn't sure she was quite cold enough to do that. And secondly, she would have to meet someone. That's not something she had ever done before, and frankly, she realized, she probably couldn't afford it. To attend a social, one had to be both properly and attractively dressed. There wouldn't be any money for that sort of thing. Her eccentric parents didn't have any close friends, so there would be no matchmaking. Perhaps she would be run over by a carriage in the road and the driver, in his pity, might lean over and become enchanted by her beauty. That didn't seem like a very good hand on which to gamble, so she imagined it would be more practical to make plans based on the notion that she would be alone.

Glancing nervously toward the road, halfway hoping for something—she didn't know what—she recalled with agonizing embarrassment the day she'd told Faith she wanted a rose. A rose. She curled her lip at a joke at her own expense. Who would be crazy enough to ask for a rose in a world where they were all lucky just to find bread? She couldn't stand to think of the way she had behaved ever since her arrival on these shores. If trials were a test to see whether the person were heavier than the atmosphere, she had failed. She had caved in to her emotional side from her first day of captivity. And she would feel shame every time she looked back on it. She would hate herself every time she thought of the tears she had shed, the cries of anguish which had escaped her lips, and worst of all . . . that she had given herself to someone, like a stupid child who hoped that love would come of lust. She gritted her teeth. She must not think of it. She had a life ahead of her now.

Suddenly, Cassie was startled by a hand that trickled along her neck like water. She gasped, spun around, and found herself inappropriately close to the most handsome face she had ever known. "Malcolm," she rasped out, then tried to compose herself. "I suppose you have come to see me off," she said, turning away from him. "I had rather hoped you wouldn't, but I thank you anyway. It was most unnecessary."

Malcolm didn't play the formal game. He made her look at him by touching her hair and said in a low, tender voice, "I'll die if you go."

Cassie's lashes flung high, but she could scarcely think of anything to say. He looked so handsome. His eyes were bluer than the sky and his sideburns accentuated the fine squareness of his jaw. "That's . . . that's ridiculous," she said, sounding like her old self. "You won't die. What are you talking about?"

He wasn't looking at her eyes, but at the piece of red hair he had loosened and was rubbing between his fingers. "I just realized I forgot to tell you something," he said in a very ghostly voice. "I should have told you sooner, but this appears to be my last chance." He looked her fearlessly in the eye and a little smile crossed his lips. It wasn't a smile of humor, though. It was a smile of relief. "You see, I've fallen madly in love with you, Cassie. And I can't let you get on that ship."

Cassie frowned indignantly, though her knees began to shake. "You don't mean that," she said haughtily, "you—"

He cupped her chin in his palm and leaned close to

her. He touched her ear with his lips and let her feel his hot breath. "I mean it, Cassie," he whispered, gradually bringing her toward him with his free arm. He did not hold her in restraint, but firmly enough to prevent her from leaving. "I like myself when I'm with you," he said, moving his lips from her ear to her neck, "I want to be the person I am when I'm with you." Cassie began to shake. First it was her legs, and then her hands, and then finally her chest. "Marry me," he begged in a whisper. "Be my wife."

At the sound of those words, Cassie collapsed into tears. Pink-faced, she tried to cover her face with a hand. She sobbed as she had never sobbed before. Malcolm gently removed her hand and saw the honesty of her tears. "What is it?" he asked tenderly. "What do you say?"

But she couldn't stop crying long enough to say it. She had just been hating herself for all of her emotional outbursts since she'd arrived in Sydney, and here she was, having a public fit. And the strangest thing of all was that she didn't care. As soon as she was able, she blurted out, "Oh, damn it, Malcolm. Go . . ."—she sniffed hard—"go tell them to sail without me."

Malcolm was stunned. "Does this mean that you'll—"

She nodded and wiped her tears at the same time.

He almost ran off to do her bidding, but paused for one last moment of self-doubt. "Are you sure?"

That made her smile through her tears. "Oh, Malcolm, I would have married you the first day I met you." She wrapped her arms around his neck and squeezed. He lifted her off her feet and swung her, burying his face in her sweet-smelling hair. They ignored the clumsy applause which broke out at the docks, remaining in their embrace until they were both ready to let go. Malcolm put her down and took her hand. "That way?" he asked, pointing at the long, winding path home.

"Any way," she told him. "Just don't let go of my hand."

He gave it a firm squeeze and led her down the wild road, far away from the crowd, and from the seas they had charted for her.

Fifty-one

"I want to wear white lace," said Cassie, wrapping her arms around his neck. The last rays of orange sun were pouring into the study from beyond a lavender sky. Cassie's smile sparkled in the shimmering magic of an oncoming sunset. "I want to wear a long gown with silver embroidery." She scrunched her nose up against his. "I look better in gold, but I want silver anyway."

Malcolm smiled distantly, but he was busy gliding his lips along her neck.

"And flowers in my hair," she went on, grinning at herself. "It's the most absurd custom in the world—plucking flowers just to put them in our hair and then watch them die. But I don't care," she laughed, "I want to wear flowers, white ones. Lots of little white ones."

Malcolm gently took her hair down from its pins. He did it with such a light touch, so sensitive to how it would feel, that it made her shiver as the loose strands fell to her cheeks one by one. "I think we should marry unclad," he teased with an entirely straight face. He lowered the sleeves of her dress so he could watch her fiery hair touch her bare, milky shoulder. "We should give the guests something more exciting. We should make the priest come bare-skinned as well."

"Malcolm, that is blasphemous," she scolded kindly.

"Was it?" he whispered against her hair with a kiss, "I'm sorry." His hands didn't seem very sorry as they set to the task of undoing her gown. He seemed in a hurry to drop it to the floor.

"Malcolm," Cassie laughed, playfully slapping his busy hands, "you know I don't believe in doing that before marriage."

He stopped what he was doing and gave her a curious look.

She met his eyes and said, "I'm joking. It's a joke."

"Oh, thank goodness." He went eagerly back to work.

"Malcolm," she said amorously, as his hands finally touched bare skin. He embraced her and rubbed the snowy white skin on the small of her back, peering over her shoulder so he could get a good look. In a sensually slow motion, he lowered her bloomers so that her bottom would gradually come to light. When at last it was bare, he cradled it and squeezed hard with both hands. "I never thought marriage could be to a man like you," said Cassie.

"Am I just the type you love and toss away?" he asked with a boyish smile, and eyes that were too busy scanning her body to look into hers.

"Absolutely," she teased.

"Well, no more, young lady," he said. "I'm tired of people just using me for my body." He led her gently to the sofa, arranging the cushions so they might be comfortable for her head. "This time, you're going to have to make an honest man of me. This time you'll have to wed me." He winked as she lay down on the sofa, naked as the day she was born. He spread her hair carefully over the pillows so that it looked sprawled and romantic. "Spread your legs," he told her, "I just want to look first."

Cassie would never get used to that strange sense of eroticism he had. At least, she didn't think so. But she knew that if she didn't open her legs, he would just coax her in that gentle way over and over until she did. So she flushed and let them spread. Malcolm wasted no time with formality. He peered between her open legs and examined her womanhood with lustful eyes and a knowing finger now and again. He always seemed to sense just when and where to touch her. "Does this feel good?" he asked her curiously, moving to a certain spot. It felt like heaven.

"Yes," she groaned, "stop teasing me."

"I'm not teasing you," he said, "I'm just exploring. It's going to be mine, after all. Hadn't I best get to know it?" He bit his lip enticingly, for even to him, that had been a devilish sentiment.

Cassie scowled. "Wouldn't you rather know my heart?"

"Of course," he smiled adorably. "I just haven't gotten up that far yet. I'll get there."

She returned his smile and wrapped her hands around his neck. "I love you, Malcolm. I love your strange ways, and I love you."

He brushed his lips against hers. "I love you, too."

"Will you open up to me?" she asked, her green eyes growing darker as the sun fell. "Will you let me look into you?"

He swallowed nervously, for this was something he had never done with a lover. But Cassie was going to be his wife, and it was different. He would bleed for her. He would die for her. He would do anything if she asked it. "Of course," he croaked nervously.

Cassie smiled assuringly. "Where do you like to be touched, Malcolm?"

He lowered his eyes uncomfortably. But then he took her hand and slowly placed it right below his navel. "I have a tender spot right here," he told her.

She tickled it with featherlike strokes. "Is that the only place?" she goaded him.

He let out a little laugh. "No," he confessed, nearly shy, "there is somewhere else."

Cassie lowered his breeches, and he let her. "Like

this?" she asked in a whisper, stroking him in steady movements.

Malcolm watched her hand move back and forth with a certain tenderness in his heart. He felt a little vulnerable, and he wasn't sure he liked it. But he tried to like it. And he gradually caved in to the enjoyment of the tender, loving way she was reaching out to him. He swallowed nervously once more. "Not quite," he said softly to his inexperienced partner, "more like this." With a gentle hand, he spread her fingers and taught her a smoother stroke. "That's lovely," he said encouragingly, "that's perfect." Then he stopped her with a hard kiss.

Cassie nearly melted under his passionate lips, which were fiercely trying to devour her. But when she felt him hard against her thigh and knew he was about to enter, she stopped him once more. "Not yet," she said. He withdrew, some loose hair falling wildly over his forehead. Cassie slid down and touched his chest with her tongue. It caused a strange look to cross Malcolm's face. She licked and suckled him, wetting him with her tongue. He studied the sensation within himself. A crooked smile crossed his lips. "Do you like that?" she asked.

Malcolm thought carefully about his answer. "Yes," he said at last, "I think I do." No one had ever done that before, and he was delighted to discover a new sensation.

She suckled and teased him until he could stand no more. "Enough of that," he said without malice, lifting her face firmly to his. "Enough of that. I'm going to take you."

Cassie opened her knees to make it easier for him. "Do you want me to make it so easy?" she asked with a giggle, "or would you rather I put up a struggle?"

He kissed away her smile. "I want you to be sincere," he said predictably. "Just don't pretend anything. Just don't pretend to be eager if you'd rather hesitate. I like the hesitation; I like the fear."

"I don't feel hesitant," she told him.

"Then show me your lust." He thrust into her with spectacular force and watched her face accept his penetration. It made him smile strangely to see her bite her lip and then, moments later, lick it. He moved in and out of her, watching her carefully for clues about when she would want it faster, and when she would want him to slow down. He was very good at noticing clues. It wasn't long before his glide was slick and wet, and she was softly begging him to push harder. Ordinarily, Malcolm didn't like such talk because he saw it as artificial—just some women's way of feigning lust—but he could tell she meant it, so he let her words curl his lip and he increased the power behind his thrusts.

At last, she began to shudder. She let out a soft, desperate cry, ripping her fingers through Malcolm's hair. The sight of her ecstasy was enough to make him follow in the wake of her waves. He exploded with violence, and forced her to take the last brutal thrusts of his passion. She swallowed them joyfully, and they brought a smile to her lips. "That was wonderful," she told him. He sat down and lifted her into his lap, kissing her hair, for he so loved the smell of it.

"Now, I believe we were talking about a dress?" he said, squeezing her tightly against him.

"Huh?"

"A dress," he said gently, tucking a piece of hair behind her ear. "You wanted a white lace dress. With silver embroidery and white flowers in your hair."

She was surprised. "You mean, you were actually listening?"

He laughed. "Well, I was storing it for later recall. Not exactly the same as listening. But I've just retrieved it, so why don't you tell me more about what you want. You can have anything."

"You're not *that* wealthy," she teased.

"Yes," he said with a kiss on her head, "but neither are your tastes extravagant. I suspect I'll be able to afford anything you could come up with."

"You never know. I could want diamonds sewn into my gown."

"This from a woman who feels flowers are frivolous?"

"Perhaps my tastes are changing," she said. "Perhaps now that it's your money I'm spending . . . "

He smiled brightly, and it made his eyes squint. "Ahh, well it looks like I'm going to need some more money then. I'll have to sell you from time to time. Is that all right?"

"Absolutely," she answered, kissing his handsomely stubbled lip, "but only to good-looking men. And you needn't charge much. I'd practically do it for free."

"Mmmm." He tickled the sensitive skin at her hip. "I can see I'm going to have to think of a different plan. Perhaps I should sell *myself.*"

"All right," she relented, "but I'm to be your only customer."

"Hmmm. Well, perhaps we could just skip the diamonds then," he grinned.

She grinned back. "I love you, Malcolm."

"Well, that's probably good since you're marrying me."

She pressed her nose against his. "I want to hear you say it again."

"What? That I love you?"

She nodded.

"Why?" It's not that he had any objection, he just didn't understand the need for repetition.

"Because," she said, cuddling her head against his chest, and loving the way he hugged her in response, "I've waited so long. I loved you so long before you ever even noticed me. I deserve to hear it a thousand times."

He smiled at her candor. Lifting her chin with a finger, he said, "I noticed you, Cassie. I did."

She blinked expectantly.

"And I love you," he said, sealing it with a kiss. For as long as he understood the need, he would never call it silly. That's why Cassie knew he would make a fine husband.

Fifty-two

Cassie and Malcolm were married in England that August so that Cassie might see her family one last time. They took a ship far more luxurious than the one her countrymen had sent for her. And when they arrived, they arranged a grand event. Outdoors in the countryside beyond Canterbury, they took their vows under an archway of white roses. It struck Cassie how different her old home was from Australia. For one thing, it was summer, where in Australia it had been winter. But more importantly, there was something about the wilderness. All of the flowers were well-controlled, growing in perfect patterns, or climbing along trellises, just as they'd been instructed. The grass had been perfectly cut, and the sweet smell of it wafted through the air. It was beautiful, and she could not have imagined a more quaint spot for a wedding, but still, it seemed so strange to see wildlife, and yet know that there was absolutely no danger.

Malcolm looked smashing as always in a well-tailored suit and a cravat of white satin. The white brought out the deep blue of his eyes, which gazed into Cassie's with sincerity and thoughtfulness as he held her hands in his. Cassie wore a gown of cream, embroidered with silver lace at the sleeves and skirt. She wore cream flowers in her russet hair, loosing several strands to float romantically about her face. She liked the dress because she thought it made her look more buxom. The top seemed to have a firm, round shape of its own that seemed quite flattering. But everyone else liked the dress because they thought it made her look like some rare wildflower with red petals on top. No one had ever seen plain old Cassie looking so stunning. In fact, no one had ever seen her dressed up.

When the last of the vows were taken and Malcolm had kissed the bride, Cassie broke into a big grin. She turned to face the crowd, her eyes sparkling up in delight, her face aglow with bridal joy. It was time to welcome everyone to the reception. And that, of course, would be an adventure in itself. The crowd and the couple moved to the white-painted iron tables settled in a cool grove of evergreen trees. A harpist began to play his metal strings, ringing through the forest like the song of nature itself. Delicious punch flowed into crystal glasses. Malcolm took the earliest opportunity to grab several crackers with caviar. He knew enough about weddings to know he wouldn't have much chance to eat.

Cassie was the first to get whisked off, and it was by her mother. Her hair in coils high on her head, Mrs. Madison wore a charming yellow dress, bought especially for the occasion. Having come into some money of late, what with the arrest of Egbert and the redistribution of the will, she was back to her old spending habits. "Oh, Cassandra," she said, her round face teary.

Cassie was stiffened by her presence, but reminded herself about maturity, reminded herself about forgiveness, and broke into a warm smile. "Well, Mother, it seems official. You have washed your hands of me." She had hoped the jest would make her mother smile, but it did not. Instead, the woman gave her a pleading look and said, "May we talk?"

It looked rather serious, and so Cassie took the woman's elbow with great concern and led her a few feet from the reception. "Of course, Mother, what is it?"

She looked into her daughter's lovely face, her hair

flame-bright in the sun. She took after the Irish side of the family, and that was pleasing. "Cassandra, there's something I've wanted to say to you ever since you returned, but I . . . I haven't known how."

Cassie cast her a sympathetic gaze and took her hand with understanding. "What is it, Mother? Go on."

Bashfully, she tilted her head. "Well, this isn't easy to say, but . . ."

"Please, Mother," said Cassie, feeling a warm glow between their hands, "please, just say it."

"Well, I . . ." she dabbed her eyes with a yellow lace handkerchief and confessed, "I didn't know when the right time would be."

"*Now*, Mother. Tell me now."

Mrs. Madison bowed her head. "Well, dear, I just . . . I just feel that I should tell you what's in my heart. Because you are my daughter, and I feel . . . well, I want to feel close to you." Cassie smiled encouragingly. "You see," she took a deep breath and then let it all out, "I sent you a batch of sugar biscuits last Christmas. And I never received a thank-you letter. Now it isn't that I don't realize you were busy, but . . ."

Cassie rolled her eyes to the heavens and privately begged for strength.

". . . but when someone gives you a gift," she continued frantically, "it takes effort and it takes thought, and when the gift isn't even acknowledged . . ."

"It didn't arrive," interrupted Cassie.

Her mother gasped. "What?"

"I said it didn't arrive, Mother. Now, if you'll excuse me." Sheena, all dressed in red, had caught her eye, and Cassie nodded in reply.

"Didn't arrive?" fretted her mother. "Well, I . . . of all the . . . I told them specifically . . . Oh how you must have been furious with me! You poor dear, you must have thought I'd forgotten. And on Christmas!"

"I'll recover. Please excuse me." She waded her way through the trees and the crowd to embrace her long-lost friend. "Oh, Sheena," she cried as the women rocked in their hug, "oh, my God. How can I ever thank you? How?"

Sheena pulled from the embrace and smiled. "Well, you gave me your brother. That was a pretty good thank-you."

Cassie burst into a laugh. "Oh, my," she said, "I still can't believe the two of you married. I still think of him as a child!"

"Well, soon he's going to have his *own* child," she said, touching her belly.

Cassie gasped. "Oh, Sheena!" She embraced her friend once more. "How wonderful! Oh, how I wish you could come live with us in Sydney."

"Well, I love you," said Sheena with a wink, "but not enough to be hanged for escaping. No, thank you. Nobody has the slightest idea who I am here, and I think that's best." She grinned triumphantly. "And besides, your brother will inherit your family's entire estate as the eldest boy, you know. I'd say it won't be such a bad life for a convict from a poor family."

Cassie squeezed her hand in congratulations. "Well, speaking of the devil, where is that brother of mine?"

"Right here," said Samuel cheerfully, wrapping a lanky arm about his bride. Ever since her return, Cassie had been shocked at his height. She had not remembered his being so tall!

Cassie pretended to be formal. "Well, hello, sir. I had hoped you would make it to my wedding."

"I wouldn't have missed it for the world," he said downing his third glass of champagne.

"Samuel," she said in all seriousness, "I haven't had a chance to tell you this, but I really am impressed at how you saved our family's estate. I don't think I could have done it. I know how hard it is, looking after their affairs. I did it for years and years, but I never thought to double-check that will."

"Well," he said stretching both arms overhead, "I'm sure you did the best you could, but . . . well, handling money now, that really is a man's job." He looked to his left and then to his right with startled eyes. "That was a joke. Please don't hit me—either of you. It was a joke."

Cassie smiled at him. "Well, I missed you, Samuel."

"Oh, God," he groaned, "you're not going to get sentimental on me, are you? I thought you were the one person I could count on not to start . . ." Sheena absolutely glared at him. "Oh, very well," he said, "I . . . I missed you, too." Her glare did not cease. "And I . . . I love you," he added, eyes downcast.

Cassie turned up her nose. "How horribly sentimental of you, Samuel. I wouldn't have taken you for such a pansy."

"What?! You . . ."

Cassie and Sheena both started laughing uncontrollably, and wound up locking arms. The three of them strolled away from the crowd to do some catching up and to share stories of times past. "You two are the one thing I don't want to leave," said Cassie as they made their way toward the sunset.

"Well, you can't have one thing without leaving another," said Sheena, stroking Cassie's back, "just as you can't take one thing without all that comes with it. We'll miss you, but you made the right choice. And we wouldn't want anything less for you." She rested her head on Cassie's shoulder as they walked on.

Malcolm, in the meantime, was left in the grueling company of Mr. Madison, who had been lecturing his new son-in-law for more than thirty minutes. Malcolm knew, because he'd continually glanced at a nearby pocket watch that an elderly man kept retrieving. "Fidelity," Mr. Madison was saying, "I have found that it is the key to a solid marriage." Malcolm checked around for any open pocket watches but saw none. "I know that a young man is tempted. Don't think I don't know that," he warned with a wink, "but it's resisting those urges that makes us married men. My wife and I have been married for . . . oh, to tell you the truth, I don't remember how many years, and that makes it a long time. But the one thing that has held us together has been our devotion to one another." Malcolm could only squint curiously. He'd heard enough from Cassie to know exactly how remarkable a speech this was. He began to wonder how long receptions last.

More than an hour and more than a half-dozen drinks later, Mr. Madison was still talking. Someone offered Malcolm some champagne but he smiled politely and said, "No, thank you. I . . . I switched to water two hours ago. Thank you." He blinked hard to awaken himself and took a deep, cleansing breath. He tried to look attentive.

"You know, I wazz ssinking offf being a doctor once." Mr. Madison was slurring a little now. "But I hate blood. I just can't tolerate the sight of it."

Malcolm nodded.

"What . . . whh . . . whhat do you ssink of that?" he asked.

"Uh." Malcolm studied the glass of water in his hand, then nodded rhythmically. "I uh . . . I think blood is a big part of it."

Mr. Madison started laughing boisterously, for no particular reason. He laughed so hard that his foot stomped involuntarily, over and over. "Oh . . . oh, that reminds me," he said, wiping his eyes, "I . . . I have more advice for you, ssson. Come sssit closer."

Malcolm had his limits. "I uh . . . I'm sitting as close as I can without being in your lap," he smiled. "Why don't you just tell me what it is from here."

The old man leaned forward as though to reveal a very important secret. "Never," he said, "never ever ever ever wear white shoes with a black waistcoat. Do you understand me?"

Malcolm bit his lip. "I uh . . . I think so."

"Because, when you sstart chasing the ladies again, and you will, because fidelity iss for morons . . . you want to look your best, and . . ." His head started to lean so heavily to one side that it looked as though he might fall. Malcolm assisted him to sit upright. "Why? Why did you do that?" asked Mr. Madison. "I wasn't going to . . . to fall." His eyes started to close. Then suddenly there was a voice as clear as a bell.

"Are you ready to go?" asked Cassie.

Malcolm looked up. "What? Uh . . . so soon?"

"Well, I've said my good-byes, and I'm ready, but we could stay a bit longer if you like."

He rose briskly to his feet. "No, no, I don't want to keep you." He offered his arm. "Well, Mr. Madison, it's uh . . . it's been a pleasure." He was snoring. Malcolm gave Cassie a weak smile. "I uh . . . I think I must have talked his ear off. Come, let's go."

The two of them walked arm in arm to the carriage which would take them to the docks. They planned no honeymoon, for Cassie thought the trip home would be long enough as it was. No honeymoon could be more exciting than going home to Malcolm's house and getting to call it her own. No shore would be more welcome than the sandy beaches of her new home in Australia. No morning would seem more grand than the one she would see each dawn as she sat across from Malcolm at the breakfast table with the early sun streaming in. No evening would be more thrilling than the ones she would know every night for the rest of her life, cradled in Malcolm's arms. "I hate to leave all this behind," she told him as the crowd grew farther and farther away in the distance.